Romance Reader 2 features:

Rendezvous in Acapulco—*Under the pen name of Katherine Edmonton, Kit Roderick enchanted millions of readers with her romantic novels. Now Kit and her husband, Collin, were in Acapulco, trying to put the pieces of their shattered marriage back together. However, they were uncertain that either desired a second chance at love. Where could Kit find the love and faith needed to rekindle their marriage?*

Love's Broken Promises—*When Cheryl arrived in Flint, Georgia, she was determined to start a new life. But because she refused to confront some vital truths about herself, happiness, peace, and a chance at love eluded her. Would she ever attempt the reconciliation that would heal the damaging pain of love's broken promises?*

Destined to Love—*Although Lezlie had been swept off her feet by Hap Austin and had married him, Travis Manning, her former boyfriend, still loved her deeply. Therefore, he was troubled by Lezlie's apparent unhappiness. After a tragic twist of fate drew them together once more, Lezlie and Travis realized that she had been used by Hap. But the truth may have been discovered too late—both of their lives were endangered, due to her innocent involvement in Hap's underhanded schemes. Hap's business provided Lezlie with money . . . but also deprived her of love. She knew she had made a mistake in marrying Hap—would she ever be happy?*

Romance Reader 2

3 NOVELS IN ONE

Three full-length inspirational romances in one volume.

Fleming H. Revell Company
Old Tappan, New Jersey

0-8007-1413-X

Renezvous in Acapulco, by Melanie Haywood, © 1985 by Fleming
H. Revell Company
Love's Broken Promises, by Celia Blaine, © 1985 by Fleming H. Re-
vell Company
Destined to Love, by Cecil B. Murphey, © 1985 by Fleming H. Re-
vell Company
Printed in the United States of America
Published by the Fleming H. Revell Company

Contents

LOVE'S BROKEN PROMISES

Celia Blaine

Chapter 1

Cheryl wiped the tears from her eyes with her right hand while gripping the steering wheel with the left. She drove east on Interstate 80, keeping exactly at the speed limit. *Why am I crying now?* She had not cried when she left the note—not even during the hurried packing of her two suitcases and typewriter. She had moved around in her room carefully and then tiptoed out of the house, having to make two trips.

Now with the lights of Des Moines far behind her, she let the tears fall. Her vision blurred, and Cheryl no longer trusted herself to drive in the dark. She pulled over onto the right shoulder and parked. As she lay her head back on the seat, Cheryl made no effort to restrain the weeping. She pulled a box of tissues from the glove compartment and let the pain gush out. "Oh, Shep—Shep—"

A tap at the window startled her. A highway patrolman stood outside the car, shining a light on her. Cheryl rolled down her window, not sure she could trust her voice to speak.

"You okay, lady?"

She nodded.

"I saw you pull over and I circled back. Found you still here. Thought there might be something wrong."

She shook her head again. Finally she opened her mouth. "I'm all right."

"You sure?"

She nodded again.

"Okay," he said. "Sorry to bother you." He turned off his flashlight and walked away. Seconds later the highway patrolman's car pulled away. Cheryl watched his taillights disappearing in the darkness ahead of her. She realized her crying had now come to an end. She wanted to continue crying but couldn't. Even so, the ache had not vanished.

In an effort to change her mood, Cheryl flipped on the radio and moved the dial from station to station. She picked up a country-and-western station. A Johnny Cash record played, followed by a female vocalist whose voice she did not recognize. She wailed about broken promises and lost love.

"That's not the kind of singing I need now," she said and turned the dial again. Even before she heard the whole sentence, she knew it was one of those shouting preachers. She flicked the radio off.

8

Cheryl started the engine and pulled onto the expressway. At that moment, Cheryl Leigh Adams felt tempted to turn back. She saw the sign ahead saying that she was approaching the Mississippi River and would soon cross over into Illinois. She eased her foot off the gas pedal, and her left hand grasped the turn signal. She hesitated only a fraction of a second and then pressed down on the accelerator.

Cheryl had made her decision and would not turn back. Her shoulders relaxed slightly, and she consciously pushed the pain to the back of her mind. She was entering a new life. The ache would go away.

As she continued driving, Cheryl could still hear Shep's voice. "I do love you. I love you very much, but—"

Cheryl banged her hand on the steering wheel. "Stop it!" she screamed and forced the vision of Shep out of her mind. She would never see him again. He would not intrude into her life or her thoughts. "It's a finished chapter," she said aloud. In spite of herself, Cheryl smiled. "As a reporter, I should have said, 'That's a thirty.' "

That moment of self-mockery lifted her spirits. She no longer thought of Des Moines, Iowa. The note she left had cut her off completely from Shep—and from Karla. But, at last, it had finally cut her off from Mother.

As her VW sped across the endless asphalt road, passing few other cars in the early hours, she wondered vaguely where to stop. How would she pick the right town? Did it make any difference? When she had thrown the suitcases into the backseat of her car, she thought only of leaving Des Moines but had little concern for arriving anywhere. A force within compelled her to keep going. No thoughts of going back troubled her. Her spirits lifted slightly as the odometer clicked away the miles.

Just before reaching Chicago she headed south. Momentarily she wondered if she would end up at New Orleans or perhaps Miami. She had never lived in the South before. Each mile and each hour, the depression lifted as the tires hummed their monotonous tune.

Cheryl drove most of the night, stopping for gas each time her tank registered one-quarter. By always staying on the expressways, she felt a sense of safety. Somewhere in Kentucky, weariness overcame her, and she stopped at a rest area. Parking near the rest rooms, with plenty of light shining on her car, she locked the doors, covered herself with her coat, and curled up.

Awakening to the sound of a recreational vehicle easing out of its space a few feet away, she stretched and finally went into the rest room and cleaned up the best she could. Then she pulled out of the area and started driving again. An hour later, she exited from the expressway for gas and breakfast. Half an hour later while sipping tea from a paper cup, she continued southward.

Although it was only mid-April, she noticed the difference in the temperature. Even more, she began to marvel at the green leaves and early signs of vegetation.

When the crimson rays of morning painted their way across the horizon, Cheryl approached Atlanta's interstate loop. Driving almost directly east, each ray intensified and seemed to point directly at her. Cheryl thought of it as symbolic of her life. "A new day and it's getting brighter and brighter," she said aloud. Once she might have seen this as a sign from God, promising happiness and a fresh beginning. But Cheryl had stopped believing in God—at least in a God who actively intervened in lives. Even though she could not see God in the early rays of morning, she could still accept this as a turning point in her life.

Cheryl glanced at the overhanging signs and realized she had to make a decision. Should she head north on the loop? Go south? Continue on through Atlanta or bypass it? Perhaps drive all the way to the coast? Hardly realizing she had made a decision, Cheryl took the southbound road. Minutes later she heard the low-flying planes above and saw signs directing traffic to the Atlanta airport.

At that moment, Cheryl realized three things. First, she was hungry. Second, the car was down to a quarter of a tank again. And third, she had not slept enough, and the heaviness of her eyes demanded that she stop.

She saw the next exit coming up: Flint. She shrugged. "Why not? One redneck town ought to be as bad as another," she said. She might stay for a week, perhaps longer. She had enough money to last at least four months. It didn't matter where she stopped.

She had escaped Des Moines. That mattered.

After driving only a quarter mile from the expressway, Cheryl's attention was diverted by the red letters of a neon sign which read BREAKFAST.

Cheryl pulled over and turned into the parking lot, only to discover that every place was taken. She drove the full length of the area and had just decided she'd go further down the road. Then she saw a man carrying a carton of coffee cups, getting into a car. Cheryl whirled around to the lane and waited for the man to back out. Since he came out her way, she reversed far enough to give him plenty of space. Then she shifted into forward gear and was ready to pull in when a compact car, coming from the opposite direction, pulled into the spot. She laid her hand heavily on the horn.

The other driver, a man, looked up in surprise. He got out of his car and smiled as he walked toward her.

"Good morning," he said and started to move on.

"Good morning? You grab my parking place, and all you do is tell me good morning?"

"Your place? I didn't realize—honestly I didn't see—"

"My VW may be small, but it's not invisible!"

"Hey, look, I'm sorry. Want me to pull back out?"

"I wouldn't want you to be inconvenienced," Cheryl said and pulled her VW bug behind his car, their bumpers touching.

"That's kind of romantic," he said. "Almost like holding hands or something." He walked around and opened Cheryl's door.

"I didn't intend for it to be anything romantic. I just wanted to stop for breakfast, but after driving through the place, finding only one spot and then—"

"Ma'am, I didn't do it intentionally. I guess my mind was on something else."

"Okay," she said as she slid out of the driver's seat. For the first time she looked at him. He was quite tall, a little too thin, and dark. Although she read no expression in his face, his dark eyes seemed to be laughing at her. "Guess I'm a little tired. I've been driving for hours."

"Then the least I can do is to buy your breakfast—"

"I don't know, I mean—"

"After all, I did take your place."

"Yes, you did."

"And I'm a prisoner here until you move your car."

"You could have looked more carefully before you just wheeled into the spot."

"You could have moved faster," he said and then smiled. "Let's not go back to that again."

"All right," she said and followed him toward the building. They found the only empty booth in the place and sat down.

A waitress appeared immediately, smiled broadly at the man, and said, "Sure good to see you again." She gave Cheryl only a cursory glance. "What you having today?"

"We'll both have the granola cereal with skim milk, and let's see, how about honeydew melon—"

"I can make up my own mind—"

"Of course you can, but since I'm paying for this, I ought to at least decide how I'm going to spend my money." He nodded to the waitress, who grinned back at Cheryl.

The waitress took the full order as she stared at the man again.

While waiting for their food, Cheryl looked around at the people. "They do quite a business here."

"Only place in this area that's open twenty-four hours daily," he said. "Food's not particularly good though."

"If it's not good, then I suppose the granola would be a good idea, wouldn't it?" She smiled, determined to make the conversation pleasant until she could get away from him.

"I noticed you didn't insist on coffee," the man said.

"I don't drink coffee. It tastes bitter to me."

"Smart girl," he said. "You can get hooked on that stuff. I have this friend who drinks coffee continually all day. He's surprisingly healthy, though."

"Yes," Cheryl said, purposefully looking past him, hoping he would realize she had no desire to talk with him.

"By the way, since we're getting so cozy, my name is—"

Cheryl held up her hand. "I never remember names so don't bother telling me."

"I always remember names," he said. "What's yours?"

"Margo."

"That your real name?" he asked, leaning slightly forward, grinning.

Cheryl realized he was quite handsome. His smile made her even more conscious of his looks. Her eyes traveled across the table and saw that he wore no wedding band. Then, realizing what she had done, Cheryl pulled herself away from that thinking. She was just getting out of one bad situation. She didn't need to jump into another. "No,"she said, "Margo isn't my real name."

He laughed. "Name doesn't suit you anyway," he said. "But I'm curious. Why did you say Margo?"

"Because," she said, "since we'll likely never see each other again, it really doesn't matter what name you remember, does it?"

"That sounds like a brush-off and a put-down."

"Hmm, then I communicate better than I thought."

Cheryl took a final sip of her milk, put the glass down, and reached for the check. His hand came down on top of hers, and she felt a slight tingle. "I—I—I can pay my—my own," she stuttered.

"Now, Margo, allow me. After all, I caused the problem, didn't I?"

Cheryl opened her mouth to say, "You certainly did," but the words did not come. Instead she smiled and said, "Good-bye."

Cheryl hurried outside and drove away before the man had time to pay the check and follow her.

"I don't need another relationship like that," she said aloud.

But he was handsome, wasn't he? a voice inside her added.

Chapter 2

Taylor Michaels studied the application longer than he needed to. Cheryl wondered if she ought to tap her nails or cough. She could not decide if he was studying the paper or letting his mind flit elsewhere.

"Uncanny," he said.

"Uncanny? My application?"

Taylor grinned, "Sorry, no. You. Your fine bone structure, high cheekbones, and that auburn hair."

"Am I applying for a beauty contest or—?"

"Sorry again. It's just—just that you resemble someone. I can't get over the uncanny likeness."

"Oh," Cheryl said, not certain what he expected her to say.

Taylor cleared his throat slowly and peered over his half-moon glasses. "Why should I hire you?"

Cheryl had already decided she didn't like Mr. Michaels and, therefore, really did not care if he hired her. As he had read her application either for the fourth time, or else extremely slowly, she had stolen peeks at the cramped office. Her green eyes had taken in the messy arrangement of files, unkempt desks, and wastebaskets that begged for relief.

"Because I'm good," she said as her eyes met his and held them. "And because you need me on the *Flint Sun*." Cheryl surprised herself. She had never talked with such bravado before. Taylor looked away.

"Hmmm," he said and studied the application.

As Cheryl's eyes swept across the room once again, her instincts yearned to bring order to the place. She also knew that her two years' experience with the *Des Moines Register* meant she could probably write better than Taylor Michaels and anyone else who worked there. *If* anyone else worked there. One middle-aged woman sat at a desk, seeming to spend her time on the phone, jotting down information, sipping Coke, and laughing a great deal. Her calls sounded more like gossip than news gathering.

"Our paper must look different to you. I mean, after working for a big-city daily."

"You don't even have a clock on the wall."

He chuckled, "And you had dozens of them in Des Moines?" he asked, not looking up.

"Those clocks regulated every minute of our day."

"Yes, I suppose."

"You know how it is. Ten minutes to deadline. Five minutes to deadline."

"We work at a slower pace here," he said.

"So I noticed," she answered, as her eyes roamed across his desk once more.

"The smallness of our space must have shocked you, too," he said.

"Looks more like a bureau office than the whole operation. Why, the food section alone on the *Register*—" She stopped momentarily and added, "Yes, quite a bit smaller."

"We have only one computer terminal here. The composition shop's located in Atlanta," he said. "Our ad staff's there, too."

"I see," she said, wishing she could at least stack the papers straight on his desk.

Taylor's black eyes peered over his half-moon glasses again. "Okay. You're hired."

"It's that simple?" she asked, remembering the long interviews with two department heads and then a ten-day wait before the *Des Moines Register* hired her. "But—I mean, don't you at least have to go through the publisher first?"

"Of course I do. But that's no problem," he said. "He trusts my judgment."

"Oh, I see," she said because she did not know what else to say.

"And you can start tomorrow," he said as he took off his glasses.

"Tomorrow? Well, I don't know. I mean, I've just gotten here and—"

"Okay, then how about starting today?" The slightest hint of a smile appeared on his face which Cheryl had decided could be any age from twenty-two to thirty-five.

"You're hiring me because you think I'm that good? Or is it because you're that desperate?" Cheryl asked, surprised a second time by her own boldness.

The dimples that formed when he smiled gave Taylor's face a boyish look, and Cheryl revised her estimate from twenty-two to twenty-eight. His face held an innocence about it that made her wonder if he didn't belong in a college journalism class. "Let's say that in my wisdom and great ability to judge character, as well as assessing our needs—"

"You don't write as pompously as you talk, do you?" Cheryl asked and immediately regretted her bad manners.

"I'm going to like you, Cheryl Leigh Adams," he said. "So when do you start work?"

"Well," she hesitated, "you see, I arrived in Flint only this morning. I don't even have a place to stay yet—"

"Left in a hurry?"

In spite of herself, Cheryl flushed.

"You didn't rob a bank or shoot the mayor of Des Moines, did you?"

Cheryl laughed. "No—just—just personal reasons."

"Personal matters I can handle. But prison escapees, murderers on the prowl, and sixteen-year-old runaways exceed my ability to cope."

"I don't fit any of those categories," she said and smiled.

"Good." He stood up. "And you need to practice smiling more often. You have the right kind of bone structure for good smiles. Fits your natural face lines."

"What?" she asked and laughed.

"Good. You laugh well, too," he said and came around and stood next to her. He stood only two or three inches above her five feet seven, and was a little too thin for her taste in men. As she revised his age to twenty-seven, she also wondered if she would like him.

"We'll talk about salary and the job. Then I'll take you over to an apartment for you to rent. That'll save you days of looking—"

"But what if I don't like it?"

"It's called the Hermitage on Old Flint Road. You don't have any furniture, do you?"

She shook her head. "No, nothing."

"That leaves nothing to discuss. The Hermitage has a one-bedroom apartment with kitchen. Furnished." He winked. "The owner is a friend of mine."

"The apartment sounds fine. The wink bothers me."

"You'll understand when you meet her," Taylor said. "Now let's get down to business." He went to another desk with papers piled high. He pulled open a drawer which contained a wild array of pencils, paper clips, and multicolored papers. He pawed through it three times before extracting a single, Xeroxed sheet. "Here. This will tell you everything and nothing at the same time. We operate that way around here."

"So I gather," she said, not trying to disguise the sarcasm in her voice.

"Almost forgot." He paused, and his dimples showed again. "You get the desk over there." He nodded with his chin. "You may keep it as neat as you like. You may dust it every morning and polish it every noon. But don't touch my desk and don't try to reform me, save me from bachelorhood, or turn me into a Democrat. Agreed?"

"I wouldn't think of urging anyone to become a Democrat," she said, surprised at her own words for the third time that morning.

"We're going to become friends," he said. "I can tell."

"I haven't decided that yet."

"But you will," Taylor answered.

"We'll see," Cheryl said and suddenly thought of the man in the restaurant. He had dark eyes, too, like Taylor. *Why didn't I at least get his name?* she asked herself and then immediately stopped thinking in that direction.

Within an hour, Taylor drove her to the Hermitage Apartments, located less than a mile from the newspaper office. The complex, spread over four double-story buildings, was enclosed by neatly trimmed shrubbery. Inside the complex, Cheryl glimpsed an array of bright red azaleas and occasional dogwood trees. "Oh, the grounds—the colors—"

"April is always the most beautiful month in the Atlanta area," he said. He pulled up in front of the apartment marked MANAGER.

Taylor knocked on the door and walked inside. "Hey, beautiful. I've brought you a real paying customer!"

"Coming!" called a voice.

The room surprised Cheryl. It might have been from the turn of the century. Every piece of furniture fitted the room. She especially noticed the brocade, hand-stitched draperies that whispered both their quality and their age.

A moment later a slight woman walked into the room, carrying a cup of tea. She smiled at Taylor and then, as her eyes fell on Cheryl, she lurched forward, spilling her cup. "Oh, so clumsy of me." Her eyes widened, and she took another step toward the younger woman. "You—you startled me."

"I'm sorry, I—"

"Nothing you did," the woman said in a distinctly southern drawl. "You—you look very much like someone I used to know well."

"Struck me the same way," Taylor said, and a look passed between the two.

"I've never been told before that I looked like anyone—"

The woman, in her mid-sixties, recovered and patted Cheryl's shoulder. "Never mind, never mind." She set her cup down on a marble inlaid table. "I'll just get you both a cup—"

"I want you to meet this young lady," Taylor said and introduced Cheryl.

"Well, you have finally brought me a woman to look at, have you? Yes, I think she ought to do quite well. You have my permission to marry her. Today. Within the hour. I'll be your witness." Her placid features gave no hint of humor, unless you looked at her light brown eyes. They danced with laughter and even Cheryl understood.

"How could I marry her when my heart still loves you?" Taylor said, attempting to look dejected. "That would hardly be fair to this red-haired damsel."

"Yes, that would be a problem," the older woman nodded.

"So I brought her here. She needs a place to stay. *A furnished apartment.*"

"Furnished? Why, Taylor, you know we don't—," she stopped, and their eyes met. "Oh," she said softly and sat down in a padded chair with the same off-white material as in the draperies. She indicated chairs for them. Her color paled.

"Yes, well, I don't actually have any furniture of my own—I mean—," Cheryl stopped, not knowing what to say.

"You see, my darling true love, she is a runaway heiress, fleeing from her wealthy-but-bigoted father. She plans to hide out here for a month until her penniless-but-pure suitor arrives and they elope together."

"Why didn't you say so?" the woman answered as she picked up her cup and took a dainty sip. "Let me—let me get you both some tea."

"Annie Laurie, you know tea rots a person's insides," Taylor said with exaggerated disgust.

"I would like a cup of tea," Cheryl said.

"She would not!"

"I certainly would—"

"You only think so," he said and turned aside. "She can have coffee back at the office. And now, Annie Laurie, let's talk about the apartment."

"Look, I don't want to be a bother—," Cheryl said and started to rise.

Taylor waved her back down. "Cheryl, this is the special love in my life—Annie Laurie Burns."

The older woman smiled and narrowed her eyes into a squint. "Actually, my name is *Ann* Burns. This hack writer decided Annie Laurie sounds more lyrical. You're normal. You may call me Ann."

Cheryl smiled. "Thank you." She put her right hand behind her full head of hair and brushed it upwards, an unconscious nervous habit.

Ann kept watching her, and then aware that Cheryl noticed, she said, "I'm sorry for being rude. The way you—you move your arms. And your face. Even the color of your hair. Well, you—as I said, you remind me of someone—"

"Someone you liked?"

"Very much." The woman glanced at Taylor. "Very, very much."

"As long as it was someone you liked," Cheryl said, trying to think of something light to add. Nothing came to mind, and she dropped her gaze.

"So, please forgive an old lady like me. Age ought to have a few privileges. Staring is one I take. Your face—such a beautiful shape with fine features—"

"Annie Laurie," Taylor said sharply, "let's not bore my newest staff writer and get on with business."

"Yes, just as soon as both of you drink a cup of tea." She rose and gestured to Taylor. "Now sit down and be quiet. This is my house and I'll not have any disgusting talk about coffee here." To Cheryl she added, "My father used to say that cultured people drank tea. I am trying to teach this would-be gentleman about life."

Twenty minutes and two cups of spiced tea later, Cheryl paid a month's rent and took the key. Ann pecked Taylor on the cheek and whispered loud enough for Cheryl to hear, "Such a pretty woman, and it makes me a mite jealous, you know."

"No danger, m'love," Taylor said. "But for bonnie Annie Laurie, I'd lay me doon and dee . . . ," he sang as he pulled open the door. "Come on, reporter, let's leave my heart's desire, and I'll show you the apartment."

As they walked toward the next building, Taylor said, "I hope you liked my friend. She accepted me when I arrived in Flint three years ago."

"And you still live here?"

"Of course."

"Oh?" she said. "I just thought—"

"You mean, do I still rent a furnished apartment? Yes, I rent one of the only two she has left. You get the other."

"You still rent a *furnished*—"

"Why not?"

"I guess it's okay if—"

"If I don't wish to be encumbered with possessions. Or tied down," he said.

"Nor do you want to vote Democrat," Cheryl said and smiled.

"You learn fast. I'm going to like you."

"I do learn fast," she said. She wasn't sure how to respond to his second statement.

He pulled her arm. "C'mon you can see the apartment later. It's yours. You've paid your rent for the month. Let's go to work."

"But—"

"You can always go home," he said. "You can't always get a fresh story." He had walked her to the door of his subcompact. "Hop in." As she got in, he pulled a stack of papers out of the backseat. "Here—skim through the *Flint Sun.* You'll see our approach and style."

"And what is your approach?"

"Lots of pictures. Mostly local events. As much information of a county-wide nature as possible. Mostly human-interest material. *And,* best of all, you get to write an editorial."

"On what?"

"On whatever delights or angers you," he said as they pulled out of the complex. "You and I are the only columnists for the paper. You also cover features, food, and religion."

Cheryl did little work that day, mainly spending her time getting acquainted with procedures. She left at four, ate an early meal, and went into her one-bedroom furnished apartment. It was clean, and aside from the small kitchen, reminded her very much of a dozen indistinguishable motels she had slept in. The bed was comfortable, and she slept well.

She awakened only once during the night. Tears ran down her cheeks. "Shep—Shep—," and slowly she drifted back to sleep.

Chapter 3

Cheryl had changed clothes three times, finally settling on her original choice, a rust-colored suit and a simple white blouse. She had bought the suit on sale two days before leaving Des Moines.

Because of her indecision over what to wear, as well as her nervousness—which meant doing half of her morning routine twice so that she got it right—Cheryl arrived at the office at three minutes after eight. Taylor had not given her a time, but at the *Register* when she worked in the food department, she arrived no later than eight unless instructed otherwise.

As she walked inside, she saw Taylor scrunched over his typewriter, staring at the machine in full concentration. Judging from the half-empty glass coffeepot in the middle of his desk and the amount of typed copy next to it, she assumed he had been there a long time. She nodded to him as he turned around and faced her direction. He did not return the nod.

Taylor laced his fingers together at the back of his head, pushed his feet forward, and slumped into his chair.

"Good morning, Mr.—"

He looked up at her and held up a hand. "Don't interrupt me for the next half hour unless it's an emergency." He whirled back and said over his shoulder, "Which it won't be." A second later he shifted his frame back toward the typewriter. Cheryl looked up and watched his furious-paced typing.

At 8:32 he got up, did half a dozen deep knee bends, and picked up the now cold coffeepot. He went into the small kitchen and set it on a burner. As soon as it had heated, he pulled out two mugs, filled them, and threw out the rest of the pot. "How do you take your coffee?" he called.

"I don't," she said.

"Cream and sugar then," he said and added a generous amount of both.

"I said I don't drink coffee."

"You have to drink coffee around here."

"I have to do what?"

"Because you also have to know how to make it."

"Your logic escapes me," she said, wondering if she ought to have worn the pale yellow dress.

"Who says it's logical?" He added another helping of sugar. "You see, I put on the first pot in the morning when I get here. You're responsible for the second. Our receptionist, Marge, makes the third if we need it. We try not to need it because she makes a terrible brew."

He walked toward her, carrying both cups. "We have another staff member. You'll meet Robbie later. He's our legman, in the field most of the time. Even does his writing at home." He extended a cup. "I hope you make better coffee than Marge."

"And if I don't?" she said, her eyes staring straight at him.

"You'll never become a decent reporter," he said, and his eyes met hers. He did not look away.

She lowered her gaze and felt herself flushing. "I—I never drink coffee."

"You can't afford to offend your boss the first morning," he said and winked. "At least wait a full week." He set her cup down on the desk in front of her. "Drink it." He pushed the cup forward; his dimples showed as his teeth gleamed. Cheryl touched the handle, and her fingers gripped the cup. She lifted it slowly and held it in midair, trying to decide whether to throw it at him. At that moment, the front door opened.

"Just in time, Marc," he said, without turning.

"In time for what?"

"In time to save my life," Taylor answered. He winked at Cheryl.

Cheryl caught a glimpse of the newcomer, felt herself flushing, and looked away from him.

"How did you know who it was?" the newcomer asked.

"You sound like a four-hundred-pound man with your heavy gait. Those metal taps make me wonder if the Sixth Army marching band is following half a mile behind you."

The tall, spare man walked over to the desk, ignoring Cheryl, and extended his hand. Taylor grabbed Marc with his free hand, pulled him forward, gave him a quick bear hug, patted his shoulder, and smiled.

Marc glanced at the cup Taylor held. "Don't you know about coffee? The latest research shows it's not good for you—"

"Neither is living," Taylor said and threw back his head. "Research confirms that one hundred percent of the population dies." His face suddenly went sober. "You see, I am not the only one who knows about facts."

"But according to an article I read in the Harvard Medical—"

"Here, take my cup," he said and pushed it into the newcomer's hand. "And, Cheryl, it's your turn to make coffee. See, I don't even have any. Make the full twelve cups, please."

Cheryl hesitated and then grabbed the pot, still careful not to look at the man. She was glad to get out of there. She hurried past the two men and into the cluttered kitchen area, which was hidden behind a row of filing cabinets. She found a coffeemaker, a can of coffee and small containers marked SUGAR, CREAMER, and ARTIFICIAL SWEETENER. She picked up the coffee can and read the directions.

"Apparently you don't drink the horrid stuff either," Marc said.

She spun around, embarrassed. "Well, uh, in our house, no—no, not much." She stared back at the dark eyes that met hers. She could not tell if he was laughing at her or merely appraising her. She turned her back to him but felt he had not looked away.

"Oh, Marc," she heard Taylor call, "you're flirting with our new reporter. Meet Cheryl Leigh Adams."

"Cheryl Leigh Adams," he repeated. "What an interesting name."

"Thank you," she said, looking away from him.

"Do they call you Cheryl Leigh Adams—all three names?" Taylor asked.

"No, just—just—I'll just use Cheryl Leigh."

"Somehow you don't look like a Cheryl to me," Marc said, now staring openly at her. "Hmmm, you'd look better with a name like Margo, don't you think?"

Cheryl slammed down the pot. "Very funny ," she whispered.

Taylor walked in and leaned against the filing cabinet. He watched her measure out the water. "Is Cheryl Leigh the name you wrote under before?"

"Any law against using just my first two names?"

Taylor shrugged. "Never let people say I squashed the creative urge in any reporter."

"Look, Mr. Michaels," she said, spilling water as she poured it into the top of the machine, "I don't—"

"Call me Taylor," he said, "except when you're angry. *Then* you call me Mr. Michaels with venom in your voice." He turned and walked away. "Oh, use half a teaspoon per cup. Too weak for me, but I'm willing to give in to the delicate taste buds of other people."

"Look, *Mr. Michaels*—"

"Not bad," Marc said. "With a little practice you can add a bit more venom."

"And, Cheryl, this is Marc Lattimer leering at you. Marc does all sorts of strange things under water."

"What your less-than-brilliant editor means," Marc said in a low voice, and Cheryl realized he spoke with flawless diction, "is that I am a physical therapist. Much of the work I do with patients is hydrotherapy."

"Which means," Taylor said, "that I want you to interview him. You have done interviews before?"

Cheryl slammed the coffee can on the table. "Yes, sir, *Mr. Michaels.* Many interviews, *Mr. Michaels,* sir."

"She learns fast," Marc said and stared at her already-flushed complexion.

"You know, I keep having this strange feeling I've met you before," Marc said.

"You see the resemblance, too?" Taylor added.

"Oh, that? Yes, but I have the feeling as though we'd met, oh, within the last day or so."

"Cheryl's just come into town—arrived when?"

"Yesterday."

"Early yesterday?" Marc said.

"Yes, quite early yesterday."

"Somehow I get a feeling I don't understand something—"

"Mr. Lattimer means that we met yesterday. At some restaurant—"

"We sort of ran into each other there," Marc said, "and ended up sharing the same table."

"Yes, we did," Cheryl said. She turned to Taylor. "About that interview—"

"Do you have a camera?" Taylor asked.

"Of course."

"Where?"

"In my car."

"Unless you expect him to climb inside the car with you for a picture, how about getting it."

"Right away, *Mr. Michaels,*" she said, glad to have an excuse to rush out of the building.

"Don't hurry on my account," Marc called. "I can waste another thirty seconds this morning."

"Yes, *Mr. Lattimer,*" she called back.

She heard the laughter behind her as she fled from the office. "What pompous, swell-headed—," she sputtered. Without realizing what she had done, Cheryl stopped and then moved her feet slowly forward. She dawdled to the end of the building, turned left, crossed the parking lot, and made another left turn. Enjoying her defiance, she leisurely searched through her purse for her keys, selected the door key, and locked and unlocked the car before finally opening the door. She slipped inside and sat down, smoothing her skirt. After checking her hair in the mirror, she reached over and pulled her camera out from under the front seat. She opened up her 35 mm camera and checked to make certain she had film. Cheryl pulled out her lens cleaning cloth and made sure no dirt particles smeared the glass. She made every motion deliberate in case the two men watched from inside. When she could think of nothing more to delay her return, she carefully locked her car, pausing to visually check the air in all four tires, and took the long way back to the office.

I don't need this job, she said to herself. *One more crack and—*

She walked back inside, her head held high. Both men sat across from Taylor's desk, their feet propped up. They were laughing. For a moment Cheryl felt awkward, and then not sure what to do, she ignored them and sat down at her desk. She pulled open each drawer and inspected its contents. Her predecessor had left plenty of paper clips and memo pads. She wondered where to find a dustcloth in the office.

Taylor came over and laid his hand on her shoulder. "You're okay, Cheryl."

She turned around and opened her mouth to reply. Taylor patted her shoulder. "For the Lattimer article, give me a front page, ten inches, a mug shot, and maybe an action one." He turned and stretched by rising on his tiptoes and reaching high. He bent forward and touched the floor. He winked at Cheryl. "Keeps me in shape when female reporters chase me!"

He walked over to the filing cabinet, pulled the top drawer open, and extracted a wrinkled jacket. He put it on. It did not fit him well. "I've got an item to cover at Flint City Hall. Be back at nine thirty. Marge ought to be in by nine. Until then, act like a big city editor and answer the phone." Before Cheryl could think of a reply, he was gone.

"Well, what do you want to know?" Marc said as he came up from behind her. He sat down next to her desk stiffly, his long legs obviously wanting to sprawl.

"Just tell me about yourself. Your work. I'll stop and ask you questions. I'll snap a couple of pictures when I'm ready. Maybe I could visit your office and snap you there."

Marc smiled. If his manners had not been as obnoxious as Taylor's, she might have liked him. He had that healthy look about him which showed in his good coloring, clear nails, and even his neatly trimmed hair. She noticed the sharp creases of his trousers and the polished shoes. Most of all she liked his eyes—definitely the best feature of his handsome face.

"My name is Marc Lattimer. That's not short for Marcus. Just Marc with a C. Very unpretentious parents. My social-security number is four-eight-three—"

Cheryl dropped her pencil. "Look, I don't write articles about comedians—especially bad ones."

"You're right, I'm a terrible comedian. I'm sorry."

"I like you better this way."

"How much better?" he said and leaned forward.

"I retract that statement." She picked up her pencil and waited for him to speak again.

"Oh, I see. I am twenty-seven years old, unmarried. Almost married once. I can give you a list of my former girl friends—"

"I beg your pardon!"

"You're pretty, young, obviously unmarried. Just thought I'd save you time about my marital status and my availability so that you wouldn't have to ask subtle questions."

"You're as insufferable as Taylor!"

"I take that as a compliment," and he smiled.

"A compliment?"

"Yes, that I could upset you. Now I'm convinced I want to know you better. Taylor said you had spirit. He's right."

"So you two have discussed me like—like some—some—"

"Like some nice young lady reporter." He smiled again. "Now you'll want my educational history." He talked in a well-modulated voice, explaining that he specialized in physical therapy and speech pathology.

"Am I going too fast?" he said.

"With the interview or your remarks?"

"Ah, Taylor said you were sharp."

"Just keep talking," Cheryl said, waiting for him to relax and open up more. She had not yet figured out her angle for the feature. She jotted a word or two as he talked.

She could describe Marc as handsome, and she could think of no other word that fit. An additional ten pounds, evenly distributed over his more-than-six-foot frame, would have helped him look robust. His dark hair curled just enough to give him a casual look. His clothes fit well, and she had the impression he looked as much at home in denims as he did in his three-piece suit.

"How did you get interested in physical therapy?" she asked.

"Because of Frankie. A little boy in our neighborhood."

"Tell me about him."

"He had been in a car accident, and after two years in the hospital, no one expected him to walk again. One summer afternoon I took him to a friend's swimming pool and put him in the water. Just had him lie on his back, and I helped him float. He enjoyed every minute of it. I did that regularly for a month. Then one day he actually wiggled one of his toes. He had never done that before."

Marc's face lit up as he told of Frankie's progress. Cheryl noticed Marc's long lashes, covering his dark brown eyes. Yes, they were brown. His heavy brows formed a perfect arch over each eye.

"His parents could hardly believe it. By the end of the summer, Frankie took a few steps. In the water he did a frog kick you wouldn't believe."

For another twenty minutes she asked questions, and Marc answered. His reserve broken, he relaxed in the chair, spread his legs out, and appraised her when her head bobbed down and she didn't see his stares.

In the middle of the interview, Marge breezed in, waved, and said, "I'm Marge. You just go ahead with your work." She placed her purse in a drawer and sat down at her desk. Almost as if waiting for her, the phone rang. Marge picked it up with her left hand as she pulled out a ball-point pen with her right. She took notes, made several "uh huh" noises, and hung up. Immediately the phone rang again. After an additional six phone calls, Marge brushed past them on her way to the rest room. She dropped a sheaf of papers on Cheryl's desk.

"What's this?"

"Grips and grins—for you."

"Grips and grins? What's that?"

"You know—they grab a plaque, grin, and move on after you snap a picture," she said. "They're all yours."

Cheryl looked at the notes, each one on a five-by-six piece of paper. The first called for her to report on a county commissioners' meeting at nine thirty and snap a picture of an award presentation. At four she had to interview a member of the South Atlanta Optimist's Club on their summer projects. Sometime during the day she would visit the Flint Nurse Care Center to take pictures of their newly opened wing. As she skimmed the sheets, she suddenly realized it would be at least eight o'clock before she would get home again.

"Am I supposed to do all of these? Today?"

Marge shrugged as she passed by again. "I only take down the information, honey." The phone rang again.

Cheryl felt Marc laughing at her, and she frowned at him.

"You wanted a busy life, didn't you?" he asked.

"Did I say that?" she said, the irritation thick in her voice.

"I assume that's one reason a person works for a newspaper."

"There are better reasons."

"Such as?" His eyes held hers until she looked away.

Cheryl flushed and felt angry for doing it. "Oh, because I want to write. Because some day I'd like to move on to a national magazine and because—"

"Love the determination in your voice," he said.

"In the meantime, I'm living in Flint and working on the *Flint Sun.*"

"Marking time?"

She glared at him. "I wouldn't put it that way."

"Oh?" Although his face betrayed nothing, she heard a distinct smirk in his voice. "How would you put it?"

"*Mr.* Lattimer, shall we go now? I'd like to get a picture of you at work, and then I can still make my call at the county commissioners' meeting."

"As you like," he said and stood up.

After they went outside, Marc suggested that she drive and that he would get a ride back for his car. Cheryl shrugged indifferently and yet wondered why she felt pleased at the arrangement.

"First you back carefully out of the parking lot and turn left."

"You don't need to be quite that explicit in your directions," she said, now wishing she had not agreed to drive him.

"Be sure to watch out for cars fighting to take your parking spot."

Cheryl almost shot a sharp retort, but the playful look on his face made her realize he was teasing. "I'm learning a lot about parking and about people," she said. She turned left and headed south on Flint Road.

"Just keep going until I tell you. By the way, where are you from?"

"Where do you think?" she answered, stalling until she could decide whether to lie or change the subject.

"Not from the South."

"You sure?"

He chuckled. "Not with that accent."

"I don't have any accent—"

"Midwest definitely," he looked at her and saw that he had hit the target. "Illinois?"

"Close enough," she answered. "You from this area?"

"Why don't you say it's none of my business where you're from," he said.

"Okay, Marc. It's none of your business."

"How about dinner tonight?"

"What?" she said and stole a glance at him.

"How else can I get to know you?"

"I'm not sure I want to know *you*—personally, I mean," she said, her hands digging into the steering wheel.

"Oh, but you will," he said. "I grow on people. I have a hypnotic effect on redheads from the Midwest."

"Look, Marc, I came into town yesterday. I meet two men—you and Taylor. You both sound alike and act alike—"

"Except there's a difference between us."

"I hadn't noticed," she said.

"I'm eligible. He's not interested."

"Why, you insufferable—"

"His lack of interest has nothing to do with you. He's still—well, maybe he'll explain it himself."

"Look, Mr. Great Lover, I'm not—"

"Turn left at the corner. And I'll remind you of this conversation the night I propose to you."

Chapter 4

Cheryl parked her car and pulled the bag with a now-cold hamburger and fries from the empty seat. She stumbled wearily toward her apartment. She had been going over her lead for each of the eight articles she expected to write before going to bed.

If I can just force my mind to function in high gear, she said to herself, *I can get those leads down on paper and then tuck myself in for the night.* She felt grateful that she had brought her typewriter instead of leaving it behind in Des Moines.

Cheryl inserted the key into the lock and turned the knob. The door across the hall opened. "You're late," the voice said.

She spun around. Taylor leaned against the door frame. He wore a Tee-shirt and cutoffs, but no shoes. "The Volunteers Club took longer than I thought. They kept insisting on more pictures—"

"And they didn't feed you anything but gooey finger foods and weak coffee."

"Right," she said, "and so—" she held up her Burger King bag.

"Oh, no," he said. "Your supper's in the oven. In my apartment."

"What?"

"I'll bring it right over."

"Taylor, I don't need games—"

"Go inside, like a nice girl reporter, kick off your shoes, and relax. Your generous boss will carry a tray over in less than three minutes."

"Don't order me around. You sound just like—" she stopped and obediently went inside. She kicked off her shoes. Too tired to argue, she fell into the hide-a-bed. At the moment she did not care if she ate or not. The luxury of lying still, no one talking to her, and her body relaxing, dulled her mind. She could feel herself drifting into sleep.

The door swung open, and Cheryl's eyes snapped open. "I must have fallen—"

"I told you to relax. I'm glad you did."

He carried a metal tray, covered with a dish towel. She could smell the fish, and it stirred hunger pangs within her. As she thought about it, she had not had a full meal since the night before. Taylor set the tray down on her lap, bowed, and said, "Mam'zel, it es ze hope of ze management that you love our food."

"Anything, Taylor, anything—" she blushed. "I didn't mean it quite like that. I meant—"

"You cannot insult me, madam," he bowed again. As he straightened, she saw his dimples showing.

"Thanks. It may be a cliché, but I needed that!"

"Put the tray in my room if I'm gone before you get up in the morning." She heard a plunk as his key landed on the tray.

"Thanks again for the food. As for the key—"

"So you can leave the tray inside the room. It's kept locked, you know."

"And then leave the key inside?" she asked.

He shrugged. "You might as well keep it."

"Wait a minute. Let's get this straight. I work at the *Flint Sun*, but—"

"I'm not offering you a sleeping invitation. Just leaving my key. From time to time you'll have to run by my place to leave or to pick up something."

"Oh," she said. "Sorry, I—I didn't mean—"

"I'm always willing to do the same for you. If you want. If not—," Taylor shrugged again.

"That's kind of you, but—"

"I thought friends did that sort of thing for each other."

"Friends?"

"I've accepted you as a friend," Taylor said.

Cheryl, not knowing how to answer, looked again at her tray. She pulled the towel off to discover that he had broiled fish and baked a squash casserole and cornbread. Taylor had even made a tossed salad. She looked up at him, touched by his kindness. "Did you really—"

"I cannot tell a lie. I do excellent cooking."

Cheryl sampled the fish. "Hmmm, delicious," she said and did not lie.

"You may not get another treat like this for a month. But since it was your first full working day, I decided to show you how friends take care of friends."

"Taylor, thanks—"

"I left a message with Marge to tell you about dinner, but you didn't call in before she left."

"I didn't know I was supposed to."

"You weren't." He turned and started for the door.

"Do I give you a key to my apartment? Is that the arrangement?"

"Don't bother. I already have one."

"You have one? How dare—"

"I've had it a long time. Another friend lived in here before you did."

"Apparently you have many friends."

"On the contrary. I'm extremely selective."

"How do I rate—?"

"Good night, Cheryl, my friend," he said and closed the door.

The key remained untouched on the tray that night.

The next morning she heard Taylor locking his door. She had been lying awake, her eyes closed, telling herself to get out of bed. She opened her eyes long enough to peek at her travel alarm. It was only six-thirty. Almost immediately she fell asleep again.

By ten to eight she had gotten up, gulped a glass of juice, and munching on toast, she was ready to leave. Cheryl remembered the tray and took it across the hall. She wanted to leave the key inside and hesitated. She stared at the small object in her hand and said, "Oh, well." After locking the door, she dropped it into the bottom of her shoulder bag.

Five minutes later she walked into the office. Taylor looked up and yelled, "Cheryl, get over to Hunter's Sporting Goods. A fire."

"Where?"

"Here." He had written down the directions. "Hurry. Fire trucks already on the scene. Interview the chief. Anyone else. If Hunter's around, don't miss him, and—"

"I've done assignments before," she said.

"Good. Then you know how to listen to an editor." He handed her a file marked HUNTER, GEORGE R. "Read it today before you write the story. We don't want to libel—"

Cheryl clenched her fists, trying not to say anything. And then realizing she was doing what she had always done in the face of authority, she unclenched her fists and took a deep breath. "Taylor, I am not a rookie. I know what to do and how."

"I didn't question that—"

"And if you don't like my finished product, you're the editor. But give me credit for having some brains."

"Love it when you get angry!"

"What?"

"Don't forget Chief Edwards. A bit brusque at times, but a good man. Get a feel for the story and plan on two pictures."

"Yes, *Mr. Michaels.*"

"And call in from there—"

"Why don't you write down my entire schedule for the rest of the day?"

He grinned. "I'm glad we're friends."

"Oh!" She whirled around, grabbed her notebook, and ran from the office.

She found Hunter's Sporting Goods store because Taylor had written clear directions. She took a shot immediately while she could still see the firemen actually battling the blaze which seemed contained in one section of the building. Having previously covered two fires in Des Moines, Cheryl knew better than to stand around and bother the fire fighters. She asked questions of onlookers, always watching the main action out of the corner of her eye.

"I reported it," an elderly man said.

Cheryl stepped up close and got her pad out, not because she needed it, but she sensed the man would pour out more information. "I was coming out of the all-night Laundromat." He pointed three buildings down. "I always do the wash early in the morning while there's no crowd and I can be alone with my thoughts—"

"And you saw the fire?" Cheryl coaxed.

"That's right. I was getting into my car and looked up. Saw flames shooting out. I ran to that phone over there," he nodded with his chin to a nearby pay phone. "Lucky I had a quarter. Almost didn't have, but I didn't need to dry the extra load—"

"And you called the fire department."

"Right. I called them, and I want to tell you, it wasn't five minutes before they pulled in here like Christmas with bells ringing and firemen jumping every place."

Cheryl asked further questions, only half listening. She did write down his name. She also jotted a few key words in her pad to jog her memory when she actually wrote the story.

Her mind raced, trying to decide how to get the kind of information she wanted.

"That's the owner," someone said and pointed to a man.

Cheryl scurried over and held up her press card, carefully covering the name of the *Des Moines Register*. "Reporter. Understand you own the store."

"Yes," he said and looked down at his feet. "And it will just about ruin me."

"Are you insured?" Cheryl asked.

"That's the only good thing about this," he answered. "Last week I insured the place. Kind of had a feeling, I did."

"A feeling?" Cheryl asked. "You mean like a —"

"Like a premonition or something. I go on those kinds of things."

"And where were you when the fire broke out?"

"Why, sound asleep at home, of course."

Cheryl gave him a quick scrutiny. "You shaved and dressed pretty fast, didn't you?"

"I was sound asleep, I tell you, when the fire started!"

"Easy, Mr. Hunter. I'm not a detective—"

"Just leave me alone," he said. "I just want to be alone."

Cheryl walked away and milled through the crowd. The fire seemed over, but remembering her two previous experiences, she knew it could blaze up again. The fire fighters would not leave until they knew for certain that no danger existed of any further flare-up.

Standing slightly away from the crowd, she realized the stench had gotten to her, making her nose run. The acrid smell of water on charred timber made her sneeze twice. She backed away where she would not breathe in the fumes and yet could observe the activity.

"I didn't see a thing," a deep voice behind her said.

Cheryl whirled around. Marc was leaning against a car, watching her. She wondered if he had been there long. She forced a smile and said, "Hello, Marc."

"Want to ask me anything?"

"No," she said and turned away from him. She walked over to a small group that had gathered. She introduced herself and asked questions. "I saw it from across the street there," a boy said.

"What were you doing out so early?"

"Helping my dad deliver papers," he said. "And I saw the fire blazing away and then the trucks coming—"

"Don't you want to know anything I can tell you?" Marc said as he stood directly behind her.

"Marc, please—"

"I don't know a thing. That's why I thought you might like a totally objective point of view. I'm also open to interviews on the subject."

In spite of herself, Cheryl laughed. "If I run out of material, I'll use your objective quotes," she said, moving toward the paramedic unit.

A man, probably in his mid-twenties, stood alone, his arm on the door, but his eyes stared at the building. Of medium height and build, he had a quickness about his motions like a finely trained athlete. He put tanks of oxygen back into the unit, but in such a way as to lose eye contact only momentarily.

Cheryl flashed her card in his face. "Anyone hurt?"

"Luckily no one was inside the building," he said.

"Any idea how it started?"

Only then did he allow his attention to shift from the blackened building. His light brown eyes swept over Cheryl's entire body, beginning with her hair and going to her feet, then up again. "Hey, you're new," he said.

"Yes, I am," she answered.

"I know I've never seen you before," he said, and his eyes took another tour. "I'd never forget someone like you."

"Obviously you've been at this a long time," Cheryl said, realizing she had stiffened. Automatically her hand touched the top button on her blouse to make sure it was fastened.

"No, I'm just beginning—"

"I mean, you've been a paramedic a long time?"

He laughed, and this time his eyes went down only as far as her waist.

"What do you do here?" she asked. "I mean, other than stare at women."

He flashed a smile, showing bright, if slightly uneven teeth. "I know all the other women reporters. I'm willing to get to know you better."

"I don't cover that many fires," she said.

"I can give you exclusives," he said.

"Let's talk about *this* fire," she said.

Another man caught his attention, and he motioned back with finger signals which his partner answered. He looked at her again. "My partner's giving me the all-clear signal. We'll be leaving in a few minutes."

"Anything about the fire you can tell me?" Cheryl asked.

"You know, you're the best looking of the women reporters. At least the best in the last two years."

Cheryl flushed and peered at the notes on her pad, wondering how to move away from him without letting him see her embarrassment.

"Hey, want to see the inside of my unit sometime?"

Cheryl felt her skin redden, but she determined not to back down. "I saw the inside of one once."

He grinned. "Fine, then how about coming into this one?"

"That one was first class. I see no reason for wasting time on one of lower quality."

"Ouch, lady," he said but smiled. "You're smart, too."

She liked his square jaw and deep voice. "Smart enough to know I need enough copy for a story. Seriously, though—"

"You don't think I'm serious about getting to know you?"

"Seriously, can you tell me anything about the fire?"

"Naw. Chief Edwards will tell you everything. They've got it under control. They'll be packing up soon, too."

"What caused it? Any idea?"

"Arson."

"You think so?"

"No question. Fire contained in one area. A back room. All the valuable stuff away from the fire."

"You mean you think the owner—"

"Everyone knew Hunter was losing money. Tried to sell the place." Cheryl felt pleased to hear Taylor's conjecture confirmed.

"May I quote you as an informed and reliable source?" she asked, not intending to use the information.

"If you insist," he answered. He stood straight and whipped off his raincoat. He flexed his bicep. "Want my picture, too?"

"She's got other pictures to take," Marc said as he pulled Cheryl away.

"Hey, sorry, Marc. Didn't know you had already claimed this one."

"Now you know, Kevin," he said, and he continued to pull her away from the paramedic.

"Just my luck," he called. "I get all the lousy fires and lose all the pretty girls!"

Marc pulled her arm until they had gotten thirty feet from Kevin. He walked close to her, enjoying the pressure of his arm on her shoulder. He pulled her tighter, which was a mistake. She slipped out of his arm and looked at him. "What do you think you're doing?"

"I think I'm protecting you from one of the biggest girl chasers around."

"I was in the middle of getting information from him for a feature story."

"Information is not what you get from Kevin."

"So you think you're God's protector of fragile women or something?"

"That's the man," Marc said and pointed to a bareheaded fireman who barked orders to a man on the roof. He whirled around and yelled at another man who stood behind him. That man took off in a run into the store. The bareheaded man, obviously the chief, stood with hands on hips and surveyed the entire situation.

"Over there, Thompson!" the chief pointed.

"Chief Edwards," Marc said. "This is Cheryl Leigh, new reporter for the *Flint Sun.*"

He nodded without looking at her. His eyes followed the fireman who had reappeared on the roof. "Jones! Back up Rawls on the other side. I want one final check!"

Jones ran off and climbed the already-in-place ladder.

"Got it contained," the chief said, still not looking at them. "If you can wait a few more minutes, I'll answer any questions."

"Of course," Cheryl said as she snapped a picture of Edwards, an arm stretched out, motioning to one of his men.

Twenty minutes later she had the information and at least two good pictures. She decided to have a cup of tea and call the office. As she approached her car, Marc was sitting on the hood.

"Hurry up, Cheryl. I'm starved."

"Starved?" she repeated and then realized what he meant. "I had breakfast an hour ago."

"So did I," he said. "I lied just now. I'll settle for coffee."

"I'm not thirsty."

"Then I'll settle for a few minutes in a quiet booth with you."

"Marc—"

"Please," he said and stood up. He moved a few steps toward her, peering down into her green eyes. "I'd like it very much."

"Okay," she said.

"Follow me. I know a quiet place two blocks from here." He grabbed her hand and started walking.

"I thought you said *follow.*"

"Aren't I leading?" he answered and tightened his grip on her hand.

Minutes later they sat in a small booth. Both settled for hot chocolate. He took occasional sips. Mostly he stared at Cheryl.

"Marc, you're a friend of Taylor's—"

"Quite a good friend."

"He said the other day that I reminded him of someone. Then Annie Laurie Burns who—"

"I know Annie Laurie, too."

"She seemed startled when she first saw me, and the two of them kept making sly glances at each other and commenting on how much I resembled someone else—"

"There's no one in *my* world like you," he said and reached for her hand.

She pulled it back slightly. "Tell me what they were talking about."

Marc picked up the cup in front of him and took a long drink. He looked away for a moment and then back at her. "Cheryl, I don't have the right to tell that story. When he's ready, Taylor will tell you anything you want to know. He's like that. And until he's ready—," Marc's voice trailed off.

"Okay, I won't ask you again."

He glanced at his watch. "I'm already late for my first patient, so I can't stay," he said, "but how about dinner tonight?"

"Don't think so—"

"Tomorrow night? Next Friday? When?"

Cheryl laughed. "Don't rush me, Marc."

"Rush? I'm talking about monopolizing your time. How can I do it, unless you give me a chance to get started?"

Cheryl said, "Give me a chance to find out how my schedule goes. Once I know what kind of time—"

"There's still a guy back home, isn't there?"

"What makes you think—?"

"He dropped you, and you're afraid—afraid of being hurt again so you don't want to trust another man. Or get involved."

"Do you charge by the hour for your on-the-spot analysis?"

"I'll call you tomorrow," he said. He grabbed the check, leaned forward and bussed her on the cheek. "You're the prettiest Yankee I've seen in a long, long time," he said in his best southern drawl.

He rushed out, but Cheryl remained in the booth. She liked Marc better than she had the day before. She smiled to herself. He was right; he did grow on her.

But he wasn't Shep.

She sighed, but then, there would never be anyone else like Shep. She felt tears coming to the surface. She shook her head as a symbolic gesture of casting him out of her mind. "I refuse to think of him again," she said aloud.

But she knew she was lying.

Cheryl ate lunch as a guest of the Flint Area Homemakers' Club where she snapped a picture for the paper and jotted down three pages of notes. Later she interviewed a housewife who had published a book on stitchery.

She had two more interviews that day and decided to go back to her apartment for a quick nap. Cheryl had learned at college how to nap when needed. She could doze off instantly and had the ability to set a mental alarm clock. She decided to grab fifteen minutes.

She slipped into her room, kicked off her shoes, and fell face down on the hide-a-bed. Almost immediately she was asleep. Exactly fifteen minutes later she awakened, stretched slowly, then sat up. She washed her face, applied fresh makeup, and left the apartment.

As Cheryl rushed toward her car, she saw Ann Burns watering the azaleas. She waved.

Ann turned off the hose and walked toward her. "My dear, I do hope you're satisfied with your apartment."

"Very much," she said as she stood next to the car, her hand shielding her eyes from the glaring rays of the mid-afternoon sun. "Peaceful here. Very quiet. The apartment is exactly the right size."

Ann moved closer until she stood less than a foot away. "I want to apologize for the way I stared at you the other day."

"Think nothing of it."

"I couldn't help it. Even now—the way you half ran to your car. She moved the same way. Graceful but fast—just like her."

Ann stared into space for a moment. Then she touched Cheryl's face. "She looked so much like you. She was a little darker, but about the same height and figure. Every time I see you go in and out of that apartment—"

"It brings back memories?"

"Oh, yes. And always with a shock. Almost—almost transporting me back to the past."

"What was her name?" Cheryl asked.

"Elizabeth. Elizabeth Frazier," Ann said. Her eyes seemed to look beyond Cheryl. "She wore a lot of rust—just like you do. Oh, how lovely she looked, kind of skipping across the complex. Do you—do you like to walk?"

"Love it. I often walk long periods of time, especially when I'm stuck with an article."

"I thought so."

"You mean I look like a walker?"

"No. I mean, well, that was the way with Elizabeth. She walked three miles every day—rain or sun. Her way of relaxing, she said. And yet, to look at her, she appeared as helpless as an infant. Every afternoon she'd come out of her apartment—," Ann stopped. "Sorry, I just got carried away."

"She lived here? In these apartments?"

"I—I thought Taylor explained."

"Explained what?"

"About the apartment—"

"You mean—you mean I'm living where—"

"Yes, my dear. I kept only two furnished apartments. Taylor had one, and she had the other." Her eyes misted, and she cleared her throat. "When she—when she left—I just never rented it again. Until you came. Somehow I just couldn't let anyone else live there. When Taylor brought you—"

"Oh, I see," she said. She hugged the older woman. "I'm sorry, Ann. I didn't know how much pain it caused you—"

"I loved her so much. Like my own daughter."

Cheryl patted Ann's shoulder, trying to think of what she could say to the woman.

"There's been such an emptiness the past year, but seeing you coming and going—it brings back memories—"

"Look, I don't want to cause you pain. I can move out—"

"Oh, no, please," Ann straightened up. "Don't do that. You remind me of her. And when I see you, I think of how much I love her."

"I didn't mean to—"

"Good sometimes to know how much you love someone," the woman said as though she had not heard Cheryl.

"Yes, I suppose it is," she answered and looked away because the words stabbed at her own heart.

"Sometimes we don't know how deeply we care until—until those people aren't around anymore."

"Yes, that's true—," Cheryl said. She stiffened and breathed deeply. She patted the woman once again. "I have to rush back to the office before Taylor decides to fire me."

Cheryl didn't wait for a reply but hopped inside the car. As she pulled out of the driveway, she waved at the older woman. Ann had not moved. She didn't wave back, only stared at the retreating car.

Yes, Cheryl thought, *sometimes you don't realize how much you love someone until you've lost him.* Shep's name was on her lips, but she would not say it aloud.

Cheryl flipped on the radio to a country-and-western station. The guitar-playing baritone momentarily caused her to listen as she struggled to blot Shep's name out of her mind. Even turning up the volume didn't blot his name out of her consciousness.

Chapter 5

Cheryl surveyed her desk. Neat. Clean. All her assignments completed. She had even written her column for the following week, which put her ahead. She glanced at Taylor's desk. If anything, it looked more untidy than a week earlier when she had first come into the office.

Taylor seemed to take pride in the disarray and rebuffed every offer she made toward bringing order or neatness. Taylor hunched forward at his desk, rereading copy. He changed a word or two and turned the page. Cheryl admitted that although he kept the most untidy desk she had ever seen, he was the best editor she had worked for.

She got up, picked up her purse, and walked out the front door.

She waved at Marge who waved back. In the full week there, she had never gotten much conversation out of Marge. The receptionist answered questions, but she never volunteered more than asked for. Cheryl began thinking of her as the great robot, with a pleasant voice.

As she drove away, Cheryl realized that for the first time since arriving, she had no work to do and no evening commitments. She thought of the situation and decided it was time to cook a full meal for herself. She had decided that at her first opportunity, she would cook amounts large enough for at least two meat dishes and freeze portions to heat up later.

She drove to the nearby grocery store, loaded her shopping cart with vegetables, a roast, and two pie shells. She hadn't thought to try the oven and hoped it worked.

Cheryl had barely walked inside the apartment when the doorbell rang. She hesitated a long second, fearing it might be Taylor with an assignment he wanted her to cover immediately.

She opened the door, and there stood Marc.

"I know you don't have anything else going tonight—"

"How do you know that?"

"Taylor told me."

"You two talk about my private life, do you?"

"Wait, let's start this over again. I called your office. You were gone. I asked Taylor where I might locate you. Then he told me. Okay?"

"Okay," she said.

"And I knew you had to eat sometime. Right?"

"Yes, but—"

"So what if I take you into the big city of Atlanta to one of the nicest restaurants—"

"Marc, thanks, but I've just walked in with two bags of groceries," she said as she walked back into the apartment and started to put the food away. She took the egg carton from the first grocery bag. "I plan to cook a full meal myself and—"

"That's okay," he said. "When should I come?"

"Not quite what I meant," she said, laughing in spite of herself. She separated the dairy products—milk, yogurt, and cottage cheese.

"Look at me," Marc said. "I have worked hard all day, without even taking time for lunch. I'm already ten pounds underweight, and when I eat alone, I only pick at my food—"

"I'm sorry about your poor eating habits—"

"I know you are, Cheryl, and that's why you have to help me. I'll waste away to nothing, and contract pellagra, scurvy, even halitosis—"

"Okay, okay," she said. "Make it six thirty. And pick up Taylor on the way."

"Taylor? You think you need a chaperone?"

"Chaperone? You make him sound like he's eighty."

"As far as romance goes, he's only good as a chaperone."

"Is that right?"

"You have no romantic ideas about Taylor, do you?"

"Of course not," she said and realized she spoke the truth.

"I was beginning to wonder a little—"

"I meant," Cheryl interrupted, "that I might need him as protection."

"Never."

"Never?"

"Cheryl, one day you're going to love me, so you might as well get used to the idea. In the meantime, my mother taught me never to force myself on a lady."

Cheryl laughed and then said, "You don't think this visit has any element of force in it?"

"No. With this visit I'm being assertive—or aggressive—whichever word you like. But I'll never make a real advance until you're ready."

"And if I never am ready?"

"I'll take my chances on that," he said.

"It's just that—I don't want to lead you on or give you false hopes."

"A boy back home?"

"That's really none of your business—Sorry, I didn't mean to sound rude."

"I asked for that one. Anyway, let me bring something. Dessert maybe?"

"As I recall, the last time we ate together you picked up the check?"

"That's right, *Margo*—"

"I was in a bad mood—"

"You certainly were," Marc answered, "but, you know, I liked your spunk."

Cheryl laughed lightly as she stacked canned goods into the inner recesses of the cupboard.

"You blew it, lady."

"Blew what?"

"That was your cue. You were supposed to say, 'You know, Marc, I liked you that time, too.' "

"I need to get busy cooking, Marc."

"I really did like you the moment you screamed at me in that parking lot," he said. "Even then I thought you were something special."

"I was so angry at you I didn't think how I felt toward you. I had waited for a parking spot, and you grabbed it. That's what went through my mind."

"But since then?"

"I don't think about the parking lot. Is that what you mean?"

Marc chuckled. "I told you I grow on people. We started out on a negative note, and we've progressed."

"We have?"

"You don't hate me anymore, do you?"

"No—"

"And you at least like me a little now, don't you?"

"Yes. Yes, I do," Cheryl answered guardedly. "A little."

"A little? How little is that?"

"Good-bye, Marc."

"We can continue this discussion at six thirty. See you then," he called on his way out the door.

Immediately Cheryl took the meat out of the cellophane wrapping. "Oh," she said aloud. She remembered that she hadn't thought to check the oven and hadn't used it since she had moved in. She turned the oven on. To her delight, it began heating immediately. Within an hour, her roast was cooking, and she had placed five potatoes on the rack next to it. Cheryl enjoyed baked potatoes, hot or cold. She then made a custard and poured the filling into the pie shells. It suddenly occurred to her that she could bake the pies in Taylor's apartment instead of waiting for her roast and potatoes to finish.

"He's probably still at the office, but I have a key," she said aloud. "And he said I might need to get into his apartment!" Cheryl laughed, wondering why she had to justify to herself going into Taylor's apartment, especially since she planned to share the meal with him. She took the two shells for banana-cream pies across the hall. She had to set one of them on the floor so she could put the key into the door and turn the handle. She pushed the door open, picked up the second pie, and gave the door a kick. It did not close.

She put both pies in the oven, set the timer, and turned to go back to her own apartment when she noticed Taylor's desk tucked into a corner. It struck her first that it was neat—especially after seeing the piles on his desk at the office.

She walked over and saw a picture of a girl in a large frame. Cheryl picked up the picture. At the bottom was written, "I'll love you always. Beth."

Beth? Elizabeth? As Cheryl scrutinized the picture, she saw where people could detect a resemblance. Same facial structure. Oddly enough, the same style of hair, worn short and curly. Next to the picture was a small jeweler's box. Without thinking about it, Cheryl opened the box and saw two matching gold wedding rings.

Cheryl didn't hear Taylor come in. He watched her reaction to the picture and the rings. "Friends don't snoop on each other," he said.

She whirled around, "I—I didn't intend to snoop. I mean, really, I'm sorry."

"Friends don't have to tell each other they're sorry," Taylor said.

"The picture? Elizabeth Frazier?"

"Annie Laurie been talking to you?"

"A little. Nothing about you."

"Good. I'll tell you what you want to know. Later."

"You must have loved her very much."

"I still love her," he said. He snapped the box closed. "Ah, my nose tells me that you have baked a pie."

"Yes, and I'm actually cooking a whole meal. You're invited to share it with me. It'll be another hour—"

"Your place or mine?"

"Mine. I'll come get you."

As she left, she called out, "I'll try not to pry again, friend."

"Delicious meal," Marc said.

"Excellent," Taylor echoed.

"Anything you don't do well?" Marc asked.

Cheryl only smiled, glad that the roast had turned out well. Judging from the portions the two men ate, they really had liked her cooking.

During the meal, Cheryl realized how comfortable she felt. Even though she had known them such a short time, it was almost as if they had known each other for years.

Even when the conversation lagged, no one felt the need to rush into a new topic. Marc and Taylor kept their conversation light, and Cheryl enjoyed the banter between them.

Odd, she thought, *Shep and I had times like this, too—with Karla as the third party.* The more Cheryl thought about it, the more she realized that during the last few months the give-and-take had gone on mostly between Shep and Karla. They had developed private jokes, which they did not always bother to explain. *Why am I just now seeing that?* she asked herself.

"If you want to sit there like the great sphinx," Marc said and tapped Cheryl's foot with his own, "we don't mind."

"Oh, sorry," Cheryl said, "I guess my mind wandered a little."

"You mean with all this high-level conversation going on, you could think of other things?" Taylor said.

"Yes, stupid of me, I know," Cheryl laughed.

Cheryl stared at her desk calendar. She had actually lived in Flint three full weeks. The days had flown by quickly, and her work kept her so busy, she hadn't thought about anything except deadlines, getting the right lead for her articles, and juggling all the entertainment events into a single week.

As religion editor, she had already attended seven different church functions, arranging to stay only long enough to snap pictures and get details on presentations, dedications of new buildings, and installations of new pastors.

In the food section, she had started receiving recipes and diet items. If she stayed, Cheryl thought she might even run a question-and-answer column on nutrition.

But today work had slowed down, and she sat at her desk, reflecting about her work. She still had not made up her mind if she wanted to remain in Flint or move on.

And what about Marc? Under normal conditions, everything would move along smoothly. But life wasn't normal right now.

She thought of Shep often, but as the days fled past, his image receded into the back of her mind. But today had been different for her. Mid-morning a tall blond man walked into the office to see Taylor. About Shep's age, he had that tennis-player look that made her think of Shep. She remembered the late afternoons when they had played tennis together. His unruly blond hair always insisted on falling down over his forehead. He had a habit of tossing his head to push the hair back.

Shep. What would he be doing right now, she wondered. She thought of calling him—not that she hadn't thought of it before. But she had no idea what to say.

Cheryl smiled to herself, glad that she had not had a phone put in. The urge to call always came late at night. By morning she would realize the impossibility of calling him.

If she called him, she would, one way or another, tell him where she was. And somehow Mother would find out. Cheryl shivered, suddenly glad she now lived so far away and did not have to talk to her. She could imagine the lecture Mother would give if she knew how to get ahold of her daughter.

"You fallen asleep?"

Cheryl looked up. Taylor stood in front of her. "Either make the call or don't."

"Make the call?" she said half-dazed.

"You've been staring at that phone for at least five minutes."

"Have I?"

"You have." He sat down on the edge of her neat desk. He picked up three manila folders and spread them carelessly on her desk. "Improves the desk thirty-five percent," he said and smiled.

"If you say so," Cheryl answered and picked up the folders.

"You know, my friend, I've tried not to interfere in your private life—"

"Thank you for that favor."

"But—is there, you know, anything you'd like to talk over with me?"

"Talk over with you?" she repeated.

"Yeah, talk over with me."

"I—I don't think so."

"Remember the night when I brought you dinner?"

"Of course—"

"I told you then I had chosen to be your friend. Friends care about each other. I care about you."

"Taylor, I'm touched that—"

"All I'm trying to say is that I know something's troubling you. You left Des Moines without giving proper notice to your paper." He winked. "I have a contact there, by the way."

"So you've gossiped about me—"

"So I know you were a good reporter. I did not ask about your personal life, and I especially asked that he *not* tell friends or relatives you had come here."

"Thanks, Taylor—"

"You wrote under the name of Cheryl Adams."

"That *is* my name."

"Of course. Just noting the fact. And I didn't cause any concern on the *Register*."

"Thanks—again."

"You don't have to thank a friend," he said and walked back to his desk.

"Maybe one day I'll want to talk."

"The offer's always open—to friends." He sat down in front of his own typewriter. Seconds later she heard the clacking of the keys.

Cheryl opened the stack of letters Marge had dropped on her desk as she rushed by. Most of them contained wedding pictures and announcements of everything from bazaars and church revivals to square dances. She skimmed through them, mentally preparing them for the people section of the paper.

She stopped at one wedding announcement and accompanying picture. After reading it over twice, she said, "Taylor, listen to this. John Bolling and Emma Craig were united in marriage Sunday—"

"So what's unusual about that?"

"They're both eighty-three."

He shrugged. "Lots of old people marry."

"That's not all. According to what they wrote, John and Emma met in grammar school, dated in their teens, and planned to marry. John served in World War One, and Emma married someone else. John never married. When Emma's husband died last year, John started calling on Emma again. Isn't that quite a story? Unreal."

"What do you mean, unreal?"

"I mean, this guy must have waited sixty years for Emma."

"What's wrong with that?" Taylor said. He now looked up at her. "He knew the woman he wanted. He waited."

"Nonsense."

"What do you mean, nonsense?" Taylor asked. He took off his half-moon glasses and glared at her.

"I don't believe he could have carried his love that long."

"Why not?"

"Oh, come on, Taylor. Somewhere he must have stopped loving her. Maybe that love rekindled later. But sixty years—"

"Some people only love once in their entire lives," Taylor said.

"Only if they choose that," Cheryl said.

"Maybe it's not only a matter of choice," Taylor said, his voice rising. "Maybe they can't help how they feel."

"We all have disappointments," Cheryl said. "And some of us—well, some of us love people very much—and lose them. But—we get over them." She wanted to add, "At least I hope we do."

"Maybe some people don't want to get over their loss."

"And some people never want to face reality, either," she said, thinking of herself.

"Stay out of other people's business," he snapped and turned around and pecked rapidly at his typewriter.

Cheryl stared at him, wondering what had upset him. "Sorry," she mumbled and continued staring at the picture. She would not be like John Bolling. She would love again.

Warm night winds swept across the apartment complex. Cheryl, unable to sleep, got out of bed and slipped on jeans and a light jacket. She tiptoed past Taylor's door and walked around the apartment complex and then circled the block twice. Other than a few cars on the road, she would not have known another soul was around. It felt good to walk in the May evening.

"If I still believed in prayer," she said aloud, "I think I could even pray and—," she stopped, laughing at her own foolish words.

"At least I know I'm getting better. I'm not tortured with memories of Shep." Although she had not been able to sleep, it was not because of him.

A hundred thoughts marched through her mind. She had gone to dinner four times with Marc. She had discouraged him from coming back, but he called at least three times a week. She liked him more, but not enough.

At last, feeling she could sleep, Cheryl headed back to the apartment. She knew an inner peace she had not felt since the day she ran from Des Moines. If she had not been afraid of awakening people, she would have started singing.

She was fishing her keys from her jacket pocket when she first heard the noise from Taylor's apartment. She stood quietly and listened.

Taylor screamed. She couldn't hear the words, but the volume increased. She put her ear against the door but could hear nothing but Taylor's voice.

"Taylor! Taylor!" She pounded on the door.

The yelling stopped.

"Taylor! You all right?"

When no answer came, she dashed into her own apartment, grabbed the key to Taylor's apartment, and struggled in the dark to find the keyhole. She finally threw the door open and flipped on the light switch. As the light went on, Taylor bolted upright in bed, his pajama top soaked with perspiration. He stared at her without saying anything.

"Taylor, what's wrong?" she asked, trying to control her voice. "Your yelling frightened me."

"Oh, uh, nothing," he said, but he did not move.

"I heard your screaming—"

"It's nothing," he said, and he finally brought his eyes into focus. "Hello, Cheryl." He smiled.

"I thought friends didn't lie to each other," she said and turned to leave.

"They don't. And I did."

"Good night—"

"Wait, Cheryl, don't go." He jumped out of bed. "Just—just sit down for a minute."

Cheryl obeyed. "For a minute maybe."

"Let me change pajamas and get a robe on—and then—then maybe as one friend to another, we can talk. I'm sorry—"

"Friends don't have to tell each other they're sorry," she said, allowing her voice to sound hard and remembering she echoed his words.

"Sometimes friends want to explain," he said. From a drawer he grabbed clothes and headed for the bathroom. "Hey, make us a pot of coffee while I'm changing, will you?"

"Might as well. I've learned to halfway like the stuff," she said.

"Then make it just a little stronger this time. At the office, it is just a tad weak." He slammed the door so he wouldn't hear her answer.

When he came out and sat down at the table, she poured his coffee. "Cheryl," he said as he picked up the liquid and took a gulp, "I'd like to tell you about Beth."

"You sure you want to?"

"I'm not sure I want to but—I know I need to—to talk to someone."

"I'm ready to listen," she said and poured herself a cup.

"I loved Beth a long time. We met in college, and I knew the first time I saw her that she was the woman I wanted. I chased her and talked to her every chance I could."

Taylor remembered the lunches together. The walks across campus. He also remembered the dozens of times he had proposed, but Beth always gave him the same answer. And he always argued.

"You see," he said and leaned forward. He took Cheryl's hand a minute and squeezed it. "I see so much of Beth when I look at you. Maybe that's why I find it easy to talk to you. You don't mind? I mean, my seeing Beth in you?"

She shook her head and returned the squeeze of his hand.

Taylor withdrew his hand and took another long drink. "Beth grew up in the church. Her whole life revolved around that building and its programs. I went a few times, mostly to be with her. I didn't *not* believe—actually I didn't think much about it all. God and the rest of it didn't seem important."

"But they were to Beth?" Cheryl asked.

"Important? Top priority for her."

"It must have caused a strain in your relationship."

"It did. But one day, Beth offered a compromise. She would go out with me every time I attended a church or religious function with her."

"Did you?"

"Absolutely," he said. "I loved Beth. I would have done anything for her."

"Did you—oh, you know, get into the religious part yourself?" Cheryl asked as she delicately sipped her coffee.

"Yes, I did," he said slowly. "Eventually God became as important to me as to Beth. Perhaps not as deeply—"

"But just as real—"

"Just as real. And as for the events that happened later, well, I wouldn't have been able to get through it all if my faith in Jesus Christ hadn't been there to hold me together."

He stepped behind Cheryl and hugged her. "You're a good friend." Abruptly he released her, picked up his cup, and walked over to the pot. He poured a full cup for himself and drank most of it in a single swallow. "Love coffee when it's just off the boil and burns your mouth." He took a second swallow and drained the cup.

Cheryl sat in silence, sipping slowly, wondering if she ought to speak. She wanted to ask questions, but sensed Taylor had closed the subject.

Taylor filled his cup again, sat down at the table, and looked directly into her green eyes. "Who's the man? The one you're running away from?"

"Shep. Just a nickname—," she stopped and dropped her gaze. "I feel as though you're starting a police interrogation."

"Me?" he smiled.

"Do you ask questions that way to shock people?"

"One of the tricks of my trade. Throws folks off balance, and they answer before they have time to think up a lie."

"You thought I'd lie?"

"No, but I didn't know if you'd answer."

"I answered your question."

"That's all you did."

"Taylor, do you want to talk more about Beth right now?"

"No," he said and looked away.

"I don't want to talk about Shep either," she said softly. "At least not right now."

"That's okay with me. Friends don't—"

"Friends don't pry. Right?"

He laughed. "You're doing well, Cheryl Leigh Adams."

"In some ways—"

Taylor cocked his head. "I'm not sure—"

"I'd like to ask you a question. Not about Beth," she said.

"Friends don't have to ask permission—"

"Cut it out, Taylor." She examined her fingers and played momentarily with the garnet stone on her right hand. "You—well, you mentioned God. Do you still, you know, believe?"

"More than ever."

She nodded. "Just asking."

"Are you a Christian—a believing Christian?" he asked.

"I don't think so. I mean, I used to be, but not anymore."

"Would it be prying," he said, and his voice became soft, "if I asked you what happened?"

"It would be prying," she said.

"You're really learning to stand up for yourself, aren't you?"

"Is that what I'm doing?"

"Sure. Set the limits. Don't let anyone intrude beyond that point." He got up and put his cup in the sink, came back to the table, and leaned down. He pecked her on the forehead. "You're a great person."

Cheryl flushed, not sure what to say.

"I'm going back to bed now. So turn out the light when you finish your coffee—"

"And don't make too much noise closing the door," she said and laughed.

"Like I said, you learn fast."

"I'm glad," she said.

"Talking to you has helped, Cheryl."

"Has it?"

"When I have those nightmares and wake up, I usually don't get back to sleep all night. But this time it's different. I know I can sleep now."

She got up and walked to the door. She opened it and pulled the key out. "I wish you were Shep," she said.

"And I wish you were Beth," he answered.

"But because that's impossible for both of us," she said, "I'm willing to settle for your friendship."

"It's the best I can offer," Taylor answered.

Chapter 6

Cheryl had spent more time rewriting an article about local politics than she had planned. Her lead paragraph hadn't gone right, and she wrote it five times before she felt good about it. She glanced at the clock and realized she had overspent her carefully budgeted time. She would be at least ten minutes late in reaching the special ceremony held by one of the airlines to honor seven of their employees, all with more than thirty years of service. She needed a good picture for the paper.

Cheryl hurried out of the building, threw her bag and camera into the backseat, and pulled out of the parking lot. The traffic light was red, and she groaned because that would delay her that much longer. Her mind flipped through other unfinished material piled on her desk. She made a mental note to call the library in the morning. She had promised to do a feature on their new computer system.

Because Cheryl had not given the road complete attention, she did not notice the green one-ton truck. It sped south. Her blinkers indicated her left turn, heading north. As soon as the light changed, she lightly pressed the accelerator.

The squeal of brakes as rubber screeched against the asphalt filled her ears. She turned her head only to see the truck bearing down. A horrified look filled the driver's face. Cheryl threw up her hands and screamed. She heard the sound of glass breaking around her. Then everything went black.

Voices kept coming toward her and then drifting away. Cheryl tried to listen. She wanted to move, to stretch her hand, anything, but she felt lifeless. With an extreme effort, she popped her eyes open. The blur before her was a man. He wore a blue jacket.

"Just lie still, ma'am," the voice said. "Don't try to move."

"She's alive," a woman's voice said. "I don't see how—"

"But how long?" another voice said. "Pretty awful crash, if you ask me."

"Please move back," the voice of the blue jacket said, and she heard people's feet shuffling. Cheryl didn't know if she actually heard sirens or if she dreamed it. It required too much effort to keep her eyes open. She closed them again.

She awakened a second time and felt herself being carried. "Please, don't," she mumbled. "I'll never get to the ceremony in time." No one paid any attention to her. She opened her eyes and tried to sit up. A strong hand pushed her down. "Lie still, miss."

Cheryl awakened again and saw only white all around her—white walls, white sheet, a white uniform bending over her. "Are you awake?" a woman's voice asked.

"Yes," she mumbled and tried to raise her head. A hammer of pain struck her, and she winced. Her mind asked, "Where am I?" but her lips refused to form the words. She tried to move her legs, but they felt chained to the bed. Nothing responded to her effort.

"We're taking you to a room now," the voice said again. "In a while you'll be coming out of it. Surgery's all over."

"Thank you," Cheryl mumbled, the words not sinking in. Or had she only thought the words? *Surgery.* Did the voice say *surgery?* How could that be? She felt herself being moved from one bed to another. She heard the wheels of the gurney rolling away. Cheryl drifted off again.

Conscious of a wet cloth gently wiping her face, Cheryl opened her eyes. Even though drawn shades diffused the light, she realized she was in a hospital room. She moved her head to the side. Whoever had wiped her face, stopped, and their eyes met.

"Nice to see you fully awake this time," the voice said.

Cheryl stared blankly. She felt the heaviness of her own body, as though someone were sitting on her. Her left arm ached, and she tried to move it but could not. Then she turned her head and understood why. A cast extended from the bicep past the elbow. Her right arm, although bandaged, did not have a cast. Instead, an IV needle and tube ran to a rack next to her bed. Cheryl raised her head slightly and peered down at the rest of her body. Both legs had casts up to the top of her thighs.

"Dear God," she whispered, "what's happened to me?" Tears spilled down her cheeks, and she could not move an arm to wipe them away.

Cheryl did not know if the door opened immediately or if she dozed off again. She turned her head, and a nurse wrapped a blood-pressure cuff around her right arm.

"Please—tell me where—where I am," Cheryl said. "What happened to me?" She found each word hard to speak, her mouth dry, and those few words drained her of strength.

The nurse patted her on the shoulder. "You've been involved in an accident."

"But where—where am I now?"

"Room four twenty-seven. Flint General Hospital."

"What time—?"

"Lie still, dear," the nurse said and placed a thermometer in her mouth. "Your doctor's down the hall. In a minute I'll tell him you're awake."

When the nurse extracted the thermometer, Cheryl asked, "What time—?"

"About nine thirty," the woman said matter-of-factly.

"Morning? I mean I left the office just before nine—"

"Evening," she said and left the room.

Cheryl lay quietly, the mild humming of the air-conditioning unit breaking the silence. Presently she heard the patter of feet in the hallway. Far away strains of a TV wafted through to her. She tried to orient herself to the room. Her head hurt so much that concentration proved difficult. She saw the switch to call the nurses. She debated whether to call and ask questions and demand answers. As Cheryl made the effort to reach for the switch, she realized she could not do it. Even though it lay six inches from her arm, she could not move either her arm or her fingers.

She moved her head slowly, taking in the entire room. That small effort exhausted her. She closed her eyes, deciding to rest a little, and then she would sit up and begin demanding answers.

"Miss Adams?" the voice said.

Cheryl opened her eyes, seeing a woman in a white uniform in front of her. It was a different face from before.

"Good morning. Hope you slept well—"

"Morning?" Cheryl asked.

"Almost eight," she answered. "Think you can eat anything?"

"I—I don't think—I don't think I'm hungry."

"How about coffee? Milk? I brought both."

"Please—what happened to me? Tell me what I'm doing here." And then Cheryl mentally saw the truck coming at her and relived the throwing up of her arms. "The truck—the truck hit me!"

"All I know is that you were involved in a traffic accident," the nurse said as she put a straw in Cheryl's mouth. "Now sip slowly."

Cheryl did as she was told, and when the black coffee reached her mouth, she turned her head away.

"Want sugar in it?"

"No—nothing."

"You sure?"

"Just—please—call my boss."

"The doctor's coming in soon," the nurse said. She left the room.

Cheryl closed her eyes again, unable to hold them open. This time a male voice awakened her. "Aha, so now you do want to be close to me."

"Marc!"

"And he's the one who will give you physical therapy when you're ready for it," Marc said.

"Physical therapy? Just get me out of—out of this—"

"Do you know what happened?" he asked.

"A truck. I saw a truck coming right at me. That's all I remember."

"He ran a red light. We've got witnesses. He also knocked your car into another car. But you were the only one seriously hurt."

"How hurt?" she asked as she looked directly at him.

"Your doctor will see you soon. Ethically, I'm not supposed to tell you—"

"Marc, tell me—"

"Okay," he said, "if you're sure—"

"Marc, it's *my* body."

"Okay," he said again. "Well, both legs are broken. Your left arm, too. Your right arm only cracked. You may need additional surgery on your left leg because the bone shattered in several places. Aside from that, you're not doing too badly."

"How bad is that?"

"Oh, you know, a couple of casts—"

"Will I walk again?"

"Nothing's impossible—"

"*Will I walk again?*"

"Cheryl, we don't know. At least not yet. It depends on what happens with your legs. They may heal all right—"

"If they don't?" she fought back the tears that threatened to overcome her. "Just—just leave me for a few minutes. I'm tired—and—I need to think—"

"I understand," he said.

"It's easy for you to understand. You're on that side of the bed—" she stopped. "I'm sorry. I don't know why I lashed out like that."

Marc leaned down, his face only inches from hers. "You're going to be all right, because you've got guts."

"I don't feel much like anything right now."

"But you're a fighter," he said. "And you've got me on your side."

"Marc—"

"And don't forget God's on your side, too."

"God? I'm not sure—not sure He's on my side." She turned her face away from him.

"He is. Whether you know it or not." He smiled and touched her fingers and squeezed them gently. "He's on your side. Always."

"On my side? He's got a strange way of showing it!"

"Sometimes God lets us go as far on our own as we want. When we realize we can't handle life without His help, *then* He shows He's on our side."

"I'm not sure I quite understand—"

"Or want to right now?"

"Or even want to," she said. "I just hurt too much."

"I'll drop by to see you later," he said and pecked her on the lips.

Cheryl didn't answer. Pain throbbed in her body, and she felt as if every joint ached and every bone was broken. If only the nurse would come right away. The news Marc had given only added to the physical weight and pain she had already felt.

"Why? Why?" she mumbled aloud. Tears slid down her face and across the white pillow.

Chapter 7

In fuller detail, Dr. Lambert explained what Marc had told her. She should expect to remain in the casts at least six weeks, perhaps longer.

"How much longer?"

"Hard to say. Depends on how your bones knit together again and—"

"But the maximum?" she asked.

"Oh, six months," he said. "But let's not think about that. Instead let's concentrate on the immediate problems."

"I guess I'm doing all right—aren't I?"

"There's the question of a nurse, you know," Dr. Lambert said in his distinct New England baritone. "You need someone to stay with you around the clock. At least until we remove the casts."

"You mean all the time—the first six weeks?"

He nodded. "After the first casts come off, and if everything goes well, you might be able to get by with part-time help—"

"A nurse? Will my insurance cover that?"

"You'll have to check that out yourself," he said. "I can only tell you that you don't have any choice—not for the next six weeks anyway."

"Isn't there a nurses' registry or something?"

"Yes," he said and made notations on a card he held. "Unfortunately, they have a limited number of private duty and practicals. The demand always exceeds the supply. But I'll have my secretary call them for you if you like."

"Please, doctor."

"However, for the next few days, the hospital can provide private-duty nurses. In the meantime," he shrugged his shoulders, "they'll do what they can to help you."

"Excuse me," the nurse who assisted Dr. Lambert said. "Your boss, Mr. Michaels, called us this morning. You're fully insured by the *Flint Sun,* and the driver who hit you is insured. And he said to tell you not to worry about finances."

"That's one load you won't have to carry," the doctor said and smiled at her. "Now you can concentrate on getting well and let the insurance people worry about paying for the nurses."

"Yes, I suppose you're right," Cheryl answered automatically. She looked at the nurse. "Mr. Michaels called you?"

"Oh, yes, not more than twenty minutes ago. Called the nurses' station. Asked us to pass the message on to you."

"Oh, I see."

"Very concerned about you. Wanted to make sure you had the best of everything."

"Yes, thanks," Cheryl said and thought, *It would help if he would come by and see me himself.* This was her second day, and so far as she knew, Taylor had not come.

Just before leaving, Dr. Lambert had the nurse give Cheryl another injection for pain. She felt her body relax almost immediately and drifted toward sleep again.

For the next week, days and nights blurred for Cheryl. She knew everything that went on, but she could not keep track of time. Had the nurse changed the IV only five minutes ago or had it been hours? Time to eat again? She had eaten only—how long ago? She stopped trying to sort it out. Nurses changed IVs, checked her temperature and blood pressure, moved her slightly in the bed, always asking if they could do anything more.

At least three times Cheryl burst into tears for no apparent reason. The crying bouts disappeared almost as quickly as they came.

"For a stranger in town, you have a good share of visitors," the day nurse said to her. Cheryl realized that a number of people had come to see her.

Each morning Marc breezed in and out and then again in the evening. Ann Burns came almost every afternoon, stayed ten minutes, and departed. A rapid succession of people came at other hours. Most of their names she did not remember.

"I'm Jim Burris," one man said. "I go to Flint Lutheran Church. Marc Lattimer told us about you."

The same afternoon an elderly man with a soft-spoken voice came, offered to read to her, which Cheryl declined, and then said as he left, "Several of us at the church pray for you every day."

One woman brought flowers from her garden. Another baked cookies and urged Cheryl to eat them. She did, although she had no appetite.

Two middle-aged housewives came promptly every morning at ten. "Marc told us about you," one of them said. "We came by to help in any way we can. We also want you to know that we pray for you every day."

The pastor came on Cheryl's fourth day. "I've been out of town," he said, "but I understand members of our congregation have visited you already." He was a tall man who looked more like a linebacker on the Falcons team than a minister. His broad neck made her wonder if he gasped for breath because of the tight collar. Cheryl wanted to reach up and unbutton his top button. "You've been the concern of many people," he was saying.

"Thank you for coming," she said.

"We want to do anything we can to help—"

"I'm doing fine, really."

"Marc has arranged for one of our women to clean your apartment once a week and do your laundry after you get home. Anything else?"

"Thank you, that's plenty," Cheryl said, and in spite of herself, tears surfaced in the corners of her eyes.

"Another family has already started preparing meals for you and freezing them. That way, once you get back to your apartment, you'll only need someone to slip them into the oven."

"That's kind—"

"We'll keep checking on you. If you can think of anything else—"

"Nothing. You've done so much already."

"Oh, almost forgot. When you get ready for another car, we'd like to help. One of our most active members runs a car business. He's an honest man. He'll help—if you want him to." The pastor smiled, and Cheryl liked the warmth he seemed to radiate.

"Why are you doing this?" she asked.

"Doing what?"

"Visiting me. Bringing me things. I don't attend your church. I probably won't attend when I get out—"

"What's that got to do with our helping you?"

"I thought—I thought you visited only church people."

"We care about people, Cheryl. You're people."

"I've just never—well, never had anything like this before." And as she spoke those words, she remembered the scene in the pastor's office. She had come out of desperation. And left angry. She had vowed never to go again. She had also assumed that all churches were like the one in Des Moines.

"Cheryl, we're not trying to push you into our congregation. We're trying to reach out to you because you're someone in need." He laid his large hand gently on Cheryl's right hand. "Would it be all right if I prayed for you?"

She nodded yes.

He prayed a few sentences, quietly, and almost immediately headed for the door. "We want to help in any way possible," he said and waved.

Cheryl decided that was the best day she had spent in the hospital. She hurt less and even omitted a pain shot in the middle of the afternoon.

To her surprise, Cheryl anticipated seeing the people from Flint Lutheran Church. But most of all, Marc's presence highlighted her day. His two daily visits always lifted her spirits.

Marc's visits lengthened. From a few minutes before work and half an hour in the evening, he started coming earlier and staying later. By the second week he reached her room by five in the afternoon and didn't leave until nine, sometimes ten. A few days later he told the nurse, "You can go home. I'll stay until the relief comes in at eleven."

On the occasions when Cheryl did not feel like talking, Marc turned on the TV and kept the volume low. If that bothered her, he pulled a paperback out of his jacket pocket and read. Occasionally he picked up the Gideon Bible in the room and read from it. But whenever Cheryl felt like talking, she always had his full attention.

By the end of the second week, he said, "You may go home in a week or so. You really need someone to stay with you."

"I try not to think about it," she said, "but I'm afraid we've got to find someone."

"I keep trying. Got a lot of friends trying too. No luck yet."

"Somehow I'm going to make out all right," she said and gritted her teeth.

"Don't be silly. I'll move in if I have to—"

"You need your sleep, too—"

"I can do it for at least a few days," he said. "Till we can find someone."

"Thanks, Marc."

"I just want you to know that not having a nurse won't stop your leaving the hospital when it's time to go."

"Marc, you've been so good—," she stopped, not wanting to cry. The bouts of depression had become less frequent, but she still found herself crying easily.

Marc kissed her on the cheek. "We're all spreading the word for private-duty nurses or even a woman who'll just sit and wait on you."

"But no luck, huh?"

"Not yet. But it'll work out. We're all praying—"

"Praying? You're actually praying for a nurse for me?"

"Of course. Why not?"

"I don't know. I mean I used to—I used to pray about things like that—once."

"You don't now? You don't believe anymore?" He leaned forward and pressed the fingers of her good hand.

"No—no I don't."

"Because of your accident?"

"I stopped long before that."

"Want to tell me about it?"

"No. Not yet, anyway." Cheryl knew that if she started, the tears would gush out. She wanted to avoid any subject that would affect her emotionally.

She closed her eyes and yawned.

"Tired?"

"A little," she answered, not opening her eyes. She needed to think about going back to the apartment. About someone to stay with her. And yet, thinking was the one thing she had tried not to do in the hospital. She wanted to go back into oblivion not remembering the past, and having no concern for the future.

At the same time, Cheryl wanted to remember. And more than remember, she wanted to tell Marc about her inability to believe, about her father and her mother, and most of all about Shep.

Shep.

He was so far away. Even so, he would come if she contacted him. But she couldn't. Not ever.

How she had loved Shep. For how long? Always? For as long as she could remember. They had gone through junior and senior high school together. They started going steady by their junior year of school.

Then college. Cheryl wanted a local college and went to Drake University. Shep had opted for Cedar Falls, a smaller college. They had offered him an athletic scholarship, and he wanted a chance to live away from home. He drove back to Des Moines almost every weekend. And when he did, they spent most of their time together. Shep's parents had laughed, "Your family ought to adopt the boy because he's at your place more than at ours."

Even the distance between them during the week did not destroy the relationship. If anything, she grew to love Shep more. She was always counting the days until Friday, and from noon on Friday, counting the hours and minutes. Everything had seemed so perfect.

Cheryl remembered how well life had gone. By attending summers and carrying extra classes she had completed her college load in three years. Immediately she got a job with the *Des Moines Register.* She worked first in the people section and later in the city news. Shep, on the other hand, took a fifth year to graduate. With the extra work of his athletic schedule, he took only the minimum hours to maintain his full-time standing. In the meantime, Cheryl's younger sister, Karla, also entered Cedar Falls. Shep and Karla made the trip to and from the college on the weekends.

Then there were wedding plans. For nearly a year, Cheryl had been making decisions about announcements, her dress, the floral arrangements. Had it not been for Mother—

Mother! Cheryl's body tensed at that word. Mother had always interfered. She had constantly tried to stop the wedding.

Mother! Why did her mind focus on her? More than anything else, Cheryl wanted to blot that name and that face out of her mind forever.

Then guilt stabbed her as it always did. Children were supposed to love their mothers. Society always taught it. Probably somewhere in the Bible it said it too. But people didn't know her mother. The parent who controlled lives, who manipulated conversations. The parent who tried to break her spirit. And Mother had almost succeeded. Karla had submitted, but Cheryl had held out. Now she was free of the tyranny.

How she had resisted. It came to a head one night in her own bedroom during Cheryl's second year of college. Cheryl had left clothes thrown across the bed and the back of a chair because she had overslept and was going to be late for her first class.

Her mother got home early and had inspected the room—which she often did. "This room's a mess."

"Mother, I didn't have time—"

"You could have gotten up five minutes earlier!"

"I overslept."

"Then you could have gone late."

"I'm sorry—"

"Sorry? You've done this repeatedly. Do I have to hire someone to come into this house just to pick up and clean up after you?"

"No, Mother."

"Then get this picked up! Now! And don't let it happen again!"

"Stop screaming at me!" Cheryl yelled. "I can hear you!" She put her hands to her mouth. It was the first time she had actually screamed at her mother. Not that she hadn't wanted to before, but she had never said the words until now.

"If you hear, then do what I say," Eloise Adams said, her hands on her hips, and her voice suddenly low, but firm.

"I will not!"

"What did you say?"

"I will not bow to your every demand like some slave!"

"How dare you talk—"

"Mother, you're not yelling at Karla or at Father anymore."

"Young woman, I am your mother."

"That's not my fault!" she screamed, aware that her voice rose. "So stop blaming me for it!"

Eloise had gone into a tirade then, threatening, arguing, wheedling, and finally, "I'll let you pay your own tuition at Drake if you're going to be so independent."

"That's all right with me. I'll even make plans to move out."

"As you like."

"And if I do, I promise you one thing," she paused only long enough to take a deep breath. "I promise that you'll never see me again. Not ever!"

A look of horror swept across Eloise's face. She turned and headed out of the room.

Cheryl followed her into the hallway. "You're not going to brainwash me and control me like you have Karla and Father."

Eloise spun around and slapped her daughter's face. "Don't you ever, ever speak to me like that again!"

Cheryl's eyes narrowed. "Don't you ever strike me again."

The incident was never mentioned again. Eloise continued to pay the tuition. An unspoken truce lay between them. Eloise said less, and Cheryl, feeling guilty over the way she had confronted her mother, was thankful nothing more was said. If her mother had continued her tirades, Cheryl might have buckled under.

In one area only Eloise kept up her complaint: Shep.

"He's not the man for you," she said matter-of-factly for at least the third time that evening.

Cheryl, addressing wedding invitations, had ignored the comment earlier. This time she put down her pen and turned slightly to face her mother. "I don't choose to discuss the matter."

"I just want you to be happy—"

"And I don't intend to allow you to choose my husband."

"I wasn't trying to choose your husband, only—"

"Only you don't want me to marry Shep."

"I hate to think of your making a mistake."

"A mistake? We've known each other since we were kids."

"That still doesn't make Shep right for you."

"Mother, get this straight. I love Shep. He loves me. You can't understand things like that, but—"

"Your love for Shep isn't enough," Mother said, and quite uncharacteristically lapsed into silence. She dropped her head and concentrated on her crossword puzzle.

Cheryl felt ashamed for speaking so harshly and said softly, "I love him. That's enough for me."

"Is it?"

Cheryl pushed the invitations aside, slammed the pen down, and stomped out of the room.

As Cheryl lay in the hospital bed, she knew Mother had been right. *Mother is always right!* She swore under her breath. *She's right about everything.* Tears fell from her cheeks.

Marc noticed the tears and wiped them with a tissue. "Need another pain shot?"

"No," she said and kept her eyes closed.

"I'll call the nurse if you want—"

"No, I'm all right."

"Cheryl, I need to say something to you—if you feel like listening, I mean."

"Of course," she said and turned her head toward his.

"I love you. Deeply. Sincerely. Hopelessly. Helplessly. And all those other words that go with it—"

"Marc, don't—"

"I have to tell you. You see, as I've been coming in here every day, I've had plenty of time to think and examine myself and my feelings."

"Marc, I—I don't honestly know how I feel about you. I love you, but—but not in the same way—"

"I didn't ask you to say anything. I just needed to tell you, Cheryl. You see, you're the first woman I've really loved. I've dated a lot, but it's different with you."

"You deserve the best woman in the world."

"I hope I'm going to get her, too," Marc said, as his hand gently brushed her hair.

"I would like very much to fall in love with you—"

"Like to?" Marc shook his head. "You don't choose to fall in love. It just happens to you. And it will happen if you'll forget that guy back home and give me a chance—"

"Subject closed," Cheryl said.

"It's always closed," Marc said. "You won't let me inside, will you?"

Cheryl felt the sting in his words. She hesitated a long minute before saying, "I will let you in. Just be patient."

"As long as there's a chance, I'll be as patient as I have to be," Marc said. "By the way, Taylor told me today that he thought he might have a lead on a nurse for you. Should know something by tomorrow."

"Taylor? Is he working on it, too?"

"Working on it? Everywhere he goes, he puts out the word. He's one concerned guy."

"One concerned guy?" she snorted.

"He's worried half-sick about you," Marc answered. "Grills me every day about your condition—"

"If Mr. Michaels has such great concern for his employee, he could show it by coming by and seeing me in person."

Marc's face clouded. "He hasn't called you?"

"I haven't heard a word from him since the day of the accident."

"Oh," Marc said.

"You don't seem very upset," she answered.

"I knew he wouldn't come here, of course, but I thought he'd call—"

"You knew he wouldn't come?"

"Why don't you let Taylor explain it himself? I'll call him when I get home and—"

"You don't have to force him to visit me—"

"Calm down, Cheryl. I simply think he owes you an explanation, that's all. The guy cares—really cares about you."

"I haven't had any evidence of that."

"Good Morning America" had just signed off, and a firm rap came on the door. "Come in," Cheryl called as she snapped off the set.

"Is it all right for me to come in?" the male voice said.

"Of course," she answered, recognizing it as Taylor's.

He came inside and looked around the room. "How are you feeling?" She saw the forced smile on his face.

"Okay," she said.

"Uh, that's, uh, good," he said as his eyes continued to sweep around the small room. He walked to the window and peered out. "Not much of a view from here."

"Not unless you like looking at brick walls."

He moved back to the other side of her bed. "I guess—I guess I ought to explain why I haven't been to see you."

"It doesn't matter," she said, trying to make it look as though it did not.

"I think I need to explain," Taylor said and sat down in a chair across from her bed.

"You don't need to—"

"It's because of Beth that I couldn't get here. I spent so much time in a hospital room with her—"

"Oh, I didn't know," she said.

"You don't know much about Beth and me," he said. "I promised to tell you when the time came. I think now is the time."

"Friends don't push for information," Cheryl said and realized she smiled at him and hoped he would tell her.

"Sometimes friends want to tell," Taylor answered, and his dimples showed. He took Cheryl's hand and kissed her fingertips.

"I told you Beth and I met in college and fell in love. Flint is her hometown. She came back and got hired on the *Neighborhood News*. They couldn't make me much of an offer. I had already had experience in newspaper work because I dropped out of college for a couple of years. So the *Flint Sun* hired me.

"Beth and I worked for rival papers, but that didn't change our relationship."

How he had loved Beth. She was everything he had always wanted in a woman. She was not only beautiful and bright, but she stood up for herself. She argued with Taylor when she believed in her cause. She also gave him a quick apology when she was wrong.

It had all gone well. Both of them planned to work in Atlanta; he on the *Constitution* and she had the offer of an editing job with a new textbook company. They also set the date for their wedding.

One Friday they had driven to Beth's parents who lived five miles south of town. On the way back to Flint, a drunk man pulled out of a side road at full speed. He crashed into Taylor's car.

Taylor remembered being knocked against the steering column and dazed for a moment. As he became aware of what had happened, he looked at the crushed body of Beth next to him.

Police arrived, and an ambulance minutes behind. Taylor heard little of the conversation and stood in a stupor. He got into the ambulance with Beth.

For thirty-three days Beth lay in a hospital bed at Flint General Hospital in the intensive-care unit. Taylor came every day and spent every possible minute with her, even though technically they allowed him only five minutes at a time. He sat by her bed for hours at a time. Occasionally he talked softly to her, hoping that she would respond. He waited for a flicker of her eyes, the slight pressure of her fingers when he touched them. There was no response.

"It looked as if she would pull out of it, then infection set in. She died thirty-seven days after the accident."

"Taylor, I'm sorry—" Oblivious of her own tears, Cheryl said, "Oh, Taylor, Taylor, I'm sorry—so sorry, I—"

He turned back to her and said, "That's why I couldn't come to see you. The painful memories. The same hospital—"

"You don't need to explain—"

Taylor bent down and kissed her lightly on the cheek. He pulled his face a few inches away and looked into her green eyes. "And every time I see you, I think of Beth. I hope you understand."

"I do, Taylor, I do," she said.

Chapter 8

"Good news and bad news," Dr. Lambert said as he entered the room. "The good news first. I can let you go home tomorrow."

"And the bad news?" Cheryl asked.

"The bad news—we still have not located a nurse to stay with you."

"Oh," she said. "Then what—?"

"Your friend Marc will surely come up with something. He's determined to find someone. So, providing you can assure me of adequate care, I'll release you to go home tomorrow."

"Thanks," Cheryl said, smiling. "Twenty-two days here is a long time."

"Quite a long time."

After he had gone, Cheryl wondered how it would be in the apartment. At least she could control her world. Nurses would not be running in to take her blood pressure and temperature every two hours, feeding her pills to sleep, and giving her injections for pain. But still, they were people, and it made the hours pass.

She decided to put it out of her mind. *It's one more step toward full recovery,* she thought. And she would recover totally. She'd show Dr. Lambert—she would not even have a limp!

That evening both Marc and Taylor came together. They had already heard the news. Neither of them talked about the problem for a long time. Finally Taylor cleared his throat, "Still haven't found anyone."

"A couple of widows from the church have offered to stay one or two nights apiece," Marc added. "And I told you I'll move in if we can't find anyone."

"If only you had a family—," Taylor said and stopped. "Sorry, I know that's a closed subject with you."

"Very closed," Cheryl said.

"Should it remain closed?" Marc asked.

"What do you mean?" Cheryl said.

"I've been thinking about this," Marc said, "and I don't think you're being fair."

"Fair?"

"I assume you have parents, and brothers, and sisters?"

"I have a sister, Karla, and my mother. So what?"

"Is it fair to them? Your being laid up, desperate for help, and maybe one of them could come and stay with you. Would either of them come?"

"I told you it was a closed subject."

"And I'm opening it up," Marc said with a wide smile. "You're one stubborn person. *Now,* would either of them come?"

"I suppose—I mean—I—I don't intend to ask."

"Look, I have no idea why you left. Okay? I get the impression that they didn't run you off. Right now, you need them."

"Need them? Need Mother? Not on your life."

For twenty minutes Marc pushed, but Cheryl remained adamant. "I left Iowa, and I have no intention of reviving that buried past."

Marc bent down and took Cheryl's hand. "Remember when I told you that God was on your side?"

"Yes. And if He is, then why can't we hire someone?"

"Why should God help us get someone when Karla could come?"

"I won't ask her."

"It might be that God wants a reconciliation to come about through this—"

"Reconciliation? Karla and I had no fight—"

"All the more reason then to call her."

"I can't. It's that simple."

"Change places with her a minute. If she were hurt and needed help, what would you do?"

"That's not fair, Marc," she said.

"Why not?"

"Well, you just don't know the circumstances of why I left and—"

"Would Karla come?" Taylor asked.

"I suppose so," she said weakly.

"Will you call her?" Marc asked.

Cheryl did not answer. She closed her eyes. Karla—sweet, wonderful Karla. How she longed to see her again. But if she came, that meant Mother— and Shep—and— "No. It—it won't work."

"Why not?" Taylor pressed.

"It just wouldn't."

"If—if you called her, would Karla come?" Marc asked.

"Of course, only—"

Both men looked at her. Taylor shrugged.

"I know—I know it sounds unreasonable but," Cheryl said, "but I—I just—just don't—"

"Would you like me to call her?" Taylor said.

"You're pressuring me. Both of you."

"Smart kid," Taylor said. "She understands."

"I understand only too well," Cheryl said. "But understanding and doing something—"

"I'll make the call for you," Taylor said.

"I can make my own calls! And stop ordering me around."

"Ah, her temper acts up now, too," Marc said, "but it won't save you, Cheryl. We're going to push you until you give in."

Cheryl's gaze shifted from Marc to Taylor and then back to Marc. "You're both probably right. But the way I left—I mean, I just took off with nothing except a note and—"

"And they're probably still worrying about you," Marc said.

"Okay," Cheryl said. "You're right. It's just—"

"I'll dial if you'll give me the number," Taylor said, staring at her.

"I'll talk—but not to Mother. Only to Karla. So ask for her. That's the only way," she said.

Cheryl gave Taylor the number, and he waited until a woman answered. "I'm calling long distance for Karla Adams, please," he said into the phone. A few seconds later he said, "Just a minute, please."

He put the phone to Cheryl's ear. "This is Cheryl—"

Karla squealed, and her voice carried loudly enough for the two men to hear a few words.

"Listen, Sis, I want to make this quick. I'm in the hospital and I—I need—," her voice broke, and she could not continue.

Marc took the phone. "Hello, my name is Marc Lattimer. Your sister was seriously injured in a car accident three weeks ago. She's still in the hospital. They'll release her tomorrow providing someone can stay with her, around the clock for at least the next three weeks. Since you're her sister—"

Marc listened and finally said, "She has only one request. She does not wish to see her mother. I hope you understand, and I cannot discuss this with you." Marc gave her information on how to get to Flint. A minute later he hung up.

"Karla promises to catch the earliest plane out of Des Moines and will probably arrive sometime tomorrow. I think I'll have the doctor keep you one more day."

Ten minutes later, the phone rang, and Marc picked it up.

"Yes, just a minute," he said. "It's for you." Marc placed the phone next to Cheryl's ear.

"Hello," she said.

The color suddenly drained from her face. For a moment, the two men thought she would burst into tears. "Mother! I expressly do not want you here. I didn't want Karla to give you any information about me. I don't want you here! Can't you understand—"

Marc grabbed the phone and identified himself. "Mrs. Adams, you're upsetting Cheryl. I'm going to terminate this call—" he paused and then listened. "Okay, I've got that."

"Karla will arrive tomorrow at the Atlanta airport at ten. I'll pick her up and bring her here myself."

"Is Karla coming alone?"

"No."

"Put the phone up to my ear again," Cheryl said. The look on her face forced Marc not to argue with her. "Now dial the number again."

He dialed.

"This is Cheryl—," she said, and the other person on the line interrupted her. "Mother, don't lecture me. I'm calling because I need Karla's help."

Again another interruption, and Marc pulled the phone away. "This is Marc Lattimer again. I'm a physical therapist—" The voice cut him off, and then he interrupted, "Excuse me, ma'am, but if you'll calm down a moment, I'll talk to you. I will not talk to anyone who asks questions and will not listen for answers." He paused again and said, "Your daughter needs help. Someone must stay with her around the clock for perhaps a month—"

Another interruption, and he listened a full minute before breaking in. "Mrs. Adams, I am the physical therapist, not the doctor, but I can tell you this much. Your daughter needs help. She also needs peace. She has a lot of pain. She'll be in casts at least another three weeks. Maybe longer. She has expressly asked for Karla. We cannot locate nurses or aides to stay with her. Her family is the last resort—"

Marc took a deep breath and said, "Mrs. Adams, please don't keep interrupting me. Taylor Michaels and I will meet Karla at the airport in the morning. Good night."

When Marc hung up, Cheryl smiled. "How lovely to listen to someone shut up my mother."

"She is a bit forceful," Marc answered.

"A bit? She's overpowering and intimidating."

"Anyway, Karla is coming. She promised not to tell Shep where you are until after she's talked to you. Okay?"

"Yes," she said, relieved that she would not have to face Shep—not yet anyway.

"Is Shep the one you've been carrying the heartache for?" Marc asked.

"How did you know?"

"How did I know? When a man like me gets interested in a lovely lady like you and keeps hitting a brick wall, I figure there's another man in the picture."

"There isn't really. Not anymore. I mean, it's something I'm working myself out of."

"He didn't throw you over—?"

"No. Actually I walked out a month before our wedding."

"Want to talk about it? I listen real good," Marc said, flashing a smile and making his voice sound like a south Georgian.

"Not yet."

"I'll wait."

"You don't need to—"

"No one forces me to wait," he said. "I like you very much, Cheryl. You know that, don't you?"

"I know you keep saying you care very much for me, and I—"

"And you answer with words like, 'Don't rush me' or 'Give me time.' And I keep telling you that I'm willing to wait."

"I'm not making any promises," she said. "I've had too many broken promises in my life."

Marc shook his head. "Cheryl, you're exasperating at times."

"What he means," Taylor said softly, "is that he's crazy about you. But you're afraid."

"Afraid? Me?"

"Afraid to love. Afraid to let go. Most of all, afraid to trust a man again."

"So now these two gentlemen have licenses to practice psychiatry!"

"No, not at all," Marc said. "I don't know what happened back in Des Moines. Somehow Shep hurt you. And the few things you've said about your father—"

"What about my father?" the anger flashed in her eyes.

"He let you down, too—by dying," Marc said.

Cheryl took a deep breath. "Marc, if I'm so tortured over love's broken promises, why do you keep coming around? Why do you spend so much time with me?"

"You don't know? I like you. Very much. Isn't that enough of a reason?"

"Doesn't sound like much of a reason to me. And I've not always been kind to you."

"Maybe it has to do with me."

"You've lost me there."

"When I was a little boy, I brought home stray cats and dogs. Once I found a baby robin with a broken leg on the ground. I made a little splint and kept feeding that bird for over a week. Learned to love the little bird."

"What happened to it?"

"Don't know. I made a nest high enough so that none of the cats could reach it. One day it was empty."

"Did she fly away?"

"I'd like to think she did." Marc stood up and walked to the window and peered into the darkness.

Taylor got up, waved to both of them, and walked out of the room.

"Wait—," Cheryl called after him.

"See you in the morning," he called without turning around.

"So anyway, as I was saying," Marc said and sat on the windowsill. "I've been in the business of searching for sicks, strays, lonely, hurting types—"

"And you singled me out because I fit into that category?"

"Don't you fit?"

"Do I?"

"Cheryl, don't you know?"

"I've just never had anyone say it that bluntly before—"

"I didn't mean to offend—"

"But you're right anyway. I am one of those hurting creatures."

"So that's one reason why I've kept coming around."

"There are others?"

"A better one," Marc said and came to the side of her bed.

"Because you're part of the medical profession and—"

"Because I'm a man and you're a woman and—"

"Marc, I'm grateful for all you've done. You've been here—"

"Evasion again."

"What?"

"Whenever I move in close, you jump. You don't have to be afraid of me, Cheryl."

"I'm not afraid."

"You are, but you'll overcome it in time. You'll see."

"Marc, please, let's just keep it as it is now. I am genuinely grateful. You've been here when I've needed you—"

"We're just beginning, Cheryl."

"Beginning what?"

"I think they call it a relationship."

"Is that what you want, Marc?"

"It's what I've wanted all along."

"Even though you know about Shep? I mean that it's not totally over with him."

"I'll wait. You'll come around."

"How do you know?"

"I don't—not for sure. But, I'm one of those guys simple enough to believe that God plans our lives. And because I believe that, I also believe that He sent you into my life."

"Marc, I've tried to tell you before, I'm—well, I'm not into this God business. I left that a long time ago."

Marc shook his head. "You must have had a bad experience somewhere along the line."

"I did. Not with God so much as with church people."

"And you turned against God because people mistreated you?"

"Marc, pull me up a little. And move the pillow to the left." She paused while he moved her. "Ah, that's better. I just get so tired of lying in one position."

"That's why you have me and all these nurses around—to move you when you need it. But when we start the physical therapy, kid, I'll have you moving around and groaning too."

"Thanks, Marc."

"I'd be happy to move you anytime."

"And thanks for not pursuing the subject."

He pecked her lightly on the nose. "Do I need to say anything more? It's your move next."

Even with the sleeping pill, Cheryl did not rest. She awakened numerous times during the night. Her first thoughts always centered on her sister. If she could have stopped with Karla, she might have dozed back off. But Mother was coming too. Why hadn't she agreed to stay away? "How much do I have to say to her?" Cheryl said aloud.

She closed her eyes, lay still, hoping to drift back to sleep. Her mind flitted from Marc to Shep and then to Karla and her mother. She finally flipped on the television and watched an all-night station which showed movies from the 1940s. She went back to sleep again, only to awaken every hour or so.

The next morning she tried not to think about Karla's arrival but found herself continually asking the nurse for the time. At noon, wearied from lack of sleep, Cheryl dozed. She did not hear the door open or Marc come in.

"Cheryl," he said softly.

"Yes," she said, fighting to open her eyes.

"They're here!"

Karla rushed into the room. She stood a foot from the bed and took in the casts and then squealed, "Cheryl, it's great to see you no matter how you look!"

Karla embraced her sister. Cheryl wanted to respond, but with one arm in a cast and the other pinned down by Karla, she could move only her head slightly. "Karla—Karla," she whispered.

When Karla released her and backed away, Cheryl saw her mother standing next to the bed.

"I asked you not to come."

Eloise Adams's eyes were riveted to her daughter's legs. "I had no idea—no idea how bad—"

"I didn't want you to come."

"That would have been cruel. A mother belongs with her daughter in times like these."

"I'm too weak to argue," Cheryl said and turned her face away.

As Marc watched the scene, he noticed how much the three women resembled each other. The mother, slightly shorter, displayed the same high cheekbones. Her hair, a lighter shade of red with specks of white, hinted that she had been even more beautiful than Cheryl in her younger days. Karla, however, had a more filled-out face and robust coloring. Her darker hair could barely be called red.

Karla stroked her sister's forehead. "We worried so much about you—all of us."

"Yes, all of us," Eloise said. "Your leaving like that. No warning. Just a silly little note. Drove us half crazy."

"Mother, I don't intend to explain my actions."

"Did I ask for an explanation?"

"Not directly, but if I don't stop you, you'll get around to it."

Eloise closed her eyes, her hands gripped the railing of the bed and she waited before replying in an even voice. "I worried about you, Cheryl."

"You read the note? I said I'd be all right. And I was—until the accident."

"But we had no idea—no idea at all—that anything was wrong. I thought you had gone off with one of those strange cult people and were selling flowers on street corners."

"I didn't."

"How were we to know? Just that note. You didn't even give your paper a notice. You even had a delivery from—"

"Mother, no lectures, please," Cheryl said. "I don't have the patience."

"You don't have the patience?" Eloise put her hands on her hips, her mouth agape. She closed it. "Yes, Cheryl," she said and bent over and kissed her daughter's cheek. "We'll talk about it later."

"Cheryl needs help," Marc said. "As I've already explained—"

Eloise turned, and with a quick sweep of her eyes, she dismissed him. "I am aware of that."

"I'm here," Karla said. "I'm prepared to stay as long as you need me."

"But your school—"

"Forget that right now. I'll tell you all about that later."

"I'll leave now," Marc said to all of them, but his eyes were on Cheryl. "I'll check back later."

Cheryl smiled and wished she could think of a reason to detain him.

Eloise's eyes followed Marc's departing figure. "Well, you didn't lose much time after dumping Shep. But I don't blame you—"

"Mother! Don't! Don't spoil this. I didn't ask you here. And now that you're here, please try not to upset me."

"Upset you? What did I say that upset you?"

"I've missed you," Karla said and kissed Cheryl again.

"I've missed you, too. Now sit down. Tell me about yourself." In asking the question she wanted to hear about Shep. Yet she was afraid of what she might hear.

Chapter 9

Seeing her mother again had caused more of a strain than Cheryl had realized. When everyone had gone, she asked the nurse to post a no-visitors sign on the door. The nurse also called Marc and Taylor, asking them not to come back.

Even though she felt extremely tired, Cheryl found it difficult to sleep. She could not get her mind off worrying what it would be like in the small apartment. How hard it had been to get along with Mother when she had the whole world to retreat to. But now she would be confined to a bed with Mother hovering over her constantly.

"I will not let her dominate my life," Cheryl said halfaloud through her clenched teeth.

"Can I get you something?" the nurse bent down and whispered.

"No, I'm all right," Cheryl said. "Just having a bad dream."

She finally asked for a second sleeping pill. As the pill began to take effect, she thought of both Marc and Taylor. Neither of them would hesitate at escorting Mother to the airport if she antagonized Cheryl too much. *Why didn't I think of that before?* she asked herself. She was asleep before she could answer.

Although the pill had lulled her into sleep, she awakened shortly before seven when the nursing staff changed shifts.

The door opened, and Marc's head appeared. He gazed at her from across the room. "Looks like you had a rough night," he said.

"Didn't sleep well," she said.

"A lot of pain?"

"No. Just—oh, Mother coming—my going home—"

"Oh," Marc said and walked over to her. He bent down and kissed her lightly on the forehead. "I don't have to stay if you'd prefer to be alone."

"Please stay. Right now I feel as if I need someone."

"That's all I want to hear," Marc said.

"Thanks," Cheryl mumbled, wondering what to say next. Right now she realized she wanted Marc in the room with her. But she had no idea what she wanted to say to him.

"Want to talk? About Iowa? Your mother? Whatever?"

"I don't know."

"Sometimes it helps—just talking."

"Maybe you're right," Cheryl answered but lay in silence. She kept staring at the ceiling, wondering where to begin. *How do I tell him so he'll understand?* she asked herself. "There are so many things—"

"Start somewhere," Marc said softly.

"The church then. I asked Pastor Weathersby and two other leaders to visit my father, and so far as I know, they never did. And my mother hated my father. They fought all the time. Even as a child, I used to overhear them when I was trying to sleep."

"And—"

"Then my father took his own life. She drove him to it."

"That's an awful lot to lay on one person."

"But she did—"

"Did she?"

"You think I'm lying, Marc?"

"No. But you may be blaming your mother for an action your father took. She didn't drive him to do anything."

"Right now, I don't know," Cheryl said. "I just feel confused."

"Cheryl, I'm sorry about your father. About everything. But, please, don't let bitterness crowd in. Don't close yourself off—"

"I'm trying not to. I'm even going to get along with Mother," she bit her lip. "At least, I'm going to try."

"And don't cut yourself off from God just because a few church people let you down."

"But they—they were the leaders."

"Peter and James and the other disciples were all leaders too, but they let Jesus down in His hour of need."

She smiled. "Okay, if you don't preach me any sermons, I'll promise to try to overcome my bitterness toward religious people."

"That's all I'm asking."

"I'll tell you this much, Marc. The folks from Flint Lutheran have helped. I guess I've never met kind people like them before."

"There are a lot of kind people in the world," he said.

"And you're one of the kindest."

"That's at least one good thing you've said about me."

"Marc, just give me time, will you?"

"Because of Shep?"

"Shep? Right now, he's a habit I've got to work out of my life. You see, Marc, I've known him almost all my life. And, more than that, Shep was—well, just Shep."

What would she have done without Shep after the funeral? He had been at her side, constantly. He hadn't insisted on talking. Everyone else had given her glib phrases like, "You'll understand all this one day" or "Your father's at peace now."

But Shep had just been there, quietly sitting by her, walking with her. Faithful Shep. How would she have survived those first weeks without him?

At school he did only average work. A passing grade was what he expected, and all he achieved. That was Shep—average, but dependable. He was her confidant and supporter, especially when she complained about Mother. No one comforted her as he had after Father's death.

She tried to remember when Shep had kissed her the first time, but couldn't, or when they had first talked about love. It was as though they had always loved each other. By the eighth grade they had started passing love notes in class.

When Cheryl finished college they talked about wedding plans. Had Shep proposed? Again, she couldn't remember, nor had it seemed to matter. Marriage had been the next step for them. For years they had window-shopped and paged through catalogs and talked of wedding rings, bridal gowns, and what kind of furnishings they wanted in their home.

When had it gone sour? With Mother, of course. Always with Mother. Less than a month before she finally left, Mother increased her remarks about Shep. "He simply isn't the man for you," she said.

"You think I could do better?"

"No," Eloise said. "Not better. Only different."

"I simply don't understand you," Cheryl answered.

"I love him like a son. I'm not against him. Please try to understand. I am only against your marrying each other."

Cheryl opened her eyes. She had never asked Mother *why*. It was strange. All those times Mother had spoken against the wedding, Cheryl had become piqued, even angry. But never once had she asked why.

Now she knew. Mother had been right again.

She swore. Why was Mother always right?

Chapter 10

Eloise arrived promptly at nine and dispatched Karla to the business office to clear Cheryl's leaving. Two members of the Flint Paramedic Unit arrived shortly afterward, wheeling a gurney down the corridor.

"Hi, pretty lady reporter," one of them said.

Cheryl smiled. It was Kevin whom she had met at the fire. "You remember me? That fire was a long time ago."

"We were also the team that brought you here after your accident," he said.

Kevin and his silent companion gently lifted Cheryl from the hospital bed to the gurney. She had expected pain, but they moved her so carefully she hardly noticed. As Kevin put her down, he smiled and said, "Now I've got you just where I want you," and he laughed. "You've still got that boyfriend, too, haven't you?"

"Oh, he's around, all right," she answered.

Minutes later they had her in the ambulance and then whisked her to her apartment. Another ten minutes and she was tucked into the rented hospital-type bed. The trip had tired Cheryl more than she had expected. She fell asleep almost immediately and did not awaken until noon. When she opened her eyes and surveyed her room, she also smelled the soup Karla had heated. "Oh, that makes me feel ravenous." It was the first time she had expressed any interest in food since the accident.

Eloise looked up from her crossword book. "By the way, I'm having a telephone installed," she said.

"A telephone? I don't need—"

"Should be in some time tomorrow," she added.

"Mother, I don't need—"

"I'll have to return home in a few days. Karla and I will probably take turns staying with you. No need for both of us to be away from home at the same time—"

"Why didn't you at least ask me first?" Cheryl said, trying to keep her voice calm.

Eloise looked at her daughter. "Maybe you don't need a telephone here, but I do. How do you think I'd feel, being so far away and unable to hear each day?"

"I didn't know you cared that much."

Eloise threw down her book and walked across the room. "I'm going out for a little air." She shut the door behind her.

"Cheryl—" Karla said and stopped.

"You think I shouldn't have said that?"

"I don't think it was necessary."

"It's the only way I know to defend myself," Cheryl said. "Unless I ward her off at every turn, I know she'll keep trying to control me. The way she tried with Father. The way she does with you."

"I don't think of it as control," Karla said as she carried the soup to the bed.

"But then, you were always the sweet one," Cheryl said.

It amazed Cheryl that the three of them could sleep in a single bedroom apartment. Karla never complained—but she seldom complained about anything. Eloise bore up under the overcrowding and lack of privacy—far better than Cheryl thought she would.

It also became obvious to Cheryl that her mother tried hard to keep the conversation on a pleasant level. Although Mother had the phone installed, she took no other initiative without first asking. Cheryl acknowledged to herself that it was nice to have a phone handy. Calls interrupting her day made the hours drag less.

"Mother," Cheryl said softly, after taking almost an hour to force herself, "I do appreciate the phone. Thoughtful of you."

"I'm glad you feel that way," Eloise said.

Cheryl breathed a sigh of relief. She half-feared Mother would start her of-course-it-was-a-good-idea lecture. Cheryl was glad Mother had the good sense to say nothing more.

At the end of the second week, Eloise announced, "I'm leaving in the morning."

"It's been kind of you to stay this long," Cheryl said, surprised at the normal tone of her words.

"I have an office to run."

"I know that, Mother."

"I'm going to be gone only a week. Then Karla and I can change places."

"But what about Karla's college work? She's missed two weeks already—"

"I'm not going back," Karla said. "I had decided to drop out in June anyway."

Eloise sighed. "So you see, there's no real hurry for her."

"But why? I mean—"

"I have a job," Karla said, and a look passed between her and her mother.

"What kind of job?"

"I hope you don't mind my leaving like this," Eloise said too quickly.

"No, Mother, I don't mind your leaving at all."

"Then it's all settled," she said. "Anything I can do for you?"

"Nothing I can think of. There—there is one thing," Cheryl said. "We've all three avoided the subject so carefully—"

"What's that?" Eloise asked.

"Shep."

"Come to think of it, we haven't talked about Shep, have we?"

"No, Mother. We haven't talked about Shep at all."

"He's fine," Karla said.

"Tell me about him. I—I want to know."

A look passed between Karla and her mother, as though trying to decide who would speak first.

"He's still in school, you know," Eloise said.

"Shep only has to finish two courses before he gets his degree," Karla added.

"I know about that. I haven't been gone that long."

"He started selling insurance right after you left. He's done well," Eloise said. "Even on a part-time basis, he's selling almost as much as the rest of them."

"That sounds like Shep," Cheryl said. "People just seem to trust him."

"His future looks pretty good," Eloise said. "Careerwise, I mean."

"What about—about my leaving?"

"He took it hard," Karla said as she walked across the room. "Blamed himself and had quite a bad time of it."

"And you know Shep," Eloise said, her voice a little too jocular, "he's not one to hold a grudge or stay down long. You used to say you could blacken his eye on Monday and by Wednesday he'd be asking you to play with him again."

"And since you hadn't sent out the invitations," Karla said, "we still have them boxed up."

"The wedding gown's ready, and you're entitled to free altera- tions—if you decide to use it," Eloise added.

Karla came over to the bed. "Don't you want to see Shep?"

"No," she answered.

"You don't even want him to know—about this," she gestured to the casts.

"No."

"Is that fair to him?"

"Maybe—maybe later, when the casts come off or when I'm ready to jog—"

"I think he's entitled to know," Karla said softly, but her dark green eyes pleaded even more.

"I don't know if I could face him—like this. I mean, I didn't give him much of an explanation when I left, did I?"

"No, you didn't," Karla said. "Just the note to us."

Cheryl studied her sister's face. "Okay, Sis, something's bothering you. What is it?"

"Just thinking about Shep. Left up in the air like that."

"In the air? I thought my note made it plain—"

"But that's not the same as saying it," Eloise interrupted.

"It ought to be enough," Cheryl said.

"Don't you—don't you love Shep anymore?" Karla asked.

The sisters' eyes met and held, and then Cheryl looked away. "I'll always love Shep—"

"Then why—"

"But I'll never marry him."

"I can't understand that," Karla said.

"Karla, how about checking the mail, will you?" Eloise said.

"It's still a little early," Karla answered and stared at her mother.

"Then I'll say it plainly. I need to talk to your sister for a few minutes, and I would like to do it alone. Please."

Karla looked at Cheryl for a long minute and then left.

"Cheryl, I still think you ought to talk to Shep. Either let him come here or call him—"

"Why?"

"He needs to hear it from your lips. Also you'd better have the right words to say when you tell him."

"You knew all along, didn't you, Mother?"

She nodded. "I suspected."

"Naturally. You suspect or know everything, don't you?"

"Cheryl, please, I—"

"Mother, I don't want to talk about it now."

"I think I'll walk over to the grocery store and buy steaks for supper. How does that sound?"

"Sounds fine."

"Cheryl, just one more thing about Shep—"

"Mother! Don't say another word. I'm tired of your interfering, your trying to manipulate. We've done well these two weeks. Don't spoil it all now."

"I'll be back in about an hour," she said. "Tell Karla she can peel potatoes if she wants. Otherwise I'll do it when I get back."

As Cheryl lay in the room alone, she pounded the side of her bed with her one free hand. "She knew! She knew all along!" The anger welled up inside her, and she stifled the urge to scream. The night table next to her bed contained a pot of tea, medications, and a pitcher of water. She swiped at everything on the table, feeling them fly and hearing them crash on the floor.

Through that single act, her anger dissipated, and she lay exhausted, feeling the perspiration all over her body. "So Mother wins again."

Cheryl remembered every detail of the day she left, as though it had been etched into her brain. The day had been unusually warm for April in Iowa. She had discarded her jacket by midday. Finding herself with a free afternoon, she came home, took a leisurely bath, lay in bed, and read.

It was Thursday, and Shep would not be home until Friday. Since he drove Karla, he would be coming by the Adams's house first.

Cheryl must have fallen asleep because she suddenly opened her eyes and realized it was almost dark. She did not know what had awakened her, but she decided she was hungry. She had not bothered with lunch. And on Thursdays Mother stayed late at the office. She debated on whether to get dressed and go out or to go downstairs and raid the refrigerator. Cheryl tried to remember if there had been any chicken left from Tuesday night's dinner.

She got up slowly, and barefooted, started down the stairs. She heard a woman's voice in the den. Since Karla and Mother sounded very much alike, she had assumed that Mother had cancelled her evening appointments and had come home early. She was probably talking on the phone.

Cheryl had reached the last two steps when she heard Shep's voice. She wondered why he had returned a day early. But it didn't matter why. She was glad he had come. She decided to surprise him. She tiptoed forward, planning to grab him from behind.

"So what happens now?" he asked Karla.

"I don't know, Shep. I don't think we can do anything."

"I love you," he said.

"What about Cheryl?"

"We've been over this a thousand times. Of course I love her—but it's well, it's different—"

"I never intended this to happen," Karla said. "She's my sister and my best friend."

"And you'd let me marry her?"

"Shep, I want her happiness and yours. And—and—yes, I would back out of the picture rather than hurt Cheryl."

"I kept trying to push you out of my mind," he said. "I didn't mean to fall in love with you. You know that, don't you?"

"Who plans to love anybody?" she said.

"It just happened."

"But Cheryl. Oh, Shep, I'm so confused. Her dress is almost ready. The invitations—"

"I don't know what to do," he said. "But this much I know, I love you. I love you. I love you."

Shep must have moved in the room with his back toward the door because Cheryl could not hear the next words he said.

"But how?" Karla asked. "How do we—you know?—"

"I don't know. I don't know. There's got to be a way for all three of us to be happy."

Cheryl turned and tiptoed back up the steps. Tears flowed down her cheeks. She held the railing, afraid that she would fall otherwise. She hurried inside her room and silently closed the door. She fell across the bed and wept.

Afterwards she lay on the bed, unable to cry anymore. Her mind sought for a solution. "It's me," she said. "If I weren't in the picture—"

That's when she made up her mind to leave. Cheryl knew that Karla would never let Shep hurt her. That quiet, self-effacing sister would deny her own happiness for Cheryl.

She sat down calmly and wrote a note to Mother, Shep, and Karla:

> I am leaving Des Moines. I do not plan to return. A am all right. Please do not try to find me. I cannot go through with the wedding. Cheryl.

She dressed and tiptoed across the room, trying to include enough things in her two suitcases to take care of herself until she could re-settle. She had a good balance in her checking account and the municipal bonds her father had left her.

She had the two suitcases packed and her typewriter. Then she wondered how to get out of the house with Shep and Karla downstairs. Unless they opened the door to the garage and saw her car, they would not know she was home. She sat on the edge of the bed, wondering if she should risk going down the steps again.

Then she heard the front door close. She raced across the room and watched as they left the house. They held hands all the way to the car. She stifled a cry and made sure she was out of view. They got into his car and drove off.

Cheryl called her editor at the *Register*. "I've had something come up which I can't explain. I have to leave the city, and I have no idea when I'll be back or even if—"

He listened and offered to give her a leave of absence.

"All things considered, I've decided to quit," she said. She hung up as soon as possible, fearing that he would pump her for information. She didn't want to add anything more.

When she came down the steps on her second trip, she saw a note propped up on the coffee table:

> Shep and I skipped classes. Have gone out for a Coke. Be back for supper.
>
> Love,
> Karla

Mother walked into the room, carrying a bag of groceries. She set it on the table and came over to Cheryl's bed.

"You should have seen it happening," she said to her daughter. "You didn't see it because you didn't want to."

"See what happening?"

"After you started working for the paper you had less time for Shep—"

"But he knew about my job."

"He never complained, did he?"

"Shep? Never."

"So you saw less and less of each other. That also meant that he saw more of Karla. They went to and from college together. It was a natural thing—"

"That's why you kept saying those things about Shep."

"That's one reason," Eloise said.

"One reason? What else?"

"Because you don't love Shep."

"Don't love him?"

"No, and you never have. I mean adult love—the kind you build a marriage on."

"You think I had only a puppy-love kind of thing going?"

"No, I think you imagined you loved him. You couldn't think of not marrying Shep. But deep inside, Cheryl, you don't love him. Not now. Not really then either."

"How dare you—"

"You're angry because I'm right."

"I'm angry because you're wrong and because you're always trying to run my life."

"Am I wrong?"

"You think I don't love Shep—"

"If your eyes had lighted up for Shep the way they light up for Marc, then I would have known you loved him."

"Oh, that's how you tell? You check people's eyes. They have to register a certain level of iridescence—?"

"How about a baked potato with your steak?" Eloise asked as she walked back into the kitchen area.

"How about keeping out of my personal life?"

"I am out, Cheryl. You've locked me out."

Chapter 11

The entire southeast faced a drought with unseasonably high temperatures. Daily reports on television showed pictures of damaged crops and predicted higher prices at supermarkets by fall. Cheryl sighed as she watched the news. Glad to be inside and away from the heat, she was also tired of all the depressing news and snapped off the set.

She looked down at her body. She had made progress. She now wore only a small cast on both legs. "You have graduated," Dr. Lambert had said that morning, "to the wheelchair. Then on to crutches."

At least she could now do things for herself. Marc had taken her outside twice. Once shopping and once for a pleasure ride. Both times she had returned exhausted and needed a long rest to recover.

Members of Marc's church continued to visit regularly. She had assumed that once she had gotten back into the apartment, they would stop. Ann Burns came by every morning and again before dark. Her visits always gave Cheryl's spirits a lift. One young couple came every Thursday, always bringing a gift—a large tomato, a cucumber, or fresh peas.

The pastor dropped in for a few minutes every week. Today as he got ready to leave, he said, "Cheryl, you seem a little down."

"Depressed a bit. Marc and Dr. Lambert say it's part of the getting-well process. I'll get over it."

"I'm sure you will. In the meantime, we're your friends—"

"I sense you mean that."

"Perhaps it sounds like a meaningless phrase," Pastor Ziegler said, "but if there's anything we can do for you—"

"Do for me? You've all done so much already."

"We'd like to do more," he answered.

"Your caring is enough," she said.

He nodded. "May I pray with you before I leave?"

"I'd rather you didn't," she said. "No offense intended, but—"

"And no offense taken," he said. He stood up and offered his hand which she took. His firm grip made her wince.

"It's just—well, I've turned off religion."

"I understand," he said.

"And then I met Marc and Taylor. Until then I didn't think I'd ever want to hear about God again. I'm still not sure that I do. But I do know that the people of your congregation—," she stopped and grappled for a word. "They—they simply overwhelmed me with kindness."

"And you've never had church people doing anything like that for you before?"

"Never!" The iciness of her voice made even Cheryl realize she had spoken more vehemently than she intended.

"You don't need to explain anything," he said. "Sometimes we church people hurt others. We don't intend to, but it happens."

"And then people like me end up blaming every church and even God because one congregation or one pastor fails," she said.

"Is that what happened?"

"Thank you so much for coming," she said as she turned her face away.

Karla remained in Flint and worked part-time for Taylor at the newspaper. She did no actual writing but learned to collect news stories and became fairly proficient with a camera. She even persuaded Taylor to let her set up a filing system for him.

Cheryl moved on to crutches two weeks early. Dr. Lambert said as she left his office, "You're making fine progress." Those few words buoyed her spirits.

She laughed as Marc took her home. "Strange, how a little thing like getting to walk on crutches can give a person such a lift."

Her spirits stayed high the rest of the day. She had her crutches and took walks across the room with them. She went into the kitchen, feeling she could once again cook. She kept a chair near the sink where she frequently sat down.

Just before seven, Karla breezed in. "Cheryl, have I got a surprise for you!"

"I've got one for you, too—" She was sitting in the only stuffed chair in the apartment, her legs elevated by a stool that Ann Burns had lent her.

Karla threw the door open, and Shep stood there. He smiled and then moved inside, not certain what he ought to do next. Karla closed the door, grabbed his arm, and pulled him into the room.

"I know it's a surprise," Karla said, "but I felt it was time to level with Shep about the accident."

"You look great," Shep said. "I expected to see you wasted away to nothing and with casts all over your body—"

"I'm doing just fine," Cheryl said. She pulled out her crutches and stood on them. "See! Just started this today." She walked across the room. Karla beamed as she watched her sister.

"So you see, Shep," Cheryl said, trying not to breathe heavily from the exertion, "I'm even two weeks ahead of the schedule and doing fine. One small cast on my left leg, otherwise—"

He moved awkwardly forward, and she sat down again. He knelt beside her chair and wrapped his arms around her. "I've missed you."

Cheryl steeled herself against returning his embrace. When he pulled back, she said, "Tell me all about yourself, Shep. How have you been doing? You've graduated now, I suppose—"

"Why did you leave like that? Not even a word. Just a note."

"Maybe some of us grow up suddenly," she said. "Maybe I understood some things I should have understood long before."

Karla sat down on the kitchen stool and watched them. Shep glanced her way as if to say, *Tell me what to say next.* Karla ignored his silent entreaty.

"Shep, it wasn't right. Our getting married, I mean."

"Cheryl—"

"Wait a minute," she said as she laid her hand on his cheek. "Shep, you're the nicest man in the whole world. The kind of man any good woman would want for a husband, but—"

"But—," he said, and out of the corner of his eye noticed that Karla leaned forward.

"But we don't love each other. Not the kind of love for marriage. I love you as a friend—a very special friend."

"I don't understand—"

"And perhaps," she said, speaking as though she hadn't heard him, "perhaps I could love you best of all as a brother-in-law."

"A what?" he said.

Cheryl turned to face Karla, and the two sisters stared at each other. Karla got up slowly and walked over to the chair. She knelt beside Shep. "You found out? About us, didn't you?" she said in a tiny voice.

"I ought to have known long before. I just didn't want to face it."

"We didn't mean for it to happen," Shep said. "We found ourselves thrown together so much—"

"It's my fault," Karla said. "I've always loved Shep, and I tried not to let it show. I didn't mean to—"

"Hey, wait. I'm not blaming anyone," Cheryl said. "Marriage wouldn't have worked for us. I also knew that as long as I was around, you would never get together."

"I wouldn't want you hurt for anything," Karla said.

"That's the trouble with you," her older sister said. "You'd deny your love for Shep as long as I was there. That's why I left."

Shep kept shaking his head. "I—I can't believe—"

"*And* I'd better be the maid of honor at your wedding or else—"

Karla hugged her sister. "If only you knew how guilty I've felt for the past year. I didn't mean to love him or try to take him away."

"I know that, so stop apologizing."

"I do love her," Shep said. "I never wanted to hurt you—"

"Listen, you two," Cheryl said. "I've had a wonderful day. I'm now on crutches. I'm feeling good. Don't spoil it all by making me cry or laying all kinds of guilt on yourselves. It's one of those happy endings. Right?"

"Almost," Karla said. "Unless, of course—unless you're talking about something going on between you and—"

"One romance at a time," Cheryl said.

Eloise Adams called three times a week, usually before nine at night. Cheryl tried to keep her voice calm and to remain uninvolved. She found that by giving simple answers and confining herself to yes and no answers, she did better. When she disagreed, as she frequently did, she simply said, "I don't agree, Mother," but added nothing more. When Eloise pressed her, she replied, "I don't care to go into it, but only to let you know how I feel."

Marc dropped in during a telephone call. Eloise had phoned to tell her that Karla and Shep had returned safely to Des Moines. They planned a fall wedding.

"So you see, Cheryl, it is working out for the best."

"Yes, Mother, for the best."

"And you knew Shep planned to start a partnership with a friend in their own insurance agency, didn't you?"

"No, Mother."

"Oh. Then you didn't know that Karla had decided to quit school so she could work for them—even before we heard from you."

"No, Mother, I didn't know."

"Shep would have opened his office sooner, but both of them, you know, waited, not sure—"

"Yes, Mother, I slowed down their plans."

"I didn't mean it that way," she answered. "I only meant that things are moving along smoothly now. Don't you think so?"

"Yes, Mother, I think so."

"Karla is quite suited to Shep. Now you realize what I kept trying to say all along—"

"Yes, Mother, you were right." Cheryl paused, breathed deeply and said, "But then, you've always been right."

Eloise hurried on to the wedding plans and then hung up shortly afterward.

Marc brought coffee over to Cheryl. As he handed her a cup, he said, "I know you're still sick. I also know you and your mother have never gotten along well—"

"Never gotten along! A masterpiece of understatement."

"Even so, that doesn't give you the right to intentionally hurt people."

"Whose side are you on?"

"Do I have to take sides?" Marc said as he added milk to his coffee.

"You'd really have to take the conversation in context," she said weakly, "in order to understand."

"In context? All I know is that from the time your mother appeared in the hospital until you hung up just now, I've never heard you say a kind thing to her. You've never treated her with any appreciation. Even when you agree, your voice has a snarl in it."

"How dare you!"

"I dare because I love you," he said.

"Who do you think you are to come in here and try to run my life? Just like Mother." Cheryl realized she was screaming at him, and yet she could not stop. She grabbed the pillows off the bed and threw them at Marc. She reached across to the water glass and grabbed it, aimed, and let go. It missed, hit the wall, and rolled across the floor. She tore at her blankets. "Everyone loves Mother! Everyone gets taken in by her! I'm always the bad guy—"

Marc grabbed Cheryl and pinned her arms down. She tried to break loose. Realizing he only increased the pressure, she stopped struggling. After she relaxed, he held her with one arm. With his free hand he stroked her hair. "I'm here, Cheryl, and I want to help you work all this out with your mother."

"What if I don't want to work it out?"

"But you need to. For your sake if nothing else."

"My sake? I'm doing fine. And the farther away from me Mother stays—"

"Distance isn't the answer," Marc said. He turned to his coffee and took a long drink. He set the cup down and walked over to the stereo he had loaned Cheryl. He put on a Montavani record.

"Cheryl, I love you. And because I love you, I want you to be perfect. Seeing anything less than perfect in you, hurts me."

"If you only knew—only knew the years—the pain—"

"Don't offer me excuses, darling," he said.

"Excuses? Listen, Mr. Lattimer, if you knew how she treated me. Even worse, how she treated my father—"

"It doesn't matter how she treated anybody," he said, his voice calm. He sat down again and listened to the music.

"Doesn't matter?" she asked.

"Cheryl, you can't change your mother. You can't control her behavior. But you *can* do something about yourself."

"I took psychology courses in college, too," she snapped.

"Then you only understood the lessons in your head, and it never got down to your behavior!" For the first time his voice began to rise.

"So now I am supposed to let my mother knock me down, punch me again, wipe her feet on me, and then smile at her and say 'Gee, thanks, Mom, I needed that'?"

"I'm saying that you need to learn to forgive."

"Why should I forgive her? I don't think she even knows what she's done to me. Or even cares."

"Cheryl, she may not know what she's done in the past. But she cares. She cares very much."

"Oh? I really don't think so."

"She came here. Even when you didn't want her."

"She came. Out of duty. Guilt. Because of Karla. She's always loved Karla and hated me."

"Do you really believe that?"

"An old friend says if something sounds like a duck, smells like a duck, and acts like a duck, you'd better believe it's a duck. So my answer is yes. I do believe that."

Marc shook his head. "Okay, but I'm sorry for you, honey."

"Don't be sorry for me. The farther our paths move from each other—"

"Discussion ended, I guess," Marc said. He got up and walked back to the kitchen. He poured out the rest of his coffee and rinsed the cup. "I think I'll go now."

"You're angry with me, aren't you?"

"Disappointed maybe."

"Because I don't love my mother?"

"Because you can't forgive her."

"Please—please don't leave. Not like this. I've been angry and stupid and—and I'm trying, Marc. It may not show, but I'm trying to like her. As far as forgiving—well, I'll work on that, too."

He sat down next to her on the hide-a-bed. He pulled Cheryl close. He kissed her warmly on the lips, and she responded. "I love you," he said between kisses.

"Marc, just don't—don't try to pressure me."

"Pressure you?"

"By trying to make me say that I love you. Give me time," she said and laid her head on his shoulder. Marc sat silently, his arm around her. The second record fell into place. After a few minutes he realized her breathing had grown heavy and that she had fallen asleep.

Twenty minutes later she opened her eyes. "Must have dozed off," she said.

"I like watching you sleep."

"Marc, I'm sorry. About all the things I said."

"I know you are," he said and kissed her on the cheek.

"I made quite a scene, didn't I?"

"I shouldn't have let you get so upset."

"You can't control the unpleasant things in my life." She took his hand and held it a moment. She brought it next to her cheek and rubbed it. "You've been so patient with me."

"I want to protect you. To help you—"

"I know that, Marc."

"And I've been praying for you, too—"

"Marc, do you know that when you get intense about something, your eyes blaze. Like just now."

"I also know that every time I try to talk about God, you find a way of diverting me."

"Right! Someone advised me never to talk about religion or politics. Otherwise you lose your friends."

"I'm not just a friend," Marc said, "and you keep shutting me off from talking about the things that mean the most to me in life."

"Mean the most?"

"Yes. Like God."

"Maybe that's something we can talk about later. Right now, I don't—I don't want to talk about God. Or about the church or about my rudeness to Mother."

"Okay," he said, "but I hope you won't wait too long."

A quizzical look filled her face. "What do you mean?"

"You already have a lot of venom in you. I hope it doesn't get worse before you do something about it."

"And you think my anger is eating away at me?"

"Answer your own question," he said, and his eyes held hers.

She forced a smile on her face. "Now you sound like a psychiatrist I went to a few times. Whenever I made a strong statement, he always turned it back to me. 'How do you feel about that?' he'd ask. And you know, Marc, I got a little tired of it."

"I didn't mean to play a game with you," Marc said. "I push because I care about you. A lot."

"And I care about you. Perhaps not as much, but I do care."

"And because I care, I want to know your pain and to share it and—and to help," he said.

"And my rejection of the Christian faith troubles you, doesn't it?"

"Yes."

"Look, Marc, I have a string of Sunday-school pins for perfect attendance. Fifteen as a matter of fact."

"And yet—"

"What do you mean by that?"

"All you've done is confirm your bitterness and disappointment."

"Okay. And do you know what soured me?"

"No. But I'd like to. I'd like very much to know."

"Here's the biggest reason. My mother and father never got along well. She treated him badly. I used to hear their voices. She kept trying to make him leave. So when they argued, I prayed."

"And—"

"Maybe that sounds childish now, but I believed that if I prayed and believed, God would answer and make my father stay."

"But he left?"

"Bingo! He left anyway."

"But Cheryl, don't turn—"

"Wait, there's more. I prayed for him to come back. To live with us or to take me to live with him. *He died.*"

"Tragedy happens in a lot of lives," he said, "and I can't give you all the answers."

"But I prayed. I prayed every day. And on Sundays the minister kept talking about God's answering prayer."

Cheryl paused, remembering one Sunday when she lingered at the door. After everyone else had gone, she asked the minister, "Does God always answer our prayers? Especially if we want something badly?"

He cleared his throat. "Sometimes we have unconfessed sins in our lives," he said, "and that means God won't listen. God hates sin." For the next ten minutes he lectured Cheryl on sin, holiness, and God's anger.

Cheryl explained about her father's leaving and how it upset her.

"Exactly what I mean. Sin in the home. Your father seldom attended church. But your mother—she tried to bring you up right. He left. He walked out on his wife and two fine children. God can't and won't bless his kind of behavior. He divinely appoints a man as the head of the household. The Bible declares that he's responsible for the care of the family."

"I don't understand what you're talking about," she said. "You make God sound mean." She walked away.

As Cheryl's mind returned to the present she said, "No, I'm not much interested in God. I gave Him several chances. If He's real then—"

"He is, Cheryl. And someday you'll understand."

"Will I?" she asked.

Chapter 12

"I want to talk to you," Eloise said on the phone, "seriously."

"You always want to talk—seriously," Cheryl said. "But you know, Mother, I'm older now, and I'm tired of listening." She hung up.

Five minutes later the phone rang again. "Cheryl, at least listen for one full minute. If you hang up after that, I won't call you again— *ever.*"

"All right."

"I know you hate me. I can't change that. But I think there are some things you deserve to know. Things you may not want to hear."

"What kind of things?"

"About your father."

"I doubt you have anything to say that would interest me. He's dead, Mother. Why don't you let him rest?"

Eloise paused at the other end and then gripped the phone. "I am coming out to see you one more time. I must show you something about him."

"If it's that important, save your money and mail it—"

"I've already booked a flight."

"I would prefer that you not come," she answered.

"Let me show you these things, and then I promise to stay out of your life completely—if you want."

"That sounds too good to be true."

"I don't make idle promises."

"All right, Mother. I'll give you that much. We'll talk. And then—"

"And then I'll stay out of your life completely if you want."

Cheryl wrote down the flight number and time. "I can drive now, so I'll pick you up," she said.

After she hung up, Cheryl sat alone in her apartment, thinking about the call. She kept wondering what her mother could possibly have to show her. Then, using her crutches, she walked across the hall and tapped on Taylor's door.

He let her inside, and she related the phone conversation. Taylor listened and offered no ideas when Cheryl wondered about what her mother wanted to show her.

"You haven't said a word about all this," she said.

"Do you want me to say anything?"

"You think I'm wrong, don't you? Wrong about the way I talked to her?"

"A friend does not judge a friend," he replied.

"But a friend speaks honestly when asked a question," she snapped.

Taylor smiled, showing his dimples. "I'm going to have to change my way of talking to you. You've gotten too clever."

"And you're quite deft at distraction," she said.

"Okay, you want it straight. Here it is: You've never forgiven your mother, have you? Even after all this time."

"No, I haven't."

"Haven't? Can't? Won't?"

"All of the above," she said.

"Then why do you want me to say anything?"

"I thought—I honestly thought that as my friend, you could at least offer advice."

"You wouldn't listen," he said.

"Try me."

"Okay, Cheryl. Pray about this. Ask God to help you forgive—"

"Oh, Taylor, you, too."

"Me, too, what?"

"Pushing this religion at me. You're sounding like Marc now."

"You asked for my advice."

"Okay, I asked," she said.

"And I told you that you wouldn't listen."

"You warned me."

"But it helps, Cheryl. Believe me, it helps."

"Look, Taylor, it's not that I'm against praying. I'm just not convinced it does any good."

"I'm not going to try to persuade you, Cheryl. Only suggest. And it works for me."

Cheryl grabbed her crutches and hobbled across the room. "I'll have coffee ready in a few minutes. And this time I'll make it plenty strong," she said and turned on the tap.

"Now who's getting adept at diverting?"

"Guilty, your honor."

"Cheryl, I've told you about Beth. I'd like to tell you a little more about her."

"Sure," she said as she measured the coffee.

"Add another half spoon, please," he said and flashed a quick smile. "You still make it too weak."

Minutes later, she let Taylor bring the cups to the table. They sat down, and she sipped the hot liquid slowly, wishing she could learn to enjoy it as much as Taylor did.

"My world fell apart when I lost Beth. That's when I turned my life over to God."

"Turned your life over to God? I mean—how?"

"Maybe I said too much in a single statement. I'll back up. For the first few weeks after Beth's death, I kept telling God how cruel He was. 'Why are You doing this to me?' I must have screamed that question a hundred times."

"Did you get an answer?"

"No," he said. "At least not the kind I can explain."

"But you did get some kind of answer? Is that it?"

"Yes. A peace inside—like I'd never experienced before. Even though I still missed Beth, I had this deep sense of Jesus Christ being right beside me, all the time."

"And you kept on praying?"

"More than ever."

"You feel it helped?"

"Very much."

"I don't see how," she said. "I prayed for a long time about my father—and he left. Then he died—"

"God didn't change circumstances," he said. "He changed me."

"You mean you learned to accept the circumstances?"

"Yes. But something else. I also realized that everyone has problems. Mine seemed bigger than others. Each of us thinks his or her tragedy is the worst in the world."

"I suppose you're right—"

"And you see, Cheryl, I didn't start out with a grudge against God."

"And I did. Is that what you're saying?"

"No, I hadn't meant it that way."

"How did you mean it?" In spite of the smile on her face, Cheryl knew her whole body had grown tense. She did not want to prolong the conversation, yet she kept responding to everything Taylor said.

"Only that I started with an open mind. That's all I meant."

"And now everything has gone well for you—"

"I've gotten a lot of answers in life, that's all," Taylor said.

"I'm glad for you—"

"Stop being so flip," Taylor said. "You don't have to turn to God, if you don't want. Stay miserable." And he laughed.

"I have been miserable, haven't I?"

The next morning Cheryl waited for her mother in the baggage claim area. She saw her mother, nodded in recognition, and indicated that she would stand where she was until Eloise claimed her luggage.

Minutes later Eloise, carrying a small suitcase, approached her daughter. "Great seeing you on crutches. You've really made progress—"

"We can take the escalator," she nodded with her head. "There's a restaurant upstairs. That way you won't even have to leave the airport."

"If that's what you want," Eloise said.

"That's what I want."

They went silently up one flight and down the broad hallway to the restaurant. A waitress came immediately and took their order.

"Okay, Mother, I'm here. I'm willing to listen." She looked at her watch. "I can even waste fifteen more minutes."

"I've been wrong, Cheryl. Wrong about a lot of things."

Cheryl resisted the urge to reply. She sat stiffly, her hands on the table. She slowly tapped her long nails against the full water glass.

"I've always been hard on you. Perhaps too hard. I'm not trying to excuse myself—"

"Good."

"But I tried to do my best under the circumstances."

"Mother, I really don't care. It's too late for us. I've gotten away from home now, and all the stored-up anger has dissipated. I don't *hate* you anymore; I just don't particularly want to be around you."

"I tried to protect you and Karla."

"Protect us?" she snorted.

"Did you ever hear me speak against your father? Even once?"

Cheryl thought for a moment. "No, I don't think I ever heard you say anything directly to Karla or me about him. But the way you treated—"

"One thing at a time. Just give me the chance to tell you the truth about him."

"The truth? I know everything about him I need to know."

"No, Cheryl. There's much you don't know."

"For instance?"

"For instance, he went away a lot. Often for weeks at a time."

"Because you sent him away!"

"In one sense, I did. In fact, I demanded it—"

"So what is there to say?"

"But you don't know *why.*"

"I think that was always obvious. You hated him."

"Hated him? I loved your father. He's the only man I've ever loved in my whole life. If I hadn't loved him, why—why do you think I put up with him for twenty-eight years?"

"Okay, Mother," she sighed, "why did you put up with him for over twenty-eight years?"

"I told you, because I loved him. You don't have to believe me."

"I don't."

"But what you don't know—," Eloise stopped, looked down at her hands, and saw they were shaking. "What you don't know—"

"Mother, please—"

"Your father was mentally ill."

"Mentally ill? That's a low trick—"

"He went away regularly for treatment. He was clinically diagnosed—" she turned and pulled her purse from the floor and rummaged through it.

"I'm not going to sit here and listen to you say those things against my father!" She pulled her crutches from the table, stood up, and started to move quickly across the floor.

"Cheryl, please—"

But Cheryl walked even faster.

Eloise dropped a ten-dollar bill on the table and hurried after her daughter. "Wait!"

Cheryl reached the door just as an older man was entering. She leaned back to avoid colliding with him and lost her balance. She fell, and one crutch slid noisily across the tiled floor.

Four people suddenly surrounded her, all offering to help her up. Cheryl had fallen on her back but kept her left leg slightly elevated, so that it did not touch the floor. Her eyes filled with tears.

"Here, miss, let me help you," a large man said as he reached down and slowly pulled her up. Someone else picked up the crutch and handed it to her. "You okay?" he asked.

"Yes, fine," Cheryl said. She pulled away and took a step. She felt a weakness hit her and sensed she was going to fall again. Eloise grabbed her. "She's my daughter. I'll help her." She thanked the people.

"Just help me get out of here," Cheryl whispered, not sure if she spoke more from pain or embarrassment.

"I'm sure we can find a place to sit down—"

"No, just get me out of here." Eloise half supported, half guided her daughter along the corridor. She held on to her as they went down the escalator. By the time they had reached the bottom, Cheryl said, "I'm all right now."

"You sure?"

"Yes. I can make it."

"May I—may I stay?" Eloise asked.

"After what you said up there, I think you'd better. You not only owe me an explanation, but you'd better be able to prove it."

"I will," she said.

Ten minutes later the two women drove out of the Atlanta terminal and onto the expressway. After a short distance, they pulled onto State Highway 139 and headed toward Flint. Suddenly Cheryl pulled over to the shoulder of the road, parked, and turned off the ignition.

"Okay, show me the proof. I don't want to go any farther."

"Let me tell you first."

"Let me see some proof!"

Eloise opened her purse and pulled out photocopied pages from the Veteran's Hospital in Iowa City. Five doctors, all on different dates, made an individual diagnosis of George Adams. Terms such as *schizophrenic* and *manic-depressive* jumped out at Cheryl. Tears filled her eyes, and she could hardly read. She dropped the paper "I—I had no idea."

"Then I suppose I did a good job," Eloise said and turned her face toward the window. "I tried to shield both of you girls so you wouldn't know."

"Why? We deserved to know."

"At the time I thought it was best. And for a long time—well, I thought he'd get better."

"But later—if you realized he wasn't—?"

"Then it was too late. I didn't have the courage, I suppose."

"Awfully hard to learn about my father now."

"I suppose it is," Eloise said.

"When your father had a serious bout and had to check into the VA hospital, I simply told you kids he was away on business. And you never knew the difference."

"But the arguing? I used to hear you at night—"

"Your father would get better and stay on top for weeks. Then, suddenly he'd get worse. Most of the time, however, I could see it coming for a week or more before he realized it. That's when I'd beg him to go back to the hospital. He always resisted."

"And you insisted?"

"Cheryl, I knew that if he was ever to get better—or even to live any kind of normal life, he could not do it without help."

"All those years," Cheryl said. "All those years, and I had no idea."

"I want you to know this much, Cheryl. I failed in a lot of ways, but through it all, I loved your father."

"I just—just had no idea," Cheryl said. And for the first time in her entire life, Cheryl saw tears in her mother's eyes.

"Whatever you think of me, Cheryl, please believe me. More than anything else, I loved him."

"If only I had known—"

"I didn't want to destroy the image of your father. He begged me over and over not to tell you girls. So I did what needed to be done to protect him."

"You did a good job. I never suspected."

"I lived in constant fear that you would find out. You especially because you and your father were so close. I feared you'd sense his mood changes."

"I suppose I did," Cheryl said. "But he'd say he was tired or complain about the piled-up paperwork at the office. Sometimes he said he was having trouble with his heart again."

"He had nothing wrong with his heart," she said. "Just another lie we made up to protect you and Karla from the truth."

"Mother, I—I wish I had known about his sickness. If only you had told me—"

"Maybe we were wrong to hide it," Eloise said. "But he was ashamed. We did what we thought was best at the time."

"You know, I've not only hated you, but in a crazy sort of way, I've been angry at him, too, for dying."

"Cheryl, no, no, don't—"

"But I was. At least now—at least now I understand a little better."

"Am I too late in telling you?"

"Oh, Mother, I—"

"Too late or not, I had to tell you. Even if it doesn't change you, I needed to get it off my own conscience."

Cheryl started to answer, but as their eyes met, both saw the pain in the other. Cheryl stretched out her arms, and her mother moved toward her. The two women embraced.

Chapter 13

"I don't want to go to your apartment," Eloise said. "Just drop me off at a motel."

"I don't mind your staying at my place. Not now."

"Maybe I'm not ready this time," she said.

"I don't understand," Cheryl said as she weaved back and forth in the crowded three southbound lanes of traffic.

"I've told you about George," she said. "Now I need to be alone and do some thinking on my own."

"I'd really like you to stay—"

"It's not that. Telling you about your father opened up a lot of things inside me," she said, her voice choking with emotion. "I just want to be alone someplace for a while."

"Will you call me?" Cheryl asked.

"As soon as I'm—as soon as I've got it sorted out in my own mind," she answered.

Cheryl stopped in front of a motel and sat in the car while her mother registered. She then drove to the room and waited until her mother went inside. Then she pulled out of the lot.

In one sense, Cheryl felt relieved that her mother had declined to stay with her. She, too, needed to sort things out. She had heard the words and read the reports. Now she wanted to let it all sink in.

As she recalled her childhood, incidents now took on a different perspective. One time she heard her father scream, "I will not go! Nothing you do can force me!" And, of course, Cheryl had assumed—"That's it," she said, "I *assumed.*"

How she had despised her mother! Flashes of insight struck at her brain as she realized how she had misinterpreted everything. As Cheryl grew into her teens, she railed against her mother. Not once had her father ever defended his wife. He would say, "I have you, Cheryl. Sometimes I feel as though no one else in the world really cares." On another occasion he hugged her and said, "You'll never let me down, will you?"

Now she knew. He had been sick, even then.

Cheryl's mind reeled from confusion. She hardly knew what to believe. But she knew Mother had not lied. The papers confirmed it all.

She could hardly believe that Father had allowed her to think those things about Mother. But then, that, too, was part of the sickness—allowing her to believe Mother had deliberately turned against him.

Cheryl pulled up in front of Marc's apartment. After stopping the car, she hobbled up to his door and rang the bell.

"Cheryl—"

"I need to talk. Desperately, Marc."

"Of course," he said and opened the door wider. She had been to his apartment once before. Today she hardly saw the almost-new furniture or the neatly vacuumed carpets.

"Marc, I'm confused. I guess that's the best way to say it."

"Confused?" he said, indicating a stuffed chair for her to sit in. He sat across from her on the sofa.

Fighting back tears, Cheryl told him what she had learned about her father. "My mind is reeling with all this. I can't believe—"

"Your father was sick. Right?"

She nodded.

"And because he was sick, apparently he did not know what he was doing," Marc continued. "Now you've heard what your mother said about all those years—"

"I hated my mother. I hated her because of what—because of what I thought she had done. Now—now I don't know what I feel."

Marc leaned back, and put his hands together, palms inward, and seemed lost in thought. Cheryl continued to tell about the meeting with her mother.

"Have you forgiven her?"

"I don't know."

"You'll have to do that first."

"I suppose you're right."

"Then you've got at least two other people to forgive."

"Two?"

"Your father. And yourself."

Cheryl stared at him. She nodded her head slowly. "Right now I was reproaching myself for believing all that garbage. And hating my father for feeding it all to me."

"Remember, Cheryl, he was sick."

"I know you're right," she said, "but still I should have—"

"Don't use that word."

"What word?"

"*Should.* It always produces guilt, demanding things of yourself that you can't change. You did what you thought best even though you were wrong."

"I'm ashamed."

"It's not too late to make up—"

"I don't know—I don't know—"

"Cheryl, there's where you need God's help. Especially in forgiving your father for taking his life and for deceiving you. And you'll need God's help in forgiving yourself."

"I suppose you're right," she said numbly.

An hour later, Cheryl sat in her apartment, hardly aware of how she had gotten there. She kept trying to sort out everything, and nothing made sense to her. The phone rang, and she picked it up mechanically and answered.

"This is Marc. Feeling any better now?"

"I'm all right, Marc—"

"I called because I can't get away right now. I have patients scheduled for the next three hours. But I'll be there as soon as I can."

"You don't need to come. Honest." She tried to make her voice sound cheerful and realized it sounded flat.

"Cheryl, I love you, and I want to marry you."

"Marry me?"

"That's the message. I don't care about all your background. I just want you."

"Marc, I—I can't deal with all of this right now—"

"Maybe not. But I don't care about your father or your mother or all the mess. I love you. Please remember that. Okay?"

"Okay, Marc."

"Well?"

"Well, what?"

"Will you? Marry me, I mean?"

"I need to think about that. Please don't push me—"

"You never know when you can catch a lady in a moment of weakness," he said.

She laughed. "Thanks for cheering me up."

"But the marriage proposal was serious. One hundred percent serious."

After he hung up, Cheryl sat in the room, aware from time to time of the aching hip where she had fallen, but the pain was not severe enough to take all her attention from the confusion in her head.

A knock on the door brought her to the real world again. She stood up, and hopping on one foot, went to the door, and opened it. "Mother? How did you get here?"

"I rented a car," she said. "May I come in?"

Cheryl opened the door and hopped back across the room. She plopped into a chair and elevated her leg.

"You always felt that I hated you," Eloise said, her voice low.

"Until today anyway—"

"I did, Cheryl. Maybe hate is too strong a word. But I did dislike you. I didn't mean to. I didn't want to, but over the years—well, I—"

"Mother, don't—"

"I knew what your father was doing," she said. "I also knew it was part of his sickness. You never thought he could do anything wrong. And you believed him, and I resented that."

"But you never tried to tell me differently—"

"Would you have listened?"

"I suppose not."

"And you would have accused me of trying to hurt your father even more," Eloise said. "So I said nothing. And because you couldn't see what he was doing to you, I—well, I suppose I began to hate you too."

"Mother, I—"

"I came here to ask you to forgive me. I failed you, and I'm sorry."

"Failed me? Oh, Mother, no, no—"

"Yes, I failed. As you grew older, you hung onto every word he said. I shouldn't blame you for that. You loved him. And a girl needs to love her father—"

"Even if it means turning against her mother?"

"I don't know, Cheryl," she said, "and I'm tired. Tired of fighting. Tired of protecting. Tired of holding anger against you for something you couldn't help."

"Mother, I've been sitting here, fitting all the pieces together in my head. I'm still confused."

"It'll take time," Eloise said. "But I know you well enough to be sure that you'll straighten yourself out."

"Thanks, Mother, for—"

Eloise stood up. "I'm going back to my motel. I've done the two hardest things in the whole world today. I've told you about your father. And I've admitted my own failure."

"I'm still in shock—"

"I've got a plane reservation for six thirty," she said. "So I had better hurry. Please forgive me, can you?"

"I don't know, Mother."

"I know how that is," she said, and she walked across the room. "I couldn't let go and forgive either. Until last night."

"What happened last night?"

"I'll tell you about it sometime," she said, "if you want to know. Maybe all I need to say now is that I've made peace. Peace with myself and with God. Even with your father. And—and I'm trying to make peace with you." She pulled the door open and walked out.

Cheryl stared numbly at the sheaf of papers in front of her. She began to read the thick file again. Each admittance to the VA hospital was listed, along with duration of stay, amount and types of medication, diagnosis, and prognosis. As she looked at the dates and tried to fit them in, she realized that her mother had told her the truth. She had believed before but seeing the dates removed all doubt. Especially the entry of his admittance from February 3 through March 27. Two days before her eighteenth birthday he had gone in. She had been heartbroken. And that was the time her father had screamed, "I'm not going."

Cheryl read completely through the file a second time.

Chapter 14

"Taylor, when a friend calls on the phone, and she's desperate," Cheryl said, "then what do you do?"

"I drop everything and rush over."

"I need you. Now."

"I'm on my way," he said, and the phone clicked.

Within five minutes Taylor rushed into her apartment. She handed him the manila folder.

Taylor slumped into a chair and skimmed through the reports. He whistled once and shook his head. When he finished, he looked up, his face questioning hers. "No wonder you needed me."

"I feel as though my whole world caved in today," she said.

"Especially where it concerns your father."

She nodded. "Taylor, I loved him so much. At the same time I hated him for dying. And his death made me hate my mother even more."

"You thought she drove him to suicide?"

"Yes—and now I've read all this, and—and Mother flew in from Des Moines just to give it to me. Oh, Taylor, he was sick. Terribly sick and I didn't know—"

"You're reproaching yourself because you think you could have done something if you had known."

"Something like that."

"Everything you believed is wrong, and you're confused."

"Confused. Hurt, too."

"You learned unpleasant things about him that you didn't want to know."

"I still can't believe—I mean, it hasn't sunk in."

"You idealized him. In your mind you built him up to be more than human, you know," Taylor said.

"Did I do that, Taylor? Really?"

He nodded. "Think about it. Think of the times you mentioned him. You painted him as the perfect parent. Maybe too perfect."

"I did love him," she said.

"What's wrong with loving an imperfect person? Does everyone have to reach a particular standard before you accept him or her?"

"You think that's the way I operate?"

"Isn't it?"

"I don't know, Taylor. Honestly, I don't know."

"Think a bit. You've got Marc slobbering all over you, and you sit around and wallow in self-pity over Shep—"

"That's hitting pretty hard," she said.

"Friends hit hard because they love each other," Taylor said. He leaned forward, his face inches from hers. "Today you get a heavy lecture from me because you need to hear it."

"Oh, I do?"

"Absolutely. You're confused and unsure of yourself. Everyone lets you down—your father, your mother, Shep, the church. And you're afraid to trust Marc and open yourself to him. You've got problems, lady."

"I know the problems," she said.

"The answers are obvious."

"I don't think it's that clear."

"It is if you want to know."

Cheryl leaned back and closed her eyes. "Okay, let me hear it."

"Step number one is called forgiveness."

"I suppose I know that, but—"

"Don't say *but*. Forgive your mother. It also means to forgive your father."

"I don't need to forgive him for anything—"

"Oh, but you do. He let you down. He took his own life. He was sick, but he still let you down."

"I guess I have held that against him."

"And you need to forgive Shep for loving Karla more than he loved you. Most of all—"

"I know. I have to forgive myself."

"I always said you were smart and that you learned fast."

"It's such a shock—"

"I knew it would be."

"You knew? Wait a minute—"

"Your mother called me yesterday. She didn't give me details, but enough. I advised her to tell you everything."

"I see," she said.

"You don't see at all," Taylor said. He got up and paced the room several times then stopped in front of her. He knelt beside her chair. "You don't see anything. You only think of poor Cheryl hurt, rejected, and—"

"You think I'm that terrible?"

"Why don't you answer that question for yourself?" Taylor said.

"Taylor, I'm so mixed up—"

"That's why I'm laying it on you so heavy," he said. "You need it."

"Maybe I do," she said. "I suppose that's why I called you, Taylor. I knew you would be honest with me."

"Count on it. Always."

She reached out and took his hands. "You're the best friend I've ever had, Taylor."

"I've promoted you to the same position in my life," his dimples showed, and he winked.

"I just need someone to tell me what to do next."

"You know what to do," Taylor said. He leaned forward and kissed her lightly on the cheek. "You don't need me to tell you anything."

"Why do you always have to be right?"

"That's why you value my friendship so much."

"Stop being so right!" but this time she smiled.

Hobbling outside with her crutches, Cheryl walked across the complex. She waved to Ann Burns, who was trimming roses in front of the office. She went past the pool area and into a secluded wooded section which Ann had furnished with two picnic tables.

Cheryl realized how tired she was from that much movement. She sat on the edge of one bench and pulled another over to prop up her leg.

She sat in the silence, listening to the soft chirping of a pair of robins nearby. A chipmunk ran up and down an elm tree. Once he approached her, stood still, sniffed, and ran off again.

"Oh, how peaceful it is out here," she said as the sun caressed her face. Both time and inner turmoil stopped, and she lost herself in the pastoral setting.

She looked above at the cloudless sky and felt a peace she had not thought possible. "I think—I think it's starting to straighten itself out now," she said aloud.

As she moved her head slowly, she saw the full green of the southern pines, with occasional oaks or elms mixed in. In the distance, the steeple of the church rose beyond the trees, seeming to reach into heaven itself.

As Cheryl stared at the steeple, a cross affixed at the top, she remembered a prayer they repeated every Sunday in the church in Des Moines. Without knowing why, she started to recite it. "Our Father, who art in heaven ... forgive us our trespasses—" Cheryl stopped. "Forgive?"

"Forgive us our trespasses as we forgive those who trespass against us—" Cheryl stopped again.

"Do I really mean that?"

Two hours later, Cheryl pulled into the parking lot at the Flint Physical Therapy Center. She pulled herself out of the car, hoisted her crutches from the backseat and walked up the ramp. She went inside. A bell under the floor mat rang.

"Just a minute—" Marc poked his head out. He saw Cheryl and rushed down the hallway. He grabbed her and held her tight. Then he pulled back and stared at her. "Something's different about you," he said. "I'm not sure what it is—"

"Something good? Something bad? What kind of difference?" and a trace of a smile touched her lips.

"Definitely good," he said.

"I love you, Marc," she said softly.

"I knew it was good," and he hugged her again.

"I got a lot of things sorted out today."

"I'm glad."

"For one thing, I've faced up to the fact that I love you. And I'm not afraid of losing you."

"You won't lose me!"

"I know that now. I didn't an hour ago."

Marc looked quizzically at her.

"I'll have to explain all that to you a little later," she said.

"I only care that you love me," he said. "And that you know I love you."

"Marc, before I say anything more, I need to make a phone call."

"Sure." He led her into an office.

Cheryl picked up the directory, found the number, and called the motel. She asked for her mother.

"I'm sorry; she checked out," the desk clerk said.

Cheryl fumbled through the directory again and found the number for the airline. She told the woman who answered that she needed to get a message to a passenger scheduled for a six-thirty flight to Des Moines.

Another voice came on the line, and Cheryl explained what she wanted. "Just a minute, please." In the background, Cheryl heard the muffled page for her mother.

A minute later, a voice said, "This is Eloise Adams."

"Don't leave, Mother."

"You want me to stay?"

"You have to stay. I have too many things I need to say—"

"You're sure this is what you want?"

"Oh, yes. Please."

"I'll stay."

"I'll be right there," she said, and Marc's voice whispered in her ear, "And I'll be with you."

"I'm glad—glad for another chance—"

"Mother, forgive me. Please—please, can you forgive me?"

Cheryl could hear her Mother's voice quiver as she said, "As long as you forgive me, too."

When Cheryl hung up, she remembered the words of her best friend who said, "Friends don't have to tell each other they're sorry." And Cheryl said to herself, "Taylor, this time you're definitely wrong!"

DESTINED TO LOVE

Melanie Haywood

Chapter 1

Neither of them spoke as they finished their breakfast in the airport coffee shop. Hap paid the check, flashed the waitress a wide grin, and folded her hand over a generous tip. Without looking to see if Lezlie followed, he loped down the terminal corridor. His long strides quickly left her behind. He paused only to show his identification card at security and continued his pace to the plane.

Lezlie made no attempt to keep up. "Not this time," she said under her breath. "We've played it your way long enough." She purposely slowed down, even pausing to read signs and posters she ordinarily ignored.

A full minute later she entered the plane and turned right into the first-class galley. Out of the corner of her eye, she saw Hap just inside the door of the flight deck, obviously waiting for her. Lezlie avoided looking at him.

"Wait," he said.

She took two more steps, stopped, and said, "I'm waiting." She did not turn around.

He came up behind her and encircled her with his long arms. Lezlie stiffened and started to pull away. He swung her around, and her shoulder bag fell to the floor. He tightened his grip and pulled her so that their faces almost touched.

"Is it all right for a pilot to kiss a flight attendant?" Before she could reply, he pulled her tighter, and their lips met.

"Don't—don't," she said and started to push him away.

"Lez, I know things haven't been good between us lately—"

"No, they haven't," she said.

"I love you."

She tried to laugh. "That's the first personal thing you've said all morning."

"Things will get right for us again. I promise."

"I—I hope so," she said and pulled completely away from him. Lezlie picked up her shoulder bag and started to move through the cabin. She paused and said over her shoulder, "I want things right between us. If—if it's not too late."

"It's not, Lez—"

"Hap, I can't hold our marriage together by myself."

"Some marriages have to make adjustments," he said.

Even without turning around, she knew the Hap Austin charm had taken over. His voice changed into a husky whisper, and a seemingly innocent smile covered his face. His light blue eyes gave him a help-less look. He had won her over too many times. Lezlie determined she would not weaken again. "It's more than an adjustment," she said and moved forward.

Hap took several quick strides and stood behind her. He grabbed her from behind a second time. He pulled her against his own body and kissed the top of her head. "We'll straighten it all out."

"You've said that before," Lezlie answered, and she realized her knuckles tightened against the strap of her bag. Her voice sounded cold, but it was the only way she knew to fight him.

"Please, Lez, give me a chance—"

"Don't, Hap—"

"I can't lose you."

"It's not so much losing me," she said and loosened the grip of his large hands. "It's more a matter of shutting me out of your life."

"Lezlie—"

"We've gone through all of this before."

"One more chance. That's all I ask."

She nodded. "One more chance."

"Darling—"

"No, Hap, don't—don't spoil it with your great-lover antics." Her brown eyes flashed, and the words flowed. "I've put up with a lot. I made a promise to you and to God. I'll do whatever I can to keep my vows. I'll try one more time even though—"

"Even though I've not kept mine?"

"Even though I don't think you can keep yours," she corrected.

"It will be different. I swear to you—"

She put her fingers momentarily over his lips. "No more words, Hap. No more promises. I want action."

"Action? Is that what you want?" he said and pulled her close for a kiss. She reared her head back.

At that moment, Travis Manning walked into the plane. He looked up and saw them. "Oh, excuse me—"

"No big deal, partner," Hap said. "Just one of those last-minute bits of loving between husband and wife."

"Didn't mean to interrupt anything," Travis said, and Lezlie no-ticed he was blushing. "I'll—I'll, uh, I think I forgot something." He turned around and hurried back off the plane.

"No need to do that," Lezlie called, but he kept going.

"I like it when we're alone," Hap said. "Just the two of us—"

"I want to get back to the rear cabin and be ready before the others arrive or—"

"Or Gladys will make it hard on you?"

"I didn't say that," she answered, but her face showed he was right.

"You don't need to worry about Gladys."

"Don't I?" she said then regretted her words. This was not the time to accuse. Instead she smiled and said, "Hap, I put in my bid for this flight, and I got it. I'm also the junior member. I don't want Gladys or any of the others to think I want special privileges."

"Especially, you don't want Gladys on your back," he said and gave her a mock serious look. "She's the Wicked Witch of the North."

"I didn't mean anything like that."

"Hey, I've known Gladys for years."

"Yes, I know."

"She's not going to chew you out."

"It's not a chewing out I'm talking about. I simply don't want anyone to think that I'm expecting anything special just because I'm married to the captain."

"But you are special," he said. He bent forward and kissed her lightly on the cheek and then on the temple.

"I don't need those sugary words," she said.

"I mean them. Every one of them."

"And you've meant them when you said them to all the other—"

"Lezlie, believe me." He burrowed his head in her dark hair, sniffing her lilac cologne. "Love that smell. Just a subtle hint. Not that overpowering fragrance some women use."

"You should know—"

"And it heightens my excitement over you," he added.

She shook her head. "Hap, I don't want to hear those words now."

"Maybe I can't shift gears so easily," he said.

"I'm not asking for a miracle overnight. But I do want honesty from you."

"I'm going to try, Lez. Things will get better. I promise."

"Don't make promises you can't keep."

"This time I mean it," he said.

"Okay," she answered, and hearing voices coming toward the plane, she removed his arms from around her. She patted her brown uniform jacket and automatically smoothed her dark hair.

"We'll talk, Lez. A long talk tonight at home. Then, after our trip to Jordan—"

She blew him a kiss and walked out of the flight deck.

"Hey, Lez, any antacid tablets back there?" he yelled after her. "Got a little indigestion. All that spicy food—"

"I'll find something," she said and hurried away.

Hap sat down in the pilot's chair and methodically checked the instruments. Today his mind was not on his work. The burning sensation seemed to get worse.

Maybe it wasn't worse at all, he thought, only that he was a little more anxious. He pounded the yoke several times. Of all the times for Lezlie to turn cold on him—just when everything was coming out so perfect.

In spite of the discomfort he felt in his chest, Hap smiled. He had made his last trip for them, and he was free. He had planned that part carefully. Some pilots never got out. Right from the beginning he told them he would take risks. He had taken every trip they offered, but now he had made enough, and he was out. He had set his price, explained the shipments he would handle with the L-1011 as well as the side trips from San Juan in the small craft.

They had urged him to continue. They had tried everything from threats to increasing his share of the money. He had not yielded. Hap knew that sooner or later, it would blow up. It always did. He had covered himself, and now he was safe.

You can't go on with that kind of business forever, he said to himself. *Sooner or later it catches up with you. Better to get out when you're ahead.* He had all the money he needed. His clients also knew they could trust him to keep his mouth shut. Reluctantly they agreed. That left only the trip to Jordan.

He hadn't wanted Lezlie to find out. That had been the biggest risk of all, hiding everything from her. And she wasn't stupid. He had a few terrible moments when the incident with the book came up. Fortunately, she had not caught on. Another slipup could happen anytime. No, he was right. Getting out was the answer.

He ought to feel relieved. Instead the burning sensation increased.

He wished Lezlie would hurry. He had just decided to push his chair back and go for it himself when she appeared on the flight deck. On a small tray she carried a bottle of Maalox, a half dozen antacid tablets, a bottle of Perrier, and a glass.

"You have your choice, captain," she said with mock courtesy.

He grabbed the liquid, unscrewed the top, upped it, and took a long swig. He pocketed the tablets. "Don't think I'll need them, but just in case."

"I'll leave the Perrier here, too," she said.

"No, take it back. I'll take a break and get my own when I get thirsty."

"You okay, Hap?" she asked.

He carefully avoided her eyes, as he laughed, "Hey, this is Hap Austin, king of the airways. One does not go on sick leave over indigestion and heartburn."

"If you're sure," she said, and her eyes searched his tanned face.

"After all that spicy stuff last night—"

"Okay, Hap," she said and went back to the cabin.

At that moment, Hap felt a slight pain in his chest. It jabbed him hard and then immediately eased off. Perhaps he shouldn't have made that flight last night. But the twenty thousand, he reminded himself, had been worth it.

An hour later, Captain Elson "Hap" Austin, senior pilot of the L-1011, pulled out of the runway at San Juan, Puerto Rico, for a flight to New Orleans with an intermediate stop at Orlando, Florida. As captain, he made his usual welcome-aboard-and-thank-you-for-flying-with-us speech. Immediately afterward Gladys and the other flight attendants demonstrated safety precautions.

As captain, he was flying and handling the communications as well. Forty-five minutes out of San Juan he wondered if he ought to take those tablets Lezlie had given him. The Maalox had not helped, and the indigestion had not lessened. Suddenly a slight pain stabbed him and then eased. Almost immediately he felt as though a huge fist had struck his chest and continued pushing. Beads of sweat broke out on his forehead, and he could feel the perspiration under his arms. He loosened his tie and collar. It hurt to breathe deeply.

Even the anxiety to get back to New Orleans, the pressure over problems with Lezlie, and the tiredness from the after-dark flight he had made to one of the small islands did not explain what was happening to him.

"You all right?" Travis asked. "You look a little pale."

"A little indigestion," he said. "You know how it goes. One of those super parties at the El Dorado—"

Travis shook his head. "You guys never learn."

"Wrong! I've learned to have fun! You, however, act like the hibernating bear in winter. No one sees you until flight time again."

"You sure you're okay?" Travis asked again.

"Hey, you studying to become a doctor or something?" Hap said and laughed.

Travis shook his head. "You know, you have to live in Latin America all your life to float those chilies and spices down your gullet."

Hap laughed and sang a line from "Chiquita Banana" and stopped. He stared at his instruments. Normally he would have joked more with Travis, his first officer, or Phil, the engineer. But right then he experienced a numbness in his left arm.

Hap immediately thought of a heart attack. *I'm only thirty-six and in good physical shape. I don't smoke, and there's no history of heart disease in our family.* His mind clicked off the symptoms he had been taught. No, it could not be his heart.

"Phil, what's the cabin pressure?" he asked, noting they were now at thirty-five thousand feet.

"Altitude just under six thousand," he said. "Looks normal."

"Thank you, Mr. Chief Engineer!" Hap said in his characteristically jaunty tone. "You get an A on your flight report for today."

"Want me to handle it?" Travis said. "You look as though you need to rest a bit."

"I'm all right," Hap snapped.

"Okay," Travis said and shrugged. "Just thought—"

"Ah, I know the eagerness of young men wishing to steer us into the stars," Hap said. He hummed a few lines of a popular ballad, ". . . discover new worlds with you by my side. . . ."

"Save us from another Hap Austin concert, please," Phil quipped. "I haven't had my tetanus shot yet."

"Ah, those of you who have no appreciation for music—"

"Music we appreciate," Phil said. "And if you'll provide some—"

"I can see I'm not appreciated here," Hap said. "I'll walk through the cabin and ask if any of the passengers can fly this plane. If so, I'll toss out my engineer and copilot."

"Or maybe we can get rid of the half-crazed captain!" Travis said, joining in the banter.

Hap pushed the button for his seat to move backward so that he could swing out of the seat. He gripped the chair a full second before a wave of darkness hit him. The fist which had kept the pressure against his chest was now joined by a heavier fist that pounded incessantly. Hap gasped. "I think—I think—," he said and crumpled.

Hap's body fell forward, as though in slow motion. Travis's left arm shot up to the center of the controls, and he pulled the automatic pilot. He pushed the button which moved his own seat backward, and jumped out and knelt before Hap.

Seeing his ashen complexion, Travis shouted, "Phil, get Gladys or one of the girls!"

He pushed the controls on the captain's chair all the way forward and the engineer's chair backward so he could stretch Hap on the floor. There was still not quite enough space for him to lie flat. Travis bent over him and applied CPR.

Phil entered the first-class cabin. He tried to make his appearance casual. He knew from his years of flying that passengers read the slightest facial expression as an ominous sign.

Gladys was serving a cocktail to a passenger. He bent over, smiled, and said, "Please follow me into the flight deck." He half-whispered, "Now."

"Excuse me," she said and turned to follow Phil.

Gladys immediately sized up the situation and grabbed the oxygen bottle and slipped a mask over Hap's face. Phil took over the CPR.

"I don't think he's breathing," Travis said, "but I'm not sure."

Phil continued the rhythmic push-release-push against Hap's sternum, counting under his breath. "One one thousand, two one thousand. . . ."

Travis felt Hap's wrist. "Found a pulse. Faint, but a pulse," he said as he wiped his own perspiring forehead.

Phil took a deep breath and sat down next to the inert body.

"Keep checking his pulse," Travis said. He hopped into the first officer's seat and called on the company frequency for instructions.

A minute later Travis said, "We land at Miami." He paused and said, "Just keep watching him."

"Pulse remains extremely weak," Phil said.

"Keep checking it," Travis barked.

"What'll we tell the passengers," Gladys asked, kneeling on the other side of Hap, "about landing at Miami?" She blinked her eyes, determined not to cry.

Travis took three deep breaths and snapped on the intercom. "Good morning, ladies and gentlemen. I trust you are having a pleasant flight. We have just been notified that Orlando is experiencing bad weather. We have been diverted to Miami. We do not anticipate staying on the ground long." He paused again and added, "We expect to set down at Miami in approximately twelve minutes, and then we'll continue on to Orlando as soon as weather permits. In the meantime, please fasten your safety belts and extinguish all smoking material. Thank you."

He turned his head to watch the two on the floor next to Hap. "Gladys, Phil can watch him. You walk back through the cabins, wearing the brightest smile you've got. Get to Lezlie and—"

"I'll take care of it," she said as she got up.

"I'd forgotten all about Lezlie," Phil said. "What'll she do if—"

"Just watch Hap, Phil. Don't think about anything except that pulse."

"She won't believe that weather business. Not after Hap announced sunshine and eighty-five degrees in Orlando," Gladys said.

"You're right." He thought for a minute. "Tell her a duct overheated, and we've had to operate at reduced thrust. That always calls for a landing at the first available spot."

"Got you," Gladys said and opened the door.

"Just keep your face—," Phil said and stopped.

She glared back at him. "I've been in this business long enough to know—"

"Cool it! You know what to do, Gladys," Travis said, keeping his voice low and calm, even though he could feel the tension building up inside his own chest.

In the tourist section, Lezlie looked up as she heard Travis make the announcement. Momentarily she wondered why Travis and not Hap had given the information. She detected a slight strain in Travis's voice. She pushed her cart a few feet farther down the aisle. "Anything to drink?" she asked, the plastic smile covering the questions in her mind.

It took Lezlie another full minute to reach the end of the section. She turned around and started toward the front of her cabin, carrying the coffee pot. Only a tiny part of her mind dwelt on the voice. She tried not to keep looking toward the flight deck. One part of her mind kept saying, *Nothing's wrong.* And yet, she felt a sense of apprehension. Her three years of duty as a flight attendant served her well. The passengers saw only a smiling, pleasant woman in her early twenties, serving refreshments.

Gladys came out of the flight deck, wound her way through the forward cabins, nodding and smiling to various people. Lezlie kept busy, but she knew Gladys was coming toward her. Even with the professional smile, the corners of her mouth betrayed a hidden tension. As she reached the galley of Lezlie's section, she gave a barely perceptible nod. Lezlie said to a woman who held up her cup, "Excuse me. I'll be right back with more coffee."

She walked into the galley and put her pot under the machine. She could not look directly at Gladys.

"We've had some kind of minor problem. A duct overheated and that means landing at the first available spot."

"Thanks for telling me," Lezlie said.

"Just thought you'd want to know." She poured a cup of coffee, drank it rapidly, and avoided looking directly at Lezlie. "Just wanted you to know," she repeated.

"Yes—yes, thanks," Lezlie answered. But as two professionals in the anxiety business, neither expressed any thoughts aloud.

Gladys turned and walked up the other aisle and back to the flight deck. She stepped inside, closed the door behind her, and took a deep breath.

"How's Hap?" she asked Phil.

"Still breathing. Barely."

"I'll relieve you," she said and knelt down.

Travis announced instructions for landing and added, "Attendants, please be seated." Moments later, the wheels of the L-1011 hit the ground and edged across the runway at Miami International Airport.

"Please remain seated while we're in Miami," Gladys's voice rose above the sound of the engines. "We expect to take off again shortly." As soon as she made that announcement, she moved rapidly through the cabins and came to Lezlie.

"I need your help in first class, please," and turned back. Lezlie obediently followed. They reached the first-class galley, and Gladys pulled her close, whispering so that no passengers could hear. "There's an ambulance coming across the runway now. Hap's had a heart attack."

Lezlie's face drained. Her lips formed words that her voice could not ask.

"He's breathing on his own." She touched Lezlie's shoulder.

Lezlie closed her eyes and leaned her head against the bulkhead. She suddenly became conscious that Gladys had continued talking. Occasional words filtered through.

"... still alive ... ambulance ... you go with him. ..."

"Please remain seated," Gladys said over the communication system. "We expect to be on the ground in a matter of only a few minutes."

As Lezlie stood in the galley, trying to compose herself, she heard a first-class passenger say, "Look! An ambulance. Something's happened."

Ordinarily Lezlie would have gone to the passenger and tried to calm her anxiety, but this time she could not think of the customer. She felt glued to the spot, wanting to see Hap, yet afraid.

The ambulance team moved into the airplane, and Gladys stood in the doorway, obscuring the passengers' view. In rapid-fire action, the two men strapped Hap onto a stretcher and were halfway out the door before Lezlie recovered enough to move toward them.

"Here, give me your arm," Travis said to her.

"Oh, yes," she said as she looked up and saw him next to her.

"He's alive, Lezlie, alive," Travis whispered over and over.

As she stepped into the ambulance, Lezlie's eyes searched Travis's face. Again her lips formed words she wanted to ask.

"I got permission to go with you," he said. "We'll wait it out together at the hospital."

She squeezed his arm and asked, "Tell me the truth, Travis. Will—will he make it?"

"Let's let the doctor answer that," he answered, avoiding looking directly at her.

Chapter 2

Events for the next half hour raced past Lezlie. She knew everything that went on, but it was like being in a speeded-up movie. She allowed Travis to help her out of the ambulance. He took her hand and guided her into the hospital. She stood emotionless in front of the Cuban woman who asked for information. Lezlie clicked off the answers in a state of numbness.

"Thank you," the woman said in her thick accent.

Lezlie did not move, as though unable to turn away. Travis pulled her arm. "Let's sit down," he said and indicated two empty seats in an already crowded waiting room.

"Just a minute, sir," a male voice said. "You are the family of Mr. Austin?"

"Yes," Lezlie said.

"Come this way, please," he said and led them out of the waiting area and into a small room. "You may wait in here."

"How—how long?" Lezlie asked.

"I don't know. The doctor is with him now."

"Please—may—may I see him?"

"If you'll just make yourself comfortable, the doctor will come in as soon as he can. There's a coffee machine down this hall," the man said and pointed.

"But how long?" Lezlie said, her voice rising.

"Just as soon as he's finished, he'll be in to see you," the man said, smiling, his calm voice assuring them that he was accustomed to outbreaks of rage or hysteria.

"Yes, of course," Lezlie said and sank into a molded plastic chair.

The first half hour from the plane to the emergency room had streaked by. The next half hour dragged.

"What's taking so long?" Lezlie looked at her watch again. "It's been at least an hour since we got here."

"Closer to forty minutes," Travis said. "They'll come back as soon as they can tell us anything."

"If they'd only tell me something. Anything—"

"Maybe it's one of those situations in which no news is good news," Travis said without optimism.

They heard the click of heels in the tiled corridor and looked up immediately. The nurse walked past.

"Thanks for coming here to the hospital with me," Lezlie said, her voice giving the first hint of starting to crack. She grasped his hand and held it tight.

"Your happiness means a lot to me," he answered and looked away.

"Thanks for being such a friend. And thanks for being Hap's best friend—"

"That's not quite what I meant," he said softly, but Lezlie did not seem to hear him. Her eyes were riveted to the door as sounds of heavier footsteps came their way. They turned and went in another direction.

"If only—if only they'd tell me something. It's the strain of not knowing—"

"Lezlie, why don't you go down to the coffee machine?" he said. "I'll wait here."

She shook her head. "I couldn't. Every minute I'd be gone, I'd think that the doctor would come to tell me about Hap."

"Would you like me to get something for you?"

"I'd rather have you stay here with me," she said. "I mean—if you don't mind."

"I won't budge," he said, and he laid his other hand on top of hers. "I'll stay right here as long as you need me."

"Strange, isn't it?" she said. "I mean you and I sitting here. Hap in there." She nodded.

"Yeah, it is," Travis said, and he remembered a time when he and

Lezlie had held hands before. She hadn't even known Hap then.

"Hap—you—me—," she said. "Strange how our lives keep twisting around each other."

"Yes," he said, hoping she would change the line of conversation.

"If it hadn't been for you," she said, "I never would have met Hap."

"I know," he mumbled.

"Travis, remember—remember when you and I first met?"

"I remember it well," he said.

"It was the first time I had been out of the United States—"

"And you were frightened to drink the water and scared of the food—"

"Constantly afraid someone would snatch my purse—"

"Lezlie, you listened to too many wrong bits of advice before you traveled."

"I know that now. But then—well, I'm so thankful that we bumped into each other. Literally."

"I'm glad, too," he said.

"I remember that day in Athens so well," Lezlie smiled. "When was it, May or—"

"April twentieth," he said.

"I remember we had come from Oslo the day before, where they still had patches of snow on the ground. Athens was filled with warmth and sunshine—"

She paused and thought of the group she had traveled with from the airlines. It had been her first big adventure since college.

Travis had not looked directly at Lezlie, trying to think of a way to change the subject. He did not want to talk about Athens. Then he felt her fingers relax. If it took her mind off the emergency room, he would talk about it, too.

"I thought you were the prettiest girl I'd seen in years," Travis said.

"Oh, come on—"

"You wore a blue-and-white outfit. The dress was tight at the waist but the skirt hung loose. Your purse matched the blue of the dress, and your white shoes had open toes. You want to know how you combed your hair that day? A little shorter and—"

Lezlie laughed. "I didn't think you noticed."

"Like I said, you were the prettiest girl I had seen in a long time."

"If Hap had said that, I would have laughed again."

"I'm not Hap."

"No, you're not. You're a friend, a wonderful friend—"

"Yes," he said, a huskiness in his voice. "A friend."

"We were total strangers until I fell and you picked me up."

"Seems like such a long time ago," Travis said.

"It was—let's see—" She started figuring backward in her head.

"Sixteen months ago," he said immediately and then wished he hadn't.

She shook her head. "You amaze me. I didn't know you had that kind of photographic memory."

"I don't," he said. "It's just that some things—well, some things people remember more than others."

"I suppose you're right," she said.

Both of them lapsed into silence. Lezlie released his hand. She leaned back in the chair, her head against the wall, and closed her eyes. She was remembering that day.

Lezlie, fascinated by the pigeons in Constitution Square, started across the broad street. Not paying any attention to where she was going, Lezlie stumbled off the curb and pitched forward.

"Got you," the man said as he grabbed her and helped her up.

"Thank you," she said. "Clumsy of me," and then she looked at him. He was of medium height and build, with blue eyes, and even features. His black curly hair was the only distinguishing characteristic.

"Glad to help," he said.

"Oh, you speak English. American?" she asked.

"Yes ma'am," he replied in a southern drawl. "Right from the delta basin of America."

"Yes, well, thanks for being so kind," she said and continued across the street. As she stepped up on the sidewalk, she immediately forgot the other American. She had come to feed the pigeons. She bought a bag of bread crumbs from a vendor and threw them one at a time to the birds. They ate eagerly, often coming within a foot of her. Lezlie stifled the urge to reach out and stroke one. "Here, have another," she called, as she tossed another crumb.

She threw out the last piece, squashed the bag in her hand, and straightened up. Two birds crept close to her, as though begging for more. "All right," she laughed, "I'll buy another bag."

"Here, take these," the male voice behind her said.

She turned and saw the dark-haired man who had helped her when she stumbled. "Thanks again, but you bought these for yourself."

"I'll get more pleasure out of watching you feed the birds," he said.

"All right," she answered and immediately tossed out the crumbs. When she emptied the bag, she debated whether to buy more. She looked up. He was standing next to her again. He held out more crumbs.

"Oh, I couldn't—"

"Please," he said and backed away.

"Well, thanks," she said and smiled. She tossed the crumbs, a small handful at a time. Then he knelt beside her, a fresh bag in his hand, and silently tossed out crumbs, too. He whistled gently to the pigeons. One of them came and pecked a crumb out of his hand.

"Maybe I need to learn to whistle like that," she said.

"I'll be glad to teach you," he answered.

Instead of replying to his statement, she pointed. "See that one? No wonder he's fatter than the others. He's always there to grab."

"Guess he moves faster."

"Let's trick him," Lezlie said. She threw a handful of bread beyond the half dozen birds who chirped near her. The large bird flew away to retrieve the food. Immediately she emptied the bag for the smaller pigeons who gobbled it up before the large creature returned.

"Ah, you're a crafty one," Travis said and smiled. "Want to feed them some more?"

She shook her head. "No, thanks. I loved it, and it was fun, but I've had enough."

"May I buy you lunch then?" he asked.

Lezlie stared at him, as if really seeing him. "I—I don't even know you—"

"I don't know your name either, but we work for the same airline."

"We do?"

Travis grinned. "I saw your tour group checking in at the hotel this morning. With your airline bags, it was no trouble identifying you as a fellow employee."

Lezlie smiled. "You must have a sharp eye. There were fifty of us."

"But I also saw you leave the group this morning—"

"I like people, but sometimes—well, I decided to walk around the city by myself."

"I often feel the same way," he said. "The need to be alone—"

"Or at least away from a lot of people. I have enough of that in my work."

"If one person doesn't make too much of a crowd, I'd still like to buy your lunch," he said.

As they started down the street, Travis Manning introduced himself and added, "I fly the New Orleans-San Juan route."

"That's incredible!"

"What's incredible? That I can fly from New Orleans—"

"No, I mean, I've just transferred to New Orleans."

"Really?"

"Yes. As soon as I get back, I'm on that hop. I took Spanish in college and speak it well enough, so I bid for that flight and—," she laughed. "Here I am, telling you my whole life story, and I don't know anything about you."

"Except I pick up falling women, and I'm kind to birds."

"And you have a nice smile," she added.

"*And* I would still like to take you to lunch."

She hesitated only a minute and said, "Okay, providing—"

"Whatever you ask."

"That we go to a genuine Greek restaurant and avoid these American tourist traps."

"Suits me," he said. He took her arm, and they headed away from Constitution Square. "You know, we need to move away from the main streets in order to do that."

"Suits me," she said.

"Fine," he answered, glad to be alone with her and doubly glad because they headed away from where they would likely run into others from her tour.

After a quarter hour of walking, they saw a small restaurant. "Let's try this," Travis said. They walked inside, sat down at a table, and when the waiter approached, Travis said, "We're Americans. We don't speak Greek."

He nodded and flashed a wide grin. "I speak some little English. What you want to eat?"

"Surprise us," Travis said and turned his attention to the attractive girl beside him.

"Now it's your turn," Lezlie Johnson said. "You tell me about yourself."

"I'd rather listen to you."

"Your turn, please."

Travis Manning told her he had learned to fly while a teen, kept up his hobby during college, and spent three years in the air force. He had been with the airline six years.

"What brought you on this tour?" he asked.

"I've always wanted to travel," she said. "After college, I went to work, and I had debts to take care of first. This is my first real vacation. That simple."

"You'll love Athens."

"You've been here before?"

"Twice."

"You must love it, then."

"I do. The Acropolis always stirs me. Your tour probably calls for a trip to the lights-and-sound program—"

"That's on for tomorrow night," she said. "I've heard it's wonderful."

"It is. But how about going there with me tonight?"

"But the others—"

"So what? You paid for the trip. You can do what you want, can't you?"

She looked uncertain for a moment and then smiled. "Yes, I would like that very much."

The waiter appeared with a kind of pancake on a large platter. He poured brandy over it and struck a match. As it flamed, he yelled, "Oopa!" Two other waiters chorused his word. As soon as the flame died, he squeezed lemon across the top and set it on the table, along with two small plates.

Later, they held hands and walked through the streets of Athens. Just before dark, they stopped at a fruit stand and bought oranges and grapes which they ate as they climbed the steep road which led to the Acropolis.

From the Acropolis they walked slowly through the main street of Athens, amazed at how different the city looked at night. They enjoyed the gentle breezes from the Aegean sea.

"You've made this an exciting day," Lezlie said.

"You're an exciting person," Travis said and then looked away from her.

"That's awfully nice—"

"I mean it," he said and then looked into her face. "I'm—I'm not very good at saying things like that—but when I say them, I mean them."

"I sense you do," she said and squeezed his hand. "That's what makes it so nice."

Travis pulled her into the shadow of a closed store and put his arms around her. He kissed her gently on the lips. Travis started to let go and suddenly gripped her tighter and kissed her again, much harder.

When he released her, Lezlie said, "You may not be awfully good at saying how you feel, but you're good at demonstrating it."

"Am I?" He pulled her close and kissed her again, long and warmly. They pulled apart but stayed in the semidarkness, their faces close to each other. Lezlie could see only an outline of his features, but she knew he stared at her.

"I already like you very much," Lezlie said.

"Me, too."

"You're—different from the others I meet."

"I hope so," he said.

"I've kept myself closed off from men lately."

"You must have had a rotten affair—"

"Yes," she said slowly. "Brief, but rotten."

"He gave you a line. You believed it, and—"

"And you know the rest. I was only one of a dozen. Fortunately I found out before I got too deeply involved."

"Is that why you came on this trip?"

"Partly," she answered. "You know, Travis, it's almost as if you can read my mind."

"Want to talk about it? About him?"

"No," she said. "Not any more. I waited until I got him out of my system before I took this trip. Honest."

"I—I hope we'll see more of each other," he said before kissing her again.

They did see more of each other. After they returned to New Orleans, they went out as often as their schedules permitted. Lezlie suspected that Travis purposely changed flights a few times in order to be in town when she was off. What she hoped he did not know was that she did considerable switching and accepted the relief flights to be available on his free days.

Their relationship might have gone on for a long time. The evening at Toni's changed everything for both of them.

Chapter 3

"You won't like it," Travis said for the third time, "but we'll go anyway."

"Just once so that I can see for myself," Lezlie answered. "I feel stupid when the others talk about Toni's."

"I just don't think it's the kind of place for you."

"Don't be patronizing," she said and smiled.

"Okay, we go," he laughed. "Anything for a lady."

Toni's, located at the edge of the French Quarter, gave the impression of being another disco, indistinguishable from a dozen other places. Two large doors, opened wide, allowed tourists to peek inside as they passed by.

Lezlie hesitated only a moment, smiled at Travis, and said, "Let's go in." The music, rising to a crescendo from a five-piece band, filled the room.

Travis guided her past the bar. They took two steps down and entered a smaller room with a glittering neon sign: TONI'S FINE FOODS. Two dozen tables, occupied mostly by couples, all bunched together, gave Lezlie the impression of every man enjoying a tete-a-tete with the woman sitting across from him. Coming closer, she realized they had no choice, with scarcely enough space between tables for a person to pass.

Despite the crowded look, the room held a sense of intimacy. The band stopped playing in the bar, and Lezlie hoped they would take a long break.

Travis spoke to two couples on the way in, and Lezlie nodded to a flight attendant she had worked with three weeks earlier. They sat at a corner table where Lezlie had a clear view of the room.

Menus on the table featured a limited food selection. But she had known that the airline personnel did not come here for the food. It had become the in place for them to meet and talk shop.

A waiter appeared immediately and without consulting the menu, Travis ordered. Lezlie's eyes swept the room. Of the two dozen tables, over half of them were filled, mostly with couples. As her eyes swept the bar, she saw a man she immediately thought of as incredibly handsome. He leaned against the bar, sipping his drink, and smiling at her. She turned her head away quickly and continued to survey the room. Seconds later she glanced at him again. He still smiled at her and tipped his glass toward her. Her eyes moved on, but they had lingered long enough to catch a better view of him. He was tall, blond, and broad-shouldered, and probably in his early thirties. He did not wear a wedding ring.

Lezlie tried to make each glance casual until she realized he had been staring at her the whole time. She flushed slightly.

Travis's back was to the bar, but suddenly as if aware of the other's presence, he turned around. He saw the man. "Hey, Hap!" he shouted. "How are you doing?"

Without waiting for an invitation, Hap walked over, pulled up a chair, and set his now-empty glass on the table. Giving Travis a bare nod, he turned his smile and full attention on Lezlie. "You aren't keeping this gorgeous creature all to yourself, are you, Travis?"

"I was trying to."

"Share and share alike," Hap said. Leaning toward Lezlie he said, "In case you did not know, this would-be pilot sits beside me on our flights—"

"This is my senior pilot, Hap Austin," Travis said and introduced Lezlie.

"Travis, you never told me what you did on the ground." Even when he talked to Travis, his eyes never left Lezlie.

"We, uh, met in Athens a few weeks ago," Lezlie said.

"You have a beautiful profile," Hap said.

Lezlie laughed. "That's a new approach. A lot better than 'You remind me of someone' or 'Haven't we met before?'"

"How do you answer those approaches?" Travis asked.

"I say, 'Then you wouldn't want to go out with me because you'd constantly think of her.' Then I try to move away before he thinks of a reply."

"Very clever," Travis chuckled.

"Excellent," Hap said as his eyes explored as much of her body as he could see.

"And when they ask if we've met somewhere else before, I use a line I once heard on a TV talk show. I say, 'Impossible. I've never been somewhere before.'"

"I don't have a new approach," Hap said, "but I do have a new problem."

"That sounds like a new approach to me," Lezlie said and laughed.

"Hap's got all the good approaches worked out," Travis said, forcing a smile on his face.

"I do need a favor. You see—uh, you two aren't getting married or something?"

"Not yet," Travis said.

"Good, because I need this favor. You see, Lez, I've been invited to this party tomorrow night. I need a date and—"

"And five other girls have already turned you down?" Lezlie asked.

"At least. I stood at the bar, brokenhearted. Then when I saw you with this fellow, I thought I would try one more time. I need you to build up my self-confidence."

"You don't seem to lack self-confidence," Lezlie said.

"The smile and bright eyes are only a mask," he said.

"Well, uh, I don't know—," and she looked at Travis.

"You surely don't mind, do you, buddy?" Hap said. "I mean, one party—"

"I don't own Lezlie. I mean—"

"Great. Thanks."

"Hey, Hap, we're scheduled to fly tomorrow—"

"Had a personal business matter come up," he smiled at Lezlie. "You see, I'm also a bit of a businessman on the side. Sometimes things come up suddenly, and I have to make adjustments. So, please, I'd like very much to take you to the party tomorrow night."

"If you don't mind," she said, looking at Travis.

"Oh, I'll be halfway to San Juan."

She went to the party with Hap. Although she knew no one when they arrived, Hap made certain everyone knew Lezlie. When someone pulled him away for a private conversation, he constantly looked back at Lezlie. Even when standing on the far side of the room, his eyes returned to her.

"You've absolutely captivated him," one older woman said to Lezlie. "I've never seen Hap so taken up with one person before."

Lezlie flushed and smiled, not knowing what to say. She knew she could not resist the magnetism he exuded. Even if he had not been constantly looking her way, she would have been staring at him.

Later, he drove Lezlie to Kenner where she lived. He shut off the engine of his Jaguar. "Let me peek at your apartment," he said. "I like looking at things like that."

"It's just an apartment."

"But I want to see it."

"But, why, I mean—," she stammered.

"I want to know everything about you," he said as his hand touched hers. Then he took her fingers in his and kissed them gently.

"Well—all right."

They walked up to her second-floor, one-bedroom apartment. She had furnished it simply with cast-offs and cheap pieces.

"Simple. Neat," he commented as he paced the entire width of the living room.

"Not much to look at—"

"Oh, yes, you are," he said.

"I mean, the *apartment.*"

Hap gazed at her for a moment. "But I meant you." He took her in his arms.

"Hap, I've got an early flight tomorrow and—"

His lips pressed against hers, and the kiss lasted a long time. He moved his lips gently across her cheeks and kissed her neck and ears. His grip on her shoulders increased.

She pushed him away. "Hap, I'm—I'm not that kind of woman—"

"What kind?"

"Who lets a man in for the night and—"

"I'm not asking to spend the whole night."

"I'm not inviting you for even part of the night," she said.

Their eyes met, and Hap smiled. "Your dark eyes burn like fire when you get upset. Did you know that?" He moved closer.

"And I'm saying," she pushed him back a little more, "I—I think we need to call it a night."

"I want to marry you," Hap said.

"Marry me?" she laughed. "You met me yesterday, we spent three hours together tonight, and now you're proposing marriage?"

"Seems like a good idea," he said.

"A good idea?"

"Because I love you."

A chill swept over her. Momentarily she wondered if he said that to every woman he went out with. "Please—don't—don't say those kinds of things, Hap. They're not funny."

"I didn't mean to be funny," he said and drew close, his lips next to her ear. "I love you."

"But—but you don't know—"

"I knew I loved you the minute I saw you sitting at that table with Travis."

"I—I don't know—," she said, realizing she was starting to stutter. "I—I mean—I—"

He kissed her on the cheek and pulled away. "I won't force you into anything tonight. But I'll see you the day after tomorrow—"

"I don't get back until—"

"I know when you get back. I'll meet your flight." He closed the door.

Long after he was gone, Lezlie stood in the same spot, as though mesmerized by his lingering presence. She could still see those incredibly long lashes over light blue eyes, and she felt the strength of his arms.

"Am I in love?" she asked herself. And she laughed at the thought of it. But as she walked across the room and looked into the mirror, she said aloud, "Well, am I in love?"

"I still want to marry you," Hap said.

"Don't tease me," Lezlie said. "I don't play those kinds of games very well."

They had just returned from a cruise on the Mississippi River and were now eating red beans and rice at Toni's. The small, crowded room buzzed with conversation, and yet Lezlie saw or heard nothing but Hap's words and the intensity of his blue eyes.

"I wasn't teasing," he said.

"Hap, you could have a dozen women—"

"I'm proposing only to you," he said. "Again!"

"This is crazy. I mean, I've known you a total of seventeen days and already—"

"Interesting," he said as he leaned forward. "Interesting that you know it was seventeen days."

"Well, I—all right, so I know exactly how many days—"

"And you love me, too," Hap said.

"I—I'm not sure. I mean I don't *not* love you. Does that make sense?"

"Not at all," he said. "I've been waiting a long time for someone like you. Now that I've found you, I'm going to marry you. It can be next week—next month—"

"Next year?"

"I won't let you go that long," he said.

"You work fast. Too fast maybe."

"That's the way I operate," he said. "I know what I want, and I go after it. And right now   "

"Hap, I—"

He tossed a handful of bills on the table and took her arm. "Let's get out of here. This isn't the most romantic spot in New Orleans, is it?"

"Does the place make much difference?" she asked.

Hap grinned. "It sounds as though you're moving in my direction." He put his arm around her and pulled her close. "I could find any place romantic with you."

"Hap, don't—"

"Don't what?"

"Don't let those words flow so easily. I'm a simple, naive girl. I don't play games of the heart."

"I'm not playing a game now, Lez."

They walked slowly down the street and into the parking lot. Once inside the car, he took her hand. "I meant it, Lezlie. Every word. I love you. I want to marry you."

"I'm flattered, but—"

"I've made advances to a lot of women, but you're the only one I've wanted to marry."

"Honest?"

"Absolutely," he said. "I've been waiting a long time for you."

"And you never married?"

"I married once, but not because *I* wanted to. But that's another story."

"I'd like to hear—"

"I'd like to marry you. That's the topic of conversation."

"Hap, I'm confused. I feel giddy and—"

"It's simple. I want to marry you. I love you. What's your answer?"

"Is that the way you always reduce the problems of the world?"

"Whenever I can," he said.

"You know, Hap, this reminds me of a time when I was in high school. It was my first date, and we were ice skating in northern Wisconsin where I lived. We raced the full length and back of the roped-off area—this boy and I—and when we got to the end, we both huffed and panted. And he said, 'I'd like to kiss you.' I was still wheezing and trying to breathe normally again."

"And did he? Kiss you, I mean?"

"Yes, because I couldn't think of what to say."

"Did you want him to kiss you?"

"I think so, but—"

"But you wanted to think it over first?"

"Yes."

Hap shook his head. "That's your trouble, Lez. You want to sit down, analyze, think it all through, and by then you've lost the moment."

"Lost the moment?"

"Yeah. That poor guy had a romantic impulse, and he kissed you. Bravo for him."

"He didn't give me much chance to protest."

"Just one question, Lez. Did you enjoy the kiss?"

"Yes. Yes, I think so—"

"And you don't regret letting him kiss you."

"Not at all."

"Then if this reminds you of that situation, let's jump into it."

"Somehow, Hap, I feel you're twisting what I'm trying to say—"

"Of course I am, but you need a push, and I'm ready."

"It's just that it's so sudden. I'm out of breath and—"

"But you love me, don't you?"

"I feel something, but I don't know. I've—I've never been in love before—real mature love."

"It's real with me," he said. "I'm sure."

"Hap, would you—would you go to church and talk to my pastor with me? He's a fine man and—"

"If you want," Hap said.

"I'd like to very much."

"I had in mind a flight down to one of the islands, get married, have a honeymoon, and head back to work. But if you insist, we can talk to anyone and drag it out."

He pulled her tight against him and held her. He whispered over and over, "I love you." Between his words he kissed her passionately.

"Yes, yes," she whispered back in response. "Whenever—wherever—"

During the whirlwind courtship, Travis called three times. Once he invited her to dinner. She said, "Oh, I'm sorry, but I do have other plans."

After the second invitation, she said, "Hap and I had already arranged to go out together."

The third time he left a message that he had called on the answering machine. She saw him two nights later at a party that many of the airline personnel attended. One of the senior pilots was retiring, and he held an open house in Kenner.

It was the night after she had agreed to marry Hap. They walked in together, while country-and-western music played on a stereo. Hap went to the bar to mix himself a drink and brought back a Coke for Lezlie.

She spotted Travis sitting by himself, sipping a drink. She went over and sat down. "Hi, Travis, I got your message—"

"You look great," he said. She wore a black dress, cut tight and fully showing her size-five figure.

"I feel wonderful," she said and smiled.

Just then Hap walked over, handed Lezlie her drink, and asked, "Travis, did she tell you our good news?"

"I was just coming to that part," Lezlie smiled and put her arms on Travis's shoulder. "Hap and I—we're going to be married."

"Married? Quite a surprise," Travis said, his face betraying no emotion.

"Yes, like Julius Caesar, I came, I saw, I conquered," Hap said and slapped his first officer on the back. "I knew what I wanted—"

"And obviously you got her," Travis said. "Congratulations."

"We're getting married next week."

"And you'll come to the wedding, won't you?" Lezlie asked.

"I never go to weddings," he said and stood up. "Excuse me, I need to freshen up my drink." He walked over to the bar and poured himself a half tumbler of ginger ale.

Lezlie walked up behind him. "Travis, it all happened so fast. I mean, I should have told you, only—only I didn't know myself until last night and—"

He held up his hand. "We had no strings on each other."

"I know, but—"

"Congratulations again," Travis said and walked across the room.

A pained expression covered his face before he turned away. Lezlie stood immobile. For a moment, she wanted to go after him, throw her arms around him, and say, "Don't be hurt, please." Realizing how silly that gesture would have been, she leaned against the bar, waiting for Hap to extricate himself from a small group, all wildly congratulating him.

Lezlie stared at Travis, sensing he deliberately kept his back to her. She realized that her eyes darted from him to Hap and then back again. For a few seconds, she wanted to say to Travis, "It's not true. I've changed my mind about marrying Hap."

Slowly she walked toward him. At that moment, a new piece of music began on the stereo, the current popular song, "Destined to Love." A deep-voiced country singer warbled, "We were destined to love, but you've turned away. We were destined to love, but now I've lost you. . . ."

At that moment, Travis whirled around, and their eyes held for a moment. Lezlie knew Travis had been listening, too.

Chapter 4

On the occasions when Lezlie met Hap's flights, Travis nodded at her and passed on quickly. At first Lezlie felt relieved. She had wanted to explain to Travis and make him understand what had happened. But since she never had the opportunity, she decided it was better to leave everything unsaid.

Three months after her marriage, Lezlie attended a farewell party for Sharon, one of the flight attendants who had married earlier, and now that she was pregnant, decided to retire. Lezlie had met her only once and came mainly to be with Hap. Most of the evening she sat by herself, watching the gaiety of the evening and Hap in the middle of the laughter. She had not felt particularly lonely, nor did she want to join in. Mostly she watched or occasionally chatted with whoever sat down by her for a few minutes.

"Get lonely for you at a party?" someone asked her. "I mean with Hap neglecting you—"

"Neglecting? Not at all," Lezlie said. "He likes people around him, a lot of people. I enjoy watching him enjoying himself."

The woman, whom Lezlie did not know, raised an eyebrow. "I

could never be so casual about it," she said and swept off to another part of the large room.

Lezlie sipped her drink and laid her head back on the comfortable sofa cushions. She closed her eyes momentarily.

"How are you, Lezlie?" She recognized Travis's voice and opened her eyes.

"Fine. And you?" Lezlie said as she sat up straight and reached for his hand.

"Are you happy?" he asked, not returning the gesture.

"Of course I am. Why—"

"I'll always be your friend. You can count on my being around if you need me."

"Travis, what—"

He got up, walked to the bar, set his empty glass down, and left.

Sitting alone, she wondered about his behavior and his question. She also wondered about her answer. She was happy—at least not unhappy. Their romantic relationship had continued, even heightened. Hap remained the smiling, considerate, charming Hap—except once.

She cut off that line of thinking. We all have bad moments, she decided. Yet Lezlie could not forget that incident, and it had troubled her for days.

She had bid for Hap's flight and finally got it. That meant that they could stay together at the Condado Holiday Inn in San Juan, which the airline arranged for its personnel. She had gone down to the pool because Hap said he wanted to nap before dinner. She got all the way to the pool, remembered her suntan lotion, and came back to the room. Since she had not locked the door, she pushed it open, and hearing Hap on the phone, tried not to disturb him. He lay on the bed, his back to Lezlie. She picked up the lotion and planned to close the door behind her.

"Don't you ever call me here again! Not ever! You hear me?"

The other party must have apologized because Hap said, "Okay, I understand why this time. But next time—don't let there be a next time. I've given you instructions—"

Hap sensed Lezlie's presence and whirled around. A hardness filled his eyes. The facial expression changed abruptly, and he was smiling again. "Okay, I understand. Now take care of yourself," he said in his finest southern drawl and hung up.

"Hap, I didn't mean to—"

He walked over to Lezlie, grabbed both her shoulders, and his eyes peered deeply into hers. "How much of that conversation did you hear?"

"Why, nothing."

"Don't lie to me," he said and shook her. "I want to know—"

"Hap, you're hurting me," she said. "Your fingers are digging into my skin." She tried to pull away from him.

"I asked you a question, Lezlie, and I want an answer now!"

"Nothing. Only your telling someone not to call you here. That's all."

"You're sure? Nothing else?"

"Nothing. Now let me go!"

He released her and almost as if he had snapped his fingers, the friendly smile returned. "Sorry, just—just an important business deal—"

"I'm your wife, Hap."

"It's a sensitive affair right now," he said, "and I wouldn't want anyone to know until it's all completed. You might innocently say something and—"

"What am I not supposed to talk about?" she asked. She rubbed the skin where his thumbs had bruised her.

"Nothing to worry your pretty self about," Hap said. "Just leave it alone right now, that's all."

"Hap, I'd like to know—to share this part of your life—"

"One of these days, I'll sit down and explain it all to you," he said. The old Hap had returned. He pulled her close and kissed her. "I'm sorry, Lez. Honest. Just a litle tired, I guess."

She kissed his cheek. "Okay," she said and picked up her lotion and left the room. But she didn't forget. And she felt guilty for not forgetting.

As the months passed, a discontent stirred within Lezlie. She could not put her finger on why. Once she had seen Hap nuzzling Gladys and then shrugged it off. Hap was apt to do that to any attractive woman. He frequently went away on business which he did not discuss and blocked every question she asked. "Don't worry yourself, darling, about this. I'm in the process of concluding business arrangements, and in less than a year, I'll be free of it all."

Something had changed in their relationship, and she could not figure out what. Hap had not lost his charm. And, in his presence, she felt no different about him than she had in the beginning. When he was away, however, questions filled her thoughts—questions she didn't want to answer.

Yet as soon as Hap returned, her questions disappeared. She would lie in his arms and silently rebuke the troublesome thoughts.

Lezlie did not fly on all of Hap's flights. Not having enough seniority often meant taking weekend flights or catching the holiday traffic. She managed to fly with Hap and Travis at least once a month on the San Juan jaunt.

In those moments when the questions flared, Lezlie reminded herself of Hap's thoughtfulness. He constantly showered her with small gifts of perfume and jewelry. The most considerate thing he did was packing her bag.

"Hap, don't bother," she had protested. "I can pack my own things."

"No bother. Besides, I like doing things for you, darling," he said as he filled the plastic flask of shampoo and checked every item.

"You're absolutely the kindest man in the world," she said, as he filled another bottle with bath lotion. "Really, Hap, there's enough in there for a couple more trips—"

"No, ma'am," he said. "I like your overnight case to be fully packed with everything. You never know when an emergency comes up. I want my wife's cosmetic case full and first class," he said.

On one trip to San Juan—a trip when she was not flying with Hap—she saw a paperback in the airport at New Orleans. It was a current best-seller. Impulsively Lezlie bought a copy and threw it into the top of her cosmetic case. She forgot about it because she didn't expect to read it until after she arrived in San Juan.

As usual, when she arrived at the Condado, she went immediately to her room. Lezlie planned to change and then relax in the pool. She often went out to eat with one of the other flight attendants. On that occasion, she opened her case to take out the paperback. It was gone.

She pawed through her neatly lined case. No paperback there. Lezlie paused, mentally retraced her steps at the airport. She had seen the book, grabbed it, and had even broken a twenty to pay for it.

"Guess I must have done something else with it," she said. "Maybe I left it on the counter." Yet she remembered stopping long enough to put the book in her case. "Maybe I only thought I did," she said.

The lost book might have remained a forgotten episode except that a week later she made another flight to San Juan. She went to the pool as usual. She returned to the room. When she opened the case, the paperback lay inside the case. "I—I must have been blind," she said. She had searched the case, and it wasn't that big to begin with. She made a mental note to ask Hap if he had seen the book when he packed for her this trip.

When Lezlie returned to New Orleans on Thursday she asked Hap about the book. "Don't remember," he said and laughed. "But if you put it inside the case, it must have stayed inside—"

"But Hap—"

"You think someone stole the book, read it, and returned it a week later?"

"Of course not, only—"

"Only what? Obviously you didn't see it when you knocked things around inside the case."

"I suppose you're right," she said.

Hap draped his arms around her and said, "We all get a little absentminded at times," and he pulled her close. Their lips met, and he whispered, "Lez, I love you, more than anything else in the world."

Lezlie consciously pushed the book incident from her mind. It simply did not matter.

Too many other problems troubled her. Not only Hap's frequent, unexplained absences, but they were living far above the income level of their salaries. On at least three occasions she tried to talk to Hap about it.

"Don't worry, darling, we're in no financial trouble."

"But look at this." She held out a list: the rent, a four-acre plot of land he had bought. She had written down conservative estimates of the vast amount of money they spent on entertainment.

Hap smiled and tore up the paper. "I told you that I was a good businessman. I've invested wisely, and we can spend a little foolishly if we want."

"A little foolishly?"

"Lez, you have no need to worry—about anything. If we get into debt or the money starts to run out, I'll let you know. Okay?"

As usual, Lezlie acquiesced. But she still thought often of their high cost of living. Yet it was more than the money and the absences.

She could not prove that anything went on between him and Gladys, but she suspected. And because she suspected, she felt guilty, almost as if she had betrayed her husband. He remained as affectionate and attentive as ever. Yet when he and Gladys were in the same room, glances passed between them that made her suspect they were more than two employees for the same airline.

Yet Lezlie could not speak to Hap about her suspicions.

She also knew that something was missing from their marriage but could never put into words what it was. She knew only that they lacked something.

One day Hap had been slightly delayed, and Lezlie went on to the plane. Travis caught up with her and walked beside her. Inside the plane, they realized they had arrived before anyone else.

"Lezlie, are you happy?" Travis asked.

"You asked me that once before," she said.

"I'm also asking you again. Today."

"Yes. Yes, I think so—"

"Just remember. I'm your friend, available if you need me," he said and walked away.

Lezlie walked to the rear cabin to stow her own bag, and the question she had been asking herself for weeks answered itself. "He's like a robot," she said. Once she said those words aloud, she could admit to herself that Hap went through the motions of kindness and concern. But always she felt even though he said the right things, smiled, and exuded charm, it was all on the surface. She wished she could dig below the surface with Hap and discover what he was really like.

No, she said to herself. *My mind's playing games. Hap is just what he is—charming and wonderful.* No man ever showed more consideration for his wife than Hap. It was real, totally real, and she could not keep on thinking this way.

A few weeks before Hap's heart attack, they had flown together unexpectedly. It was not one of her regular flights. She had substituted at the last minute because of a death in the family of one of the other attendants.

When they reached the Condado, Hap said, "Lezlie, I—I made other plans for this evening. It's an important business deal."

"Okay," she said, trying not to seem disappointed.

"I have to leave right away, and I'll be back late."

"It's okay, darling, I trust you."

"If I had known you'd be on this trip with me—"

"Hap, I don't mind being alone. I've been alone before, you know."

"You're the greatest wife in the world," he said. They got to the room a little before 8:00 P.M., and Hap left almost immediately. "Probably be back a little after midnight," he said, "so don't wait up for me."

Lezlie tried to stay awake by reading. But by midnight her eyelids became heavy, and the print blurred. She turned off the lamp, and slept.

The door opening and closing startled Lezlie. She sat up. "Hap? Is that you?"

"Yes," he said. "Don't turn on the light. Just go back to sleep."

She looked at the luminous dial of her travel alarm. "It's nearly four."

"Ran a little late, that's all," he said. He went into the bathroom and closed the door.

A minute later Lezlie went to the bathroom. When she opened the door, she saw that he had stripped off his clothes. He was examining cuts on his right leg and arm.

"Hap—"

He looked startled. "Go back to bed, Lezlie!"

"What happened?"

"Just a little—a little car accident," he said.

"But you're hurt—"

"I'm fine, just fine," he said.

She took the washcloth from his hand and carefully wiped the cuts. Hap always carried a miniature emergency kit in his luggage. She said, "Wait a minute," and brought back the kit. She found Mercurochrome and painted the cut liberally. "Not deep," Lezlie said.

He winced, "I'll be all right. Honest."

"Anybody hurt? I mean seriously?"

He shook his head. "If anyone asks, Lezlie, tell them I've been here all night."

"What?"

"Please, don't worry," he smiled. "Nothing immoral or illegal. I was with a couple of businessmen who had a little too much to drink. We had a minor accident. I would prefer not to be involved if—you know—if anyone asks any questions."

"But, Hap, why would—"

"Don't ask stupid questions! Just do what I say."

She dropped the bandage she had started wrapping around his leg. "Bandage your own—"

He hobbled behind her. "Darling, I'm sorry. Honest. I guess it does hurt. And I took my hurt out on you."

Hap held her, and his words purred in her ears. But this time, she found herself inwardly resisting.

No one asked them any questions. On the flight going back, he complained that he had a bad headache and let Travis do the flying while he handled the radio.

A week later, Hap announced, "Lezlie, I'm going to bail out of the flying business."

"Is that what you want? Really want?" she asked.

"It is."

"But why?"

"I've been flying these planes for twelve years!"

"Then why quit now?"

"I don't need to work. I've invested enough for us both to live comfortably and do the kinds of things we want for the rest of our lives."

"You're sure you mean it?" she asked.

"Why not?"

"Well, I—I like my job and—"

"But wouldn't you rather be free to travel everywhere with me? We'd be together all the time."

"If that's what you want, Hap."

"It is," he said. "In six weeks—that's all we need. Six weeks."

"Okay," she said and hoped her face expressed a happiness she did not feel inside.

"Right after we come back from Jordan," he said.

"If that's what you want," she said again, feeling her words sounded mechanical.

"We'll celebrate our first anniversary in the Middle East and let it be the beginning of a hundred great things ahead of us," he said. And Hap's charm almost pulled her back into its spell again.

"Hap—," she said and hesitated. "Hap, something—something's

happened to our marriage. Something I don't understand, and I'm confused and—"

"We'll straighten it all out once I leave the airline," he said. "Trust me."

"Can't we talk about it?"

"Okay," he said. "But not today. Later."

As Lezlie sat in the emergency waiting room, she said aloud, "So now is later."

"What?" Travis asked.

"Just talking to myself," she said. "Hap promised to talk with me later. Now is later. Much, much later."

"Lezlie, he's still alive—"

"It may still be too late," she said.

Travis stared at Lezlie, trying to decide what to say. At that moment they heard heavy footsteps outside the room. The door swung open, and a balding man in a white jacket paused. He looked over the top of his glasses. "Mrs. Austin?"

"Yes," she said and stiffened. Her eyes searched his features, but she could read nothing.

"I'm Doctor Mills." They shook hands, and Lezlie introduced Travis.

"Please, doctor—"

"Your husband suffered a severe myocardial infarction and that means—"

"May I see him? Is he still alive?"

"He's alive, but you see—"

"Then may I see him?"

"First I want to explain to you the seriousness of his condition."

Lezlie stood. "Doctor, let me see him now. After I've had a chance to see him, you can tell me anything. But please—"

He held up his hand, nodded his head gravely. "All right, this way. He may not feel like talking—"

"Just let me see him," she said and moved toward the door. The doctor took her arm and led her down the corridor. Travis slumped in the chair.

Travis did not know how long Lezlie was gone. He closed his eyes and might even have fallen asleep. He jumped up as Lezlie walked into the room, accompanied by a nurse.

"Would you like something to calm you?" the woman asked.

"Nothing, nothing," Lezlie answered and sank into the chair across from Travis. She looked up, and their eyes met. She opened her mouth, but no words came out.

Travis sat down next to her. He took her hands in his. As if on signal, she grabbed him and held tight. Then the tears came.

"He—died," she managed to say.

Chapter 5

"You're beginning to look like a human being again," Travis said. "For the first time in two months I can see life in your eyes."

"It's been hard," Lezlie said. "But I'm all right now."

"Or you will be as soon as you put a little weight back on."

"Yes, I did lose a little."

"A little? Your clothes hang on you, and you have that gaunt, haunted stare of a woman suffering from malnutrition—"

"Stop it! You're supposed to cheer me up," she said. "That's depressing."

"Didn't mean to depress, just to encourage you to fatten yourself up a little."

"I'm trying," she said.

They sat in a bakery coffee shop. Lezlie had just completed a return trip from San Juan. Although not the same flight with Travis, he had managed to meet her and drive her into the city.

"This is the first time I've had any appetite in weeks," she said as she dug into her second blintz.

"Since Hap's death, you mean."

"Yes—since Hap's death."

"I'm not trying to be cruel," Travis said. "I think it's important to say words like that and keep saying them until they no longer have any emotional impact to them."

"You're right," she said and took another bite.

"Lezlie, I can't believe you're still going through with your trip."

"Hap planned it," she said.

"But Hap's dead. Push all of that away—"

"Look," she said and stopped eating. With her fork poised in mid-air she pointed it at him and took a deep breath. "Look, Doctor Freud, you've been helpful to me. I don't know what I would have done without you. You've been right about a lot of things. But don't try to talk me out of this trip. I am going."

"If that's what you want."

"It's what I have to do."

"Then I won't argue anymore."

"Hap planned this trip. It was important. He had an errand to do, and since he can't take care of it himself—"

"You're going in his place."

"I have to go. That's one of the things Hap said in the hospital."

"It's your life—"

"Travis, why are you trying to talk me out of this trip?"

"I simply want you to put Hap's death behind you and start living again."

"I have," she said and took another forkful. "See. I'm eating and enjoying every bite." She smiled and patted his hand across the table. "However, this is an item of unfinished business. It's the last thing I have to do for Hap."

"I know when to shut up," Travis said and smiled. "But why did he want to go to Jordan?" He tried to sound casual.

"Didn't he tell you?" The surprise registered in her face.

"Tell me? I didn't know a thing about it until you told me."

"You were his best friend."

"I was?"

"You certainly were—"

"Then it's news he didn't share with his best friend."

"Hap thought more of you—more of you than anyone," she said. "He liked you. And you know, Hap didn't like other men very well."

"But he sure liked the women—I'm sorry, Lezlie. I didn't mean to say that. Just a dumb attempt at humor."

"But true."

"True? How do you know?"

"I didn't at first. I suspected and then hated myself for suspecting. But after his death I overheard things. Little bits of gossip, and I know Hap wasn't—well, wasn't always faithful—"

"But he loved you," Travis said. "He really did."

"I know that. That's what makes it so strange. As much as Hap knew how, he really did love me."

Travis signaled the waitress for a refill of his coffee.

"As much as he knew how?"

"You knew him as well as anybody—"

"Maybe too well," he answered and looked away. "Sorry, I don't know why I'm saying things like that."

"Don't you?"

"Is that a question I'm supposed to answer?"

"Not necessarily," Lezlie said. She pushed her plate away and took a sip of the coffee. "It's just that you could have told me so many things—"

"No I couldn't."

"You mean you wouldn't."

He shrugged. "However you want to say it."

"But you knew—"

"Suspected—suspected a lot of things."

"Then, Travis, why—why didn't you tell me? You said you were my friend."

"Would you have listened?"

"I—I'm not sure. I hope I would have."

"But you might have told me to take a hike."

"I could never say that to you. Not ever."

Travis flushed and played with a spoon for a moment. "When do you leave? For Jordan."

"Thursday on an afternoon flight to Atlanta then JFK and then direct on Alia."

"When does your plane leave New York?"

"Seven thirty or something like that. I can check it. Why?"

"Just a question to change the subject," he said and smiled. "I'm also wondering when you'll be back."

"Probably I'll stay ten days. I'm not sure, but at least a week."

"Is there that much to see in Jordan?"

"No, silly. I'll cross over to Israel and maybe even Egypt later. I've never been to the Middle East, and I want to see as much as possible."

"You going alone?"

"I am now," she said, looking down at her finger where she had once worn the diamond-studded band.

"You're not wearing your wedding ring?"

"I took it off to help me adjust to my new life."

Travis took both her hands in his and squeezed them. "Clumsy of me. I didn't mean to stir up any painful feelings."

"You didn't—really."

"I should have married you myself," he said and grinned. He released her hands and looked away from her. "Then we'd be making plans like this together."

"Maybe that's what should have happened," Lezlie said. "You know, I'm going to have another blintz." She signaled the waitress and pointed to her empty plate and raised one finger. "Since I'm going to have to put on weight, I might as well do it the fun way."

"You're beautiful no matter what weight," he said, his eyes not meeting hers.

"I didn't know there were any honestly shy men around any more," she said. "Maybe you're the only one left."

"Maybe," he said.

"Anyway, I'll always appreciate everything about you, Travis. You've been a wonderful friend."

"You sound as if we'll never see each other again," he said.

She laughed.

"It's good to see you smiling and laughing," he said. "Again."

"I do have to move on," she said. "I've still got several things to do. I may need to buy a new suitcase. A small one."

"You don't have enough?"

"I have to deliver a present. You see, that's the last thing Hap mentioned at the hospital. It's a coat Hap had specially made, hand sewn even, for some business-connected friend, Habib Taisir. Ever hear of him?"

"No, can't say that I have, but then I never knew about a lot of things Hap involved himself in."

"I didn't either," she said, and sadness veiled her eyes.

"Did I say anything wrong?"

She shook her head. The waitress served the third blintz. She took two bites, put down her fork, and pushed the plate away. "I still get a little moody at times, that's all."

"Hap's still—"

"No," she said, "it—it doesn't have anything to do with Hap."

"Then what—"

"Perhaps—perhaps after I've come from Jordan I can tell you."

"Whenever you're ready to tell me anything—"

Lezlie took a final sip of the coffee. She got up. Travis laid a five-dollar bill on the table and took her arm. He stifled the urge to put his arm around her.

Outside, Lezlie indicated she was going in a different direction. He hugged her lightly and kissed her cheek. "Lezlie—"

"Yes?"

"If you need me—for anything—"

"You didn't even have to say that," she said. "I've always known you were there."

He kissed her cheek again, let go abruptly, and turned. Over his shoulder he called back, "See you later."

The next morning the insistent ringing of the phone awakened Travis. He picked up the offending instrument, his eyes still closed. He expected a voice to ask him to take an extra flight. "Hello," he said without enthusiasm.

"This is Lezlie."

He sat up, suddenly alert. "What a lovely way to start out my day."

"I need you—"

"I can come over right away."

"It's not that urgent. I just need to talk to you. I'm confused and depressed—"

"Say no more. I'll shave, shower and—," he said, now out of bed and unbuttoning his pajama top.

"Thanks," she said. "But it's not *that* urgent. How about lunchtime? Say noon?"

"I'll be there."

"You know where I live?"

"I know the building. Hap never invited us peons in, you know."

"Oh, no I didn't—"

"I'll be there at noon," he said and hung up.

Travis arrived early and looked up at the magnificent building on St. Charles Street. Three stories high, shaped in an L, with carefully mowed lawns and grounds, it resembled a resort hotel more than an apartment complex. As he walked into the lobby, he saw the security guard sitting behind a long counter, watching closed-circuit television of all the floors. He smiled genially at Travis.

"Mrs. Austin's apartment?"

The security guard consulted a sheet. "Your name, please?"

"Travis Manning," he said as he looked around. If the lobby were this carefully decorated, he wondered about the apartment itself. From outside the building he figured they paid at least five hundred a month. He now revised his figure to seven.

"She's expecting you. Three B." He nodded toward the elevator. "I'll ring Mrs. Austin that you're on your way up."

"Thank you," Travis said as he turned toward the elevator. He wondered if he ought to have worn one of his better suits. His ready-made brand looked out of place standing next to brocaded wallpaper. When the elevator door opened, he smiled. It would have disappointed him if the floor had not been carpeted. "All the comforts of home," he said under his breath as he stepped inside.

A minute later he had barely touched the bell when Lezlie opened the door and stood back.

Travis stepped inside and surveyed the interior from the foyer. "I'm not sure if I should bow or take off my shoes," he said, his eyes staring at the marbled foyer.

Lezlie flushed. "It is a bit—"

"Does it come with maid service?"

"Yes, but—," she stopped. "You're laughing at me."

"No, not laughing. Just overwhelmed."

"Forget the apartment—"

"How can I? I'm still looking at it."

"Then stop." She put her arms around him and kissed him on the cheek.

"That helps," he said.

Lezlie took Travis's hand and led him into the living room. He tried not to focus on the light-wood furniture which could duplicate a picture window he would expect to see at an expensive furniture store. At the opposite end of the carpeted room, he saw the dining table. A silver candelabra for a centerpiece confirmed the touch he had expected. "Who decorated?" he asked as he decided the rent must run a thousand dollars a month.

"All Hap's work. Every single piece."

"It doesn't seem like your touch."

"As soon as the lease expires, I plan to move out."

"Can't you afford to stay here?"

"It's not a matter of money," she said.

"Of memories?"

"The wrong kind of memories," Lezlie said and led him into the kitchen where she had already set plates in the breakfast nook. "I hate that dining room. We used it often because Hap liked it. I think it's simpler and cozier here."

Travis stared at her as she moved quickly around the kitchen. She wore a chocolate brown skirt, which fit snugly around her hips. The blouse, tan with appliquéd initials on the pocket, highlighted her brown hair and dark eyes. "Brown's your best color," he said. "You need to wear it more often."

Lezlie smiled. From the microwave she took out two plates. Travis smiled at the combination. Fried plantains next to red beans and rice.

"Ah, you know how to please a man."

"You're easy to please," she said.

"Maybe you're right," he answered.

"Travis, is that why you stay in New Orleans? Hap said you could have moved up by bidding for Chicago or San Antonio. He said you stayed because you liked the Cajun food."

"That's one reason."

"There are others?"

"Yes."

Travis stared at Lezlie, cleared his throat and said, "Where else can I find a rich young widow who knows how to cook my favorite meal?"

Lezlie smiled and sat down next to him.

They ate in silence. Travis stole glances at Lezlie. Her face was drawn, and twice she opened her mouth as if to say something and didn't. She took small bites, mostly picking at her food. Travis pushed her plate away. "You make me nervous, moving your plantains from one side of the plate to the other. Why don't you talk to me instead?"

"I had all kinds of things to talk about when I called. Now—," she paused and got up. She took her plate and emptied it into the garbage disposal. "And now, I can't think of any of it."

"Or is it that you don't know how to start talking about whatever is bothering you?"

"You think that's it?"

"Of course. I know you pretty well. Remember?"

Lezlie flushed. "I suppose you do."

"So what's the problem?"

She moved directly in front of him and stared down into his blue eyes. "How much do you know about Hap? Before we were married, I mean?"

"That's never a fair question for a lady to ask another man," he said with a smile on his face.

"Let me try it another way. How much do you know about Hap's financial situation?"

"Nothing. Honest."

"Please don't lie to me," she said.

"I'm not lying—"

"Remember, I know you pretty well, too."

Travis gave a deep sigh and looked away. "I honestly don't *know* anything."

"What do you suspect then?"

"That's not a fair question, either."

"You mean you won't tell me?"

"I mean, what do you want to know?"

Lezlie continued staring for a long moment and then walked across the room. She opened the drapes and stared out at the traffic below. "I need information. I'm confused and—"

"And what else?"

"At the moment mostly confused," she said. "Especially since I've been going through his papers."

"What have you found?" he asked.

"I'll show you."

She walked into the spare bedroom which Hap had used for an office. Moments later she returned with a small metal box. She laid the box on the table, opened it, and strewed the contents on the table in front of Travis.

He whistled. "No wonder you asked."

Before him lay deposit books from banks in Switzerland, Argentina, and Portugal. Stacks of bearer bonds, bound by a double rubber band indicated, after a cursory examination, a value of at least one hundred thousand dollars.

"A lot of money," Travis said, fingering the bank deposit books.

"I'm not sure about all the currency exchanges," she said, "but the deposits and bonds total somewhere in the neighborhood of a million dollars."

"Then you're a very, very wealthy woman," he said.

"Is it legitimate money?"

"What kind of question is that?"

"How would you feel if you were in my place and discovered all that?"

"You didn't know about it? About any of it?"

"Not a hint," she said. "He said he was a businessman too, but—"

"I'd say quite a businessman," Travis said. "And he never told you about—about this?" he indicated the contents from the box.

"Nothing."

"Not ever?"

"Only—only one time," she said, suddenly remembering.

"Tell me."

"Three, maybe four weeks before his heart attack, we had breakfast in San Juan before the flight. . . ."

Lezlie slowly ate a fruit bowl while Hap wolfed down his three-egg omelet. He had almost finished eating, and they had spoken little during the breakfast. He stopped, reached over, and took her hand. "Lez, if anything ever happens to me—"

"Happens to you?" she laughed. "You mean thirty years from now?"

"If anything should happen—and I'm not trying to scare you," he said.

"Okay, Hap," she said. "Guess I just didn't want to talk about something like that."

"If anything happens to me, go to Travis. He's the only person I trust."

"Of course, Hap, but—"

The Hap Austin grin flashed across his face. "Good ole Travis—"

"Hap, are you trying to tell me something?"

"Nope. You know accidents happen. Just wanted to prepare you—" He stopped and chuckled. "Once in a while a man thinks about the future. About his wife—the children he hopes to have—"

"Hap, I don't know anything about your business or about your investments—"

"You don't need to know anything right now. But you'll never have to want for anything in your life. Not ever. I've been holding the golden goose that produced golden eggs. Now I've accumulated enough, so I'm releasing the bird."

"Hap, I don't understand," she said, leaning forward.

"Hey, don't worry about it. I'm just telling you that I've taken care of finances for you."

Lezlie, remembering nothing more that Hap had ever spoken, rested her hand on Travis's shoulder. "His mood changed then, and he smiled, letting the charm take over."

Lezlie methodically picked up the contents of the box, stacked them neatly inside, and closed it. She pushed it to the far side of the table and sat down. She laid her hands on his. "Now you see why I asked you the questions I did."

"I'm afraid I'm not the one to ask—"

"But you were his best friend. You knew him—"

"Lezlie, I was not his best friend." He pulled his hands away and pounded on the table. "I was not his best friend!"

"But I always thought—"

"Hap never *had* a best friend!"

"That's a cruel thing to say," she said, her face ashen as though Travis had slapped her.

"I didn't mean to be cruel. Only honest."

"But Hap always spoke about you—"

"Lezlie, you were his wife. You were married to him for nearly ten months. Why don't you tell me about his financial status?"

"I didn't know anything. He kept it all very private."

"You didn't know *anything?*"

She shook her head. "Just today I remembered the key to our safe-deposit box. I haven't even been there yet."

"Was the box in both your names?"

She nodded. "But I never opened it. No, once. A few days after we married. I put a copy of our wedding license in it and a few government bonds I inherited when my aunt Martha died."

"But didn't he ever say anything?"

"Only that he had invested wisely. He hinted that his investments in real estate and the commodities market were paying off big. He promised that after we returned from Jordan—"

"What then?"

"Then he would retire."

"Retire? Didn't that strike you as odd? He had exactly thirteen years with the airline."

"Travis, did you ever try to get straight answers from Hap when he didn't want to give them? He smiled and twisted and avoided all that."

"But you kept asking questions?"

"For a while. After a few months I decided that I'd wait until he wanted to tell me."

"But he never did," Travis said to himself.

"He'd say every once in a while that we had enough money put aside for the rest of our lives. He frequently bragged that money could always make more money for people who knew how to do it."

"That sounds like Hap."

"It's made me, well, afraid—"

"Afraid? Of what?"

"That—that Hap did something illegal."

"A lot of people do illegal things in this world. Jaywalking, cheating on their taxes, padding expense accounts—"

"You wouldn't."

"You think you know me that well?"

"I think I know you that well."

He cleared his throat. "I think it's time to change the subject. When do you leave for Jordan?"

"I've already told you—Thursday."

"Yeah, you did."

"Travis, I have a favor to ask."

He stood up. "I'm always willing to do anything for you."

"Go to the bank with me."

"You mean now?"

"If you can. If not—"

"Are you afraid of what you'll find in the safe-deposit box?"

"Yes, I am."

"Grab your purse," he said. "Let's go."

Fifteen minutes later, Travis pulled his car in front of the First National Bank. They walked inside to the section for safe deposits. Lezlie showed her key, signed the book, and both of them followed the clerk to the vault. After inserting the bank key and her own, Lezlie withdrew the box. She and Travis went into a small room.

"Let me know when you're through," the woman called as she returned to her desk.

"Open it," Lezlie whispered.

He pulled the top up. On top lay files with birth certificates, the marriage license, and envelopes marked: SIGNIFICANT INFORMATION. From the bottom, Travis picked up a five-inch thick envelope. Both of them saw it, and their eyes met momentarily.

Travis pulled the unmarked manila envelope out and ripped the end off. He dropped its contents on the counter. Lezlie gasped.

Two stacks of thousand-dollar bills fell out.

"Where—where did it all come from?" she asked.

"You haven't any idea?" he said, but she saw the accusation in his eyes.

"I haven't the slightest—"

"Okay, play it your way." He picked up the money and put it back in the envelope. He turned and opened the door. "I'll wait for you in the car."

"Travis, wait a minute—"

"No, you wait, Lezlie. I don't play games with people. And I don't like people playing them with me."

He slammed the door and walked out.

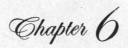

Chapter 6

Lezlie walked out of the bank and hesitated as if not sure she wanted to get into Travis's car. He motioned to her to get in. He did not get out and open the door. As soon as she sat down, he started the engine and pulled out of the parking lot, heading back toward St. Charles Street.

"Travis, if only you'd tell me—," she stopped in mid-sentence.

His grim eyes stared straight ahead. He hunched slightly forward as his foot pressed down on the accelerator. He soon exceeded the speed limit.

"Won't you at least talk to me?" she asked.

He said nothing but concentrated on driving.

Involuntarily, tears slid down her cheeks. She searched her purse for tissues. Travis handed her his handkerchief. "Here," he said and looked away again.

"Thank you," she mumbled and wiped her eyes. She turned her face away from him and stared out the window.

Abruptly Travis turned left, pulled over to the curb, and parked. He shut off the engine and slowly turned to face her. "Lezlie, I'm stupid about a lot of things, but don't pull a con job on me."

"I'm not trying—"

"Don't ask me to swallow all that innocence—"

"Just what are you trying to say?"

"You don't know?" he asked, anger in his voice.

"Listen to me, Travis Manning. I haven't any idea what you're yelling about. Say it straight if you want to find out anything. Or accuse me. Then I'll know how to deal with you."

"You don't know a thing? Not one little thing about all that money?"

"Honest. Not a thing."

"You had no idea about the nice little package of thousand-dollar bills?"

"Travis, I never saw them before you opened the envelope."

Travis rubbed his cheeks and shook his head. "Crazy, but I believe you."

"Believe me? Why shouldn't you? What's crazy about that?"

"What's crazy about it? You live with a man for nearly a year. He's got a couple of million dollars lying around in cash, and you don't know anything about it. You didn't even know it existed."

"I didn't."

"That neat little metal box was in your apartment all the time, and you never even opened it? Not once?"

"Never."

"Lezlie, that's not like you. I always thought you were your own person. Independent—"

"I was. Maybe I am. But with Hap—well, with Hap it was different."

"You changed for him?"

Lezlie breathed deeply and looked directly at Travis. "I did it his way to save our marriage."

"Was it that bad?"

"It wasn't *bad*. Just that—Hap had his own way of coping with life. I conformed to his way, that's all."

"You mean, like no questions?"

"Yes. If the questions had to do with anything personal. Otherwise—"

"Otherwise, the center of charm."

"Exactly. He knew all the jokes and imitated more comedians than anyone I know. He smiled, and every woman melted around him. But when we were alone—"

"He was like a different man?"

"Not *like* a different man. He *was*, totally different."

"I didn't mean to pry or to put Hap down—"

"I didn't feel you were doing that, Travis. That's not your style."

He flashed her a quick smile and shook his head. "It's just so—so incomprehensible that he kept you absolutely ignorant. And that you stood for it."

"Hap wasn't a bad guy, Travis. In other ways he was so gentle and thoughtful. Our eighteenth-century-style apartment—you know why we moved there? I admired the limestone colonnades. When we saw the gardens and fountains and the gorgeous waterfall, well, he insisted we move in. He really wanted to please me."

"Did you want to live there?"

"No," she said and looked away. "But Hap thought it pleased me. He did so many little things for me. Like—did you know, he always packed my cosmetic case for my trips? Always. That may not sound like much, but that tender gesture—"

"It doesn't sound like Hap. I would have expected you to pack for him."

"Every once in a while, he'd open up a little. I think that if he had lived, in time he would have told me everything."

"Maybe you wouldn't have wanted to hear it," Travis said.

"Maybe you're right."

"But he never told you anything—not a single thing—about his business dealings?"

"No," she said, probing her memory again. "Well, he did talk a little about the Jordan trip. Not much about the business part of it, but—"

"Tell me about that, Lezlie. As much as you remember."

"He got excited about the trip. He kept saying that it was the big event." She thought of the half-dozen times he had referred to the trip. "The time he talked the most was when a man delivered the coat."

"What coat?"

"That beautiful fur coat I told you about. It was made of different kinds of fur but all beautiful looking. I recognized mink and sable. Each section in small pieces about six inches long—"

"Forget the fashion show, Lezlie—"

"Sorry, it was just such a beautiful coat. Anyway, the man delivered it, and Hap hung it up in the closet. He made a phone call right after that and wrote down, Habib Taisir, Tyche Hotel, Jordan. He left the paper next to the phone. When I asked about it, he picked it up, and stuck it in the coat pocket. He said that was to tell him where to deliver the coat."

"That's all?"

"He said that it was a present for Taisir's daughter. And that Taisir had helped him in investing his money in an international pool. We were going to Jordan to surprise him because he doted on his daughter, an only child."

"But anything more about the business?"

"No, except that when we returned, he was going to resign. He said that by then all his investments would have paid off, and we could live anywhere in the world we wanted."

"You didn't press him for details?"

"Like I said before, did you ever try to press Hap for information he didn't want to give you?"

"Right. Subject closed."

"That's why I didn't know anything."

"I believe you."

"I should have pressed him more. I really regret that I didn't."

"Lezlie, we all have regrets," Travis said and started the engine again.

Chapter 7

Lezlie held the ticket in her hand. She tapped her long fingers on the envelope. *Am I really doing the right thing?* she asked herself. And then answered immediately, *I have to do it. I have no choice.*

She laid the ticket on the table, straightened up, and walked into her bedroom. The suitcase lay on the bed half packed. She finished putting in the clothes she planned to take. She was ready to close the case when she remembered the coat. It hung in the closet in the spare bedroom. She walked in and picked it up, admiring again the beautiful fur and style of the coat. As she took it off the hanger and walked back into her bedroom, she remembered another conversation that she and Hap had had.

"It's for the daughter of my friend Habib Taisir," Hap said.

Lezlie examined the coat, especially noting its styling. "Just how old is Mr. Taisir's daughter?" she asked.

"Don't know for sure. Why?"

"It's obviously a woman's coat. Certainly not that of a child. I just wondered."

"I guess she's about twenty, more or less," Hap said and smiled. "A little too young for me I think."

Lezlie laughed. "I wasn't thinking of that. However, when you take an expensive coat like this to a young woman, it does raise some doubts in a wife's mind."

"Ah, but don't forget, you'll be with me."

"Yes, that's right."

"In fact," Hap said, "why don't you wear it?"

"Wear it?" she asked. "I thought it was a gift."

"It is—but I thought you might like to have an opportunity to wear it."

"Hap, you mean, you want me to smuggle it through customs by wearing it?"

"Oh, something like that," he said.

"But that's dishonest."

"Dishonest? What do you mean?" he answered, and a strange look passed across his face.

"I mean, are you trying to cheat customs out of import duty?"

Hap laughed. "Oh, maybe a little."

"That's not right," she said.

"I'm not trying to smuggle in a million dollars in diamonds or—"

"But if we bring it in illegally—"

"You'll be bringing it in as your coat, see? Try it on." He held the coat while she put it on. "Hm," he said. "Perfect fit. So that's your coat. I'm giving it to you as a gift from your husband."

"Then when we get into Jordan, I decide I no longer want it and give it to Mr. Taisir's daughter. Is that it?"

"Well, if you decide to give it away . . . ," he said, leaving the sentence hanging in the air, "What's illegal about that?"

"I don't know," she said slowly. "It's not quite honest and that bothers me."

"Ah, c'mon, you're just afraid of risks and adventure."

"No, Hap, it's just—well, I'm just opposed to anything dishonest, that's all."

"You've never asked questions before about things legal and illegal!"

"Asked questions? I didn't know anything like that had come up before."

"You never worried about the gifts I gave you," he pointed to the necklace she wore. "Those are genuine pearls. You never asked where I got the money. You never asked about the trips we made—"

Lezlie paled. "You mean—you mean, you've been involved in something illegal?"

Hap leaned against the door frame, his face wreathed in smiles. "No, not at all."

"Wait a minute, Hap—"

"Just teasing," he said.

"Hap, don't play games with me," Lezlie said. "You know how I feel about things like that. At least I've tried to tell you—"

"Oh, here we go, getting religious again. Is that it?"

"Maybe it is, Hap. I've tried to tell you before that because I'm a Christian—"

"Because you're a Christian, you're always looking for something wrong to pick at!"

"Is that what you think I mean by being a Christian?"

"No," he said, smiling broadly. He came over to her and put his arms around her. "I suppose I'm just a little miffed, and I don't know how we got into this discussion."

"We got into this discussion," she said, "because you wanted to cheat customs."

"Look," he answered. "It's not anything illegal about the coat, but if you're upset about it, when we go through customs if they ask anything about it, we'll just tell them that we brought it in and intend to give it as a gift. Then if they want to charge any duty—"

"All right," she said. "Maybe I got a little too worked up about that."

Later she wondered if she allowed Hap to soothe her because she wanted to be soothed and she wanted peace. Even more, she did not want to believe that Hap could be involved in anything illegal.

"This trip to Jordan is important," Hap said. "To me and to us."

"I'm not quite sure why the trip is so important," Lezlie said. "We've taken trips before. Like the time we went to Lisbon—"

"This is a bit of a business trip," Hap said. "Most important, it's the last business trip we'll have to make."

"I'm still not sure what you mean—"

"Look, Lez, I have financial connections all over the world. Now I'm bowing out of the rat race and investing in projects here in the good old USA. I need to make the trip to Amman as a final gesture to Taisir and then—"

"Then it's over?"

"Absolutely," he said. "Then we can concentrate on our marriage."

"All right," Lezlie answered quietly.

"Honey, I want you to know that you're the best thing that's ever come into my life." He kissed her on the cheek and pulled her closer to him.

"What brought that about?" she asked.

"Just thinking about the future. Maybe reviewing the past a little bit."

"Every woman likes to think she's the best thing in her husband's life."

"And you are!" He kissed her lightly on the lips.

"I'm glad," she answered, and then wished truthfully that she could have said, "And you're the best thing to come into my life." She wondered why the words didn't flow from her lips.

* * *

Lezlie sat on the edge of her bed, staring at the now-closed suitcase. She was going. She had committed herself. Yet she did not want to go.

She fell back on the bed, her head resting on the pillow. She covered her eyes with her left arm. "Oh, God," she said aloud. "I feel as though I've made such a mess of my life. Where did I go wrong? How did I get turned around this way?"

She stopped speaking abruptly and sat up. "I was praying," she said. Lezlie realized that for the first time in more weeks than she could remember, she had prayed.

"God, I feel as though I have no right to talk to You. When things went well in my life, I seemed to have lost my need to talk to You. Now that everything has turned upside down, I'm talking to You again. I'm sorry I neglected You. Help me know if I'm doing the right thing. Help me in knowing what to do about this money and all the other things that are troubling me."

Lezlie lay down again, and for the first time in several days she felt at peace. She reached over and opened the drawer of her nightstand. She fumbled around, and under several sheets of paper she found her Bible. She pulled it out and stared at its cover for a minute. It was worn, more worn than she had remembered.

Her father had given her that Bible when she left for college. She opened the cover and saw his large scrawl: LEZLIE. AS LONG AS YOU USE THIS BOOK, YOU'LL NEVER GO WRONG. YOUR FATHER.

Tears filled her eyes. She had not used that book, at least not for a long time. She flipped idly through the pages and opened it to the Book of Psalms. "Blessed is the man who walks not in the counsel of the wicked, nor stands in the way of sinners, nor sits in the seat of scoffers; but his delight is in the law of the Lord, and on his law he meditates day and night."

Tears blotted out the words, and she could no longer read. She closed her eyes. Even though she had not thought of that Psalm for a long time, the words of the following verses came to her. At least once a week they had recited the first Psalm together.

". . . for the Lord knows the way of the righteous, but the way of the wicked will perish."

Lezlie stood in line to board the Delta L-1011 with the group going into first class. She knew there were plenty of seats from New Orleans to Atlanta. There was a reasonable assurance that from Atlanta to New York she would have no trouble. As an airline employee, she would be on standby for Alia Airlines. Lezlie decided not to worry about it. She had made her decision to go to Jordan. It would work out, she knew. She brought only one suitcase and a flight bag which she carried over her shoulder. Even though she might be gone for at least ten days, she had learned long ago how to travel light. She walked in and sat down in the first-class cabin. For a moment she thought of the hours of travel. There would be seventeen hours of actual flying time from New York to Amman. Although the plane would stop in Vienna for fuel, the passengers would not be allowed to leave the plane. She had her Bible and two books in her flight bag. She would read and hoped she could sleep during the long trip. Of course she might meet some interesting people on the trip, but for a moment the sense of aloneness stabbed at her. She closed her eyes, not wanting to think about it.

"Excuse me, but may I sit next to you?"

Lezlie looked up. Travis bent down and said again, "May I sit next to you, ma'am?"

"What are you doing here?"

He stood there smiling, a briefcase in his hand. He wore an open shirt, a light jacket, and jeans.

"I'm going to take a trip. Didn't I tell you?"

"No, you didn't," she said as Travis sat down next to her.

"Yes, I'm going to Jordan, Israel, and perhaps even to Egypt."

Lezlie smiled. She touched his arm. "Thank you, Travis. Thank you very much."

"Thanks? For what? For going on a trip?"

"For going with me."

"Lezlie, there isn't anything in the world I wouldn't do for you. Not anything."

She patted his arm. "Thanks," she mumbled again. She looked away from him, surprised at how the words had touched her and how pleased she was to hear them. Then a feeling of guilt overcame her for being pleased.

"Do you feel like talking?" he asked. "Or would you like to rest?"

"Do you think I need to rest?" she asked, smiling at him.

"You've got dark lines under your eyes that even your makeup won't hide; so, yes, I think you need to rest."

"Is that an order, a suggestion, or a request?"

"I'll tell you what, you relax like a nice lady, and I'll sit here and read. If anything goes wrong with the plane, I'll awaken you and then we can go into our magic act and save it."

She smiled, closed her eyes, and leaned back. A minute later she said, "Travis, this may sound silly, but—"

"I don't mind silly talk, " he said.

"May I—may I hold your hand for a little while? Just until I relax?"

"Of course," he said and squeezed her hand gently. "Here, take two of them."

"No, one is enough. I just need the sense of someone being with me."

"I understand. And I am with you."

She closed her eyes and laid her head on his shoulder. Travis could feel her body gradually relaxing. When he was sure she was asleep, he kissed her gently on the forehead. "I love you, Lezlie Austin," he whispered.

Chapter 8

Alia's flight 264 arrived at 11:30 A.M., half an hour behind schedule. With the eight hour difference in time, Lezlie's mental alarm clock told her it was still the middle of the night. Sleepily she and Travis left the plane and moved into a large open building. Minutes later suitcases appeared on carousels. The crowd from the plane surged forward, grabbing for their luggage. Travis pulled Lezlie back, and they watched as passengers pushed and tugged to get their suitcases. Once the crowd cleared, they retrieved theirs.

Lezlie draped the fur coat over her arm as she carried her flight bag and single suitcase to the counter for inspection. She laid the suitcase down and opened it. The custom's official looked up at the coat. He felt its fur and said, "Pretty, very pretty."

"Yes," she said. "I brought it as a gift—"

"Yes, very pretty," he said, as he deftly fingered through her clothes. He nodded to her and said, "You may take it now."

Lezlie shut the suitcase and moved on. Travis had stood in line right behind her. He whispered, "Don't worry about paying duty on that now."

The crowd had almost disappeared, and for a moment they wondered if they would find a taxi. One pulled up almost immediately. It was a battered Volvo with the word *taxi* in English and Arabic script next to it, which they assumed said the same thing. They got in, and the driver put their luggage in the trunk.

"Tyche Hotel," Lezlie said.

Even though it was midday in the new time zone, Lezlie found she could hardly keep her eyes open. Her body told her it was barely morning. During the taxi ride, she put her head on Travis's shoulder and slept. She had only a vague impression of the land as she peered out once or twice. It seemed to be nothing but rocks with small patches of grass pushing its blades through cracks. The next recollection she had was Travis shaking her gently. "We're here, Lezlie," he said. She opened her eyes, taking a few seconds to orient herself.

The driver carried their luggage inside the hotel, and Travis tipped him in American dollars, while Lezlie went to the desk. Travis, much to his surprise, acknowledged that the Tyche compared with any good second-class hotel in the States. He stared at the well-vacuumed red carpet in the lobby.

A minute later Lezlie returned and handed him a key. "This is yours, room two thirteen, next to mine."

"Oh?" he said, smiling.

"You expected us to share a room?"

"I didn't know what to expect," he said. He turned and picked up both their suitcases.

"Wait just a minute," Lezlie said and returned to the desk. The clerk, a tall stocky man, glanced up at her and said, "Yes, madam? There is something more, please?"

"I'm trying to locate someone," she said. "I think he stays here."

"But of course," he smiled, showing large, uneven teeth.

"His name is Habib Taisir."

The clerk's face registered momentary shock. He quickly looked down. "We have no such person registered in this hotel," he said and started to move away.

"Are you sure? I mean with all the rooms here, and you haven't checked your register—"

"We have no such guest in our hotel," he said with an expansive smile.

"Perhaps he works here," she insisted.

"Excuse me, madam," he said turning completely away from her. "I'm quite busy as you can see. I have never heard the name before."

Lezlie stood at the desk, wondering how she could locate him if he had no connection with the Tyche Hotel. Yet she vividly remembered seeing the words in Hap's handwriting. She tried one more time. "Excuse me."

The clerk turned around smiling, "Yes, madam?"

"Are you sure there is no such person here?"

"Positive," he said.

"Perhaps he stayed here." She thought back quickly. "Three months ago. Could there have been someone registered here approximately three months ago named Habib Taisir who left a forwarding address?"

"I do not believe so, madam."

"Would you—would you check your back files and let me know if you can locate him?"

"But of course, madam. If I can locate Mr. Taisir, I will inform you."

She thanked him and walked back to Travis. After Lezlie explained that the clerk had never heard of Taisir, Travis said, "You're tired. Let's go upstairs to our rooms first. Later on we'll decide what to do."

"It's just that I've traveled so far for this one purpose—"

"Right now you need a rest," Travis said. "You've been this long in getting here, another hour won't make much difference, will it?"

"I suppose you're right," she answered wearily. She started to pick up her own suitcase, but he had already grabbed both of them. She did take his briefcase and her flight bag. They climbed the steps to the second floor instead of waiting for the elevator. Travis set the suitcase down by her door, took his briefcase, and went to his own room.

"Take a nap, Lezlie. Call me when you wake up."

"That's fine," she answered wearily and went inside. Instead of unpacking as she had planned, Lezlie dropped the suitcase in the middle of the room and fell across the bed. She drifted into a deep sleep almost instantly.

When she awakened, pale streaks of light streamed into the room. She opened her eyes and lay silently, trying to figure it out. It had been midday when she had come into the room. She glanced at her watch. It showed 12:00 central time. Allowing for the eight hours difference, that made it 8:00 in the morning. She had slept through the entire day! She picked up the phone and asked to be connected to Travis's room. "Hello," he answered after the second ring.

"I'm afraid my nap went into overtime," she said.

"I thought so."

"I'm sorry—"

"I fell asleep, too. In fact, you awakened me."

"Then I don't feel so bad," she said. "How about breakfast?"

"Give me half an hour, and I'll tap on your door."

"Bye," she said and hung up. As she laid the phone back in its cradle, she saw something protruding from under her door. She got up, walked over, bent down, and picked up an envelope. She saw no writing on the outside. She opened the envelope and extracted the single piece of paper. Printed in all capital letters were these words: THE RUINS OF JERASH, NOON TODAY. ALONE. The initial T was printed at the bottom. *How strange,* she thought.

Half an hour later Travis tapped at her door, and she opened it. She wore gray slacks, a thin blouse and a light jacket. Travis wore a gold shirt and slacks with matching blue sweater.

"Ready for breakfast?" he asked. "That is, assuming they're open."

She nodded and then handed him the letter. "Here, read this."

He started reading it as they went out of her room and walked down the corridor. "What do you make of it?" he asked.

"I guess Taisir's trying to play games with us. It sounds awfully cloak and dagger—"

"Lezlie, don't get off on that one. I'm sure there's a reasonable explanation."

"Of course there is. But unless he's wanted by the police or owes the hotel money, you'd think—"

"Let's think about breakfast instead," he said and took her arm.

They walked downstairs, came to the desk, and were going to ask directions to the dining room when they noticed a sign on the wall: BREAKFAST FOR GUESTS SERVED IN THE SNACK BAR.

Travis shrugged, and they continued down the hallway past the gift shops. They had no trouble finding the snack bar because of the noise level. It was already filled with people, all involved in conversation. Long rows of tables had been set up. Each place setting had a coffee cup, a hard roll, butter and jam. Waiters ran back and forth with coffee and tea.

"Not exactly bacon and eggs, is it?" Travis asked.

"You won't get bacon in Jordan or Israel anyway, dummy," Lezlie said with a laugh.

"Right. I'd forgotten they don't eat pork."

They sat down in two empty places and each began to eat a roll. A waiter appeared, poured hot milk in the cup, and then filled it with coffee. Lezlie smiled at the woman sitting next to her. She wore a name tag identifying her as Virginia Hislip from Atlanta, Georgia. Her name tag also read PRESBYTERIAN PILGRIMAGE in bold blue letters.

"I don't think I've met you yet," Virginia said as she turned toward Lezlie.

"We're not part of this Presbyterian Pilgrimage," Lezlie answered.

"Oh, I am sorry," the woman said in her cultured southern accent. "I assumed everyone here was part of our group."

"No, we came on our own."

"Oh, then I think you came to the wrong breakfast. This was a special breakfast for our tour group."

Lezlie and Travis looked at each other. Their eyes asked the question, "Should we leave?"

Virginia patted Lezlie's hand. "Don't worry about it. You're here now. No one will mind."

"Yes, perhaps you're right."

"You're not with our tour group, but you are Americans?"

"Yes, we are."

Lezlie took a bite of the large roll and found it delicious. She unwrapped a small cube of cheese which she spread on top of the roll and took a bite. "Hm," she said, "very good. Not quite American style—"

"Yes, I don't ordinarily like cheese and bread for breakfast," Virginia said "However, I agree, it is quite delicious."

At that moment a man stood in the middle of the room and clapped his hands a couple of times. Almost immediately all talking subsided. "I need your attention, everyone!"

Travis and Lezlie looked at him. He appeared to be about forty years of age, heavy, with brown-graying hair and sparkling blue eyes. He wore dark-rimmed glasses. "Sorry folks," he said, "but we've only got ten minutes. The buses are in front of the hotel right now, so please hurry."

The activity level intensified, and the man across from Travis gobbled down his roll and spread a second with marmalade. Others called the already harried waiters for a last cup of coffee.

"So nice sitting with you," Virginia Hislip said as she daintily wiped her mouth. "I so wish we could have gotten better acquainted, but—," she shrugged as she pushed her chair back.

Within five minutes Lezlie and Travis found themselves alone in the large room with three waiters hovering over them.

"Maybe we should have waited and eaten in the regular dining room," she said.

"This is enough for me," Travis said. He grabbed a second roll from an empty place setting next to him. After breaking it in half, he generously spread it with cheese and took another bite.

"You wished for a guide to the ruins of Jerash?" the wide-faced taxi driver asked. "You are so lucky because I am the best guide in all of Amman."

"Yes, fine," Travis said as he opened the door for Lezlie.

"No one must come to our country of Jordan without seeing this magnificent site."

"Then by all means, we will see it," Travis answered.

"It is but half an hour's drive from this hotel, and you will see one of the most magnificent sites in the world," he said as he began his commentary.

Lezlie carried the coat with her and draped it across her lap. She tried to appear interested as the guide told them facts they had not particularly wanted to know.

"It was first known as the ancient city of Gerasa," he said in a singsongy voice, "and while it is not mentioned in the Bible, it has a magnificent history, rising two thousand feet on the Transjordan plateau."

They arrived ten minutes before noon. Lezlie folded the coat across her arm as she got out of the taxi. They stood momentarily waiting for Taisir to approach her.

"Ah, is it not a magnificent view?" the guide said. "Did I not tell you of this?"

"Yes, yes, you did," Lezlie answered, not wishing to be rude. Her eyes moved beyond the guide. Half a dozen Arabs stood behind tables, selling curios. Two women haggled for a moment, bought a bracelet and a carving, then walked on. Lezlie saw no one else around. She faced Travis. He shrugged.

"Ah, but we cannot stand here all day," the guide said. He came between them, grabbed their elbows, and urged them up the path leading to the ruins.

"Must have been quite a place at one time," Travis said as he stared at the long columns lining what had once been a road.

"*Magnificent* is the word," the guide said. "The Romans conquered this area in sixty-three B.C. after it had been ruled by Syrians and Egyptians. Under the great Roman Pompey, it became a city-state and a center of trade between Petra and the Orient."

"Ah, yes," Travis said as he moved a few feet ahead of the guide. "What is that?" he pointed to what he recognized from pictures as Hadrian's Arch.

"This magnificent arch, erected in the year A.D. one twenty-nine in honor of the visit of the emperor Hadrian—," and he stopped, realizing that Lezlie had not followed. "Come, nice lady, and I will show you—"

"She is not much interested in this part," Travis said quickly. "You must show me, and she will look around by herself."

"By herself? Without explanation?" he said, throwing his arms into the air, and he said something in Arabic. "Yes, come, I show you." He led Travis down the partially restored Via Antoniniana Street.

Lezlie waited in the center of what was obviously a plaza. As Travis moved off, she saw that three buses had pulled up. People poured out. She recognized them as the same people she had seen at the hotel. They gathered in separate groups as a guide called them together. She stood out of the way, separated from them. She could hear one guide speak. "This ancient city of renown has been a commercial center for many historic cultures, dating back to several hundred years before the births of Christ and Mohammed. . . ."

Lezlie pretended to listen but shifted her gaze, wondering if she ought to remain there or move on. Other small groups filled the plaza. She stared at the stone road. Each stone, almost the size of a modern brick, made her think of the months it must have taken slaves to cut, polish, transport, and finally construct the road. She turned as she heard another bus pulling in. The group that had been standing near her moved on. The guide said, "We now go toward the amphitheater." At that moment Lezlie realized that a man had moved up behind her. In a low voice he said, "Do not look at me but walk straight ahead."

She started forward, and he walked beside her.

"We are going toward the temple of Zeus," he said and pointed ahead.

"All right."

"I believe you have a small package for me, Mrs. Austin," he whispered.

"A package?" she asked. "Not a package—"

"I did not come to waste your time," he said. "Please do not waste mine. If you will hand me the parcel—"

"Who are you?" she asked.

"You received my note?"

"I received a letter which I assumed was from Habib Taisir."

"Then is it not simple? Give me the parcel, and I shall leave, and you shall have accomplished your task."

"But I don't have a *parcel,*" she said. "You see—"

"I do not want excuses," he said, and his face inched closer to her. She could smell the garlic on his breath. "I have come for the parcel. Either you have it or—"

"Let me explain—," she said, staring at him.

"Please explain," he said. "But do it quickly."

For the first time Lezlie noticed his features. No matter how she tried to stretch it, he could not have been more than thirty. If he were only thirty, she reasoned, how could he possibly have a grown daughter. He was shorter than she was, at most five-foot-six. He was extremely thin, and very dark like a typical Jordanian with an olive complexion.

"How old is your daughter, Mr. Taisir?"

"My daughter? I have no daughter. I came for the parcel."

"You have no daughter?"

"I did not come to talk about children. I met you so that you could hand me the parcel."

"I'm sorry, I do not have a parcel for you. But about your daughter—"

"I have no time to waste," he said and bent closer. "Give me the parcel," his voice sounded threatening. "Now!"

"I have no parcel," she said, hoping her features looked more defiant than she felt.

"Then why do you waste my time?"

"Waste your time? I came to the hotel, looking for you. The clerk denied any knowledge of you and then—"

"I have no time to waste further," he said. They both looked up as another group of tourists moved toward them. She saw Virginia Hislip and gave her a brief nod. Taisir noticed it and saw Virginia smile and wave at her.

"I told you to come alone."

"I'm not with her—"

"I'll contact you again," he said. He walked quickly away across the paved street of Jerash toward the amphitheater. She lost sight of him as he mingled with a group. A few minutes later she returned to the taxi, still carrying the coat. Travis had been chatting with the guide. He noticed the coat and asked, "He didn't show?"

"I'm not sure," she said.

"What happened?"

Lezlie quickly explained and added, "I just could not believe he was Taisir without some kind of proof."

"That does sound a bit strange," Travis answered.

"It doesn't make sense," she said. "I mean, that man simply could not have a daughter my age. If he wasn't Taisir, how would he know I had something for him? Why did he call it a parcel? Hap said it was a gift. But that man acted as though it was a package I was delivering like a messenger."

"Maybe he came as a representative of Taisir," Travis said. "Maybe Hap had told him he was bringing a gift."

"All I know is the man was rude, and if he was a representative of Taisir, why didn't he tell me?"

"His lack of English, maybe?" Travis asked.

"More than that. In fact I—well, I just don't like the feel of any of this."

"Maybe we shouldn't have come—"

"Maybe," she said. "But I had to come. That was my first reason."

"Your first? You mean there were other reasons?"

"There were two."

"What's the other?"

"Maybe I can tell you that later," she said.

They returned to the Tyche Hotel just before sunset. They picked up their keys at the desk and walked upstairs. Travis unlocked her door, took the key out, and handed it to her. She started to say something, and with a quick glance into her room, she gasped. "Something's wrong," she said.

He followed her inside. "Wrong?"

"Someone's been going through my things."

"Oh, come on, Lezlie—"

"I'm serious," she said. "Someone's gone through my things."

"Everything looks pretty neat to me."

"That's what I mean. Neater than when I left." She tossed the coat on a chair and went immediately to the opened suitcase.

"The maid probably did it. Look, your bed's neatly made."

"The maid's been here, but it's more than just straightening."

Her suitcase was open on top of the dresser. "I can tell by the way someone stacked my clothes."

"Seems fine to me," Travis said.

"Let me show you," she said. "See here, I always put my underwear on the side with the pockets. Just a habit I guess, but always there." It was on the other side of the suitcase.

"Are you sure?"

"Positive."

She looked through the clothes in the suitcase and pawed through her flight bag.

"Anything missing?" Travis asked.

"I don't think so," she said as she pushed open the door to the closet. "No, everything's here."

Their eyes met. "The package," Lezlie said. "They came here to get it—whatever *it* is."

"But that's crazy—"

"Crazy or not," Lezlie said, "someone has been in my room, searching for it." She sat on the edge of the bed. "You know, this doesn't make sense to me."

"It doesn't make sense to me either."

"I mean, think about it. My husband has a coat made for the daughter of a business associate. It's a gift. I'm bringing it as a present from my husband. I arrive here, and a man hassles me for a parcel that I don't have. He insults me and runs away. Hours later I return to the room and find out it's been rifled."

"Unless—"

"Unless what?"

"Let me see the coat," Travis said.

She picked it off the chair where she had thrown it. Travis examined it carefully. It consisted of a variety of skins arranged in sections approximately six inches long. The coat bore no label other than HANDMADE BY MARSHA. Travis felt the fur carefully and then the lining. He could discover nothing unusual.

"You thought Hap had someone sew in a kilo of cocaine, I'll bet," Lezlie said.

"I don't know what I thought," he answered, but his face showed her that was exactly what he thought. "All I know is there must be an explanation for this."

"I don't know what's going on," she said, "but I've made up my mind. I'm going to leave tomorrow."

"What about Taisir?"

"I did what I knew to do about contacting him. He obviously got my message through the clerk or from someone behind the desk. I'll arrange to go into Israel tomorrow. He can contact me or follow me. Otherwise—"

"Otherwise, you'll take the coat back home and then decide what to do with it."

"I don't know what else to do."

They ate dinner in the hotel dining room. In many ways it reminded them of a European hotel, the menu offering a wide selection of fish with both American- and European-type meals. After dinner they decided to go for a walk. The evening had cooled off. She put on a sweater, grabbed her purse, and strapped it over her shoulder. They walked from the hotel down a steep hillside. The streetlights had come on, and they could see fairly well.

Amman seemed to be one series of hills after another. They commented on the small houses, all made of stone or concrete blocks, which dotted both sides of the street. High walls enclosed many dwellings with bars covering windows and doors. In front of most of the houses they saw parked Volvos, Mercedes, and Peugeots. "I'd call this concrete city," Travis said.

"If you look on the hillside and see all the stones and rocks, you can see why. It makes cheap building material."

"I suppose you're right," he said.

They continued downhill in silence.

They approached an area where the streetlight had burned out. They could see enough so that they would not stumble on the sidewalk. Travis moved closer to Lezlie and was just ready to take her hand. At that moment, a man jumped out of the shadows and grabbed Lezlie's purse. He might have gotten away with it, but as he jerked on the shoulder strap, in a reflexive action she struck him with her arm. Her blow knocked him off balance, and Travis tackled the man as Lezlie landed a wild kick on his shins. Travis knocked him to the ground. He struggled with the attacker, but Travis, being larger and heavier, held the attacker down. Lezlie bent over, grabbed an arm of the assailant, and bent it behind his back.

Travis helped the man get up, keeping his arm bent behind him. Travis propelled him into the street so they could see his face.

"You're the man who claimed to be Taisir," Lezlie said.

"I am Taisir. Please let me go."

"You've gone to an awful lot of trouble and underhanded tactics," Travis said. "We want an explanation."

"Who are you? You are not Captain Austin."

"I am *Mrs.* Austin's friend," Travis said. "Tell us what is going on."

"What is going on? Yes, am I not asking the same question?"

"You search my room. You try to steal my purse—why?" Lezlie asked.

"Why? Did you not start this? Did you not ask for me at the hotel?"

"Yes, I did—"

"And did you not bring me a parcel from your husband?"

"What kind of parcel?" Travis asked.

"A parcel." He shrugged. "Who can say? Perhaps," he gestured with his hands, indicating the size of a shoebox.

"My husband gave me nothing like that—"

"Then why do you waste my time?"

"Yes, I—I think I made a mistake," she said.

"That is not your mistake, Mrs. Austin," Taisir said. "Your mistake is trying to withhold what must be handed over to me."

"Wait a minute," Travis said. "You don't go threatening Mrs. Austin—"

The small man took a step backward and paused as though making a great effort to control himself. Travis released his arm. Taisir straightened up and said, "Sir, you do not know me. I do not know you. Nor do I know this lady. She asked for me. She claims to be the wife of Captain Austin. If she is his wife, then she knows what I want and she has it for me."

"But all I know is—"

"Lezlie, you have no parcel," Travis said. "There's obviously been some misunderstanding."

"Then why did you ask for me?" The man asked, his chin jutting forward.

"I know you had some business dealings with my husband. He— he said you had a daughter—a daughter about my age and that I was to—"

"Do not confuse me," he said. "I have come to collect the parcel. Give it to me. I take it. I leave. You do not see me again. I do not conduct any more business with Captain Austin."

"My husband—my husband died of a heart attack two months ago," Lezlie said.

Shock filled Taisir's face. "Died? But—but the parcel—"

Travis laid his arm on Lezlie's shoulder. "We're going back to the hotel. This lady has no package for you, sir. Leave her alone, or we'll call the police." They turned around and headed back up the street toward the Tyche Hotel.

Travis looked back once and saw the man standing in the darkened street as they walked together. Taisir yelled at them in Arabic. Even though they did not understand a single word, his meaning was clear.

Chapter 9

Lezlie and Travis sat at a corner table in the Zeus Lounge at the Tyche Hotel. Soft music in minor keys played in the background. They scarcely noticed. One couple sat in the middle of the room, speaking quietly in Arabic. Lezlie and Travis sipped Cokes and didn't talk for a long time. Travis signaled the waiter for another Coke, which he brought immediately.

"I'm confused," Lezlie said.

Travis took her hand in his. "I'm glad I came with you to Jordan."

"I'm glad too," she said. "I don't know what I would have done without you."

"You're not just confused, you're scared. Why, you're actually shaking—"

"Maybe just a little chilly, I think," she said, trying not to look directly at him.

"You're scared, and you're confused."

"Scared. Confused. That says it pretty well."

"Want to talk about all of this?" he asked.

"I think I need to," she said, "except I don't know what to say."

"Let's just talk."

"I need to sort it all out in my head," she said. "Number one, Hap said he was coming to Jordan to give a gift to Taisir's daughter. A coat. He said the daughter was about my age."

"Taisir has no daughter so that means—"

"Either he's an imposter or—"

"Or that Hap wasn't telling the truth."

"That's what troubles me most," Lezlie said. "That Hap might lie to me."

"Maybe he wanted to spare you—"

"Spare me what?" she asked.

Travis shrugged. "Just—just a guess."

"Travis, you're a good friend. You were Hap's best friend. You don't need to cover up—"

"Best friend!" He slammed down the glass he had been sipping from. "Lezlie, this is the second or third time you've called me Hap's best friend. I was not, am not, and never have been his best friend. I doubt Hap ever had a best friend!"

A shock wave slapped Lezlie, and she sat speechless.

"I'm sorry," Travis said. "I shouldn't have said all of that."

"No, no, it's all right," she answered.

"Your face tells me otherwise."

"I'm shocked—but I'm glad you told me the truth."

"Rotten of me—"

"No, Travis, not rotten at all. I'm afraid I assumed some things, and I was wrong."

"Maybe you were wrong."

"Perhaps it's time for you to tell me about Hap."

"Lezlie, I really don't have anything to tell you."

"You're holding back on me."

"Am I?"

"Apparently I lived a sheltered life with Hap."

"Maybe you did."

"I should have realized that. Like the day you got mad at me at the bank, accusing me of knowing about that money—"

"I'm convinced now that you didn't know. I apologized for that, and I'll apologize again if you want."

"I'm not asking for apologies," she said. She leaned forward and took both his hands in hers. "Apparently I never knew Hap at all."

"Maybe—maybe you didn't want to know about him," Travis said softly.

She nodded her head. "You're right. I didn't."

"But why, Lezlie?"

"If I had known, our marriage would not have lasted as long as it did."

"You mean that?"

She nodded her head again. "Yes, I'm a very old-fashioned girl in some ways. You know how the words go. There was a marriage ceremony when I said things like 'For better or for worse.' "

"A lot of people make promises."

"I meant them."

"But Hap didn't."

"He meant them. He simply couldn't live up to them."

"But you loved him?"

"Loved? I know he swept me off my feet. I made promises to him and to God. I didn't want to face the possibility of what 'worse' might mean. So I tried to close all that off."

"Were you happy, Lezlie?"

She pulled her hands away and fidgeted with her purse. "About as happy as most—no, that's not true. The last three months I was miserable."

"I had a feeling that was the case," he said.

"Did Hap—you know, did Hap ever say anything?"

"Are you kidding?"

"No, I'm not. I thought he might have confided in you."

"Confided?"

"I thought Hap might have said something."

Travis said, "He was the one man with the jokes, always good for a laugh. He was the center of fun at any party, always one to liven up any atmosphere. But serious talk? Not Hap."

"He was the same way with me," she said. "When he wasn't laughing, he shut up and said nothing. When I tried to talk to him about feelings or things of a serious nature—"

"Lezlie, I worked with the guy for years. I know."

"I should have known," Lezlie said.

"Even if he had talked to anyone," Travis said, "I would probably have been the last—"

"Why do you say that?"

Travis took a sip of his Coke, stared at her for a moment, and then said, "He was afraid you'd leave him, and I would chase you again."

Lezlie tried to smile. "That you'd chase me?"

"Hap knew I loved you."

"He did?"

"He used to kid me a lot about it. Said it was obvious."

"He knew that?" she said, a puzzled look filling her face. "I never knew," she said as her voice grew husky.

"You never knew? What did you think was going on? I mean those dates, the times we had together—"

"I thought I was your friend."

"You were, Lezlie, but you were more."

"You never told me."

"I—well, I—I," he stuttered, looking down at his fingers. "I just don't do well talking about things like that, but—." He took a deep breath and then looked into her eyes. "Lezlie, I don't know how to say this very well—"

"Don't apologize. Just say whatever you need—"

"I love you," Travis said, and their eyes held each other.

"You do?"

"I loved you that day in Athens. I've always loved you—I still do." Lezlie dropped her gaze. "I never knew. Honestly."

"Would it have made any difference if you had known?"

"I'm not sure," she said.

"You still would have married Hap, wouldn't you?"

"I don't know," she said. "I—I don't think so."

"Ah, c'mon, Lezlie—"

"Do you know why I accepted his first invitation?"

"Because he asked you."

"Because he asked me, *and* because you didn't say anything to indicate that it made any difference to you."

"Oh," he said. "I guess—well, I just didn't think that you would—could—love me."

"The only time—the only time I ever thought you really cared for me was the night at the party—"

"When they played 'Destined to Love'?"

"Yes," she said and dropped her head. "I saw hurt on your face—"

"And I loved you even then, Lezlie."

At that moment a waiter came up behind Travis, handed Lezlie a note, and walked away. She opened the slip of paper, read it, glanced around, but could see no one else. She handed it to Travis. The note read: THE PARCEL. I MUST HAVE IT. NO MORE GAMES.

"What shall we do?" she asked.

"I don't know," he answered. "Except I think we ought to leave Amman—right away."

"Maybe you're right."

"Want me to arrange the trip home?"

"Home? Oh, no," she said. "I'm going to Israel first. Remember?"

"You still want to do that?"

She nodded. "I *am* going to do it."

"If that's what you want," he said. "I'll go to the desk and find out about arrangements."

Ten minutes later Travis returned. "We'll have a taxi waiting for us in front of the hotel at eight in the morning. It'll drive us as far as the border. Apparently there's a kind of no-man's-land for a mile or so, and Jordanians can't cross over. They'll arrange for a taxi to meet us on the Israeli side."

"Sounds all right to me."

"Otherwise we'd have to fly out of here to Egypt and then from Egypt into Israel. This seems the simplest way."

"I'm game," she said.

"They also told me at the desk that it will take a couple of hours to get through customs. They're very strict going into Israel."

"What have we got to lose?" she said. "I don't have a package. We've thoroughly checked the coat."

They talked together another half hour and then collected their keys and went upstairs to their rooms. As he unlocked Lezlie's door, Travis said, "I'm going to stay here with you tonight."

"Don't spoil it, Travis," she said. "I mean, I'm not open to that kind of thing."

"I'm going to stay in the room," he said, "so that if Taisir or anyone else tries to get in, I'll be here to protect you."

Lezlie walked into the room, leaving the door ajar. With her back toward him, not wanting him to see the flush on her face, she said, "I'm sorry. I thought—"

"I know what you thought," he said. "I'm telling you what I mean."

"I would feel safer—"

"Be right back," he said.

He hurried to his own room and returned shortly with pajamas and a shaving kit.

Later he took one of her pillows and an extra blanket from the closet and slept on the carpeted floor next to the door.

The next morning they entered the waiting taxi. The driver put their two suitcases in the front seat next to him. He smiled when they got in and indicated that he did not speak English. He mumbled, "Border," in English, and they nodded.

They scarcely paid any attention to the road. It was dry and rocky. Travis rested his head on her shoulder, and she tried to concentrate on looking out the window. Instead she saw only her reflection. Over and over again she replayed the events of the past two days. So much had happened that she had not been able to sort it all out. Signs printed in Arabic and English began to appear on the highway, indicating they were near the border, and finally that they were approaching Allenby Bridge. The taxi crossed the bridge, and the driver pulled to the side of the road. He shut off the engine and turned around.

"I'm going to take you to the border, Mrs. Austin," he said in English. "But first, if you will kindly hand me the parcel—" He pointed a gun at her.

"I don't have a parcel!"

"You do not understand Israeli customs," he said. "They will take everything out of your suitcase and your purse. They will even search your body. You cannot hide the parcel from them."

"I told you—," she said not sure what to do and wishing that Travis were not asleep. His head still rested on her shoulder, and then he slumped forward. In a split second he grabbed the arm that held the gun and with his other hand gave it a karate chop. The driver dropped the gun. It fell to the floor in the backseat. Travis scooped up the weapon and pressed it against the back of the driver's head. "Now let's move on to the border."

"But you cannot get through customs with the parcel—"

Travis pushed the gun into his scalp. "Drive."

A minute later the driver stopped outside an isolated building. Armed soldiers walked around. Several buses pulled in behind them, followed by two taxis. It took only a quick glance to see how the system worked. People laid their suitcases outside the building. A customs worker carried them inside.

Travis slipped the gun under the backseat, reached forward, and grabbed the two suitcases. He opened the door on his side and got out. Lezlie picked up the fur coat and her purse and started out on her side. She looked at Travis. "What about him?"

"With all those armed soldiers around he's not going to shoot us. Besides he's got to get out of the car and into the backseat to retrieve his weapon."

Travis pulled out two bills and dropped them on the driver's lap. The man sat immobile. "Thanks for the ride," Travis said.

"You will not get the parcel through Israeli customs!"

Travis slammed the door and hurried around to the other side. He carried both suitcases while she took the briefcase and flight bag. They entered the long building where people stacked their suitcases, and then lined up to go inside.

They put their suitcases down next to others. An official-looking man in a green military uniform, wearing a name tag which they could not read, pointed at them to go through a door. They walked inside and showed their passports. Lezlie went into a room where she was given a body search. Travis was searched while he stood next to the passport control. They moved a few feet ahead and saw suitcases piled in front of them. They realized they had only to find their suitcases, claim them, walk up to the counter, open them, and have them inspected.

"There's ours," Lezlie said and moved forward. Travis put his suitcase and briefcase on the counter first with Lezlie behind him.

"You travel together?" the customs man asked, his English precise and very American.

"Yes, together."

"We hope you will like our little country," he said and smiled. He took every item out of Travis's suitcase, checked the lining of the case and then said, "You may put it all back inside." He did the same with the briefcase.

Travis picked up his suitcase and briefcase and walked out of the way.

"And now, miss, will you open your purse please?" He followed the same procedure with the purse, the suitcase, and the flight bag as he had for Travis. He stared at her coat. "Such a beautiful coat you carry," he said. "I've never seen one like it before."

"Yes," she said. "It is unusual."

He touched it. "Very soft fur. Perhaps a bit too heavy for this time of year, I think."

"Yes, you're right. It is heavy for this time of year."

"You bought it in Jordan?"

"No," she answered. "I brought it with me from America."

"Very beautiful," he said. "Very beautiful. A very nice coat." He felt the fur again. His fingers nimbly pressing various pieces of fur. "You must be careful with this coat. It is expensive. People may try to steal such a beautiful coat."

"Thank you. I'll be careful," she said.

After the man had searched through all her luggage, he marked an X on the outside of the suitcase and handed back her purse and flight bag. She took them and walked over to the exit. Travis was standing just inside the door, waiting for her. She started to go outside, and he pulled her back. "Uh, let's stop for a cup of coffee or something first," he said.

"But I don't need—"

"You need a cup, really," he said.

He nudged her, and they walked over to a small window where a man sold coffee, tea, and soft drinks. He purchased two cups of tea in paper cups. They sat in a corner and drank slowly. He leaned forward and whispered, "I saw Taisir outside. He was talking to a taxi driver."

"What should we do?"

"I'm not sure," he said. "I need to think."

He closed his eyes and rubbed his chin. A minute later he looked up. A group of people suddenly came into the building to go through customs. He could hear buses stopping out in front and people's voices speaking in hurried English. It was then that Travis knew what to do.

Chapter 10

Travis nudged Lezlie and nodded in the direction of a group of people coming out of the building. "Remember her?" he whispered.

She searched the group for a moment and said, "Yes, that's Virginia somebody-or-other. She wears a name tag. If we can get closer, we can find out her last name—"

"Her name is not important right now."

He pulled her back against the wall. They waited until a group of more than twenty people had gathered outside the customs building. Travis furtively glanced at the taxi. He no longer saw Taisir. A white Mercedes, parked next to the taxi, slowly pulled away. A thin man sat in the backseat, but Travis dared not stare long enough for a positive identification. Slowly he and Lezlie headed outside.

Members of the Presbyterian Pilgrimage group placed their suitcases in a pile on the sidewalk. Two Israelis came and packed them in the storage compartment under the large red-and-white Volvo bus. Travis shoved his and Lezlie's suitcases in with the others. He watched until the porters packed them inside the bus.

"Now what?" Lezlie asked.

"Follow me," he said.

They waited until people started boarding the bus. There were two doors. Most of the people went in through the front although a few of them entered by the back door. He took Lezlie's arm and started moving casually toward the back door.

She whispered, "But what if it's full?"

"Then we'll say we made a mistake and get off."

"Do you think we can get away with it?"

"Let's get on, darling," he said loud enough for others to hear.

They sat near the back and carefully avoided looking at anyone. They both put on sunglasses and kept their heads low. From the corner of his eye, Travis counted the seats. When it looked as though everyone had gotten on, he saw there were still three empties. He sighed. "I think it's going to work," he whispered.

A tall man stood up in the front of the bus, looked over the group, and announced, "We need to be sure that everyone has boarded. Logan, are your folks here and accounted for?"

The man sitting in front of Travis looked around and yelled back, "My group's all here." Two others answered the same thing for their groups.

The tall man announced, "Then I guess we're ready to go."

As the bus rolled out, Lezlie rested her head on Travis's shoulder, careful not to look out the window. As they pulled away, Travis saw that the taxi driver got out of his car and walked toward the door of the customs building where people were still streaming out.

A short Israeli stood up in the front of the bus, holding a hand microphone. "Good morning, ladies and gentlemen. I am your guide during your trip in Israel. You may call me George. We are now entering into Israel from the north side. We are heading toward the ancient city of Jericho. . . ."

"And now we are stopping here in Capernaum," George said, "and we are going to a restaurant where you will taste the famous Saint Peter's fish for which this region is known."

"A fancy name for carp," the man in front of Travis chirped as the bus stopped.

People began standing up, stretching, and moving toward the doors. Lezlie and Travis waited until most of the others had gotten up. They stood up and inched into the aisle.

"What do we do now?" Lezlie whispered. "We're away from that horrible Taisir, but our bags are still in this bus."

"Let's go inside while I try to think of something," Travis said.

They looked ahead and saw a pathway of bougainvillea in shades of red and pink lining both sides. Further on they came into the dining area with tables in the open air. Trellises of bougainvillea added decoration and protection from the full glare of the sun. Waiters hopped busily from table to table, serving guests who had already come from other tour buses.

As they approached the tables, Travis hesitated, not sure if they ought to chance sitting with the Presbyterian Pilgrimage group.

"Excuse me," a voice said behind them. They both turned around. "I'm Wayne Smith," he said. "I'm the head of this pilgrimage."

Lezlie immediately recognized him as the man who had made an announcement at the Tyche Hotel. She looked at Travis, waiting for him to speak.

"We're stowaways," Travis said. "Or whatever you call it on a bus."

"Yes, I know."

"We'd like to explain to you what happened."

"Please do," Wayne said, his pleasant southern drawl belying the seriousness of his face.

"May we sit down and buy your lunch?" Travis asked. "I'd like to tell you what's happening. I think I could do it better over food."

"Of course," Wayne smiled. He led the way and asked the waiter for a table for three. He also explained that they were part of the pilgrimage group.

"Except," Travis said, "we are paying for our own."

Wayne raised an eyebrow. "You do have money, then?"

"Of course," Lezlie said. "There's no problem with money."

Wayne sighed audibly. "I'm glad you've got money. But if you have, then why—"

"We also have airline tickets. We really haven't done anything illegal," Travis said, "other than stealing a ride on your bus."

"It's just that we want to avoid—," Lezlie started.

Travis held up his hand. "Let me try to explain it, Lezlie," he said. He looked down and read the name tag so that he was sure of the man's name. "Look, Wayne, we do have a problem. We encountered trouble with some people in Amman. They tried to rob us near the Allenby Bridge."

"The man even had a gun," Lezlie said, "and Travis took it away from him."

"Naturally I didn't carry his gun through customs. I had to get rid of it," Travis said. "We had arranged for a taxi to take us into Israel after we passed through customs. But we saw one of the members of the gang talking to the taxi driver—"

"So you got into our bus," Wayne said.

"Our luggage is also in the bus," Lezlie added.

As though having a sudden inspiration, Travis said, "Maybe this will work. You still have a few empty seats on the bus we rode on, right?"

"Yes," Wayne said slowly as though realizing what was coming.

"Let us pay you—anything you want. Then we can go with you to—where?"

"Tonight we are staying at a kibbutz in upper Galilee. The next night we will sleep in Jerusalem," Wayne said.

"Can you let us tag along with you until we reach Jerusalem? We'll pay," Travis said.

"Well, I suppose—," Wayne said considering the situation. "But I don't know how much to charge. It may also complicate sleeping and eating arrangements—"

"At least let us go with you for now," Travis said.

"We'll give you cash," Lezlie said.

"I suppose it's all right," Wayne said, "but if you've eluded them—"

"We eluded them at the border," Lezlie said, "but they may keep looking for us."

"And Doctor Smith," Travis said with a smile, "I don't think they would harm you, but if you are worried—"

"I'm not worried," he said.

"At the first sign of any trouble we leave you. That's our promise," Travis said.

"It's not the danger I'm thinking of," Wayne said. "It's the whole purpose in our being together on this pilgrimage and—"

Lezlie handed him five one-hundred-dollar bills. "This ought to cover any expenses we might incur and take care of your inconvenience." She dropped the money on the table. Wayne stared at the bills but made no effort to pick them up.

"That's an outrageous amount. Far too much."

"Money is not a problem with us," Travis said. "We got on your bus because we believed our lives were in danger."

"I understand that," Wayne said. A waiter appeared and carried a plate stacked high with pita bread in one hand, and in the other, a tray containing a small dish of lettuce soaked in olive oil and vinegar, and next to that, a plate of cut-up tomatoes. In the center of the table they saw a bowl of sesame butter.

Wayne looked at the food. "Do you know how to eat this?" he asked.

"I'm afraid I don't," Lezlie answered.

Wayne took the top pita, tore the round, flat bread in half, then pulled the two sides of the bread apart. "They also call it pocket bread. And you can see why." He picked up some vegetables and stuffed them inside. Lezlie and Travis began doing the same.

"Now," Wayne said after a few bites, "here are the problems from my point of view."

"I guess we only thought of our dilemma," Travis said. "Sorry."

"First," Wayne said, "this is a religious pilgrimage. I think it's important for you to understand that. Even if you stay only a couple of days with us. You see, we're Presbyterians—"

"I'm an Episcopalian," Travis answered.

"I'm Baptist," Lezlie said, "I mean, sort of."

Wayne smiled, and his blue eyes looked playful. "That's about right then. Presbyterians probably stand somewhere in the middle in theology and church structure. But it's more—"

"I'm also a Christian," Lezlie said not looking at Travis.

"So am I," Travis said turning his gaze toward Lezlie. "And as a believer in Christ, I have no problem being with a religious group."

"I don't either," Lezlie said.

"We have worship services together each day—"

"I'd enjoy being with you," Travis said.

Wayne nodded. "Second, this is too much money. I'll figure out the approximate cost and let you know tomorrow—"

"Take the rest as a contribution," Lezlie said.

"I'd rather not."

"Please do." Lezlie pressed.

Wayne shrugged. "It's really too much—"

"You helped us when we needed you," Travis said. "That's worth more than money."

Wayne smiled, picked up the bills, folded them, and put them in the breast pocket of his safari suit.

"By the way," Travis said, "how did you know we were on the bus?"

Wayne smiled. "I saw you get on."

"Why didn't you say something then?"

He chuckled and took a bite of his pita bread. He chewed slowly and paused. "The way you got on made me realize that you weren't boarding the wrong bus by mistake."

"And you let us get on? Why?"

Wayne smiled and rubbed his jaw. "I don't know. Maybe I felt sorry for you. Maybe I sensed you needed help."

"Whatever the reason, thank you," Lezlie said. "And God bless you."

"Oh, He does! And quite well."

"You've been very, very kind," Travis added.

They suddenly became aware that most of the members of Wayne's group had finished their meal and were milling around, snapping pictures, and gradually moving toward the buses.

"Let's hurry and finish this pita so that we can have our fish. Then we'll have to get aboard," Wayne said and winked.

Fifteen minutes later they hurried inside the bus and sat in silence as they pulled away from the city of Capernaum. The guide pointed out restoration projects going on and outlined the biblical history of the city of Capernaum. Lezlie and Travis sat looking at each other but saying nothing. He took her hand in his, and she squeezed his in return. He pulled Lezlie close and put his arm around her. He whispered, "I love you."

"I—I think I love you too," she said.

"You don't know?"

"I'm still too confused to know anything for certain, but I think—I think I've loved you for a long time."

"Me, too," he said and kissed her on the top of the head.

"Travis, when we get to this kibbutz where we're staying tonight, do you suppose we could talk?"

"We will definitely talk," he said.

"I'd like that," Lezlie answered and closed her eyes.

"We are now pulling into the kibbutz called Ayelet Hashahar," the guide said. "A kibbutz is a collective settlement in which not only the production but also the household is communal. This particular one was founded in nineteen fifteen by young people who emigrated from Russia. They came here when this land was absolutely arid. The settlers worked under hard conditions during the first decade, particularly suffering from the lack of water and isolation from other Jewish settlements. Their members increased very slowly. Today it is one of the most prosperous kibbutzim in Israel. They are one of the larger fruit producers in the country and have developed diversified farming and livestock enterprises. Their beehives are the largest in Israel. In the last few years they've added fish ponds, getting their water supply from canals which have been constructed by this kibbutz. More recently they've added a bookbinding shop and a guest house. The guest house gives a large number of visitors the possibility to tour the upper Galilee region and to gain an insight into kibbutz life."

The passengers on the bus looked around as the bus turned off the highway, making a right turn into Kibbutz Ayelet Hashahar. Many of them expected primitive-looking buildings. They all expressed surprise when the bus pulled up in front of a modern building. To the left they saw five buildings which resembled motel complexes in many American cities.

"This really is different," someone said.

"I expected to be camping out," another replied.

Lezlie and Travis followed the others as they got off the bus and waited for their luggage. Wayne arranged for them to have rooms next to each other. They washed up and went to dinner that evening. Immediately after dinner, as they walked across the lobby of the main building, Lezlie said, "Let's walk around the grounds."

"You don't need to ask me a second time," Travis said. Hand in hand they strolled past the buses and down the paved road, which was wide enough for only one car. Darkness had settled in, but enough light shone from buildings that they could see where they were going.

"Travis," Lezlie said as she slowed down. "I told you I came on this trip for two reasons. First, to meet Habib Taisir and give him the coat. I guess I blew that one—"

"You tried. That's all you could do."

"I still don't know what I'm going to do about the coat—"

"We'll figure that out," he said. "Right now let's enjoy being here with these people."

"All right," she said and started walking rapidly again. They came to a fork in the road. A bright light shone, and they could see flowers planted along the side of the road. Lezlie bent down and picked one. She smelled it and indicated disappointment because it lacked a fragrance.

Travis watched her silently for a moment. Then he said, "You mentioned you had a second reason for coming."

"Yes," she answered slowly. "I've been trying to figure how to say it best."

"Just start," he said.

"Travis," she said, "I'm a Christian. By that I don't mean merely that I'm not a Muslim or a Hindu—"

"I understand."

"I really believe in Jesus Christ, like I told Wayne Smith."

"I believe, too, Lezlie."

"But with me, it's—well—different."

"Different? How?"

"God used to be important in my life. From the time I was thirteen, when I joined the church, I've believed that Jesus Christ is important."

Travis put his arm around her waist, and they started up a slight incline. "Yes," he said. "I understand that."

"Somewhere along the way I got away from God," Lezlie said.

"It happens to a lot of us," he said.

"But I really turned away—"

"When? Why don't you tell me about it?"

"During college I suppose is when I started backing away from God. First my studies kept me so busy I missed a Sunday or two at church. After a while, it became a habit not to go and—"

"Eventually you became a religious dropout?"

She smiled, and even in the dusk he could see her features. "That's one way of saying it. All I know is that I backed away from God."

She paused, waiting for Travis to reply. He cleared his throat. "And?"

"So," she said, taking a deep breath, "in time I ignored God's influence in my life. Then I met you—and finally Hap."

"And you married Hap."

"And the marriage wasn't right, not even from the first day."

"Then why did you marry him?"

"I don't know. I lost my head. He rushed me. Perhaps I fell in love with the idea of being in love, getting married—"

"Thanks for telling me all that, Lezlie."

"That's not quite all. About two weeks before Hap's heart attack something happened to me and—," she hesitated and looked into his blue eyes. "I've been wanting to tell you about it but didn't know how."

"I'm listening."

Their schedules allowed for Hap and Lezlie to have four days together from Sunday through Wednesday. Early Sunday morning Hap said, "What do you want to do today? Anything—just name it."

"Do you mean it? Anything?"

"Of course," he smiled. "We can fly to L.A.—"

"I know what I'd like to do."

"Of course. Just name it."

"I'd like to go to church."

"Be serious, Lez. How about Las Vegas or New York?"

"I am serious, Hap."

"I don't go for that kind of stuff," he said. "You know that."

"Yes, I know."

"You're not angry, are you, baby?"

"Angry? No. But I've decided to go anyway. Alone or with you."

"Don't get on that religious kick again."

"Again? I've talked about God maybe three times since we were married, and you call that a religious kick?"

"Which makes it three times too many," he said. He jumped out of bed and strode into the bathroom, slamming the door behind him. She heard him turn on the shower. Lezlie lay in bed several minutes unsure of what to do. Then she made up her mind. She got up slowly.

Lezlie walked into the kitchen, started the coffee, and hurriedly cooked breakfast. When the bacon was extra crisp as Hap liked it, Lezlie went to the bathroom and opened the door. "Breakfast is ready."

He came almost immediately, sat down, picked up his fork, and scooped up the scrambled eggs. He didn't even notice that Lezlie had bowed her head to pray.

"Well?" Hap asked after he had finished his eggs and bacon.

"Well, what?"

"Well, what are we doing today?"

"*I* am going to church—"

"Cut it out, Lez—"

"I'd like to have you go with me," she said softly, not meeting his gaze.

Hap took another bite of his toast and a quick gulp of his coffee. "I don't care very much about religion."

"I'm going. It's important."

"Important? Not to me."

"Important to me."

"Suit yourself!" he said and slapped the cup against the saucer. "Suit yourself, lady—"

"Hap, I want God in control of my life. I want Him to be just as important to you."

"Important? You've mentioned Him three times in a year. I don't see that makes Him important. You're just trying to rile me up and throw a wrench into everything—"

Lezlie pushed her plate away. "I'm leaving as soon as I can get dressed. I don't even know where I'm going to church, but I'm going to drive until I find one. Then I'm going inside and sit in a worship service. I'll be back after that."

"I don't expect to be here. I'll be gone for the entire day."

"I'll see you when you get back," she said, struggling to keep her voice level.

Their eyes met for the first time, and she did not look away. It was the first time Lezlie had ever defied him. He got up, knocked the chair over, and walked into the living room. She finished her coffee before she followed him.

He sat stiffly in a stuffed chair, his jaw clamped tight, and his eyes vacant.

"Hap, would it help if I said *please*?" She hoped her voice had the right kind of lightness about it. She kissed his cheek and pushed back a lock of his blond hair.

"Lezlie, I want you to listen to something, and then I don't want to talk about it anymore."

"I'm listening," she said and sat down on the sofa, trying to appear relaxed.

"I know about God, church, and all of that. I've heard sermons. I've even read the Bible myself. Believe it or not," he stopped, stood up, and started to pace the room. "I can even quote the Twenty-third Psalm."

"I believe you," she answered. "And that ought to make you want—"

"But sometimes," he interrupted. "Sometimes a man knows he's gone so far in the opposite direction that there's no turning back for him."

"There's always a chance to turn back," she said, tears instantly filling her eyes. "That's what I'm trying to do now."

"You can probably make it," he said turning his back on her. "But I've gone too far."

"Don't. Don't," she said jumping up and coming behind him. She put her arms around him and laid her head on his shoulder. "Hap, God will always forgive you—anybody."

Gently he unwrapped her arms, turned around, and pushed her away. He looked into her eyes. "I'm not interested. I thought I made that clear."

"Maybe if you would come with me just this one time."

"I'm not interested. If I ever become interested, I'll tell you before I talk to anyone else."

"But you won't go with me today?"

"Not today or next week or at any time!"

A quarter of an hour later, Lezlie left the apartment. She got into her car and hardly realized which direction she had taken. She drove until she saw the steeple of a church up ahead. She looked at her watch. It was 10:38. Even though she realized most churches did not start that early, she parked across the street from the church. Lezlie hesitated only a fraction of a second before getting out of her car.

Lezlie never did notice what kind of church it was. It did not matter anyway. She was there. She could sit in silence.

Lezlie had expected an emotional feeling, but none came—not then or later. She sat in a pew near the back in the empty church. Gradually people drifted in, filling up the room. Just before 11:00 a pianist started to play. Minutes later the robed minister and choir marched into the sanctuary from a side door. She sat through the entire service.

At the end of the hour-long worship service she exited by a side door so she wouldn't have to talk to anyone. Even though she had had no emotional experience, in the quietness of her own heart Lezlie had settled the issue. Whatever the cost in her marriage she would face it as it came. God would be first in her life.

"And so," Lezlie said, "I determined to acknowledge God once again in my life," She stopped and laughed. "Funny, I'm more emotional now telling you about it than I was when it happened."

They stopped and Travis pulled her close. "I'm glad you told me, Lezlie. It means a lot to me."

"You understand what I'm trying to say?"

"Yes, I understand," he said. "And when we marry, we'll—"

"When we marry?" her eyes widened.

"Don't interrupt! *When* we marry, we'll start our life together as two people who want God to be the center in their lives."

"You mean—you mean you feel the same way about God as I do?"

"I don't know if it's the same way, but God is important in my life. I was baptized a year ago at Christ Church Cathedral in New Orleans."

"You mean—"

"Yes, I mean, I found God," he said. "And you had a lot to do with it."

"Me? How?"

"When I lost you to Hap, I knew how much I really lost and—well, I felt so terrible, that I finally turned to God."

"I never knew—"

"It didn't seem important to tell you. Until now."

"I'm glad you did," she said, and the glow in her eyes said it even better than her words.

Travis pulled her tight, and their kisses lingered.

Had they walked back the way they started, they would have seen a white Mercedes entering the grounds of the kibbutz.

Chapter 11

The next day they boarded the bus, which headed south toward Jerusalem, going by way of Haifa, the plains of Megiddo, and Caesarea. Twice in the morning the bus driver noticed the white Mercedes and then again in the afternoon. *Many white Mercedes this year,* he said to himself as he drove on.

By nightfall they reached the foothills of Jerusalem. They went immediately to the expensive Diplomat Hotel. Wayne arranged for rooms for both Lezlie and Travis. He put Lezlie in room 128 near the elevator and on the lobby floor. Travis stayed across the hall.

They changed, showered, and decided to join the Presbyterian Pilgrimage group in the dining hall for dinner. They left the room and walked toward the elevator. Suddenly a man approached from behind.

"There is a gun in Mrs. Austin's back. Walk slowly ahead, and we will go outside the hotel."

"We're not going anywhere," Lezlie said and stopped. "You won't shoot me. Not here anyway."

"I'm tired of games and tired of playing. I want my parcel. Give it to me, and I will leave you alone."

"Lezlie, don't antagonize him," Travis said, at the same time wondering what he could do. He turned slightly, looked down, and saw that Taisir did have a gun at Lezlie's back.

"I am serious," Taisir said. "I will kill if you insist. But I will have the parcel." He nudged Lezlie with the gun, propelling her forward. She took a small step and then a second one, stalling for each precious second. She sensed that once outside the building in the darkened parking lot, they would be helpless. If they were going to escape from Taisir, they had to do it before they left the lobby.

"Do you want to search the room?" she said.

"I searched your luggage in Amman, and I did not find it," he answered.

"Then that should tell you we don't have what you want," Travis said.

"It tells me only that you have cleverly hidden it so that I cannot find it. Is it that you wish to bargain? Perhaps you have given it to someone else to carry for you. Maybe one of the people on the bus carries it."

"You followed the bus?" Lezlie asked.

"But of course. We waited for you outside customs. When you did not hire a taxi, it was only a simple matter to figure out you had taken one of the tour buses. You were clever, but we found you."

They approached the elevator just as it opened. Wayne was standing inside, going down to the dining room. He caught the glint of the gun and the stranger. He lurched forward, just as the door started to close. He grabbed for Taisir and missed, falling on the carpeted floor. His action was enough to distract Taisir who instinctively jerked away. As he did, Travis grabbed the arm holding the gun. Being both taller and more powerful, Travis twisted until Taisir groaned and dropped the gun. It fell silently to the floor.

Travis continued twisting, and Taisir dropped to his knees. Travis grabbed the gun with one hand as he pulled Taisir to his feet with the other. Wayne, fully recovered, grabbed Taisir from the other side.

"Let's get him to my room," Travis said. "We need an explanation from this fellow."

The four of them walked down the hall into Travis's room. They pushed Taisir into a chair. "Now we're ready for you to talk," Travis said.

Taisir stared at Travis, then at Lezlie, and finally at Wayne. "Who is this one?"

"Just a friend," Lezlie said.

"If I must talk, it will be to both of you only," Taisir said and sat stiffly in the chair.

"You will talk if we want you to."

"You will not shoot me, that much I know," Taisir said.

"Perhaps I won't shoot you, but I might rough you up a bit." Travis doubled his fist and shook it in Taisir's face.

A look of fear crossed Taisir's face.

"It's all right, folks," Wayne said. "I have plenty to do. If you need me I can stay, otherwise—." Without giving them a chance to argue, he walked out of the room. The couple turned their attention back to Taisir.

"Now, we want an explanation," Lezlie said. "Tell us exactly what's going on."

"You wish an explanation?" Taisir said. "Do you think I understand myself?" He loosened his tie, took a handkerchief from his pocket, and wiped his face. "You are the one who brings confusion to all of this. You asked for me in Amman. That was the arranged signal. I came to you because you said your name was Austin. Then you force me to chase you everywhere. You want an explanation? First, you give me one."

"We've got the gun," Travis said. "So you tell us." He pointed the gun at Taisir. "I don't plan to shoot you, but I might have an accident if I get too nervous."

Taisir stared at the gun, swallowed, and lowered his head. "All right," he said. "What is it you wish to know?"

"How does the organization work?"

"I can tell you only that the drugs leave the countries where produced in many ways. I do not know much of how that works. I have been told that more than one courier is involved, beginning from packaging in places such as Turkey. One way these goods travel is to the Caribbean and then into the United States. I know little of how that happens."

"But you know that Hap Austin acted as a courier from San Juan to the United States."

"Yes," he mumbled.

Lezlie looked as if she had been slapped. She turned her head toward Travis. "You mean Hap—"

"Ran drugs?" Travis said. "Probably."

"How? How could your people smuggle them in?" she asked. "Especially these days when security is so strict?"

"Ah, many ways," Taisir said, and he relaxed momentarily. "We work with airline people and others."

"Airline people? Why?" And then she realized why.

"You ever been searched?" Travis asked Lezlie. "I don't think I've ever had anything I carry on examined. Have you?"

She shook her head.

"That is how we work. Sometimes the person carries one, even two kilos in a bag. Other times it is put there secretly and taken out after that person reaches the United States."

"But Hap—I hardly know what to say," she said. "Hap? In drugs?"

"Lezlie, I'm surprised that you had no inkling."

"None. Not at all," she said in a dazed voice. "Hap told me nothing about his business. I didn't suspect—"

"Or didn't want to suspect."

"That's not fair," she said as tears formed in her eyes.

"Isn't it? Isn't it fair?"

She stiffened momentarily and said, "Maybe that's the real answer. I kept asking him questions and demanding answers, but I didn't really want to know."

"I'm sorry, Lezlie."

"You—you suspected didn't you? Even before Hap's heart attack you suspected?"

"Yes," he said. "I had no proof, but I suspected."

"Why didn't you tell me?" she said, her eyes blazing. "Why? You owed me that much!"

"Would you have wanted me to tell you?" he said. "Should I have come up to you and said, 'I suspect your husband is dealing in drugs'? I couldn't have done that!"

"Travis—I—suppose you couldn't have, could you?" She laid her arm on his shoulder.

Taisir, seeing they were concentrating on each other, jumped up, knocking Travis over on top of Lezlie, and bolted for the door. He fumbled with the handle momentarily, opened it, and was gone before Travis could struggle to his feet. Travis got up, and raced after him with Lezlie trailing behind. Taisir had disappeared.

"Do we call the police?" Lezlie asked.

"And tell them what?"

She thought for a moment. "I'm not sure."

"We need to figure something out," Travis said. "I mean, Hap talked about Habib Taisir, right?"

"He said he wanted to give a gift to his daughter," she answered.

"It turns out either Taisir has no daughter, or he's a phony."

"But he's so persistent," Lezlie said. "I wonder if—"

"If Hap lied?"

She nodded.

"He lied about a lot of things, didn't he?"

"He lied mostly by silence," she said.

"That's still deception," Travis answered. He took Lezlie in his arms and said, "I'm sorry. I shouldn't have been so harsh."

"It's true, though," she said. "And maybe you needed to say it."

"But he was your husband, and you loved him."

"He was my husband," she said. "I don't really know how I felt. I know now that it wouldn't have lasted."

"It wouldn't?"

"You remember the morning of the flight when Hap had his attack? You saw him kissing me in the first-class galley?"

"I remember."

"I was trying to give him an ultimatum that morning," she said. "Either we straightened out our lives, or I planned to leave."

"Did you tell him that?"

"No, not quite," she said. "I told him we couldn't go on the way we were. He promised me that once we got back to New Orleans, we'd talk and straighten out everything."

"Did you believe him?"

"I don't know," she said. She nestled her head against Travis's shoulder and closed her eyes. "I think he would have tried. I'm not sure he could have kept his promises."

"But you never suspected about the drugs?"

"As I think about it now, I'm convinced that he was trying to get out of the drug dealing, that is, if he was really involved."

"You're still not convinced he was dealing in drugs."

Lezlie pulled away from Travis. "I'm still confused about the whole thing. I want to know, and yet—yet, I don't."

"I'm positive he was involved," Travis said.

"How do you know?"

"Lots of reasons."

"Suppose you tell me just one."

"If I do, will you listen?"

"All right," she said weakly. "I need to know the truth."

"To begin with," Travis said, releasing her and walking over to the window. He pulled the drape open. It was an inside room, and he could see into the lobby. "Hap used to kid a lot about dealing with drugs. Never anything I could put my finger on, but he'd always tell me what the scuttlebutt was about drug activities. On at least two occasions I felt as though he were trying to recruit me."

"Recruit you?"

"You ought to have heard the pitch. Lots of money, adventure, and not many risks. Or so they say."

"If Hap was involved, how did he do it?"

"A lot of ways. One of them involved two pilots who worked together. One of them would charter a private plane. It would fly over the island, and radar would track the plane. Then a second plane would fly directly under the first. All this at night—"

"So radar could not detect the second plane?"

"That's one of the tricks. There are others—"

"Such as—"

"Stowing heroin in personal gear or hiding it among the equipment in places where no one would easily discover it. I heard about one mechanic who managed to reach certain planes immediately after they landed and carefully extracted all shipments. Hap was the one who told me about that fellow. He said he'd heard about it at Toni's. That was one of the times he tried to make a pitch for me to join him."

"When he kept telling you about drugs and shipments?"

"Yes, and how easy it was to get away with it. Of course he always said these were things he heard."

"He seemed to hear a lot," Lezlie said.

"He also said some of the drug dealers worked with flight attendants who concealed drugs on their bodies, even in secret compartments in their bags—"

"In their bags?" Lezlie's face went white. "Oh, no!"

"What is it?"

"Wait a minute," she said softly. She dashed for the door. "I'll be right back. Less than a minute later she returned with her overnight case. She dumped it on the bed. "Check that one out, will you?"

She fell into the chair, dazed. Travis picked up the case, and felt around the inside and outside. Discovering nothing out of the ordinary, he scrutinized it again. "You think this has a hidden compartment?"

"I'm sure of it," she said.

He raised an eyebrow and searched again. Finally he asked, "Ever hear of a suitcase with a false bottom?"

"Who hasn't?"

"This one doesn't have a false bottom," Travis said, "but—" He pulled and pried around the corners of the lid. "Apparently it has a false top." He pulled it open, exposing a cavity inside. "And I suspect—" He probed all four sides of the bag. "Ah," he said, "another clever idea." The back side of the bag also held a cavity approximately two inches thick by eighteen by twelve. "Enough space in your case to smuggle in quite a bit, I would guess."

"I almost caught on," she said. "I'm so stupid for not catching on."

"Or maybe you really didn't want to know."

"Maybe, or was it just that I was so trusting?"

"How did you almost catch on?" Travis asked.

"It was a strange experience," she said. "It was one of those flights I made without you two. I knew I'd be alone all night, so I bought a book at the airport to read. Instead of slipping the book into my purse, I dropped it into the case. I forgot all about the book until we got to the hotel. I knew it was in my bag, and you know Jose, that bellhop who always carries our bags?"

Travis nodded.

"Just like other times," she said. "He took my bag up for me while I registered. When I came up later and opened my case, the book was not there."

"Are you sure?"

"That's not the end of the story. During the next trip I made to San Juan, again Jose carried up my baggage. When I went up to the room and opened the suitcase, guess what?"

"The paperback was in your case."

"Exactly. Definitely there."

Travis frowned. "How did you explain it?"

"I—I didn't," she said. "I just didn't know."

"You know now, don't you?"

"Jose switched cases. It seems so obvious now. You know Hap always packed for me. It sounds silly when I talk about it now, but he was always doing crazy things. He insisted on doing that for me, always making sure I had a full tube of toothpaste, shampoo—you know."

"So that's how he did it," Travis said as he pounded his fist against the wall. "What a cheap thing to do, using you."

"He probably used his own bag too."

"I wouldn't bet on it," Travis said. "He took risks, but he always made sure he was covered—," he stopped quickly. "Sorry, Lezlie. I had no right to make that kind of accusation."

"But I appreciate your protective instinct—"

"It's because—," he said and started to turn away.

"It's because why?" she said.

He turned back and stared at her. "It's because I love you," he said.

"I know you do."

"I've always loved you," Travis said. "Always."

"Travis, I—," but she never finished her sentence. He grabbed her and kissed her passionately on the lips. She clung to him.

Chapter 12

Travis and Lezlie left the Diplomat Hotel on foot in the early light of morning. As they walked up the ascending driveway, they glanced over their shoulders, expecting Taisir to appear at any minute.

Following a map they had obtained at the desk, they began the four-mile journey to the walled city, walking rapidly through a residential area, largely downhill. Travis grabbed her hand and half raced forward. Each felt the closeness of the other.

Lezlie saw the wall first. She pointed. "Oh, look," she called. Although it was still half a mile ahead, they stopped, lingering to enjoy the beauty of the moment.

"Let's hurry up and get a close look," Travis said as he stepped forward and pulled Lezlie's arm. They reached the walled city but remained on the opposite side of the street in order to obtain a better view. "Let's take a few pictures," Travis said as he reached in his hip pocket for his camera.

"If you like," she said.

"You don't want any?"

"No, it's not that—"

"What's wrong with a picture?"

"A picture never captures what we're seeing now," she said.

"I suppose you're right."

"That's why I seldom take pictures," she said. "I like to remember in my mind and relish all the good things of an event. A picture captures only a single moment, and it's flat, without depth, and hardly takes in the grandeur."

"You sound like a poet."

"Or a romantic," she said and took his hand once again. "Why don't we walk around the city?" She consulted the map. "It looks as though it's not more than three miles."

"Sure, why not," he answered.

They approached the old city from the west side following Hativat Yerusualayim Street. They crossed the street and walked beside the great wall. "I never realized it was so high," Lezlie said. "I thought perhaps a dozen feet or more—"

"Overwhelming," Travis said as they clasped hands.

They paused long enough to buy a necklace with a crusader's cross made of olive wood from a street peddler. "I love it," she said, as Travis placed it around her neck.

A few feet ahead they came upon a small stand where two men sold bread baked in a circular shape, dark, and crusty with sesame seeds on the outside. They bought one each and munched on them as they walked northward along the wall.

When they reached the north side, the wall took a sharp right turn. "Oh, look at the view," Lezlie said, realizing they had reached the highest point. A street sign declared they were seeing the green hills of Mount Scopus.

"I think that's the way enemies came toward Jerusalem," Travis said. "They came over those hills."

"Hard to believe that so much of what we read in the Bible took place here," she said.

They continued on and reached the end of the north side of the wall, which took a sharp right turn again. They started down the east side. Lezlie marveled as she caught her first view of the Mount of Olives. "So much history here," she said. "My father used to read the Bible to us and now actually to see these places—"

"It is hard to believe," Travis said. He paused to snap pictures of the scenery. Just as he was putting his camera away, he noticed a blue Volvo at the top of the hill, slowly moving toward them. He had seen that Volvo earlier, and then he silently chided himself. In a city like Jerusalem there must be twenty blue Volvos. Yet even as he did, instinctively he knew it was not just any Volvo. This one moved slowly, causing the few cars coming down Ha-Offel Street to swerve, and more than one honked. His eyes searching the road ahead, Travis understood why the car moved slowly. After another hundred yards the sidewalk simply disappeared and the road narrowed, leaving space for only two cars.

He paused for a moment not sure what to do. He took out his camera again, pretending to take more pictures. "Lezlie, don't look now, but there's a light blue Volvo about four hundred yards up the hill. Do you see it?"

Lezlie surveyed the entire area carefully, smiling, and said, "Yes."

"I'm not sure if Taisir's in the car, but I saw that car on the road coming up. I think it's after us."

"What'll we do?"

"As soon as I put my camera away, take my hand, and let's start walking. Be ready to run."

He pointed to a wall on the opposite side of the street which acted as a barrier on the side of the hill. "We'll have to jump onto that." The wall was less than three feet high.

"I like it when you try to get protective," she said, trying to keep the panic out of her voice.

They tried to appear normal although both of them knew they were now walking faster.

He took one quick glance backward. "Now! We've got to run," Travis said, "or he'll cut us off for sure." The Volvo had pulled away from the curb and was picking up speed.

"Quick! Cross here!" Travis shouted as he pulled Lezlie across the road toward the concrete wall.

She followed him but turned instinctively as the blue Volvo careened around the curve, braked and skidded, swinging into the left lane. Lezlie jumped up on the wall and fell across to the other side with Travis beside her. The Volvo's left fender scraped the wall, making a grating sound, but it continued downward without decreasing speed. They climbed up on the foot-thick wall and sat down. Lezlie's hands shook, and her eyes brimmed with tears. "He tried—he tried to kill us. To run us down—"

"Just hang on," Travis said. He put his arms around her, and they clung together until she began breathing normally again.

"I think we can go down to the bottom of the hill now," Travis said.

"But if they're down there—"

"I doubt it."

"Why? If they tried to kill us—"

"They don't want you dead, Lezlie," Travis said. "They want the parcel, remember? They were trying to frighten us."

"They succeeded. I am frightened. If only I knew what this was all about."

"Let's go back to the hotel," Travis said. He draped his arm around her as they walked slowly down the hill. Both of them kept their eyes alert for a blue Volvo. They did not see any car fitting that description.

Once they reached the traffic-filled intersection, Lezlie said, "I'm all right now."

"Are you sure?"

"You think I'm one of those dumb females you see in the movies who just stands around and screams while men fight?"

"No, I don't think so at all. I saw you in action in Amman," he said and chuckled.

She returned his smile, and they continued walking at a normal pace. They crossed the street to a bus and taxi stand. Travis signaled a cab. One pulled up immediately. "Diplomat Hotel," he said.

When they reached the hotel, they went immediately to Lezlie's room. As Travis had expected, someone had searched it during their absence. The prowler left just enough evidence to let them know that he had been there—three or four articles in the wrong place—but not enough for it to look obvious to anyone else. The room still had a well-kept appearance.

"They've been here and searched," Lezlie said.

"I figured that," Travis answered. He went to the closet and pulled out the fur coat which still hung there.

"Somehow this coat has got to be the key," he said. "But I can't figure it out." He took the coat off the hanger and carried it over to the desk. He turned the light on and held the coat against the light. With his fingers he carefully felt every inch, including the sleeves which he turned inside out. "It just doesn't make sense," he said.

"What do they want?"

The phone rang sharply. They looked at each other and went to the phone together. She picked it up but held it so they both could hear. "Hello?"

"Good morning, Mrs. Austin. I hope you slept well last night," said the unmistakable voice of Taisir.

"Quite well," she said and started to hang up.

"And I understand you almost had an accident in the old city this morning. I am so pleased you were not injured."

"Look, Mr. Taisir, I don't know anything about a parcel so just leave me alone!"

"Then I speak plainly. You were to bring me five hundred thousand American dollars. Give me the money, and you'll never see me again. You will not leave Israel until you hand it over."

"Five hundred thousand?"

The line went dead.

Travis took the phone out of her hand. "At least we know what he's after now don't we?"

"But I don't understand. The money in the safe-deposit box and the bonds—should I have brought them?"

"Are you kidding? If the customs people at Amman hadn't confiscated it, the Israelis would have."

"That's right," she said. "Then what is it? Or where is it?"

"I don't know." He picked up the coat again and searched it one more time. Each square was carefully sewn together on the front and quilted on the inside.

"Hap said the coat was a gift. I'm positive he said that," Lezlie said. "Maybe he meant a box or something else."

"You talked to him in the coronary care unit, Lezlie. What did he say there?"

"Really he didn't say much. Just a few words."

"Think about it. Carefully. Tell me everything that happened when you went in."

Lezlie straightened her shoulders and took a deep breath and then pushed the door open leading into the coronary care unit. A noiselessness permeated the room, and Lezlie wondered if she should tiptoe. Her clicking heels broke the silence. She walked to the nurses' station. Before she could say anything, the nurse looked up and said, "Mrs. Austin?"

She nodded, not knowing what to say. She wanted to ask a dozen questions, but she could not seem to get the words out.

"Are you Lezlie?" the nurse asked.

She nodded again.

"He keeps calling for you. I can let you stay for only a few minutes."

"How—how bad—"

The nurse said, "Please follow me." She led the way down a short hallway into a room. The door was open, and the windows were covered by a curtain. She whispered, "He's very weak. Remember that."

Lezlie nodded again, and she went into the room. At first Lezlie didn't recognize Hap. He lay covered with a thin sheet. A hospital gown was draped loosely around his body, but his chest was left bare. Tubes ran from his nose, arms, and chest to the machines around the bed. Color had drained from his face, giving him an ashen complexion and causing him to appear much older. She laid her hand on his cheek. "Hap," she half whispered.

His eyes fluttered as though trying to wake up. His lips moved, but she couldn't hear what he was saying. He raised his left hand, motioning her to come closer. She put her face next to his and fought inwardly not to let tears show in her eyes. They surfaced anyway. Hap opened his mouth and formed words but seemed unable to make the sounds.

"Don't try to talk," she said softly. "Save your strength for—for later."

"Lezlie—"

She took his hand, careful not to press where the needles were stuck in at the wrist. She kissed his cheek. "I'm here, Hap. I'm here."

"Lezlie—love you—love—"

"Don't exert yourself, Hap," she whispered. She let go of his hand and rubbed his cheek again. The stubble of his blond beard felt rough against her fingers.

"Taisir—Tyche Hotel—Amman—the last—"

"You want me to give it to him? To take the coat to him?"

He tried to say more, but Lezlie could not distinguish between his words. She nodded, acting as though she understood and again urged him not to exert himself anymore.

His eyes fluttered again, and he lightly squeezed her fingers. A smile covered his face, reminding her what her husband had looked like only hours earlier. Her eyes kept moving toward the heart monitor, and she could see that it was very irregular. She backed away from the bed and leaned silently against the window. The tears ran down her cheeks. She defiantly brushed them away with her hand and tiptoed back to the bed. She leaned over and kissed his cheek. She rubbed his neck and gently stroked hair out of his face. Lezlie had no awareness of how long she stood next to Hap.

A nurse touched her shoulder. "You'll have to leave now, Mrs. Austin."

Lezlie nodded and said, "Just—just a minute." The nurse left.

"Hap, so many things we need to talk about. Please get well so that—," her voice broke. She leaned forward and kissed him gently on the lips. His eyes fluttered, and he opened them wide. The blue irises sparkled like the Hap of old. "Lezlie, I—I—believe—told you—first—"

"Yes," she said, "and I'm glad." She kissed him again. "Now get well. We have a lot of things to straighten out. Together."

His eyes closed again. Lezlie stared at the inert form, then turned abruptly. She wanted to run down the hallway and out of the hospital. Instead she walked quietly out of the room and down the corridor.

"What do you think he meant about Taisir?" Travis asked.

"I'm not sure. I felt at the time he was saying to take the coat to him at the Tyche Hotel, and when I did, that his business would be finished. I think he wanted out."

"You really think he meant that—that he wanted out of the business?"

"I've thought about it a hundred times," Lezlie said. "And of course I don't know. But I go on the hope that that's what he did mean."

Travis reflected silently for a moment. "What do you think he meant by 'I believe'?"

"I tell myself that he wanted me to know that he had decided to get his life straightened out and—and that he believed in God."

"I'd like to believe that, too," Travis said.

"He knew about me—about my trying to get life sorted out. When I think of that hospital room and his last words—"

"Hap would never have said he believed if he didn't," Travis said.

"He may have deceived me in a lot of ways, but he wouldn't—not where God was concerned," she said.

In a coffee shop, less than two miles from the Diplomat Hotel, Habib Taisir sipped Turkish coffee with two other men. "How long must we continue this game?" the tall man asked in Arabic.

"Tomorrow is the last time," Taisir said. He fingered the demitasse for a long moment and then said, "I have been patient enough."

"No," the tall man said, *"We* have been patient enough."

"It is not my fault."

The man held up his hand. "I do not want excuses, only the money. If not—"

Taisir blanched. In English he said, "I'll have it for you or—"

"There is no *or,"* he replied in English.

Chapter 13

Travis opened the door to Wayne Smith's knock. "Thanks for coming. We need your help."

"Anything," he answered. "I've discovered a lot of adventure with you around."

"We haven't meant—"

"You've already made this pilgrimage a distinct experience," he said smiling.

Travis laughed. "We didn't plan it that way."

"So long as you're both okay, I don't mind the adventure."

"We need one more bit of help from you."

"Anything that's not illegal or immoral," Wayne said, and his eyes twinkled.

"We need to get to Tel Aviv so we can return to the United States," Travis said.

"We're afraid of being followed," Lezlie said.

"They followed us yesterday into the old city."

"They even tried to run us down," Lezlie added.

"Do you have a plan?" Wayne asked.

"Yes, we do. I've made reservations in the name of Mr. and Mrs. Carl Johnson. I got the schedules, and I used a pay phone in case they had tapped our room phone."

"This really sounds cloak and dagger," Wayne said.

"We didn't want to take any chances."

"I can't say that I blame you."

"Now I'm going to make calls from this room for a plane tomorrow afternoon for Tel Aviv. I hope that will throw them off the trail."

"Sounds like it might," Wayne said.

"Now here's where you fit in." Lezlie said. "And we hope you will help."

"I told you I would do anything I could."

"We thought you'd feel that way," Travis said. "You announced this morning that eight people wanted to go for a tour of Tel Aviv in a minibus this afternoon."

"That's right."

"Here's what we want you to do. Number one, we want to leave our suitcases here, and then if you could get them to the United States—"

"Of course, but where would you pick them up?"

"You're from Atlanta, right?"

"Right," he said.

"Just leave them in Atlanta, and we'll pick them up as unclaimed baggage next week after your return."

"No problem there as far as I'm concerned."

"Thank you," Lezlie whispered.

"When the eight people get on the minibus, could they carry on my briefcase and Lezlie's shoulder bag? That way when we leave the hotel, it will not look as though we're going anywhere special."

"I don't think that would cause any problem."

"Now, all we have to do is figure out a way to leave the hotel without being observed by Taisir or whoever spies on us around here."

Wayne smiled. "I suspect you already have that figured out."

"You're right. It's rather simple, but I think it will work."

At 11:30, Travis Manning ordered lunch for two to be served promptly at 1:00 in his room. He carefully placed the order and repeated it again that he wanted it promptly at 1:00.

At 1:00 a waiter knocked at the door.

"Yes?"

"Room service."

"Ah, ah, just a minute—," said the voice. Then came noises sounding as though someone were getting dressed. After delaying as long as he felt he could, he slowly opened the door. Standing behind it, he said, "Bring it right on in."

The waiter brought in the meal on a tray, set it on the table, and held out the check for him to sign. The waiter looked into the face of Wayne Smith. A flicker of confusion flashed across his face and immediately disappeared.

"Thank you," Wayne said, signed his own name, and wrote under it FOR TRAVIS MANNING. The waiter moved toward the door. "Oh, just a minute," Wayne said. "I want to give you a tip."

"Thank you, sir."

"Now where did I put my wallet?" He felt his front and back pockets. He scratched his head. "I was sure I had an ample supply of shekels—"

"Does not matter, sir," the waiter said, backing toward the door.

"Oh, it does matter, I can't let you leave without a tip."

"If you say so, sir."

"Oh, well. Suppose I give you American currency. Is that all right?"

"But of course," he said. He lowered his head, and as he did so, he stole a quick glance at his watch.

"Do you have change for a twenty?" Wayne asked.

"No, sir, but I can get it for you. Or bring it back later, or—" Beads of perspiration had broken out on his forehead.

"I don't want you to go to all that trouble," Wayne said. "Let me see, I must have something smaller." He walked over to the window and pulled the drapes open. He could look directly across an open courtyard and into the lobby. He saw the figure of one of the people who had come on the pilgrimage. Recognizing Wayne, she nodded and waved vigorously. Wayne turned around and peeled off three one-dollar bills. "I hope that's satisfactory?"

"Oh, yes, sir. Very."

"You're sure now?"

"Yes, quite sure," and hurried out the door before Wayne could say anything more.

After placing the order at 11:30, Travis and Lezlie waited in the room. Shortly before 12:00, the phone rang. Lezlie answered and said, "Yes, it is."

A voice answered, "Hello, this is room service. I am terribly sorry to disturb you, but the person who took the order did not make it clear whether you wanted American coffee or Turkish."

"American."

"Thank you. And again, pardon me for bothering you."

"Not at all," Lezlie said as she hung up.

Lezlie jumped up and squeezed Travis. "How did you know that someone would check to make sure?"

"Just a hunch," Travis said.

Five minutes later they walked to the back of the hotel and found the exit. They stayed out of sight until 12:45 when the minibus was scheduled to leave. They waited for the signal. Two long blasts followed by a short one. Just as they came even with the building and had to step out where they could be seen, Virginia Hislip screeched, "My wallet! My wallet! It contains all my travelers checks and my money! My wallet! Where's my wallet?"

Immediately five people gathered around her, shouting questions, and yelling instructions. "Did you search your purse?"

"Maybe you left it in your room."

"When was the last time you looked for it?"

"Did you check the bus last night?"

"What about the front desk?"

During the diversion, the two walked rapidly without looking around, climbed into the minibus, and sat in the back. A large man sat next to the window on one side and an equally large woman on the other, obscuring the view of any curious person. Travis and Lezlie slunk down as far as possible without trying to appear to be hiding. There was always the possibility that the driver was one of Taisir's spies, but they took that chance. Both wore sunglasses and Travis had bought a beret which covered most of his hair.

"Let's go, driver," the fat man called out. "We're all here now, and we're in a hurry."

"Yes, sir," the driver said and pulled out.

As soon as the minibus pulled out, Virginia Hislip, seeing the vehicle from the corner of her eye, stopped digging frantically in her purse, and said, "Oh, look everyone. I found it!" Virginia thanked them for their concern. Immediately the crowd dispersed. She walked back into the hotel and back to the lobby and sat down in a chair. From her vantage point she could see the activity at the front door. She could also see room 127. A minute later she waved at Wayne.

Once they reached Tel Aviv and the bus pulled into the business section, Travis and Lezlie asked the driver to let them out. They took the fur coat, the briefcase, and the flight bag. "Have a beret," he said and tossed it to the driver. They waved good-bye to the others and walked two blocks. They hailed a taxi and drove to the airport. They walked rapidly, but Travis turned around, feeling as if someone were behind him. A man bumped into him, knocking the briefcase out of his hand. "Oh, so sorry," the dark-haired man said and smiled. He and Travis both bent down at the same time to retrieve the briefcase. As he stood up again, a second man was behind him. Travis could feel a knife blade pressing into his back.

"Guess our ploy didn't work," Travis said.

Lezlie had already figured out that the man behind Travis held a weapon.

"Mr. Taisir says that you have something for him. We are happy to collect it so that you will not have such a heavy load on your trip back to America." He smiled and spoke in excellent American English, even though his features betrayed his Middle Eastern origin.

"We gave it to Taisir this morning in Jerusalem," Travis said. The two men looked at each other as if to say "Is that so?" In that split second Travis swung himself around and knocked the man with the knife off balance. He kicked at the other man. Lezlie, reacting as if they had planned it, kicked the second man in the groin, and he toppled over, writhing with excruciating pain.

The tall man dropped the knife. For a moment he and Travis looked at each other; the knife lay on the sidewalk between them. The assailant took one step forward. "Don't try it, buddy," Travis said. The man hesitated.

A taxi pulled up, and Travis yelled. "Here!"

The man's attention diverted a second time, Travis grabbed for the knife. He fell to the sidewalk and struggled to get up. As the man advanced, Lezlie swung her purse and knocked him backward, enough so that Travis was on his feet again before the assailant regained his balance. The two attackers stared at Lezlie. The one now recovering from the kick in the groin lurched forward in an attempt to seize Lezlie's purse. She spun away from him, and he grabbed the fur coat which she was now wearing. He pulled at the coat, and she jerked away from him. She heard the threads tear. She whacked him again with her purse. He let go and backed off. As if commanded, the two attackers turned and ran, one hobbling behind the other.

The taxi driver looked at the American couple. "Something is wrong?" he asked.

"No, nothing," Travis said. "Here's a lovely knife for you. Just realized we can't carry those things on the plane with us."

The puzzled man took the knife and stared at them as they walked away.

"I'm so glad you came along," Lezlie said. "I don't know what I would have done without you."

"I'm glad I came too."

"Do you think God planned it this way?" she said. "I mean our being together like this?"

"Yes, I believe He just might have."

They moved over to a corner of the busy airport and paused long enough for a lengthy kiss. Then they passed through Immigration and Passport Control to wait for their plane. Three hours later they were airborne. They held hands between kisses.

"It still bothers me," Lezlie said. "About the money."

"Me, too," Travis said. "It just doesn't make sense, does it?"

"And this coat business," Lezlie said. "I'm glad I brought it because it turned colder than I expected, but aside from that—"

She slipped the coat from off her shoulders and was going to ask the flight attendant to hang it up for her. Lezlie saw a rip at the bottom of the coat caused when the man had jerked on it. "Oh, well, I can sew that easily enough," she said, fingering the torn spot. As she fingered it, she looked at the two-inch gash and turned to Travis. "I think I've suddenly figured it out."

"You have?"

"I've been wearing the five hundred thousand dollars," she said calmly. Keeping her voice low, she handed him the coat. She pulled back the torn hem, exposing the tip of a thousand-dollar bill. "I think there are probably two or three bills in each section," she said.

"That's unbelievable," Travis said as he examined it closely. "From the outside there's absolutely no way to tell that there are bills in there."

Lezlie suddenly giggled with relief. "I bet I've been wearing the most expensive coat in the whole world."

"What do we do now?" Travis asked.

"I'm not sure," she answered. "What do you think?"

"As soon as we get back to New Orleans, let's call the narcotics people. They can handle it from there."

"I agree," Lezlie said. "Right now I just want to get back to New Orleans."

"I want that, too," he said. "To get back home and to be with you under normal circumstances."

"Something else," she said.

"What's that?"

"I love you, Travis."

"You're sure?"

"Positive."

"Not just 'I think I love you' the way you said it before?"

"I have no doubts." Their eyes held each other for a long moment. He put his arm around her. "I've waited a long time for you to say those words."

"I haven't been ready to say them. Until now. I had to get a few things straight first."

"You mean your feelings about Hap?"

"Partially. Other things, too. That I was doing the right thing in loving you. That I had a right to happiness."

"A right to happiness?" A furrow creased his forehead.

"Maybe that's not the way to say it," she said and thought for a moment. "It's just that—that I made a lot of mistakes."

"Don't we all make mistakes?"

"Of course, but now I—well, I've got it sorted out, and I believe God has forgiven me."

"I know He has," Travis said.

"It's just that—oh, you know, we make wrong choices. It's as though God has a wonderful plan for us, and we're always hindering it from happening."

"Or maybe *trying* to hinder it. I don't think we really do—at least not in your case."

"Now I'm not sure what you mean."

"I've known that eventually you would come to me. And you have. Even though I lost you to Hap."

"You knew I'd come to you. How?"

"I can't explain it. Just a kind of knowledge. Maybe I could say assurance."

"Assurance? Now you've really lost me."

"Maybe, Lezlie, somehow I knew we were destined for each other."

"No question about that," she said. "I only wish I had recognized it sooner and then I wouldn't have—"

"Don't," he said and kissed her. "Forget the past and the mistakes. We've got the future ahead of us."

"That's what really matters. You, me, and God—," Lezlie stopped suddenly, and she kissed him. She paused only long enough to whisper, "I love you," before their lips met again.

RENDEZVOUS IN ACAPULCO

Melanie Haywood

Chapter 1

Katherine knew her love for Collin had died. She wondered when it had happened. They had been happy in the beginning. Had she awakened one day to discover she did not love her husband anymore? No, she couldn't think of any particular moment of insight. There was Reggie, of course. . . .

Quickly Katherine's mind hurried on, not wanting to think about that time. Even now she did not want to think about Reggie.

She idly glanced at Collin's even features. How deeply she had loved him once. *Such a long time ago,* she thought as she sighed.

They had stopped talking about feelings, substituting facts about schedules, deadlines, and finances. Finally they didn't even bother talking about facts. Indifference replaced love. Eventually resentment crept in and finally hate superseded both.

Divorce could have solved the situation. They had even talked about it once. Yet she had held back.

Why? she asked herself.

She didn't know, except that she had never been able to let go, even though everything within her told her that the situation was hopeless.

She had no solution—only a problem. Even the trip only postponed the inevitable.

She looked at Collin again, as his head rested against the seat. He was smiling.

"What can you possibly be grinning about?" Katherine asked.

"I'm not grinning. Just smiling peacefully."

"We've been on this plane five mintues, and already you're leaning your head back with your eyes closed with that silly smirk all over your face."

"Just thinking pleasant thoughts," Collin replied without opening his eyes. "And how wonderful Acapulco will be."

"The muggy heat is miserable there this time of year. Nobody goes to Acapulco in July."

"Eight years ago it was just as hot," he answered, moving his head slightly as if to burrow into the upholstery.

"That was different."

"Yes," he said, "very different."

She turned her head and glanced out the window. Katherine always hated this part of any flight, and the waiting made her nervous.

She hated sitting in the plane, waiting for everyone to board, and waiting for the sound of the engines starting. People were boarding, moving everywhere. She looked at her watch. There was another eight minutes until scheduled departure time—if the plane left on time.

"Are we going to start squabbling?" she asked in her low voice.

"No, my dear. Not at all." He patted her arm.

She recoiled. "You know I hate your doing that."

"But don't you want people to see us as an affectionate married couple?" He reached over and laid his hand on her knee.

"Collin, please. You'll mess my dress," she said as she pulled the travel magazine out of the wall pocket in front of her.

He patted her lightly, a slight grin covering his face again. "Yes, dear," he said as he dropped his hand.

Collin leaned back, closed his eyes, and shut out the sounds around him.

Katherine tried to read but could not concentrate. She had spoken sharply and knew it. *Why do I keep acting this way?* But she didn't even wait for herself to answer. She shook her head as if to clear away the disturbing question.

A woman's high-pitched voice broke into her thoughts.

"Oh, Tom, look! Our seats. Right in the front row."

"Yes, I see them," replied the soft bass voice behind her.

"I never dreamed they'd move us into first class," the woman said.

Katherine peeked from half-closed eyes to inspect the couple. She guessed their ages as late forties or early fifties. The wife, of medium height, parted her cropped salt-and-pepper hair in the middle and pushed it back in natural waves. Her light blue eyes gave her otherwise sharp features a softness. She wore an undistinguished style of suit in chocolate brown, which Katherine would have described as one step up from bargain basement. The husband, who was well over six feet, wore a tan tweed sports coat over an aqua golf shirt and what looked like first-time-worn gray slacks that bagged. She guessed the slacks had come from a slightly better-quality store. As she saw Collin finger the crease of his own impeccable ones, Katherine recalled a time when any ready-made suit would have seemed like good quality.

Collin gave them a cursory glance and closed his eyes again.

"Oh, Tom, the upholstery. I wonder if it's real leather. Oh, of course it isn't, but it's so soft. And the seats—don't you love the color scheme? All these shades of brown and tan!"

Katherine didn't hear the husband's reply, but his voice had the kind of lilt that equaled the woman's enthusiastic pitch.

"Excuse me," the woman said, leaning across the aisle and looking at Katherine. "Are you going to Acapulco, too?"

"That's where the plane lands next," Katherine said without taking her eyes from the magazine. Katherine hated talking to strangers. She hated even more to have her privacy interrupted.

Collin knew how she felt. He leaned forward, faced the woman, and smiled. "Yes, we are. Your first time to Mexico?"

"Oh, my, yes," the woman said. "We've wanted to go there for years."

"And now we have the chance," her husband said.

"I've dreamed about Acapulco for six years," the woman said.

"Sometimes dreams are more beautiful than reality," Katherine said, still not looking at the couple.

"And sometimes reality exceeds our wildest dreams, too," Collin added. "Especially in Acapulco—"

"You've been there before?" the man asked.

"Yes, we've been there before," Katherine said and dropped the magazine into her lap. She closed her eyes with a weary sigh.

"And we loved it, too," Collin said.

"Maybe you'll tell us all about it. The places to see. What to avoid and—," she stopped. "I'm sorry. You're strangers, and I'm babbling away. I'm always doing that to people I don't know."

"Yes, we don't know each other," Katherine said, as she snapped the magazine closed and pushed it into the pocket in the wall. She pulled out a copy of *Vogue* from her purse and flipped through its pages.

"But we can change all that," Collin said as he reached across his wife and extended his hand. "I'm Collin Roderick. This is my wife, Katherine."

"I'm Millie Reaves," the woman replied. She then introduced Tom, who reached across the aisle and shook Collin's hand.

"Would you like to trade places with me?" Katherine asked, giving her husband a look that barely masked her anger.

"Of course not. I'd like you to get acquainted with the Reaves, too."

"If I'm disturbing you, Mrs. Roderick—," Millie said.

"Of course you're not," Collin answered. He smiled, his white teeth contrasting with his dark complexion. "Tell us about yourselves. Where are you from?"

"Oh, we're from Chicago, along the north shore. Waukegan."

"We're from Chicago, too. Lake Forest."

"When we got on the Chicago-to-Dallas flight, I noticed you both in the waiting area," Millie said.

"You observe people a lot, do you?" Katherine said.

Millie laughed. "Not very much. But you're such a stunning person that you make people want to look at you."

Katherine's simple gold and diamond jewelry sparkled in the sunlight inside the TriStar's window. Suddenly feeling warm, she took off her white lace shawl, which she had added to combat the overhead vent. She wore an ice blue crepe dress. Her navy leather shoes and handbag complemented the outfit. Fresh-water-pearl manicured nails and the casually chic hairstyle completed the picture of Collin's wife.

In spite of herself, Katherine smiled and looked directly at Millie for the first time. "Thank you very much."

"Are you a model?"

Katherine laughed. "Good heavens, no."

"I thought maybe you were. Not only the dress, but the graceful way you walk. The perfect match of shoes and purse—"

"No, I'm a writer." She added, "A novelist."

"How exciting! What have you written?"

"My last one was called *Too Late for Love.*"

A puzzled look on Millie's face faded almost immediately. "But that's by Katherine Edmonton—"

"My maiden name," Katherine smiled. Her flawless teeth and hazel eyes accented her smooth complexion.

"I've read your books. In fact, it's because of your book *Forever and Ever Love* that we wanted to visit Acapulco."

"We've always wanted to visit it anyway," Tom said, "but after Millie read *Forever and Ever Love,* it became an obsession with her."

"I loved that book. I read it three times. I even packed a copy in my suitcase. When we get to Acapulco, would you autograph it?" She blushed. "Sorry, I don't mean to gush all over you—"

"My dear, any novelist finds herself flattered at hearing responses like yours."

"Well, you see, I wanted to go to all those places that Hillary and Randolph visited. You made the story alive and the romance so—so tender."

"It's Millie's favorite book," Tom said and chuckled. "One year she gave away ten copies for Christmas presents."

"I'm touched," Katherine said. "I never dreamed one of my books could affect anyone—"

"The story—," Millie said. "I felt as though I knew Hillary and Randolph. They're real people to me. Sometimes I think of what they would be doing now. How they loved each other and—"

"Remember, Millie," Katherine said, "books exaggerate life. A novelist can make a story sound more beautiful than reality."

"I—I'd like to ask you a question about the book," Millie said. "Of course."

"Is it based on your own experiences?"

"Well, yes, in a way, but—"

"Oh, I knew it! Didn't I, Tom?"

"Yes," he said, leaning forward. "She used to say that it had to have been a true experience."

"No one could write with that kind of emotion if it wasn't experienced," Millie said.

Sensing Collin's eyes on her, Katherine suddenly felt uncomfortable. "Have you—have you read my other books?"

"Yes, I have. I've read three others."

"Then you've read them all," Collin said. "And each one gets spicier than the previous book."

"And each one sells better than the previous book," Katherine said, giving her husband an icy smile.

"Yes, I've noticed that—that they've gotten more explicit—"

"You don't approve?" Katherine said.

"Approve? I hadn't thought of it that way. Perhaps you spoiled me with *Forever and Ever Love.* You said so much and yet you allowed the reader to visualize—"

"Explicit sex is in these days, you know," Katherine said.

"And what do you do, Collin?" Tom asked.

"Oh, I write too. Nonfiction."

"My husband means," Katherine said, "that four of his nonfiction books have sold almost as much as one of my books grossed, not counting movie rights."

"I wasn't actually saying that," Collin said and gave his wife a smile he didn't feel. "But it's true."

Tom thought for a minute, "I—I don't remember reading anything by you—"

"Oh, Collin is one of those acclaimed writers," Katherine said, "who gets good critical reviews, but the public still doesn't buy his books. He has a loyal, if somewhat elite following."

"Perhaps after we return home, I'll be able to read one of your books."

"Yes, but check the discount stores first," Katherine said. "They often stock his books there."

Collin laughed, "Ah, yes, my wife does have a way with words, doesn't she?"

"Are you doing research on a book in Acapulco?" Tom asked, trying to put the conversation on safe ground.

"Partially. I'm writing a new book about Mexican political policies and how they affect our country. But mostly I'm here for—well, a special reason." He took Katherine's hand, brought it to his lips, and kissed it. "We're having a second honeymoon."

"More like a first," Katherine said. "Eight years ago it wasn't much of a honeymoon."

"I'll bet everyone calls you Kit," Millie said.

"Everyone calls me Katherine."

"Oh, it's just, uh, I'm sorry—"

"I used to call her Kit," Collin answered. "But that was a long, long time ago."

"Where are you staying?" Tom asked.

"The Princess Hotel."

"Oh, we've read about it. And seen pictures. What beautiful surroundings—," Millie said.

"You'll be able to get a glimpse of it as you drive from the airport," Collin said. "It's *the* hotel of Acapulco."

"You've stayed there before?"

"Hardly," Katherine said, the sarcasm obvious in her voice.

"No, we stayed at an older hotel—"

"A euphemistic word—"

"At the Casa Blanca."

"Why, that's where we're booked," Millie said. "The brochure says it's one of the best second-class hotels."

"*Second-class* is a kind description," Katherine said as she pushed the button to move her seat upright.

"You didn't like it?" Millie asked.

"We did. Very much," Collin said. "My wife means that we didn't have any money then and just barely managed to pay for everything. Now that we're rolling in the green stuff, it gives us a different perspective about life."

"Oh, I see," Millie said and settled back in her seat. She locked her seat belt and felt the texture of the chairs. "I love the color scheme in here," she said to no one in particular.

Katherine sighed, picked up her magazine, and read with an intense gaze.

Collin, thinking of the partially formulated plan in his mind, said, "By the way, when we reached the airport, how about sharing a taxi?"

"Well, that's awfully nice," Tom said, "but—"

"Tom, because the Casa Blanca is about the farthest hotel from the airport, taxis don't like making that trip. We'll grab the cab, then get off at the Princess, and you can go on."

"That's awfully kind of you," Millie said. Then seeing the look on Katherine's face, she continued, "But we'll manage. We like to be friendly, but we don't want to impose."

"Impose? Of course not," Collin said, flashing his warmest smile. "It's not often that I meet such congenial people."

Katherine raised her left eyebrow and looked at her husband. He took her hand in his. "You know, Katherine, that gives me a great idea."

"I'll bet it does," she said under her breath so that only her husband could hear.

"We can switch over to the Casa Blanca."

"Really, Collin—"

"You know," he said, leaning in front of Katherine and facing the Reaves, "we have a lot of memories tied in with that hotel."

"But we have reservations at the Princess—"

"I'd like to go back," he said and then looked at his wife. "Back to room four ten."

"You remember the room number?" Katherine said, the surprise in her voice overcoming the blankness of her face.

"I remember everything about the Casa Blanca."

"I—I didn't think it meant—and, it was a long time ago."

"Good memories don't always disappear with age," he said, "or through disappointments in life."

"Really, Collin, I don't think—"

He turned his full attention to his wife and said softly, "We said we'd give it one more chance, didn't we? Let's start where we left good memories."

She stared into his eyes, saying nothing.

Collin turned his attention to the Reaves again. "All settled. We'll do just that. Then we can show you around the city—especially old Acapulco—and enjoy it ourselves."

"That would be wonderful, if it's not too much trouble," Millie said to Collin, but she looked at Katherine.

"Trouble? Not at all. I think it will make our second honeymoon even more pleasant for us." He put his arm around Katherine and squeezed her gently. "Maybe even a little bit more romantic."

"Collin, please," she said and took his arm off her shoulder.

"So don't argue," Collin said, avoiding Katherine's gaze. "It would give me pleasure to show you around. Unless you don't want our company—"

"I can't think of anything more exciting. Can you, Tom?"

"Sounds pretty good to me."

Collin started telling them about the city and some of the special places he and Katherine had visited eight years earlier. "But best of all, at least we thought so, was this little hole-in-the-wall restaurant. Cheap food, but delicious. The owner knew only two songs in English, which he would walk around singing to us in a heavy accent."

"What were they?" Tom asked.

"Bet you don't remember," Collin said as he looked directly at Katherine.

" 'Drink to Me Only with Thine Eyes,' " she said softly, "and the other was 'Always.' "

"Odd couple of songs," Millie said.

"Yes, but he sang them to us every time we came in."

"Oh, I would like to go there and meet him," Millie said.

"Yes, it would be splendid," Tom agreed. He leaned back in his seat and closed his eyes.

"Anything wrong?" Collin asked, noting the dark rings under Tom's eyes and his gray pallor.

"Just a little tired—"

"Tom had a bout of sickness recently," Millie said.

"Hey, don't mind me. I'm listening, but I'm just going to sit here quietly. Okay?"

"Then it's settled," Collin said. "As soon as we clear immigration, we'll take a taxi to the Casa Blanca, and then call and cancel our reservations at the Princess."

"Are you sure you know what you're doing?" Katherine asked quietly.

"I know exactly what I'm doing," he said as he patted her hand, "darling."

Katherine leaned back and closed her eyes. She remembered the Casa Blanca. Could she ever forget it? It was located on a high hill overlooking the bay. What a dream world it had seemed to her then.

If only their lives had stopped at the Casa Blanca.

If only. . . .

The memories flooded Katherine's mind as she pictured that white building, which seemed to guard the bay.

She suddenly found herself thinking again of *Forever and Ever Love.* It had all been so long ago. But even eight years later, she remembered every word of the prologue. Funny, she hadn't thought of that opening scene in years.

Yet now she couldn't stop thinking about it. The words repeated themselves in her mind.

Waves lashed wildly against the rocks below, sending a spray upward that struck Hillary's face. The rising winds whipped her hair in front of her eyes. Gray black clouds loomed overhead, ready to burst.

She poised, standing straight, like a swimmer making herself ready before a dive. Hillary's vision blurred as tears streamed down her cheeks. "Oh, Randolph, why—why—," she sobbed.

She inched forward and looked down at the rising waves. For a moment she saw herself tumbling forward, her body smashed by the surging power of the waves. Instinctively she shook her head and backed away.

"Hillary!"

She could not hear the voice that called to her from the top of the cliff. He cried out again and raced down the uneven path. He stumbled and caught himself just before falling headfirst on the gravel.

Hillary turned around and stood motionless for a minute,

breathing rapidly. She opened her eyes and recognized Randolph racing toward her. She took a few steps toward him and stopped.

He reached her, grabbed her by the shoulders, and shouted, "I was afraid you would jump."

"No, I—I couldn't," she said, "even if you hadn't come—"

"I tried to get back earlier. I really tried."

"Randolph, I didn't think—I didn't think you'd come back."

"But I did come back," he said, realizing they were both shouting above the waves and the wind. He pulled her close and whispered in her ear, "I came back because I love you."

"I want to believe you," she said. "I've always wanted to believe you, but—"

"I'm back. We can start over."

"Can we? Can we really start over?"

"Yes, Hillary—"

"I love you," she said as she looked into his dark eyes.

Their lips met. He held her close, not wanting the kiss to end. When he released her, he took her left hand in both of his. He slipped a plain gold band on the third finger.

"Randolph, I—"

"You only get to wear it a little while. Then we'll make it official."

"You still have it," she said and felt fresh tears rushing to her eyes.

"I never got rid of it. I've kept it and looked at it a dozen times a day."

"You're sure?" she asked, her eyes searching his for an answer.

"Till death do us part," he said. He put both his arms around her and pulled her close.

"If only I could believe—"

"You can," he said.

"Can I? What about Victoria?"

"Who's Victoria?" he said as he threw back his head and laughed.

"Don't play games with me," she said. "Not about this."

"Okay," he said. He took her hand, and they started up the path. "It's over with her."

"Randolph—please, are you sure? Absolutely sure?"

"I told her good-bye, and she's leaving in the morning."

"And you'll never see her again?" Hillary asked.

"I put the ring on your finger, didn't I?"

She twisted the gold band on her finger. "Yes, it's just that—"

"Just what?"

"Doubts, I guess."

"That you love me?"

"No, Randolph, never about my love—"

"About what?" he asked.

"It's yours I've doubted. I still do."

Chapter 2

As they moved through the immigration lines, the two couples became separated. For the first time, Katherine had an opportunity to speak to Collin. "Are you crazy? Why did you insist on going to the Casa Blanca?"

"Why not?"

"We can afford better," she answered.

"Didn't we plan this trip as a chance to rekindle the dying embers of love?" he said.

"That's what we said," she answered, "although not quite so literarily."

"Then let's go back to the place where we felt close to each other."

"Did you really feel close there?"

"Yes," he said as they walked up to the booth behind an elderly couple.

"And you think we'll find it again by going back there?"

"I don't know. I'm willing to look anywhere or try anything."

"But this sudden change of plans—"

Collin pulled her aside. "Look, I can't force you to go there," he said, a hardness filling his voice, "but I thought you would at least try—"

"You really want to go to the Casa Blanca?"

He pulled her back in line. "I want something different from what I have now," he replied as he handed the woman at the immigration counter their passports.

Minutes later the Reaves rejoined them in front of the airport. Collin slipped a five-dollar bill to an airport porter who flagged down the next taxi. Less than three minutes later they were riding toward the city. Collin acted as tour guide, pointing out places of interest. In laborious Spanish he asked the driver to circle through the grounds of the Princess Hotel. "You have to see this place," he told the Reaves. "It's the most beautiful hotel in the world."

"But you never actually stayed there?" Tom asked.

Katherine laughed. "Our last week in Acapulco, we had so little money we cut down to one meal a day and walked everywhere!"

"But we did hitch a ride out here once and walked through the gift shops and the lounge," Collin said.

Katherine smiled. "It was fun."

"We pretended we had struck it rich with our writing and had rented a suite of rooms."

"We wore our best clothes so that we didn't look too much out of place," Katherine said, remembering.

"Ah, yes, but life has changed drastically for us since then," Collin said. "Perhaps we might spend one night here before we return to the States. We always promised ourselves that once we'd made enough money, we'd stay at the Princess."

Forty-five minutes after leaving the airport, they arrived at the street leading up to the Casa Blanca Hotel. The taxi turned right and wound its way slowly up the hill. Katherine leaned back in the seat and closed her eyes.

"You okay?" Millie asked.

"Fine," she said and then forced herself to look at the hotel as it came into view. It was an enormous structure with high walls, recently whitewashed. The name, in six-foot-high letters, needed fresh paint. "I'd forgotten how old everything looked," she said.

The cab pulled into a circular driveway. In a grassy middle section they saw a fountain that once had sprayed out water under the gaze of colored lights. Palms nestled on either side of the fountain.

"How beautiful," Millie squealed. "Oh, isn't it, Tom?"

Tom, who had been sitting in the front seat next to the driver and had said nothing for the previous half hour, smiled, and turned slightly to look at his wife. "It is. We're going to have a grand time here."

"Why, Katherine, this is where Hillary and Randolph had that love scene in chapter four in *Forever and Ever Love*. I recognize the balcony above the fountain. This is the spot, isn't it?"

Katherine smiled. "You're too perceptive, Millie."

"Think of how many times I've read the book and talked about it. I'm dying to pick out other places. I hope you don't mind—"

"I'm flattered."

"Please don't tell me. I know I'll discover them myself."

"I'm sure you'll recognize most of them."

As they got out of the car, Tom leaned against the vehicle for a minute.

"You all right?" Collin asked.

"Yes, just felt a little weak."

"Probably the altitude. Affects some people like that."

Collin didn't wait for Tom's response. He sprinted across the open court and the tiled floor to the desk. The porter placed all their bags in the lobby.

"My friends, the Reaves, have a reservation, but we don't. I assume you have a room for four or five nights," Collin said as he gazed at the room boxes behind the clerk. Most of them held keys.

"We can, of course, accommodate you," the slender Mexican said in heavily accented English.

"If it's available, we'd like room four ten. We stayed there once before."

The clerk turned around, pulled the key from box 410, and laid it on the counter. "Yes, it is available." He pushed the registration card in front of Collin.

After signing, Collin handed the clerk a ten-peso note. "Would you call the Princess Hotel and cancel my reservation?"

The clerk beamed. "Of course, sir. At once, sir."

"Oh, by the way, a porter worked here a few years ago. Manuel. Is he still here?"

"Yes, still. He works today in the evening. He will also work again tomorrow morning. You wish him to do something for you?"

"No, nothing," Collin said. "He once treated us kindly." Collin turned and walked toward Katherine who stood near the baggage. The hotel porter picked up the key and luggage, and they followed.

"Remember Manuel?" Collin asked.

"Could I forget him?" Katherine answered and then turned her face quickly away. She didn't want to remember Manuel, yet to her surprise, she remembered vividly.

"I suppose both of us have more memories than we want to face," Collin said as he entered the elevator behind his wife.

Inside the room, Collin looked around. It was the same indistinguishable color, with the same drab cotton curtains covering two small windows. Katherine pounded the mattress. "The bed hasn't gotten any more comfortable. Probably the same mattress. But then what can you expect when your husband insists on going native—"

"Don't spoil it, Katherine," he snapped and then smiled to soften the effect. He tipped the porter and watched him leave. After he had gone, Collin walked across the room, unlocked the door leading to the patio, and went outside. It overlooked the old section of Acapulco Bay, just as he had remembered it. "We had good times then," he mumbled.

"Yes, we did. *Then,*" Katherine said and her lips took on a hard set.

Half an hour later, the two couples met downstairs and took the hotel's courtesy car into the old marketplace. The Reaves responded much as Collin had on his earlier visit. He enjoyed watching their enthusiasm. Tom sat under a mango tree in the plaza while the others explored the curio shops. "I'll just watch people and relax," he called after them. "Take your time."

After an hour, they returned to the plaza. "Come on, Tom, I want to show you El Brazero," Collin said. "It's not far. That's the cafe we told you about earlier."

Katherine slowed her pace as they approached El Brazero. Twice she started to speak, and then as if marshaling her courage, she lifted her chin and walked on.

The open front of the cafe gave passersby a complete view of the inside. Mexican art decorated the two side walls. An overhanging awning of coconut palm leaves glued to sun-baked tiles helped achieve a sense of smallness and intimacy.

They sat at a table in the middle of the room, which gave them a full view of the entire building.

"Dingier than I remembered," Katherine said, "and I didn't remember it as exactly luxurious."

"Never mind," Collin said to the Reaves, "they make the finest fruit drinks in Acapulco."

"Collin ought to know. He's tried every one of them. He almost lived on papaya and pineapple. He lost ten pounds, besides."

The waiter came and took their order, which Collin gave in Spanish. The waiter smiled at Collin's imperfect pronunciation. They watched him go behind the counter and mix the papaya juice with ice and sugar. They heard the whizzing of the electric blender. Minutes later the waiter brought four papaya drinks in oversized goblets.

"Hmm, as good as I remember," Collin said.

"Delicious," Millie said.

"Unusually good," Tom added.

"A little too sweet, I think," Katherine said and pushed hers aside. "Or perhaps I've just lost my taste for things like this." She looked directly at Collin.

"Thanks for bringing us here. I love the atmosphere, the smell of the food," Millie said. "I've been watching that woman over there—," she nodded with her head. "What's she doing?"

"Frying tortillas," Collin answered. "Right on the grill. They don't grind the flour for the tortillas anymore as in the old days. They come already made—like loaf bread in the States. But otherwise, you see the rest of the food prepared from start to finish."

Tom took Millie's hand. "A wonderfully warm place, isn't it?"

"Everything and more," she said and stopped. "Hey, wait a minute. This place fits into your book, too. This is where Randolph proposed to Hillary, isn't it? Oh, don't answer. I know it. You described the woman cooking her tortillas and the smell of fried corn in the air."

"You're right again, exactly right," Katherine said, her eyes focused on Collin. "Some of my best love scenes took place in El Brazero—in my book, I mean."

"Oh, I just can't believe all this," Millie said. She touched her husband's hand. "Just beyond belief."

"Yes, Acapulco is—," Katherine answered.

"Oh, Katherine, I didn't mean the city. I was talking about *you*.

To actually sit here in Acapulco with the author of my favorite book!"

"Isn't God good to let us come here?" Tom said as he and Millie smiled at each other.

Katherine raised an eyebrow as her eyes met Collin's.

"We prayed about it a long time," Tom said. "And we're so grateful for the way it worked out."

"We asked God to lead us," Millie added, "and He did."

"Do you like the papaya drink?" Katherine asked. "Collin says they make the best ones in Acapulco."

"Katherine, don't change the subject. I'd like to hear what they're saying about God," Collin interjected.

"I didn't mean to be rude—"

"No, no," Tom said and leaned slightly forward. "We don't want to make you uncomfortable."

"It's just that we're not used to hearing people talk about God and praying," Collin said. "But we don't really mind, do we, Katherine?"

"Not unless you're the holy-roller type," she said with a brittleness in her laugh.

"I hope we're not. Sometimes we might get carried away—"

"Then I won't hesitate to stop you," Katherine said. "And we're having such a lovely time in Acapulco. The weather is absolutely perfect—"

"Katherine, wait a minute. Don't do that."

"Do what?" she asked Collin.

"You keep changing the subject and interrupting our friend."

"This is supposed to be a fun vacation. I don't want to sit in some sidewalk cafe for hours and argue about God."

"Look, folks, I'm sorry—," Tom said.

"But I'd like to hear," Collin said.

"Let's forget it," Millie said. "If Katherine doesn't want to hear—"

"I can only speak for myself. I'd like to hear. But neither of us is very religious."

"We weren't either," Millie said, "until about four years ago."

"Did some kind of light from heaven shine down on you?" Katherine said but without any trace of hardness.

"No," Millie said and smiled. "We had everything going for us in life and then we had some real problems—"

"And the problems," Tom said, "made us realize we needed help. That got us started in our search for God."

"And God changed our lives."

"What do you mean *changed?* How?" Collin asked. "Just exactly what do you believe about God?" Katherine asked.

"I don't think you want to hear everything," Millie said, "but I'll tell you this. We believe God loves us."

"You don't sound like holy rollers," Collin said, smiling, and then sipped his papaya drink again. "Actually, your statements are quite orthodox."

"Collin took a course in Christianity back in graduate school. He thinks he's an expert on religion."

"All I want to say is that Christ's involvement in our lives adds meaning," Millie said, "and purpose."

"He gives us strength to meet the hard problems in life," Tom added.

"Of course if you find it necessary to believe in God in order to cope with life, then I'm glad for you," Katherine said. "And now, maybe we ought to order another drink. Anyone want a refill?"

"Katherine, don't you believe in anything?" Millie asked.

Katherine thought for a moment. "I'm not sure."

"You're thirty-one," Collin said, "and you don't believe in anything?"

"There are two things I definitely *don't* believe in. That's divorce. And abortion."

A look passed between Katherine and Collin. He turned away as though he'd been struck on the face. He spooned liquid from his drink.

"We don't believe in those things either," Millie said, "but—"

"But?" Katherine asked.

"Please don't stop there. Maybe you need to move toward a positive faith in something."

"Maybe I don't want that."

"And you have that right," Millie answered.

"Honey," Tom said, "I think we are being a little pushy."

"Anyway, I'm perfectly content with my life the way it is," Katherine said.

"Are you?" Collin asked without meeting her eyes.

"Look, I'm sorry," Millie said. "I had no right to push you—"

"Yes, you didn't have any right," Katherine said and smiled once again. "But I forgive you."

The conversation limped along with Tom asking Collin questions about Acapulco. Katherine stopped listening. She remembered a dozen conversations she'd had with Collin as they had held hands at a corner table. She especially remembered the last time they had come to El Brazero.

Collin had just finished an interview with an important Mexican official about selling oil rights to American companies. The interview had gone extremely well. Collin could hardly contain his excitement when he met Katherine at the cafe.

"He told me everything—nothing held back. The dummy thought I wanted to hand him a pile of money, I think," Collin laughed and launched into a question-by-question description. Katherine had said little.

He finally stopped and said, "How did your writing go today?"

"Collin, I don't want to spoil your wonderful day, but—"

"Sure, what is it?"

"I'm pregnant."

"Pregnant? You sure?"

"I haven't been to a doctor if that's what you mean. But I'm sure—absolutely."

The excitement drained from his face. "Uh, well, that does complicate things, doesn't it?"

"I know we said we'd wait until we both finished our books—"

"I don't see how we can afford a baby right now. With what I made on the previous book and the advance not yet here on this one, we're just scraping by now."

"I know," she said, realizing that she was close to crying.

"Honey, a baby just doesn't fit into our plans right now."

"What are you saying, Collin?"

"There are alternatives, you know."

"Not as far as I'm concerned."

Off and on for the rest of the day, they discussed and figured. Katherine recalled how Collin had argued from the point of economics. In another year they would have enough money to think about a family. But right now, he argued that they couldn't swing it. She felt hurt that he thought of their child in such calculating terms.

Then they argued over how the pregnancy had happened, neither wanting to take the blame and both feeling trapped.

"Okay, we'll cut short our stay in Acapulco and—"

"You act as though I deliberately did this," Katherine said.

"We both had a lot to do with it, didn't we?" Collin said. At that moment, the owner of El Brazero picked up his guitar and strolled among the tables, singing a love song in English.

Katherine took her husband's hand. "I love you," she whispered.

"And I love you, too," he said.

"A forever and ever love," she said as she squeezed his hand and listened to the thickly accented words of the song.

At that moment, Millie's voice penetrated her thoughts. "Hope we're not boring you, Katherine," she said.

"Oh, uh, no, just my mind wandering."

"They're asking about a cruise," Collin said, the slightest hint of reproach in his voice.

"Oh," she said, "how nice."

"With our packaged-but-private tour, we get a free cruise on the *La Fiesta*. Is it a good trip?" Millie asked.

"Oh, yes, as I remember," Collin said. "Take it at night if you want the romantic flavor. In the daylight it's largely sightseeing. Fabulous homes of movie stars like John Wayne and Frank Sinatra. They'll point out the house where John and Jackie Kennedy spent their honeymoon."

"The day tour by all means," Millie said.

"Then how about the four of us doing it in the morning?" Collin said. "The boat docks half a mile from here. We have to pass it on our way back to the Casa Blanca."

"Splendid," Millie said.

"*La cuenta,*" Collin called out for the bill as he caught the waiter's eye. The man rushed over to the table, making a slight bow as he laid the check on the table. He waited for Collin to peel two bills off his small roll of Mexican currency.

"What happened to the old man who used to play his guitar and sing?" Collin asked. "I've missed him today."

The waiter shook his head and said slowly. "No longer he is with us."

"Did he quit?" Katherine asked. "I thought he owned the place."

The waiter shook his head. "No, no *señora. He is ... muerto,*" he said. He picked up the money and walked away.

"Dead," Collin said in English.

"I'm sorry," Millie said. "I know you wanted to hear him again—"

"Many things change," Katherine said, her voice brittle. "Nothing remains the same."

A young girl approached their table with a string of crosses and star-shaped stones on strips of rawhide. She held them up and said in English, "Wish to buy, pretty lady? Nice for you."

They all said no. After several additional attempts, the little girl went away.

"Poor child. Probably not more than six or seven," Tom said.

"Often the family lives by what the children sell on the streets," Collin replied. "A hard way of life."

"Our oldest grandson is six—I shudder to think how I'd feel if he had to do something like that to help the family eat."

"It's a different culture," Katherine said matter-of-factly.

"Yes, I suppose," Millie answered. "Still—"

"You mentioned a grandson? How many children and grandchildren do you have?" Collin asked, glaring at his wife.

"Two daughters and two sons. The older son has the six-year-old. The girls are both married, and the younger son just completed college this year."

"Sounds like a great family," Collin answered.

"It is. They all helped pay for this trip."

"Makes you proud of them, doesn't it?"

Tom nodded. "Yes, it sure does."

"You have any children?" Millie asked.

"Yes," Katherine said.

"No," Collin snapped.

"I mean, we had a son," she said.

"He died," Collin said.

"Oh, sorry, I—"

"You had no way of knowing," Katherine said.

"You meet people all the time," Tom said, "who seem to have everything in life. You hardly realize the pain and heartbreak that lies behind their smiles."

"I'm sure that's just as true with you," Collin said.

"No one is immune," Tom said.

"You two don't look as though you've ever had any heavy setbacks," Collin said. "You're both so—so together."

"We've had our share, too," Millie said. She put her arm around her husband and dropped her gaze. She didn't want them to see the tears forming in her eyes.

Chapter 3

Unable to sleep, Katherine got up at the first full light. She grabbed fresh clothes, tiptoed into the bathroom, and silently closed the door behind her. She dressed casually in slacks and a knit shirt, and then walked out of the hotel. She felt restless and broke into a jog until she had passed the hotel complex. She slowed down to a normal pace, realizing that she had begun to perspire.

Over the years Katherine had discovered that long walks helped her relax. Often when stuck in her writing, she found a brisk two-mile walk relaxing. Afterward the work flowed again.

Continuing down the hill, she heard the soft chirping of a bird but didn't bother to look for it. Muted echoes of traffic from the main street, half a mile away, carried upward. She could see the belching diesel buses crawling forward. She stared at the bay and tried to count the yachts, but at that distance she found it impossible. Tripping on an uneven section of the road, she decided she needed to watch her feet instead.

Five minutes later she stopped, suddenly aware of where she had been heading. She stood in front of the open building with the hand-lettered sign above the door: LA VERDULERIA. She smiled to herself and then walked up the three steps into the store. The walls, now marred with stains and fingerprints, had once been painted aqua. A single counter extended the entire width of the twenty-foot store. An electric cooler contained milk and eggs. From the ceiling hung lamps which were lit only at dusk to conserve the expensive electricity. On top of the counter, she saw exactly what she'd expected: baskets of fruit.

Eight years earlier, she had walked to that store every day, carefully selecting mangoes or oranges for their breakfast. They could afford nothing better. They had decided that fruit was not only cheap but nourishing. Occasionally she bought one papaya for variety.

As in former days, she picked up several pieces of fruit, feeling them for firmness and ripeness and quickly discarding the bruised. Instinctively she raised a mango to her nose and smelled. "How much?" she asked in Spanish.

"One peso, señora," the old woman behind the counter said, not looking directly at her.

"Ah, don't cheat me because I am a gringo."

"How much do you offer, señora?" Although the woman gave no sign of recognition, Katherine remembered her.

"Twenty centavos," Katherine said and smiled.

"Now you cheat me," the old woman replied, but Katherine saw the first hint of a smile on her lips.

After bartering back and forth, the woman said. "Fifty centavos," as she held before her the large, golden red mango.

"You are a hard woman," Katherine said and pulled a handful of coins from her pocket.

"No, señora, today I have let you steal from me." The woman smiled broadly because they had both struck a good bargain.

Katherine handed her the fifty-centavo piece, and then hardly realizing what she had done, Katherine laid two pesos in her hand.

The woman frowned and looked up at her. "Señora—"

"Gracias, señora," Katherine said and walked out into the full light of the morning.

"*Vaya con Dios!*" the woman called after Katherine. The expression meant "Go with God."

Katherine laughed. Years earlier she could have bought four mangoes for fifty centavos—and she would have enjoyed the breakfast. Today she looked at the fruit and remembered too many things—the scrimping, the going without. She also remembered the emotional support she had given Collin. She had encouraged him each evening as he edited and retyped his manuscript.

Katherine suddenly wanted to hurl the mango down the street and completely out of her sight. At that moment she looked up to see a boy trudging up the hill behind a bent-over man. The child, probably ten years old, dragged a basket of woven hats. He kicked a beer can in front of him.

"Hey, muchacho!" Katherine called and tossed the mango. The boy looked up and caught it, staring questioningly for a moment. When he saw the Anglo smile, he clutched the basket in one hand, the mango in the other, and darted up the street.

Katherine stood in the road and laughed. She watched until the boy disappeared out of sight. Then she turned and walked to the bottom of the hill. She made an abrupt complete turn and half ran back to the hotel.

As Katherine approached the building, she saw Collin in the lobby, speaking on the telephone. Apparently, she decided, he had awakened, found her gone, and had wondered what had happened to her.

She opened her mouth to call out. His back was to her. She heard his voice. Although she didn't catch all the words, she did hear him say "darling."

As if slapped, Katherine backed away, moving behind a post to prevent Collin's seeing her if he turned around.

"But I've been tied up. I've tried to explain—"

A second later she heard him say, "We're not staying at the Princess—"

Then again, "Look, darling, it's a long story and—"

At that moment Collin apparently heard Millie's high-pitched laugh. "Look, I can't talk now. I'll—well, I'll get back to you later. I'm staying at the Casa Blanca—"

"I said I'd get back to you later." Collin looked up then and waved at Millie. "Yes, señor, at one-thirty this afternoon. Hasta luego." Collin hung up as Tom came into view.

"Good morning," Millie called out. "We tapped at your door and nobody answered—"

"Yes, well, I—uh, found Katherine gone and—"

"I just went for a walk," Katherine said, moving toward them as though she had just come in.

Katherine's eyes met Collin's. She could see the questioning in his eyes as to how much, if any, of the phone conversation she had heard. "Delightful walk. Very refreshing."

Collin quickly dialed another number. "Just be a minute," he said. He waved to Katherine and signed with his fingers, "Two minutes." Collin spoke in his labored Spanish to set up an appointment for the following afternoon.

The hotel's courtesy car pulled up almost as soon as Collin joined the others. As they got into the vehicle, he said, "After breakfast, I want us to take in two places. First, we'll take a cruise on the *La Fiesta,* which should last until lunchtime. After lunch, we'll see the world-famous cliff divers at Quebrada. How does that sound?"

"The divers interest me," Tom said. "I saw them featured on TV a couple of years ago."

"Absolutely perfect. Anything you want to plan suits us fine." Millie's enthusiasm even seemed to lift the frown from Katherine's face. Although she said nothing, she turned her full attention toward buffing her nails.

Collin looked up and saw Manuel coming toward him. He was wearing a cotton shirt with embroidered flowers on the lapels. The middle-aged Mexican smiled at him. "How very good to see you again, señor."

"You remember us?"

"But how could I forget?" Manuel answered. "Could I forget the loving couple who stayed here until their money ran out? At one time I thought I would have to pay your hotel bill for you!" He was short and wiry, but his deep voice sounded as though it ought to come from a large man.

"Manuel took pity on us," Collin said. "Twice he sneaked us food from the kitchen when we didn't have the money to buy any."

"I didn't realize you had it so hard," Millie said.

"I was expecting an advance on my book. The debts kept piling up. I had to do the interviews and research here in Acapulco in order to finish it up."

Manuel walked to the other side and bowed his head slightly at Katherine. "Señora, is most good to see you again. Often I have remembered you both as you stood up there—," he pointed to the balcony. "Ah, I saw the light of love in your eyes for each other. Such special love. I could not allow the manager to put you out."

"But the money came through," Collin said.

"And Mr. and Mrs. Roderick treated me graciously," the porter added. "Very graciously."

Just then the desk clerk called to Manuel. "I shall hope to be seeing more of you this week," Manuel said and hurried away.

"I see more and more reasons, Collin, why you wanted to come here," Millie said. "This place—what marvelous memories it must hold for you."

"It has memories all right," Katherine said. "Many memories." She didn't raise her eyes, but continued buffing her nails to a gloss.

Collin draped his arm around Katherine and patted her shoulder. "Yes, we have many special memories of Casa Blanca."

She jerked his arm off her shoulder. "Keep your arm off me and stop that patting!" She looked at him and then at the Reaves. She dropped her purse, jumped out of the car, and half ran down the driveway. Her short heels twisted in the gravel, impeding her.

Katherine ran as far as the end of the driveway, then stopped. She walked slowly across the road and stared at the bay. Although it was only a few minutes before nine, the heat had already begun to penetrate her clothes. Her hair felt limp. Hearing footsteps behind her, she said, "Just leave me alone. Just leave—"

"I didn't mean to intrude," Millie said.

"Oh," Katherine spun around, "I'm sorry, I thought—I thought Collin—"

"I volunteered to talk to you," Millie said. "Sometimes it's easier for a woman to talk to another woman—"

"I—I'm sorry, I—"

"You don't need to apologize or explain."

"It's just ... just that I've been depressed ... and confused," Katherine said as though not hearing Millie.

Millie stopped two feet away, waiting for Katherine to continue.

"Collin and I haven't been happy. Not for a long time."

When Millie didn't answer, Katherine said, "We've been virtual strangers for—for the past six years and—"

"And yet you wanted to try again?"

"I wanted to. Now I'm not so sure he—"

"Give him a chance, Katherine. Give yourself a chance."

"But there's another—another problem or two. Things I'm not sure I can cope with."

"I always feel that if a woman cares enough for a man, she'll fight for him."

"But what if she doesn't care enough?"

Millie stood beside Katherine and faced the bay. "The water's so blue, isn't it? This view alone makes me delighted we came here."

"I've been rude to you and Tom," Katherine said. Her lips trembled and every word seemed forced. "I—I just don't understand—," she stopped abruptly, smiling self-consciously. "Maybe that's why I write torrid love stories. I feel strongly, but I can't always express my feelings in person. I'm touchy and—"

Millie draped her arm around Katherine's shoulder. "You don't need to explain to me, my dear. I don't mind listening, but you don't owe me anything."

"You've been kind, and I've treated you rudely. Even from the time we met on the plane."

Millie smiled. "That was only surface rudeness. I figured it was more fear of opening yourself up than rudeness."

Katherine turned and faced the older woman. "You understood that—even back on the plane?"

"Yes."

"But—how? I mean—"

"I don't know. I'm not any special kind of mind reader. But Tom thinks I have a kind of gift." She laughed lightly. "I can read people's eyes. Sounds strange, I know."

"Yes, a little."

"You see, I look at people—at their eyes. I seem to know how they feel."

"Like reading minds, only you read eyes?"

"Tom says it's like that. It is—oh, more of an intuitive feeling. A sense of understanding."

"How accurate are you?" Katherine asked with half a smile. "Eighty percent of the time? Fifty?"

"Please don't mock me," Millie said.

"Sorry. I'm just not used to—" She stopped and looked into Millie's eyes. "Okay, what do you see?"

"What I've seen since I met you on the plane."

"What's that?"

"Pain. A lot of pain."

"A safe guess—"

"Loneliness. Confusion. Even about this trip. About your feelings toward Collin—"

"And you felt sorry for me?" Katherine said and pulled away.

"If you like using that word. I'd prefer to think that I sensed your need for a friend. I wanted to be that friend."

"Did my eyes tell you that I'd accept you?"

"They told me you wanted to, but that you're afraid to trust."

"You read that much correctly. I—I am afraid to let my guard down."

"That's why I'm standing here, Katherine. I care enough to try."

"Oh?" Katherine said and then looked away. For a moment neither of them spoke, and then she asked, "What did you read in Collin's eyes?"

"Let's—let's talk about you instead."

"Oh, some dark mystery brewing. Is that it? Just like in one of the books I write."

"Katherine, I care enough to cut through the garbage you keep throwing in my path."

"Garbage?"

"You strike people as tough. In control. But that's all on the surface, isn't it?"

"Is it?"

"Because I read that, I responded to Collin's invitation."

"But I didn't want you to—to even share the taxi with us."

"I know that. I also know that *underneath*—"

Katherine stared at Millie. "Thank you. You're right—underneath, I wanted you . . . somebody . . . anybody. . . ."

"And I'm here."

"Maybe . . . maybe a little later. I can't talk. Not right now."

"As I said, you don't have to explain—"

"But I want to. Just, just not now."

"Fine. Now let's go back to the car." She slid her arm around Katherine's waist and led her away from the road.

An hour later they finished their coffee at a sidewalk cafe and then boarded the *La Fiesta*. They walked the long gangplank into the double-deck cruise ship. Tom trudged slowly behind the others, saying he wanted to smell the air and watch the people boarding while the others moved on inside.

Collin found four seats on the upper deck, but out of range of the protective covering. Millie thanked him for having insisted they wear hats and sunglasses.

"You don't realize how devastating that sun can be on our white skins," Collin said. "That plus the reflection from the water."

"And it's a three-hour cruise," Katherine said.

Collin explained, as soon as Tom joined them, that on the deck below a Mexican band would play for most of the trip so people could dance. They would hear a short commentary in both English and Spanish as the boat went out. The ship also provided free drinks for passengers.

The boat, almost full, reverberated with the noisy squeals of children running across the deck. The band struck up its first song, a kind of calypso number. The couples saw a wide variety of nationalities represented. There were many Spanish-speaking people who wore tee shirts and carried bags from places such as Colombia and Trinidad. Two black families sat at one side, trying to speak to an Oriental woman. Local Mexicans had brought their own snacks and were passing them around in a joyous kind of picnic with each other. Two dark-skinned teenage girls lay prostrate on the deck under the direct heat of the sun. Two boys, obviously their boyfriends, also wearing nothing but skimpy bathing suits, stood nearby. Collin and Katherine had to climb over the two girls.

Collin looked at Tom. "Are you all right? You seem a bit sluggish or something."

"I'm getting older," Tom said. "I can't keep up with you young kids, you know. Don't pay any attention to me. I'm doing okay."

"Like I said on the plane, Tom was, oh, kind of under the weather before taking this trip," Millie hurriedly interjected. "But I'm watching out for him."

"You sure?" Collin asked.

"Of course," Millie said. "Oh!"

"What is it?" Katherine said.

"This boat. It's exactly what you described in chapter eight. This is where Randolph and Hillary have their big fight over Victoria, isn't it?"

"You're a real sleuth," Katherine said.

"You've made this trip so exciting for me already," she said and quickly hugged Katherine. "I just couldn't ask for a better and more marvelous vacation."

Tom had leaned back in the molded plastic chair. His head rested against a post. With his dark sunglasses, Collin could not tell if his eyes were open or closed.

"Tom, honestly, are you feeling okay?" Collin asked. "You don't look quite right. Montezuma's revenge hit you?"

"No, not at all. A little tired maybe."

"He didn't sleep well last night," Millie said, "but I'm his number-one nurse."

"Okay," Collin said.

Millie took Tom's hand in hers and sat as close to him as her bolted-in-place chair would allow.

"Let's stroll a little, shall we?" Collin asked, but even with his smile, he showed he didn't mean it as a question. He took Katherine's hand, and she followed.

Collin found a vacant spot on the right side of the boat, facing the bay. Engines churned, and along with the increasing volume of the Mexican band below, the noise made it impossible to talk in a normal tone. He smiled.

"Okay, let's talk," Katherine said.

"It wasn't so much to talk," he said, "just . . . just wanting to be alone with you for a few minutes."

"Tell me the truth, Collin. Did you bring me here to scold me for my behavior at the hotel?"

"I brought you here so that we could be together."

"Okay. We're together," she said, her face blank.

"Remember why we came to Acapulco? To try to patch up our lives."

"Yes," she said, "Maybe I simply don't understand."

"What's to understand?" he said, a smile on his face.

"You *say* we're trying to patch things up. One minute you seem honest about it, and then, oh, I don't know—"

"C'mon, what are you trying to say?"

"Then other times—like when you stare at me, not aware that I know you're doing it—"

"Yes?"

"I almost feel—well, as if—as if you hated me."

"If I hated you, do you think I'd go through all this?" His arms swept toward the bay. "An awfully expensive trip to spend with someone I hate."

"Maybe . . . maybe I'm . . . oh, I'm sorry, Collin. Of course you're trying."

He put his arm around her and gave her a hug. "Of course I'm trying. Very hard, my dear. Very hard."

Katherine wanted to ask, "What about Loretta? You called her 'darling.' Either Loretta or someone else." But she could not ask that question. Instead she said, "Collin, you're sure—absolutely sure—you want us to try again?"

"We can't go on the way we've been, can we? Two strangers in the same house."

"No," she said softly. "I don't suppose we can."

After fifteen minutes, they rejoined the Reaves. Tom had straightened up, and he waved as they approached.

"You look as though you've had a transfusion," Collin said.

"Guess I had a quick nap," he answered.

"You slept with all this racket?" Katherine asked.

"Must have," he said. "And I've missed some of the beautiful scenery already."

"Ah, but the best is still ahead," Collin said as he cocked his head to hear the captain's commentary, first in Spanish and then in English. Collin added bits of information he had picked up about Acapulco and pointed out places the captain didn't mention.

Katherine moved away from the others and strolled along the full length of the deck, observing people more than the view. After several minutes she went to the port side, where she stood alone, staring at the bay.

What am I doing here? she asked herself. *Why did I think we could ever work anything out together? Any feeling between us died long ago. Why did I agree to this trip? I must have been crazy.* Over and over Katherine asked herself these questions. She was so absorbed in her introspection, she neither heard nor noticed that Collin walked up behind her. He stood next to her, his eyes on the far shore.

He moved slightly forward and gently laid his arm on her shoulder, but the suddenness of his action startled Katherine. In an automatic action she whirled around and knocked his arm away. Their eyes met.

"Collin, I—"

"Sorry," he said and turned his back on her. He returned to the Reaves. For the rest of the trip, he never looked directly at Katherine.

A few minutes before the end of the trip, she said, "Collin, I wanted to—"

"Oh, look," he said, turning to the Reaves, "you can see a commercial ship just coming over the horizon." He pointed. "See!"

Katherine turned away, feeling the color rising in her cheeks.

When the cruise ended, Collin grabbed the Reaves' arms and pushed them toward the exit, inching past people and heading for the gangplank, as though trying to be among the first people off.

"What's the hurry?" Tom asked.

"Hungry, I guess." He laughed and slowed down, dropping their arms. "Maybe just restless after three hours in that confined space with all the noise. I had forgotten how much racket—"

"You didn't seem to mind it when we took the cruise eight years ago," Katherine said.

"Maybe I'm older now," he said, "and wiser."

Ten minutes later they reached the Crazy Lobster restaurant. "We've never been inside," Collin said. "They cater mostly to Americans, and they charge accordingly."

"Collin promised that if we ever came back, we'd eat here," Katherine said, trying to sound pleasant.

"Then let us buy," Tom said.

"Nothing doing," Collin said. "Being married to a wealthy wife and being moderately successful myself, I could never allow that, sir." He laughed and patted Tom on the back. "Besides, this is the fulfillment of my dreams. We're all going to eat the most expensive items on the menu, and I'm picking up the check."

"I'm really not very hungry," Tom said.

"And I'm not much of an eater," Millie added.

"Get it anyway. For once I want to order the best and be able to leave half of it on my plate!" He laughed.

"We walked down here almost every evening," Katherine said. "Especially during those two weeks while Collin waited for the advance. We'd buy a soft drink or sometimes fruit from a street vendor. Then we'd stroll by here and read the menu."

"Yeah," Collin said and smiled, "and we'd decide what we had already eaten. I nearly always chose swordfish steaks."

"Then we would walk over to that row of *bañas,*" Katherine pointed at small thatch-like roofs over individual chairs. "The city provides them. In the early evening, cooling breezes from the bay roll over you. It's absolutely delightful."

"And as we ate our fruit, we could smell odors from the Crazy Lobster."

Across the street two women had been bargaining with a curio seller. They watched as the Rodericks and the Reaves walked into the restaurant. One nodded. "See who just went in over there?"

"Of course," her blond friend replied.

"Strange coincidence. I mean, our being in Acupulco at the same time—"

"Nothing strange at all," the sultry-voiced woman said. "Come on, let's go."

"Go? Over there?"

"Why not?" she said with a laugh.

"But—but—"

"Let's go," she said, and her voice hardened slightly although the laughter did not disappear from her face.

They hurried to their rented car, put their purchases inside, and then waited another full minute before going into the restaurant.

A young waiter met them at the door and led them toward a corner table. They had to walk past the two couples. The blond followed the other woman. As she reached Collin's chair, she let her purse strike his back.

"Oh, excuse me—"

Collin glanced up, and their eyes met.

Chapter 4

Collin sat in his chair, as though paralyzed. Suddenly he spun around, his arm almost upsetting his water glass. "Loretta!"

She turned and smiled but did not move.

"What are you doing in Acapulco?" he asked too loudly as he left the table.

"Probably the same as you," the blond said. "A vacation. Why else would anyone come here?"

"Yeah, guess you're right," he said and hugged her.

"Collin, you look grand," she said as she pulled away and stared at him. "Been in Acapulco long?"

He shook his head. "Arrived yesterday."

"I've been here a couple of days."

Loretta's tanned skin, earned by two weeks under a sunlamp in her lower Manhattan apartment, gave her the appearance of one who had been in the tropics a long time. Her long hair, pulled back and tied high on her head, made her appear taller than her five foot four. Her white pumps and purse matched her white linen dress. Two bracelets on her left arm, also white, were of the same shade as her sculptured nails. She wore an orange bead necklace that matched the color of her lipstick.

"You look stunning," he said.

Katherine flushed at the scene before her. In an attempt to appear casual, she turned to Millie. "Did you enjoy seeing the celebrities' houses?"

Tom, who saw Katherine's discomfort asked, "Someone from Lake Forest?"

"I never saw her before in my life," Katherine said. "Either of them."

"Sorry. Just presumed—"

"I know *of* the blond. I just never met her before."

"Yes, I did," Millie said. "Fabulous houses." But her attention remained on the scene six feet away. Tom made no pretense of carrying on a conversation. He simply stared.

"And you know my assistant, Laura," Loretta was saying.

Collin nodded. "Good to see you again."

"Great meeting you like this, Mr. Roderick—"

"Uh, uh, why—why don't you come back to our table and meet my wife and our friends? Maybe even join us."

"How kind of you," Loretta said.

Collin led them to his table and introduced Loretta Kingsley and Laura Patterson.

"Why, Mrs. Roderick," Loretta said, "I've heard so much about you from Collin." She smiled, showing a full set of even teeth.

"Strange. I've never heard a word about you," Katherine said, "from Collin, I mean." A thin smile appeared on her face and vanished almost immediately.

Loretta opened her mouth, not sure of what to say next. She smiled again.

"You've earned quite a reputation," Katherine said, "in the literary world."

"I've worked hard."

"Oh, yes, and word does get around about how hard you have worked."

The waiter appeared suddenly with two chairs. He started to pull another table next to where the two couples were sitting.

"Oh, no," Loretta said to the waiter. "We'd like our own table. Over there—in the corner."

The waiter bowed his head and walked away.

"Loretta is my editor at Empire Press," Collin said to the Reaves.

"It's always a pleasure to work with Collin."

"Yes, I'm sure it is," Katherine said and then opened her menu.

"Loretta edited the first two books I did at Empire. Only moderately successful. I don't think they would have bought my third if she hadn't influenced the editorial board."

"I saw real possibilities in Collin," she said.

"Yes, I'm sure you did," Katherine said without looking up.

"She was right," Collin said, turning his attention solely upon the Reaves. "The book proved quite successful."

"It must be exciting to stick your neck out for someone when it pays off," Millie said.

"I saw quality in Collin's writing," Loretta said, glancing at Katherine. "He's probably one of the most gifted writers in America today. I'm fortunate to be associated with him."

"Oh, yes, indeed," Katherine said.

"I've always thought an editor's job must be exciting," Millie said. "So much responsibility—"

"Yes, I suppose it is," Loretta said, still looking at Katherine.

"Oh, Loretta's a top editor—the best at Empire. Promoted right to the head of the nonfiction department almost overnight."

"Almost overnight," Katherine said, "how interesting."

"Loretta, if you're going to make your appointment," Laura said, "We'd better—"

"Yes, you're right, thanks." She smiled at her assistant and started to follow Laura, who nodded and moved on. "Oh, and I enjoyed meeting all of you. Especially you, Mrs. Roderick."

"Yes, it is rather nice to meet my husband's editor—especially one who admires him so much."

"Perhaps our paths will cross again here in Acapulco—"

"Perhaps they will."

"I'm staying at the El Presidente," Loretta said. "You must come over and join me for dinner one night."

"Yes, perhaps, if we can work it out," Collin said. "We're sort of booked up for most of our time here."

"Where are you staying? The Ritz? The Princess? The—"

"The Casa Blanca," Katherine said and smiled.

"Oh, yes, such . . . such atmosphere there," Loretta said and smiled too. She waved and walked away from the table. Laura was already seated in a far corner where neither Collin nor Katherine could see them without turning around.

"Don't know about the rest of you," Millie said, "but I'm hungry. Just being in that fresh air on the bay gave me quite an appetite."

Collin avoided looking at his wife as he said, "I'm glad you finally got to meet my editor."

"I'm not very hungry," Katherine said. She took a Valium from her purse and washed it down with water. "I'll just have a glass of wine."

"Do you think you ought to? Mixing Valium and wine—I mean, it's none of my business, but—," Millie stammered.

"Right. None of your business." Then seeing the pain reflected on Millie's face, Katherine reached over and squeezed her hand. "See why I need a Valium? I'm even rude to *you.*"

"I'd like to eat any fish that's dead," Tom said as he continued to study the menu.

Later, Katherine picked at a fruit plate. Collin tried to appear hungry, but he left most of the food, after moving it around on his plate. The Reaves ate heartily.

Immediately after lunch they hailed a cab and drove to the cliffs at Quebrada. They arrived just before the first diver made his plunge off a ledge, 150 feet high, into a shallow ocean pool.

An hour later, they returned to the hotel. The Reaves went to their room. Katherine, glancing at her watch, noticed it was almost half-past one. "You have an appointment, don't you, Collin?" she asked.

"Yes . . . yes, I do."

"An important one, I suppose."

"Yes, I made it only this morning—"

"You'd better hurry. You wouldn't want to keep anyone important waiting for you, would you?" she said, consciously keeping her voice breezy.

"I'd better go on—"

"Unless . . . unless you'd rather—oh, forget it," she said. Katherine turned and walked toward the room without looking back. She hoped Collin would follow.

By the time she had gone up the flight of steps, Katherine realized that Collin was not following her. As she turned and walked across the open passageway above the fountain, she saw Collin getting back into the taxi. She raced to her room, hurriedly unlocked the door and went inside. She fell down on the bed.

The tears flowed.

"He's not worth it," she said between her sobs, beating the pillow with her fists. "If I had any sense at all, I'd divorce him. Or at least walk out on him."

The crying subsided, and she lay silently on the bed. She knew where Collin had gone.

She wished she didn't care.

Collin returned three hours later. She recognized the sound of his footsteps as he walked down the passageway. Katherine quickly wiped her eyes and then rolled over onto her stomach. When Collin opened the door, she rolled back over slowly and looked up through what she hoped would pass for sleepy eyes. "Back already?"

"Already? It took longer than I thought. It's after four-thirty."

"Oh, is it?" she said.

"Let me tell you what happened," Collin said. "I had this interview with Señor Ortega. He laughed at my poor Spanish, but I think he also appreciated my trying to use his language. He kept telling me that I was different from other Americans who came to see him."

"You had a good afternoon then," Katherine said. "With Mr. Ortega, I mean."

"Excellent—"

"Just the two of you for three hours—"

"Are you accusing me of something?" Collin asked.

"Accusing? Since when do I, your wife, have the privilege of accusation?"

"You sound like one of those dumb women in your novels—"

"Then, Collin, the next scene calls for you either to, A, lie your head off, B, walk out and slam the door, or C, confess that you've been hiding terrible secrets from the innocent woman who waits patiently and lovingly—"

"If this were a novel, I'd probably write the next scene with, D, where the hero pops the smart-mouth on her smart mouth!"

"Oh, my, then let's go to option A. Tell me about your visit with Señor Ortega . . . that long, interesting visit."

"Katherine, I came back here with good news and all I get is stupid arguing and—"

Katherine held up her hand. "I offer a truce. Speak, and I'll listen."

"You will?"

"Promise," she said.

"Well, it proved to be better than I expected. He ushered me into his office. He pulled out this huge file and actually let me read through all of it. Most of the correspondence was in English. I don't think Ortega understood just how much information he had. You see—"

A knock at the door interrupted him, and Collin raced to answer it. Manuel stood there, holding a tray. Collin thanked him, tipped him heavily, and brought the tray inside himself.

Katherine looked up. "Champagne? What's the occasion?"

"To the success of the book. To our relationship. To all kinds of good things," Collin said. He popped the cork on the champagne and poured his wife a glass. He then poured a Coke for himself.

"You're not having any?" she said as she took the glass.

"I haven't had a drink since—I mean, for a long time," Collin said.

"Oh? I hadn't noticed."

"Let's drink to our relationship. To a beautiful resolution of all our difficulties."

Just before dark, the hotel car arrived to pick up the Rodericks and the Reaves. Millie appeared in the lobby alone. "Tom's not feeling so well tonight."

"Anything serious?" Collin asked.

"He just said he wanted to enjoy the peace and quiet. He likes being alone sometimes."

"So do I," Collin said and glared at his wife.

"I hope you don't mind—my going along with you," Millie said.

"I'm glad you came. Let the old stick-in-the-mud stay home if he wants. We'll have a good time anyway," Collin said.

The drive to La Paloma Blanca took twenty minutes. The driver parked, and they got out and went inside the hotel. The elevator stopped at the seventh floor.

They left the elevator, turned left, and walked down a long hallway. Instead of an outside wall, a reinforced, three-foot-high railing ran the entire length. Although made of masonry, it had a width of less than six inches.

"Gorgeous place," Collin said aloud, his hand on the ledge.

"Yes, beautiful, isn't it?" Millie said. "And you can look out over the bay and see the lights."

"We celebrated here," Katherine said, "Just before we left Acapulco."

Collin paused to look over the railing.

"If anyone ever fell," Millie said, also looking over, "there would be no chance of survival, would there?"

Collin whirled around and stared. Then he smiled. "Not much."

They approached the bar, which served complimentary drinks and had a wide variety to choose from. Collin and Millie declined. Katherine hesitated and then said, "I think I'll have a glass of wine."

"Do you think you should?" Collin asked.

"Why not?" She moved back to the bar.

Collin shook his head. "You've already had a snoot full—"

"If you call a couple of drinks a snoot full . . . and of all people to be commenting on how much other people drink—" Katherine grabbed two glasses and followed behind Collin and Millie, drinking the first.

"I liked it so much, I thought I'd have a second," she said and handed the empty one to a waiter standing nearby. She glared at her husband.

They sat near the end of a long table that was covered with a simple white cloth. Across the room were other tables, all placed at angles providing a clear view of the buffet tables and the small stage.

The maître d' nodded at them to go through the line. "We have the finest of Mexican cuisine as well as foods from Spain, Puerto Rico, Costa Rica, Peru, Argentina. . . ." As he rambled on and pointed to various items of fish, meat, and vegetables, Collin took small portions, spreading them on his plate to make it appear that he had taken more. He had no appetite.

As they ate, Collin kept asking Millie questions about her grandchildren. To Katherine it was obvious that he was not really listening to the answers, as though he merely wanted to avoid silence.

"Oh, Katherine," Millie said. "Why didn't I catch on when we walked in here?"

"Catch on?"

"Hillary and Randolph—they came here, didn't they?"

"Yes, you're right again."

"Sounds almost as if you memorized the book, instead of just reading it," Collin said, trying to keep the conversation light.

"Oh, and one of the high points of the book took place here, too," Millie said. "Hillary finds out about Randolph's past, and she struggles over whether she can forgive him."

"Yes, as I remember the book," Collin said, "Hillary had quite a time forgiving." He riveted his eyes on his wife's face.

"You have to understand Hillary's makeup. She had been betrayed by another man before she met Randolph—," Katherine said.

"And she treated him as though he was no good because of *her* problem—"

"Really more because of his lack of sensitivity to her needs," Katherine said. "Some men think of nothing but their own needs—"

"Excuse me," Collin said, "I think I'll have another helping of that black-bean combination. Anybody else want anything?"

The women shook their heads.

An hour later complete darkness had settled over the bay, with only flickering lights from yachts penetrating the covering.

A not-very-funny stand-up comedian tried to warm up the audience with empty prattle and double entendres. Katherine decided he was more vulgar than clever. One American group laughed as though they had never heard such humor in their lives. They swung a banner announcing their home city every time the punch line came.

After fifteen minutes, though to Katherine it felt more like an hour, the comedian introduced a six-piece brass band and a strolling violinist. They walked on stage, played one number, and walked off the other side.

The comedian returned with another attempt at humor. This time, even the group with the banner only cackled. He then introduced two flamenco dancers. They, purportedly, re-created a folk dance from northern Mexico. Katherine questioned its authenticity, but they performed well and loudly. The audience applauded enthusiastically.

After two numbers, the band walked onto the stage, played one song, and danced off again. Then three couples in Mexican costumes appeared.

Katherine leaned over and whispered, "It's getting a little stuffy." She nodded toward a man sitting nearby, smoking a pipe. "I'm going to stand over against the balcony and breathe the fresh sea air." She pushed her chair back to get up.

Collin pushed his own chair back so quickly it almost fell. "I'll go with you."

Katherine shrugged. "Suit yourself."

"Hope you don't mind our leaving you for a few minutes," Collin said to Millie.

"Go right ahead," she said, her eyes riveted on the performers.

Katherine was already leaning against the balcony when Collin reached her.

"Here, let me give you a better view," he said and picked her up, seating her on the ledge. As he faced her, he put his arms around her.

"Remember when we came here before?"

"Yes ... I remember ... very well."

For a moment, both of them allowed their minds to travel back to their earlier trip to La Paloma Blanca. It had been the night after Collin had received his ten-thousand-dollar advance. They had chosen La Paloma Blanca as their place of celebration.

"In fact," Katherine said aloud, "we even stood at the back. Near this spot, I think."

"You remember even that?"

She nodded. "You put your arm around me and pulled me close. Then you kissed me."

"If only our lives had stopped then," Collin said.

"But they didn't stop, did they?"

"No . . . no, they didn't."

"You have a good memory, Katherine. You never forget anything, do you?"

"I wish I could forget," Katherine said, as she realized his body was pressing against hers. His mouth, only inches away, seemed to move closer. She made a feeble attempt to push him away.

"I wish you could have forgotten, too," Collin said. "But I remember quite a few things. The way our lives fell apart. Your accusations and screams. Then your long silences and rebuffs when I tried to talk."

"Collin, please, I—"

"I haven't forgotten the locked bedroom either. Or the accusations of my having affairs with other women!"

"Didn't you?"

"Who are you to make accusations, Katherine? You've probably slept with half the men in Lake Forest!"

"How dare you?"

"Want to know how I dare? Because I know what an evil, ugly, unforgiving shrew you are—"

"I hate you!" she screamed, knowing that with the noise of performers only Collin heard her words. "I hate you. I intended to make your life as miserable as you've made mine."

"You've done a great job then," he said. "You haven't even added a new approach. The old words still work. You've been saying the same things since Reggie's death."

Katherine pushed him away from her. "Just get away from me. I don't ever want to see you again!"

The music neared a crescendo. On the stage six pairs of feet stomped in an unceasing rhythm. The audience, caught up in the mood, clapped in time to their movements. The dancers put on a most athletic performance.

At that moment, Collin laid both his hands on Katherine's shoulders, and stared into her hazel eyes. He shook her gently, but his anger was obvious as he snarled at her. "To think that once—that I once thought I loved you! You're the most miserable woman in the entire world, and you want everyone else to be as miserable as you are!" Although his lips scarcely moved, the words came through loudly, pounding in her ears.

Katherine's eyes widened. "I never knew you hated me so much!"

"Then you never stopped to listen! You were too busy screaming at me!" His words sliced her like a new razor. She'd noticed cold indifference in his eyes before, but this black hatred was an unexpected blow.

Katherine pulled her right arm free and slapped his face. Tears filled her eyes as he grabbed her arm and the pressure of his fingers squeezed tighter. Then, as if something inside him had snapped, he released her and walked away.

Chapter 5

Collin sank down on the steps outside La Paloma Blanca. His head rested in his hands. "Oh, God, what have I done? Whatever got into me?"

Katherine, in the doorway, took a step toward him and stopped. She had no idea what to do next. She stopped, as though frozen to the spot, and stared at him.

People came and went, several of them brushing past Collin. One woman commented loudly in Spanish that he was drunk. Collin didn't even look up.

Although the temperature hovered in the eighties, Katherine could see Collin shivering. He mumbled again, "What have I done?"

Slowly he seemed to gain control of himself, and he sat upright, staring into space. Collin sighed deeply and then shuffled to the bottom of the stairs. He moved to one side, half hiding himself in the shadows.

"Oh, there you are!" Millie called out. "You okay, Collin?"

He made a feeble attempt to nod.

"The way you rushed out up there! Would you like me to call a doctor?"

"Just—just leave me alone," he mumbled.

"But, Collin, I—"

"Nothing. I'm okay." Grabbing the handkerchief from his hip pocket, he wiped his eyes and blew his nose. He looked up and saw Katherine standing next to Millie.

Their eyes met. He tried to turn his head away, but he could only stare. "Katherine, I—I—"

"Must be something you ate," she said quickly.

"It just didn't occur to me that you were sick," Millie said.

Katherine turned to the driver who leaned against the car twenty feet away. "We'll return to the Casa Blanca now," Katherine called. "Mr. Roderick is ill."

The driver hurried to them and took Collin's arm. "Come, señor, I help you to the car."

Collin jerked away. "I'm okay, really—," and then his eyes met Katherine's again. He felt his legs collapsing, and the driver grabbed him.

"Por favor, señor," he pleaded. "I shall help you." Collin no longer resisted.

Collin felt a blackness strike his head as though he would pass out. He shook himself slightly and rested his weight on the Mexican's arm. The driver opened the front door. "Sit you down here, next to me, and I watch out for you good," he said.

Then he hurried around and let the women into the backseat.

During the ride back to the hotel, none of them spoke. Once Millie laid her hand on Collin's shoulder and pressed it gently. As soon as the car halted, Katherine opened the door and slid out. She darted down the driveway.

Collin stared for a minute, as if uncertain what to do. "Katherine, please—"

"Katherine!" Millie called. "Don't make me chase after you again! Please—"

Katherine stopped but did not turn around. "I suppose this is beginning to become a habit. Running away, I mean."

Millie caught up with Katherine and laid her hand gently on the younger woman's shoulder. "Is something wrong?"

"What did you see? At La Paloma Blanca, I mean?"

"See? Well, Collin rushed from the room. I turned around, and you were leaning backward against the railing of the balcony, holding on with one hand as though you were reaching for Collin with the other. Then, a second later, you rushed out, too."

"You—you didn't hear anything?"

"Did I need to?"

"What do you mean?"

"Skip it," Millie said.

"You know, don't you? You know how Collin feels about me?"

She nodded.

Katherine shot her a quizzical look. "How?"

"Let's just say I read it in his eyes."

"You said something about that before. But . . . but I don't understand."

"Don't try to understand, dear."

"But he—he—"

"He hates you?"

"Yes. Desperately."

"But he didn't actually say that, did he?"

"No—oh, I don't know. But I've never seen him so angry before. And in the end he just walked away from it, as though it was all meaningless."

"In a way, it is. But I think that right now Collin is feeling angry with himself."

"Yes," Katherine said.

"That, too, I mean," Millie added.

"That, *too?*" Katherine turned and faced Millie. "I get the feeling I'm missing pieces of a puzzle—"

"Katherine, dear, I want to say one thing to you. You're one of the luckiest women in the world."

"Me? Lucky?"

"Yes," Millie said. "Lucky because you're loved by a man like Collin."

"Loved? Millie, maybe you've been reading too many of my novels."

"Have I?"

"Absolutely. Or else you're reading a love story that ended years ago."

"I only know what I read in Collin's eyes."

"In his eyes?" she snorted.

"Katherine, I'm not trying to involve myself in your lives. I'm your friend. I love Collin, too. Forgive my intrusion."

"I'm not angry. It's just that . . . that every time I turn around, you seem to be present, and you know almost as much about our lives as we do."

"I only meant to encourage you, Katherine."

"I believe you," she said, "but—"

"Just one other thing—," Millie stopped. "I'm sorry, forgive me." She started to turn around.

"What other thing?"

"I'm not trying to meddle, honest, but—"

"But, what?"

"I've been praying for you. For both of you."

"Thanks, Millie. I'm not very keen on religion—"

"Sometimes God speaks to me," Millie said, ignoring Katherine's words. "I don't mean I hear voices or anything like that."

"How does God speak to you?" Katherine took a step closer, not sure where the conversation was leading. She wanted to run away from the hotel and get away from everyone.

"I get a kind of feeling inside."

"Oh," Katherine said. She turned and started to walk away.

"Wait. As long as I've said that much, I'll add just this, and I'll leave you alone."

"Okay, Millie."

"You two can make it. You and Collin."

"What? After what we've been through?"

"You have more going for you than either of you realizes."

"Like what?"

Millie stared at Katherine before answering. She moved forward and patted her shoulder. "I'm beginning to sound like a snoopy old woman and I don't mean to do that. Let's drop it," Millie said. "I—I only wanted to encourage you."

"Yes, I think it best to drop it."

"I need to run up to the room and see how Tom is," Millie said as she turned abruptly.

For several seconds, Katherine watched Millie walk briskly toward the hotel lobby. Then she turned again and headed down the driveway. She had almost reached the end when she heard Collin call her name. She picked up her pace. After she nodded to the night porter and passed out of his sight, she broke into a jog. She reached the road and hesitated momentarily, looking both ways. With the help of the dim street lights, she turned right and saw that she would be able to see as she rushed down the hill.

Katherine quickened her pace. She thought she heard Collin calling her again, but she wasn't sure. Her breathing became labored, but she didn't care. She wanted to get as far away from her husband as possible. Then she remembered the shortcut.

When they had been to Acapulco before, they had discovered a well-marked public shortcut that led down a steep flight of concrete steps. It cut off half a mile and came out behind the old market. Katherine bounded down the steps.

After the first dozen steps Katherine realized the lights were growing dimmer. Because of the steepness, she slowed down, not wanting to trip.

"Katherine! Wait!"

Without looking around, she knew he had started racing down the steps. She could hear his feet pounding as he raced toward her. She increased her speed, determined not to stop and not to turn around.

She felt his hand brush her shoulder, and she dodged out of his grasp. In doing so, she turned her ankle. Katherine stumbled and fell to one side, her shoulder striking the wooden fence. She flipped forward, hitting her knees. Throwing her hands out to catch herself, she went forward and rolled down two more steps before she slumped forward.

Collin reached her just as she landed. He knelt down and put his arm around her shoulder and lifted her head. "Katherine—"

She opened her eyes and stared at him. "Why don't you let me fall the rest of the way?"

"Please, I—"

"I'm already hurt. Please stay away. You cause me more hurt and pain every time you come near me."

"Please, please, listen—"

"I didn't know you hated me so much," she said, and the tears flooded her eyes. She jerked free and in doing so, wrenched her shoulder. She cried out from the pain. She looked down at her palms—scratched and bleeding. She touched her knees that had scraped the cement. One of them bled slightly.

"Please, at least let me try to explain—"

Katherine leaned against the wooden fence. "You don't have anything to say to me. You said it all at La Paloma Blanca."

"Let me help you up, at least."

"I don't need your help," Katherine said, gritting her teeth and at the same time wondering if she could even stand up.

"Just shut up! I'm going to help you up—"

"I don't—I don't need your help," she said and burst into tears. The pain in her shoulder stabbed at her.

"I told you to shut up. We'll talk at the top." He put his arm around her and pulled her slowly upward. Katherine winced with pain but shook her head. "I'm okay. Really."

When she was upright, he asked, "Can you put weight on your foot?"

"I think so. I—I turned my ankle—"

"I saw it happen. Now, can you walk on it?"

She leaned on the foot. "It's sore, but I think I can."

"Are you sure?"

"I think so," she said.

He kept his arm around her. "Just lean on me. Let's move slowly. If it hurts, tell me."

"I can make it. Honest."

"I can carry you—"

"Silly. We'd both fall like Jack and Jill."

Collin saw a smile on her face between the tears.

"Okay, relax then. One step at a time." She winced after the first step, and he scooped her into his arms.

"I'm too heavy—"

"Quiet, lady," he said and took another step.

When they reached the top, he sat her down gently on the top step. He knelt beside her and took off her shoe. "Your ankle has already swollen a bit."

"I'll soak it later. I'm fine . . . really."

"Let me carry you—"

"Please. I want to walk. I'll go slowly, but on my own steam."

"Okay," he said and helped her stand. He wrapped his arm around her waist and pulled her close. They trudged toward the hotel.

A concrete ledge ran parallel with the road in front of the hotel. Just as they approached the entrance, she said, "I'd like to sit down for a minute. I'll be all right."

He helped her to the ledge and sat down next to her. Neither of them spoke.

He finally said, "Can we—can we talk?"

Katherine did not answer but turned her head so that she stared at him in the half light.

"Katherine, we've both made life a complete hell for each other."

"It's been that, all right."

"And yet you wouldn't let me go," he said. He kicked a small stone and watched it roll into the darkness. "I felt trapped."

"What do you feel toward me now, Collin? Anything other than hate?"

"I don't hate you. Not now, anyway."

"You don't?"

"When I ran from the balcony and later, when I sat on the steps, I knew then that I didn't hate you."

"What *do* you feel?" she asked, watching his face carefully.

"What do *you* feel, Katherine?"

"Empty. Maybe confused."

"What happens now?" he asked.

"I've been thinking, Collin. All the way back from La Paloma I've been turning something over in my mind." She hesitated, her gaze not leaving his face.

"Okay," he said, "what?"

"Would you—would you be willing to try again? To make something of our marriage?"

"I don't know if that's possible. Not now."

"Maybe you're right," she said softly. "It's just that—well, you asked me on this trip as a chance to try to salvage our marriage."

"But that wasn't my real motive—I planned to make life so miserable for you that you'd demand a divorce."

"I've already figured out that much. I just want . . . I just want to give it a try."

"After what I—"

"We said we'd give it one more chance."

"Yes, we said that."

"Collin," she said and took his hand in hers. "I've had to face up to some things about myself. I . . . I . . . saw myself through your eyes tonight. And I didn't like what I saw." She pressed her hand on his, and her nails dug into his palm, but she seemed unaware of her actions. "Collin, I want to try. Just—just give us a chance."

"Katherine, do we have anything left? Anything to build on?"

"Memories."

"Some of them are pretty awful," he said.

"But we had good ones, too. Especially here in Acapulco."

"Yes," he said. "We did."

"And we've got something else."

"What's that?"

"Anticipation."

He repeated the word. "I don't know that I have the ability to anticipate. Not after all we've done—"

"But—please, can't we try?"

"Can we?"

"Is it dead, Collin? Everything you once felt for me?"

"I don't know."

"Then we're back at the old impasse. But, I want . . . I want to love you, Collin. The way . . . the way I did eight years ago."

"Can we turn time backward?"

"I don't want to turn anything back. I just want to try again."

"Katherine, you can't say that you love me. Yet you won't release me."

For a moment she didn't answer but turned and stared at the city lights below. When she spoke, her voice was so low he had to strain to hear her. "Okay, I'll make a deal with you."

"A deal?"

"We said we'd give it one grand try in Acapulco. Regardless of your motive in asking me here, that's what I agreed to. Let's do that," Katherine said. "Let's wipe away as much of the past as we can and try."

"But if our attempt fails?"

"Then I'll file for divorce as soon as we get back to Lake Forest. No strings."

"None?"

"I'll leave your life forever. I promise."

"You really mean that, don't you, Katherine?"

She started to answer, and then her voice seemed unable to respond. She nodded. She took his other hand in hers and raised them both to her lips and kissed his palms gently. "I mean it as completely as I've ever meant anything in my life."

"How do you know I'll do my best? That I'll try?" he said.

"I'm willing to take the risk."

She stood up abruptly and took small steps toward the hotel. "Let's go back. To the room."

Collin came up behind her. He hesitated for a minute and then put his right arm around her shoulder. "I'll do anything I can. We did love each other once, didn't we?" He left his arm there, not sure if he ought to move it or not.

"Yes, once," she said. She put her left hand lightly on his. They crossed the road and started into the courtyard. She stopped and spun around. "Collin, I don't know how to begin. I've repelled you for so long—"

"I don't either," he said and chuckled.

"I feel like a sixteen-year-old on her first date," Katherine said, "wanting you to kiss me, and yet afraid that you will."

"I guess I feel a little like that, too," he said. He took her hand and looked down at his feet.

"Let's—let's stand up on the balcony and look down at the fountain," she said. "That is, if you want."

They started walking again. "Memories and anticipation," Collin said. "I like the sound of those words."

They held hands as they walked up the driveway.

Chapter 6

"Be patient with me," Katherine said as she lay in bed next to her husband. "I feel as though my head is whirling from all that's happened in the past two days."

"Along with a throbbing head, a bruised knee, and—"

"Yes, along with that, too," Katherine said. She lay on her back, her hands at her sides. Their bodies almost touched. More than once she wanted to turn over and stroke the hair on his chest as she had done in the past. But too many painful memories prevented her from moving her hand toward him.

Yet, despite her inhibition and despite the pain in her foot, knee, and shoulder, Katherine felt at peace, even though sleep eluded her. Tonight she had no knots in her stomach, and she didn't even consider taking her usual sleeping pill.

Her mind flitted from one subject to another, especially to the memories of happier times in Acapulco. She thought also of herself and of how she had changed in the past two days.

"I've learned something about myself," Collin said softly.

"What's that?" she asked.

"I realize now that I could never really hate you. But I felt so—so desperate—so trapped."

"Maybe we're both learning a lot about ourselves," she said softly.

She wanted to ask, "What happens next?" but the words would not come to her lips. *What happens when we leave Acapulco? What happens if we can't find enough common ground to reestablish our marriage?*

"I meant my promise, Collin—I mean about—about letting you go—if you still want your freedom."

"At least we'll have resolved something when we leave here," he said. "We'll know we're going to make it together or we part completely."

"Yes," she said softly, "One way or the other."

"I—I want to love you, Katherine," he said. "I just don't know if I can—can give it my best."

"You want to back out?" she asked, feeling a sudden pounding in her chest.

"No," he answered. "Right now I want to try. I don't know if I can live up to it—"

"Collin, I said I'd take the risk."

"I'm willing. With all I have within me, I'm willing to try. That's the best I can tell you tonight."

"That's all I'm asking," she said, feeling the churning in her stomach slowing down again.

Collin turned his head and kissed her lightly on the cheek.

Katherine wanted to turn her face toward his. She wanted their lips to meet, but she couldn't make her body respond. Not yet. Perhaps tomorrow night—or in a few days.

"You know, I can't understand what's happened to me," Collin said, inching slightly away from her. "I mean, all the bitterness and hatred have vanished. It's as though those feelings never existed."

"I'm glad—"

"Can such intense emotions change so rapidly?"

"Someone said that hate is actually the other side of love," Katherine answered.

"The worst part—the real bitterness," he said, "built up because you never let me explain. About what happened that night—"

"I was in too much pain then," Katherine said.

"Will you—will you let me explain? I don't mean now . . . but before we leave Acapulco?"

"I can't promise, Collin," she said, "but I'll try. Just . . . just give me a little time before we dig that up. Please."

"Okay," he said and squeezed her hand. He held it for a few seconds and then let go.

"Katherine," he said, "even if . . . even if things don't work out for us, and we can't . . . can't talk about that night . . . somehow it doesn't matter so much anymore."

"I can't say that, Collin. Not yet anyway."

"Maybe you will," he whispered. "Later."

"Maybe."

Collin sat up, leaning on his elbow. "Do you—do you feel like talking? Or maybe just listening to me a little?"

"I—I don't feel like talking—"

"I'm sorry," he said. "I guess I forgot about your pain."

"It's not the pain—the physical pain, Collin. It's simply that . . . you know, it's harder for me to . . . to talk about the things I feel deeply. You're different. You used to discover yourself as you talked about feelings."

"Maybe that's why I'd at least like you to listen."

"I'll listen."

Collin pulled himself up to a full sitting position, stuck a pillow behind his head, and leaned against the headboard. Katherine sat up next to him and laid her hand lightly on his.

"For a long time I've felt like an intruder. Maybe it doesn't make sense to you," he said. Katherine wished they had left a light on so that she could see the expression on his face.

"I'm not sure," she answered.

"I used to imagine myself as standing outside our house, peering through the window. I could see you sitting at your desk, writing away. I could even see me sitting in the den reading. But at the same time, I felt as though I didn't belong there."

"I shut you out. Is that what you mean?"

"Katherine, I'm not trying to blame you. I've done enough blaming. No, it's . . . well, here we are in Mexico and for the first time in years, I feel as though I belong inside the house."

"That sounds like a positive statement," Katherine answered.

"I—I'm not even sure that my feelings rate on the positive side of the scale. Maybe . . . maybe the best I can say is that they're now in neutral."

"But that's a positive move, isn't it?"

"Sure is," he said and chuckled.

"Collin . . . would you . . . would you just hold me. I'm not asking for anything more. Just wrap your arms around me for a minute."

Collin took Katherine in his arms and she turned over on her side. They lay in silence, hearing muffled noises outside. Collin's breathing became even, and Katherine slowly pulled away.

She lay flat on her side of the bed and tried to sleep but could not. She tried relaxing one part of her body at a time, beginning with her feet. By the time she reached her head, her mind raced along myriad paths. "This is crazy," she mumbled to herself.

Maybe fresh air would help. She crept out of bed and tiptoed across the room. Katherine unlocked the door leading to the patio, went outside, and quietly closed the door behind her.

She walked over to the railing and leaned forward, gazing at the city below. The brilliant lights of the early evening had largely disappeared. Only isolated rays pierced the darkness, except in the new section of Acapulco where the lights never went out. She could see thousands of glowing colors from the hotel area.

As Katherine thought of the hotels, she remembered Loretta Kingsley. *That's what bothers me the most,* she said to herself. *They planned this sweet little rendezvous here in Acapulco—they must have!* She slammed her hand against the rail and swore.

How dare Loretta flaunt herself before Katherine?

And yet . . . Collin had seemed genuinely surprised when Loretta showed up at the Crazy Lobster. Their meeting had obviously not been part of the plan.

If they had a plan, she reminded herself.

On the other hand, Collin had never attempted secrecy about

Loretta. For the past three years, Katherine and Collin had gone separate ways. Katherine had made it clear that she didn't care what he
did or where he went so long as she didn't have to know about it.

Loretta Kingsley. Why, she asked herself, at this stage of the game,
was she getting jealous?

"I don't know," she said aloud, "I really don't."

"Don't know what?"

She spun around. "Oh," she said, "you startled me."

"I must have fallen asleep. Then I awakened and thought I'd come
out here with you. Okay?"

"Of course," she said.

He came beside her and took her hand. They stood in silence, staring at the city, letting the soft breeze caress their skin.

They remained motionless, each of them thinking private
thoughts. They did not hear the door of room 408 open or the soft
slippers of someone walking across the concrete floor.

Moments later Katherine heard a sound, like someone crying, but
she wasn't certain. She cocked her head. Yes, she heard it again—
from the next section of the patio. It took a few seconds for Katherine's eyes to adjust enough to recognize Millie, who had been leaning on the railing. Then Millie turned away and walked slowly over
to the small metal table and sat down. She hunched forward, her
back to the Rodericks. She sobbed again. Katherine quickly put her
fingers on Collin's lips, and then with her mouth next to his ear, she
whispered, "It's Millie. She's crying."

Collin tiptoed over and leaned against the masonry that separated
them. "What's wrong, Millie?"

Millie straightened up and pulled her robe tightly around her
shoulders. She didn't turn around. "Nothing."

"You're crying," Katherine said.

"Yes, I am," she said softly.

"Look, Millie, if you don't want our interference—"

Millie turned around and faced the couple. "No, wait. I didn't
mean to be rude."

"You weren't rude," Katherine said.

"It's just that, oh, I don't know quite how to express—"

"You don't have to talk about it," Collin said, "that is, unless you
want to."

Millie grabbed a tissue from her pocket and wiped her eyes. She
walked over to the barrier between the two patios. "Thanks for your
concern. Mostly, I was praying."

"Then something *is* wrong."

She laughed. "No. Maybe you'd call them joyful tears."

"Joyful tears? That's a new one on me."

"You don't know how much this trip means to me. Even more to
Tom. Just being able to visit Acapulco is a miracle in itself. On top of

all that, getting to meet you two. You've done so much. You've lavished your time and money on us—"

"We've enjoyed it, too—"

"And to travel with my favorite author," she went on. "A chance to actually visit all the spots where Hillary and Randolph went. Well, it's—it's just more than I could ever have expected."

"You make me sound like some kind of saint," Katherine said.

She laughed again. "I'd rather think of you as an answer to prayer."

"A what?"

"Just what I said. An answer to prayer."

"That's the first time anyone has called me that."

"You see, Tom and I prayed for God to make this a very special time for us. You've helped make it special."

"I'm touched, Millie, but—"

"No buts," Millie said. "Both of you—you've been marvelous."

Katherine shook her head. "You've seen how we squabble with each other—the anger between us—and yet you say things like that—"

"You think I'm a little strange?" Millie said, and Katherine thought she saw the outline of a smile on her face.

"How you could say such kind things about us and yet know—"

"I know that I love you both," Millie said. "I know that beneath your separate pain, you're fine people."

"Wait a minute, Millie," Collin interrupted. "Do you know why I insisted on your accompanying us from the airport in the taxi? Why we came here to the Casa Blanca instead of the Princess? Why I've taken you everywhere with us? At least, originally?"

"Does it matter?"

"It does to me," he said softly. "It matters that I explain."

"If it helps you—"

"I did those things because they upset Katherine. And . . . I hoped it would make you a little more sympathetic toward me."

"Oh, Collin, you still don't understand. It doesn't matter *why* you treated us kindly. At least, it doesn't matter to me."

"You amaze me all the same."

Millie reached across the barrier and touched Collin's hand. "Sorry. You're trying to say something, and I keep changing the conversation."

"I needed to make sure you understood."

"I'm listening, Collin."

"We have one lousy marriage. I didn't mind making it lousier—for a few days. I wanted you and Tom to see a kind and long-suffering husband married to a harridan."

"I'm not exactly stupid, Collin. I know Katherine didn't want us."

"But I changed, Millie. You know that, don't you? I really want you around now."

"Of course, I know that." She grabbed Katherine's hands. "I also know that both of you are special people."

"Special?" Katherine said. "Confused, maybe. Even a little desperate—"

"Don't!" Millie snapped. "I will not listen to you say such things about yourself."

"But they're true—"

"Are they?" Millie said. "You think you're so awful, but I choose to see the good in you, and the potential."

"You're amazing," Collin said.

"Collin, we often do things with the wrong motives, and they still work out right."

"Millie, I—I'm not always good at telling people how I feel," Katherine said, suddenly glad for the darkness so that she didn't have to look directly into Millie's eyes. "But you're one of the most unique and special people I've ever known."

"Right now, I just feel thankful."

"Yes, although I'm still not sure why—"

"Mostly I'm thankful to God for making all this possible. That's what I was doing when you spoke to me. Thanking God."

"Millie, I love you, and I don't mean to cut you off, but you know I don't relate to God or this praying business," Katherine said.

"Am I offending you?"

"Not at all. It's just that—"

"You'd rather I didn't talk about God?"

"No, not really. It comes naturally for you. And I know it's real. For you."

"Do you also believe, Katherine, that our coming together was no accident?"

"I'm not quite sure what you mean."

"Has it occurred to you that this was a divine rendezvous in Acapulco? That God planned it and worked it out for the four of us to meet on the plane?"

"Guess I never thought about it."

"You see, as a Christian I try to be aware of God's involvement in my life. I don't believe in fate or coincidence or even accidents."

"Maybe you're right," Katherine said. "Who knows?"

"That's why I came out here to pray. My heart was so full of happiness. I tried to sleep, but I could only think of the wonderful things God has done for Tom and me. And I believe God used you and Collin to make them happen—even though you weren't aware of it. Does that make sense to you?"

"If you feel it makes sense," Katherine said slowly, "but I'm not quite ready to accept that kind of attitude."

"In my head I understand," Collin said. "As Katherine told you, I once took a course in the Christian faith. You're actually expressing more of a Hebraic Old Testament attitude toward God than what one sees reflected in the New Testament writings."

Millie leaned over the wall and hugged Collin first and then Katherine. "I've said enough about my faith. You caught me out here and—"

"We asked the questions," Katherine said.

"I honestly didn't mean to give you answers you didn't want to hear."

"Maybe we need to hear them," Katherine said, "except . . . maybe we're not ready."

"Maybe not," Millie said, "yet."

"But if we decide to learn more about God, you and Tom are the people we'll come to. Okay?" Collin interjected. He kissed her cheek.

"Good night," Millie said and went back inside.

Katherine and Collin stayed on the patio. They walked slowly to the other side and stared at the lights again.

"Collin, what if—what if she's right?"

"Maybe so; after all, Hindus believe in kismet, Muslims in—"

"I didn't mean that part," Katherine said.

"I didn't think you did."

"Collin, what if—what if Millie's right? About God being involved? What if God planned this rendezvous in Acapulco between us and the Reaves?"

"Okay. What if?"

"Then maybe there is something to all of this God business."

"I suppose there might be," Collin said. "It's not that I'm an atheist, you know."

"No, Collin, I don't know anything for sure. Not anymore."

"Maybe that's my trouble, too. I thought I knew what I wanted and now I'm not sure either."

"I wish I could be sure," Katherine said.

They stood together in silence. Katherine wanted to drape her arm around him and kiss him, but she hesitated. *Is it courage I lack,* she asked herself, *or is it that I sense he wouldn't know how to respond?*

She turned slowly, wanting to say something, wanting to touch him so that even if her words wouldn't come, perhaps the pressure of her slim fingers would let him know how she felt.

Collin turned back toward the room. He yawned. "I'm getting sleepy now." He went inside.

Katherine stayed in the same spot, silently cursing herself for holding back. *Yet what if you made a move and Collin rebuffed you?*

the silent voice asked.   *I don't know,* she answered herself. *Maybe I was too scared to risk it.*

Finally Katherine tiptoed back into the room. She locked the door. Collin had left the light on in the bathroom with the door half closed, allowing in just enough light to enable her to see.

Collin lay sprawled across the bed on his stomach, his mouth open. As she watched his even breathing, Katherine thought of the nights they had spent in room 410 before. He hardly looked any older, although a few flecks of gray now showed through his dark hair.

Katherine caught a reflection of herself in the mirror. Collin had always told her she was too thin, but beautiful. He had once told her, "Your dark hair and hazel eyes hooked me the first time I met you."

"Such a long time ago," she said, half aloud.

It was a whole lifetime ago. She had worked as a reporter for a northside weekly paper—her first job after college. A mutual friend had told her that Collin had signed a contract with Empire Press. That made him an almost-celebrity, especially since Empire Press was one of the leading New York publishers. It made Collin newsworthy to readers along Chicago's north shore.

She remembered she had not done well on the interview, and he had actually fed her answers to questions she hadn't thought to ask. So it had been a terrible interview, but she had written a first-class article.

He had also done a good job in learning about Katherine. He'd invited her to dinner the following evening. A series of dinners followed, where Katherine had made contact with other writers. After six months, they knew they loved each other.

Katherine had begun to try writing fiction, which was what she had wanted to do all along. The newspaper paid her a wage, helped her learn her craft, and gave her the spare time to write. She wrote two novels, neither of which sold. Collin finally read them, and at first gave her offhand suggestions. After a few months he began teaching her how to construct a plot and delineate characters.

When Collin signed a contract for the second book with Empire, it meant his going to Acapulco for research on one major chapter. They married two days before the trip, and Katherine quit her job. She decided to set her novel in Acapulco. Collin helped her in the actual writing.

One day she moaned, "It's almost an autobiography."

"So what?"

"Except for throwing in Victoria as the other woman—"

"Honey," he said patiently. "Most early novels are autobiographical. You write what you know about first. Then you move on to other things."

Many nights as they drifted off to sleep, Collin would whisper, "Good night, Hillary," and she'd respond by calling him Randolph.

Hillary and Randolph.

Yes, she remembered. Maybe too vividly.

Her mind moved back to their last night in Acapulco. She had lain next to him, her head on his chest. "Collin, I didn't think I could ever love anyone as much as I love you right now," she had whispered.

He had moved then and held her tightly as he kissed her with a kiss that seemed to go on forever.

Stop it, she said to herself. *That happened eight years ago. Stop remembering.*

Silently Katherine crept into bed, lying as close to Collin as she could without touching him. She could smell the cologne he always used. No matter how much money they earned, or how expensive their clothes, Collin always bought the same inexpensive cologne.

Collin rolled over, and in his sleep, draped one arm across her shoulder. Katherine smiled and felt at peace.

God, if You exist, make this work for us. Please.

Chapter 7

Katherine opened the door to Millie's soft tapping. Immediately she saw the tired lines in her face. Even her eyes had lost their luster.

"Apparently you didn't sleep much last night, even after our talk," Katherine said, frowning.

"No, I was up a lot," Millie answered.

"That's too bad," said Katherine, "because we've got a couple of great ideas for today."

"I hope we won't spoil your day, but—"

"You're not going?"

"Afraid we'll have to cancel out," she said.

"Too tired?"

"Oh, it's not that. Tom just doesn't feel up to it. I'd rather stay with him."

"Shouldn't you call a doctor?" Katherine asked. "I know one who speaks passable English."

"We've decided to stay around the hotel today. If Tom feels better, we can swim or sit by the pool. Besides, I'd like to read *Forever and Ever Love* again today."

"You sure?" Katherine asked.

"Positive. And I might even take a long walk on my own."

"We can be back by lunch," Collin said.

"No, Collin," Millie answered, "that's not necessary. You've been too kind to us already."

"We enjoy being with you."

"I know. But really—"

"Okay," he said.

"Anything we can pick up for you or Tom?" Katherine called as she headed back toward the bathroom.

"Nothing. Honest. We'll be fine."

After she had gone, Collin said, "What rotten luck."

"You mean having to go out with just me?" Her smile diffused the barb.

"No, I was thinking of the Reaves."

"All this way and then Tom gets sick—"

"The first real vacation they've ever had."

"Poor Tom. Not only miserable himself, but he's getting cheated out of so much."

"But," Collin said, "maybe it's just as well. I would like to have a little time with my wife. Just the two of us."

They stood together in the middle of the room. Katherine now wore nothing but a towel wrapped around her. "Collin, just your saying that touches me."

"I mean it."

For a moment she didn't answer. Her eyes searched his face as though he might say something further. Standing on her toes, she kissed his cheek and then put her arms around him. "Thank you."

Collin bent down and kissed her lightly. "You know, I think I'd forgotten that I married a beautiful woman."

"You married me eight years ago!"

"Ah, but you've improved with age. Honest."

"Collin, thank—," she turned her head away.

He pulled her back and saw her eyes filled with tears. "I meant that, too."

"I know you did. That's why I'm going to start crying in a minute."

"Crying? Why?"

"Because I'm trying so hard, Collin—"

"Aren't we both trying?"

"Yes," she said, "but. . . ."

"But what?"

"I guess I'm scared," she said.

"Scared it won't work?" he asked.

She nodded. "Last night—when I asked you to try, I felt so sure. But now this morning—"

"This morning you're not so sure. Is that it?" Collin said.

Katherine nodded.

"I guess I feel the same way."

"It's just that—like a minute ago. You called me beautiful, and you kissed me—"

"Something wrong?"

"Not at all," she said. "Only—only that my mind keeps asking it-

self if you did it out of some kind of feeling or because you thought it
was the appropriate thing to do or—"

"You've always been the analytical one," Collin said. "You always
have to ask *why,* don't you?"

"Maybe that's the reason I write novels. When characters do something in my books, I start probing for the reasons."

"And you can't accept things as they are, can you?"

"I want to, Collin, I want to very much."

"Then accept things the way they are."

"I suppose my trouble is I'm not sure of the way things are."

"That again sounds like one of your heroines talking to herself,"
Collin said. He patted his wife's cheek. "Just stop trying to read
things into everything that happens."

"Yes," she said, "maybe that's part of the trouble."

An hour later they breakfasted at the hotel. Collin chose the fruit
plate, a combination of papaya, bananas, oranges and watermelon.
Katherine selected the full five-course menu, beginning with bacon
and eggs.

The night before they had asked Manuel to arrange for a rented
car. When they went downstairs at eight-thirty, Manuel stood with
the keys in his hand and pointed to a blue Fiat. Collin took the keys,
tipped Manuel, and pulled away from the hotel.

Collin drove leisurely down the hill and turned left at the bottom.
He parked near the old market. Because few tourists were walking through the area yet, hawkers of tee shirts, curios, and baskets
converged on them. As politely as possible, they warded them
off. The couple walked slowly through the open square, holding
hands. An ornate Catholic church dominated the far end of the
square.

"Collin, I'd like to go inside."

"Inside? Why?"

"For—for a minute, please."

Collin shrugged. "Might be worth looking at. You know, even
among the poor, they built beautiful—"

"Alone," she said.

"Alone?" he asked. "Well, if that's what you want—"

Katherine let go of his hand and took several steps toward the
building. Although it was fairly old, she noticed the outside had been
freshly painted. In bold blue letters above the entrance she saw the
words CATHEDRAL LA NUESTRA SEÑORA DE LA SOLEDAD. Katherine
read the words aloud twice.

She took two more steps, suddenly not wanting to go inside. But
having told Collin she did want to go in, and alone, she took a deep
breath and walked up the dozen steps toward the opened wide doors.
Even before she could see him, Katherine heard a priest intoning the

Mass. A handful of people, mostly older women, knelt in the back pews.

She paused at the door. Almost immediately a boy galloped up the steps, holding out a handful of rosaries. "Want buy, nice lady?"

Katherine shook her head and stepped inside.

Minutes later Katherine came out and took Collin's arm. "Okay, I'm ready."

"Enjoy yourself in there?"

"Enjoy? I don't know. It was peaceful."

"If you say so," he answered. "I can't think of its being peaceful when a lot of other people are around and the priest's speaking the whole time."

"I—I wasn't listening. Hardly even noticed that."

"Oh."

"I—I just . . . well, had to go back there."

"Go back?"

"I went there once before," she said carefully not looking at him.

"When?"

"Didn't I tell you?"

"Not that I remember."

"I did. When we came to Acapulco before."

"Oh," he said a second time.

"It was . . . well, when I had to make up my mind about—about the baby. Even before I told you."

"And you prayed, I suppose?"

"Yes, I did, Collin."

"And God spoke to you through the voice of an angel—"

"Don't play the cynic with me, please, Collin."

"Sorry," he said as he held up his hand for a peddler with leather hats to move on. "Guess I'm still not comfortable talking about—about that."

"But I did pray that day."

"You did? Why?"

"I felt miserable. I wanted the baby, and I knew you'd be unhappy about our having it. I felt like killing myself. I was just miserable."

"Katherine, I had no idea—" He spun her around and looked at her.

"I couldn't tell you how badly I wanted our baby. Ours, Collin. Maybe it's because I'm a woman and having a baby—it's like—it's like having something special that belongs to both of us."

"I guess I didn't understand a lot of things."

"Don't feel bad about it, Collin. I had to figure out my own feelings. I also had to be able to stand up to you."

"So you—you found courage at the church?"

"Courage? I don't know. Calmness maybe. I can't explain it. Only a sense that—that it would be all right. I knew you'd give in."

"I'm glad I did."

"But Reggie died—"

"But he lived first. And he was a special child, wasn't he?"

"Yes, Collin, very special." She took out a handkerchief and wiped her eyes. "Sorry. I guess—I guess I've made life awfully miserable for you."

"We've made it miserable for each other."

"Maybe we have," she said.

They fell into silence as they returned to the Fiat. They drove along the main road into the newer section of Acapulco. They stopped for coffee and then drove to the Acapulco Princess Hotel.

"The structure always reminds me of a pyramid," Katherine said as they pulled into the parking lot.

"Absolutely unique," Collin said.

They strolled through the lobby of the hotel, both remembering the time when they had wanted to stay at the Princess.

"Remember how we gawked eight years ago?" Collin said as he nudged his wife. His eyes followed a group of American tourists. Collin and Katherine walked behind them into the gift shop. Two couples from the group kept saying "Ah" and "Oh, look" as they spotted a new item, picked it up, and showed it to each other.

"Now that we can afford to buy here," Katherine said, "I don't see anything I want."

"Neither do I," he said.

They left the shop, and after glancing at the beauty salon and three windows displaying leisure clothes, they walked out the back of the hotel and headed toward the beach.

"After dodging all the people here, I'm glad we're staying at the Casa Blanca," Collin said. "I'm enjoying the privacy and quietness of the place."

"Cemeteries are quiet places, too," Katherine answered.

"That sounded like a snide remark."

"It's just that I resent being cooped up there. Practically no one around but the Reaves. Almost as if we have the hotel to ourselves."

"You don't like the Reaves?"

"Of course I like them. Very much. Only—"

"Only what?" Collin asked, and then before she could answer, he said, "You like a lot of people around—but no one getting close to you. Millie has touched some soft spot inside you, and it makes you uncomfortable."

"I don't think I'd put it that way," she said, trying to keep her voice calm. They stopped at a small bridge leading from the hotel to the outside courtyard. The architect had created a miniature lagoon with flowing waters and real-looking cliffs at both ends.

"How would you put it?"

"I don't know, Collin. Just that—well, I don't like the tone of your voice."

"Okay, skip it," he said and moved on.

"Wait a minute, Collin. Something's bothering you. What is it?"

"Nothing. Nothing at all." He grabbed her hand and pulled firmly. "Let's walk down by the beach." They moved away from the hotel and from the swarm of people who kept bumping into them or forcing them to swerve to avoid collisions.

"I like standing up on the bridge," she said.

"Let's just get out of here. Back to the car. Somewhere else. Anyplace. Just away from here. Then we can talk."

"We can talk here, Collin. I can hear you."

"With all these people milling around and pushing past us?"

"Why not?"

He hesitated as though weighing his words. "Okay. Okay. I'll start with this. I can't stand this crowd. I'm tired of swarms of people. Maybe I'm just the kind of guy who needs privacy and quiet, even when I'm not writing."

"I've not tried to—"

"You like people around. Chatter and noise and music and—"

"I like being sociable. People enjoy coming to our parties—"

"It's more than that. You have to have crowds around."

"I'm a people watcher. Part of my profession," she said and smiled.

"No, that's not the reason, Katherine. And you know it!" He started to turn back.

She grabbed his arm. "Don't talk to me in a tone like that and then turn away. What are you trying to say?"

"I'm trying to say that you want to hide. You hide in the noise and in the cocktail parties and—oh, skip it."

"No, we won't skip it. Exactly what do you mean?"

"Look, I want to make something of our marriage. I really do. But as we walked across the lobby, well, it just got to me, that's all."

"What got to you?"

"The people. The crowds. The—the racket. I can't stand that kind of life anymore. I like people. But only a few at a time. I want to know a handful. Care about them. But I don't know how to get close to fifty people at a time."

"You think I like crowds to avoid intimacy?"

"All I know is that we've had an endless line of parties and crowds at our house—"

"How would you know? You haven't been to half of them!"

"Half is about all I could handle!"

"And where were you the other half of the time? With your little blond editor, reading galleys?"

Collin put his hands in his pockets and stared at the beach. He sighed. "Okay, I provoked this. But I can't stand all the people milling around me. I'm going back." He started to cut across the grass. "Coming?"

"No."

"Look, let's just get out of here and then—"

"I know enough Spanish to order a cab when I've had my fill of human life again. When I've saturated my mind and soul with noise and laughing voices and happy smiles then—"

"You sound like one of your dopey heroines now."

"How would you know? You never read anything I write!"

"Why should I? You and your characters have no connection with reality!"

"What would you know about reality? If you know so much about the subject, then you should also know about responsibility." Katherine's face contorted, and she felt her throat constricting as she added, "You've certainly proven that you don't even know the meaning of that word."

"You won't let anything go, will you? You never let a man forget."

"Why should you have the luxury of forgetting when I remember every day?"

Collin opened his mouth to speak and then closed it. He clenched his fists as fire blazed in his dark eyes. He turned his back and walked rapidly away. After ten yards, Collin broke into a half run as he disappeared from sight.

Katherine stood silently, watching him go. "Why did you say those things?" she asked herself aloud.

To which an inner voice responded, *I don't know.*

Katherine turned in the opposite direction from where Collin had gone. She walked back into the hotel. She wanted people around her. She wanted to hear voices and see the movement of people. But Collin was right about one thing: She didn't want involvement with any of them.

Could—could he be right about other things, too?

Once she allowed her mind to ask that question, Katherine could no longer escape the probing of her inner voice.

Mechanically she walked into the lobby, found the coffee shop, and sat at a table in a far corner. She, who always kept her eyes roving and watching people, now stared at the empty water glass in front of her. Without looking up, she said to the waiter, "Coffee. Black."

For over an hour she sat at the table, sipping coffee, allowing a waiter to fill and refill her cup. She drank without tasting.

What if he is right?

Chapter 8

Collin slammed the car into park and snapped off the engine. Two seconds later he sprinted across the lobby of the Casa Blanca and paused at the desk long enough to see that the key to 410 was gone. He turned, ran to the steps, and bounded up three at a time. As he raced down the tiled hallway, he saw Katherine leaving the Reaves' room. She paused, looked up at him, and then turned away without any sign of recognition. She opened the door to their room.

"Katherine, please," he said, grabbing the door before she closed it. He stepped inside and spun her around. He saw that tears filled her eyes. "I'm sorry. Just plain dumb of me—"

"Don't say anything more," she said. Katherine sat on the edge of the bed. Tears broke suddenly and flowed heavily. When her sobs subsided, she looked up at him. "I'm not crying about you and me."

"What's wrong then?"

"Tom."

"Tom? What happened? An accident?"

She sobbed again and tried to speak, but couldn't. She buried her face in her hands.

Collin knelt beside his wife. "Please, tell me. What's wrong with Tom?"

"Oh, Collin," she said, brushing tears away with her hands, "he's sick. Very sick. He should never have made this trip."

"What kind of sick? On the plane he seemed okay. A little tired maybe, but—"

"I think he's dying."

"Dying? How do you know that?"

"I don't." She choked back several sobs. "I mean, not for sure. Only I felt—I had the sense of—of what was going on between them when I was in there just now."

"Your writer's imagination, maybe?"

"No. My writer's intuition."

"That's generally pretty accurate," he said, hoping to put the conversation on a lighter level.

"Collin, I—," and her voice broke. Katherine lurched forward, dropping her head on his shoulder, and cried silently. Collin held her tightly, wisely saying nothing.

After a few minutes, and through broken sentences, Katherine said, "Millie mentioned that Tom hadn't been well."

"We both noticed he didn't look well."

"But it's more than that. I knew when I saw him on the plane, but my mind wouldn't admit it. Did you notice," she said, her voice growing stronger, "that no matter how warm it is, he always wears long-sleeved shirts and a jacket?"

"Now that you mention it, but I assumed he had a typical tourist reaction to the water and the temperature."

"And no energy, remember?"

"Katherine," he said, his left hand touching her face lightly. With his other hand he pulled a handkerchief from his pocket and gently wiped away her tears.

"Oh, Collin, we've been so busy with our squabbles—and in the next room a man's dying. And we didn't even take the effort to notice ... or to care."

"I'm sorry," he mumbled and gently stroked her hair.

"Just hold me a minute, Collin. Just hold me so that I can shake myself out of this. Hold me, even if you don't love me."

Collin wrapped his arms tightly around Katherine. She struggled to control her breathing and to relax in his arms.

Finally she pulled away. "Collin, thank you. This is one time you were here when I needed you."

"Katherine, let me tell—"

A tap at the door interrupted them.

"I'll get it," he whispered and got up. Katherine walked into the bathroom. Collin heard her blow her nose and then the sound of running water.

Collin opened the door. "Millie! Come in."

Her untidy hair and the dark circles under her eyes made her look old and shrunken. "Thank you," she said softly.

"I was just coming over to ask about Tom."

Katherine appeared from the bathroom with freshly applied lipstick. Her puffy face showed the marks of her crying, but Millie didn't seem to notice.

"Can I get you something?" Katherine asked.

Millie shook her head.

"I can ring for room service—"

"No, I'm fine."

"Or we have Perrier water—"

"I came over because Tom and I feel we owe you an explanation." Millie walked over and sat in the only chair in the room. "We didn't intend to deceive you."

"Deceive us? What do you mean?" Katherine asked. She sat down on the bed directly in front of Millie. Collin sat next to his wife and held her hand.

"Tom is," she dropped her eyes and twisted her hands, "well, very sick. His heart."

"Millie, I'm sorry—," Katherine said and started to get up.

"No, wait, let me tell you," she said, her voice calm. "We've known about his condition a long time. He's getting progressively worse, as the doctors predicted."

"Can they operate or give him medication or—?"

"There's no cure."

"But surely, with the new drugs and heart research—," Collin said.

"We've tried everything. We've been to the best doctors and medical facilities in the country."

"And there's nothing—absolutely nothing?" Katherine asked.

"One thing. A transplant."

"Then by all means, he ought to have one," Katherine said. "It's not a matter of money, is it?"

Millie shook her head. "He may not be a good risk for a heart transplant. We're waiting for an answer from Stanford University Medical Center. They've been the leading researchers."

"They haven't turned Tom down?" Collin asked.

"No. But we don't know if they'll accept him. We're waiting, that's all."

"How long do you have to wait?"

She shrugged. "We're hoping for an answer soon. Another week. Two, maybe."

"And if they turn Tom down?" Collin asked and then hated himself for such a crude question.

"The children knew Tom and I have always wanted to visit Acapulco. And as I told you, especially after reading *Forever and Ever Love*. They also knew I'd never make the trip without Tom. So our kids and friends at church had a private fund-raising drive. No one told us about it until they collected enough for us to come."

"What a thoughtful thing to do," Katherine said. "And we came," Millie said.

"I'm glad you did," Katherine said as she leaned over and clasped Millie's hands.

"We knew Tom might give out anywhere along the way."

"Is he—bad?"

"We talked to his doctor about an hour ago. He's increasing the medication. Tom's resting now. By morning he may feel fairly normal. No way to tell. Or he may take three days to perk up."

"And nothing except a transplant," Collin said half aloud.

"Enlarged heart, especially on the left side," Millie said, almost as if reciting from memory.

"I don't know much about this sort of thing," Katherine said.

"It means that his heart doesn't pump enough blood. Only about twenty percent of the blood leaves the heart, and because most of it stays there, it causes clots and—," Millie's voice broke. She looked at Katherine momentarily, and the tears flowed.

"Millie, I'm sorry, so sorry." Katherine came around beside Millie and wrapped her arms around the smaller woman.

Millie finally raised her head. "We didn't want to spoil your trip—"

"Hey, don't worry about that," Collin said.

"It's just that—we decided not to talk about it to anyone else. We've lived with this. We—well, we know what to expect."

"You've put up a brave front," Katherine said.

"It's not a front, honest. I'm crying. And I cry every few days. Especially when I think about losing Tom—"

"Don't think about it," Collin said.

"No, I want to think about it. I want to face it."

For a moment no one said anything, and then Millie sat up, reached out, and took a hand of both Collin and Katherine. "I seem to need to cry once in a while. Then I'm fine. Tom and I just felt that it wasn't fair to hide this from you any longer."

"Thanks for telling us."

"When we talked to you about God in the restaurant, I wanted to tell you then."

"Why didn't you?"

"Oh, it didn't seem to fit. You see, well, it's because of God we can handle all this now."

"And I made nasty remarks—," Katherine said.

"Don't apologize. I touched painful spots in you, and you reacted, that's all."

"Even so, I'm sorry—"

"You see, Tom and I had a comfortable life. No major problems and then—well, then this thing with his heart. It made us think seriously about life. About what's important . . . about God."

"I think I understand a little better now," Collin said. "And I taunted you in my own way, too."

"Forget all that. You've been kind. We felt we owed you an explanation."

"Millie," Katherine said, and the tears formed again in her own eyes, "I don't know what to say—"

"Don't say anything."

"It's just that it's such a load—"

"A load? I never think of it that way."

"I mean what you're going through. Watching Tom go downhill—"

"But I love him."

"Doesn't it get to you?"

"Of course it does. And I feel afraid sometimes. Lonely. I even get angry at God."

"Millie, I admire you. You have so much strength."

She blushed. "I have friends who give me emotional support. Our pastor helps. Mostly, God gives me strength when I feel depressed—"

"Your faith means a lot to you," Collin said, "doesn't it?"

"It's what keeps me going. Both of us. Tom takes it so well. He has his bad times, but he accepts all this better than I do. When I get low, he's the one who encourages me."

"You're such good people," Katherine said. "Why *you?*"

"Good?" she answered. "I'm not sure about that. We're just like everybody else. In fact, we weren't a whole lot different from most people before Tom got sick. He tells everybody that it took a bad heart for God to change him and to show him what's really important in life." She smiled and stopped.

"Please, go on," Collin said. "This time I want to know."

"So do I," Katherine said.

"Each morning Tom opens his eyes and looks around. And if I'm still in bed, he takes my hand. Then he prays outloud, thanking God for giving him one more day to live. And then he prays for strength—for me." Millie stopped and pulled a handkerchief from her pocket. She wiped her eyes.

Even Collin felt his eyes misting.

"Tell me about Tom," Katherine said. "I mean, before all this, and what changed him?"

Millie told them their story, slowly, sometimes pausing to cry. Other times the sparkle in her eyes returned. They had been active members of the PTA. Tom had involved himself with both the Kiwanis and Optimists. At church she taught in the nursery department, and Tom ushered. Then their church held a series of meetings. A medical doctor from Florence, Alabama, had visited their church with a group of ten lay people. They had held four evening services and small group studies during the day.

"About that time Tom and I realized how sick he was. Those meetings came when we searched for answers. We kept asking God why this illness hit us."

Millie especially remembered the second night and how it had affected Tom. They had lain in bed, talking long into the night. Tom had said, over and over, "Honey, this is the most wonderful thing I've ever heard in my life. I don't know why I didn't understand it all before."

And Millie had said, "Maybe we weren't listening then."

That whole year just prior to the meetings had been difficult. Their son Martin had been suspended for four days in his last year of high school—caught with marijuana, which he admitted he smoked. Their daughter Julie, a year and a half younger, had already started moving with the wrong crowd and they had worried about the kids' wild activities and lack of interest in family and academics.

"When Tom changed, it seemed to change the entire family," she said. "Julie and Martin snapped out of it."

"Remarkable," Collin said.

"If you could have seen the difference in Tom, perhaps you'd understand. He became like a new father to the kids. Attentive. Spent time with them. He talked about God and prayed with them. The kind of things he'd never have done before. And since then—"

"It's been a good life together—other than Tom's illness?" Katherine asked.

"It's been a beautiful time. About as perfect as life could be. So you see, I wouldn't want all that changed. If it took Tom's illness to make us come to our senses—," she stopped and smiled at them. "Does that make sense?"

"I think so," Katherine said and squeezed her husband's hand.

"It's just that both of us know what's important in life. Tom says every once in a while, 'If I die tomorrow, I've had so many good years.'"

"Thanks for telling us," Collin said.

"Thanks for understanding," Millie said.

"We do. And maybe . . . maybe we might talk more about God. After Tom's feeling better," Collin said.

"I'd like that."

Maybe next time we'll be more receptive," Katherine said. "At least . . . at least I know I need something."

"Look, I'd better get back to Tom," Millie said, rising. "But I love you both. I really meant it when I said God answered our prayers. You have been so special to us."

As Millie reached the door, she turned and smiled.

"Wait a minute, Millie," Katherine said. "Remember—remember on the plane you said you bet my friends called me Kit? Oddly enough, my friends *used* to call me Kit. Even Collin did once, back when we came to Acapulco before."

"Then I was right," Millie said.

"Would you—would you call me Kit?"

"I take that as a very special invitation."

"It is."

Millie walked back inside, hugged Katherine quickly, and said, "I feel honored."

"Not half as much as I do," Katherine said.

"See you later—Kit!" And she was gone.

Collin looked at his wife. "Do you want me to call you Kit, too?"

"If you want to."

Chapter 9

Collin and Katherine did not leave the room. They called room service to bring up their evening meal. They spoke little to each other, neither one sure of what to say.

An hour after dark, Collin showered and slipped into bed. Minutes later Katherine did the same. She lay in the darkened room, unable to sleep. She felt listless and weary but had no desire for sleep.

She fought an impulse to touch Collin, because they had been strangers in bed too long. She lay flat on her stomach, careful not to move, allowing Collin to think she had taken a pill and gone to sleep almost immediately. She listened to his breathing and realized that he, too, lay awake beside her.

"Collin," she whispered.

"Yes?"

"Where did we go wrong?"

"You don't know?"

"I don't mean Reggie," she said. "It started long before that."

"I don't know," he said. "Eight years ago I didn't think anything could pull us apart."

"We had drifted," she said. "And you know, I never realized that until—until this afternoon."

"What happened this afternoon?" he said as he rolled over, and lying on his side, moved his face next to hers. Katherine turned over on her back and said nothing. She felt an intense delight with Collin so close. Impulsively she kissed his lips and then withdrew her face.

"What was that all about?" he asked.

"My way of saying I'm sorry. I failed you, Collin. I let you down."

"Let me down?"

"Yes," she said. "Success sometimes blinds people. It did me. I forgot what was important in life."

"I wish you could have said that before—even a year ago."

"You mean—you mean it's too late now?"

"I mean I tried a hundred times to talk to you, and every time I tried—"

"I know," she said. "I stopped you. I didn't want to hear, Collin, because . . . because I think I wanted to blame you . . . for everything. For Reggie's death, of course, but for more than that."

"More than that?"

"For the personal misery of my life. For my own emptiness even with my literary success. For our failed marriage, for everything I could think of."

"Katherine—Kit, I've never heard you talk this way before. Not ever."

"It's not often that I get so honest with myself and about myself," she said.

"Kit . . . ," Collin stopped. "For once I've run out of words."

"Then why don't you tell me? Tell me what really happened. You know, *that* night."

"You sure you want to hear?"

"Collin, please, I have to know. I have to know everything, and I want no details spared. You can't be half as brutal as I've been on myself this afternoon."

Collin moved away from Katherine and got out of bed. He walked over to the single window, which opened to the patio. Collin pulled the curtain back and stared at the mosquito-net wiring. "I suppose I have to tell you about Loretta Kingsley first."

Katherine felt a pain stabbing at her, fearing what he might say, but knowing she had to hear. She said hoarsely, "Tell me."

"How did Loretta come to occupy so much of my time? I don't honestly know. When your success grew, you went away for two or three weeks at a time with your talk shows and autograph parties. I didn't seem important anymore, as though you had outgrown me. Maybe I was jealous. Maybe I resented your success when all the time I felt I was the better writer—"

"You are better, Collin, much better."

"That's not the issue now," he said. "I blamed you for the rotten state of our marriage. If you'd stay home more. If you'd be more attentive to me. I once told Loretta that you were more married to Randolph than you were to me."

"In a way, I suppose I was. And I'm—I'm ashamed."

"When your second book hit the big time and then your third, I felt I had no wife. By then we had grown so far apart, we had nothing to say to each other anymore."

"Collin, I—"

"Maybe it even hurt my male ego, being *Mr.* Katherine Edmonton. Not that people called me that, but I felt I was always in your shadow."

"I didn't mean to do that," she said softly.

"Probably I could have handled even that," he said as he slowly paced the room, "except—"

"Except what? Don't hold back."

"I felt as though I had become a kind of house pet. I could escort you to parties or celebrity functions, but otherwise you had little use for me."

"Forgive me—"

"But most of all," Collin said, holding his hand up to silence her, "I needed encouragement. I'm a good writer—a darn good writer.

But I had bad times—moments when I would have given anything if you had only said, 'Darling, how's the work going?' Or if you had even picked up one of my manuscripts and read—"

"I did—I've read everything you ever wrote."

He stared at her. "When?"

"When you weren't around. I always made certain I put everything back carefully. And you know, Collin, I envied you."

"Envied me?"

"You have a gift—a talent—in your writing that I'll never develop. I may sell more books but *you're* the writer."

"If you had only told me—"

"I couldn't, Collin. I couldn't."

"And because you couldn't," he said and stared momentarily into space, "I found a comforting shoulder in Loretta."

"So tell me, Collin. Tell me everything."

Slowly Collin told his story. Loretta had been more than kind to him from the beginning of the writer-editor relationship. She had sent small gifts. There were phone calls. Mostly she had listened when he talked and had encouraged him to share his problems.

"Above all, I think she really cared about developing me into a top nonfiction writer."

Loretta offered him the sympathetic ear that Katherine withheld. Most of all, she had been there to comfort him after Reggie's death.

He remembered so much about Reggie's death. It was late September, and the trees had lost most of their gold and red leaves. Blustery winds had whipped around their corner apartment. Katherine's second novel had been picked up as the featured selection by several book clubs. One critic had called *Forever and Ever Love* "a stirring first novel of innocent love."

"Remember how things went then?" he asked.

"Yes," she said. "Autograph parties. Talk shows in New York after three days in Boston and D.C."

"I promised to take care of Reggie those ten days," he said as if in a daze. "Now comes the hard part to tell." He took a deep breath.

Katherine lay in the darkness, waiting for Collin to go on, yet still afraid of what he might tell her.

Loretta had come into Chicago. As he later learned, she had made the trip because she knew Katherine was gone. She had called him, and he'd arranged for a baby-sitter, and then driven into Chicago. They met at the Palmer House.

Collin, who seldom drank, had given in when Loretta insisted on a cocktail. Then he had had a second. He may have had as many as five, he couldn't remember. Loretta had tried to persuade him to spend the night with her.

"Nothing happened that night, Katherine," he said. "I swear it."

"I believe you," she said.

"But, not being used to that kind of drinking, I wasn't at my best when I got home. After the sitter left, I tiptoed into Reggie's room. He lay there, spread-eagle, sound asleep. I laid my hand on his cheek and pushed the hair from his face. I even kissed him on the cheek."

Collin walked back to the bed and sat down next to his wife. He took her hand, and without realizing it, pressed it roughly. "That drinking must have finally hit me. I just grabbed the blanket the sitter had used and fell asleep on the sofa."

For a minute he couldn't go on, and Katherine felt the pain in his heart. She sat up and leaned toward him, laying her free hand on his shoulder, and gently massaged his neck.

"I woke up at nine-thirty the next morning," he said. "I thought of Reggie first, wondering why he hadn't cried. He never slept that late."

He had gone into the baby's room. The instant Collin saw his son, he knew something was wrong. Reggie lay with his face turned down into the mattress. Collin screamed as he grabbed his son. Remembering lessons he had learned in CPR, he brought the child out of the crib and laid his body on the floor. He tried mouth-to-mouth resuscitation. He pushed gently on the child's sternum. Even as he went through the motions, Collin knew it was too late.

Grabbing a fresh shirt and trousers, Collin fumbled with them, and then scooped up his son. He ran to the car. Driving without heeding any speed limits or signs, he narrowly avoided collisions at two different intersections. He didn't care, and he scarcely noticed.

He reached the emergency room of the hospital. A nurse took Reggie out of his arms. A woman behind a typewriter asked him dozens of questions, which he answered mechanically. Someone else took his arm and ushered him to the waiting room. After that, Collin's mind went numb. He could only see his son lying on the floor and not responding to the CPR.

A doctor called him into a small room. They sat down, and after a lengthy silence in which the doctor's eyes rested on Collin's feet, he said, "I'm sorry, Mr. Roderick. Your son was dead on arrival. We tried to revive—"

"Dead? Is he really dead?"

"We tried everything, you understand."

Collin didn't hear anything after that. The doctor had gone through enough experiences with patients to realize that after he said *dead,* Collin heard nothing. The doctor kept speaking, partially from his own uneasiness, partially because he wanted the father to understand.

The third time he explained, Collin seemed to hear it. He said it once again.

"We have labeled it SIDS, which means Sudden Infant Death Syndrome. We have no evidence that your son smothered—"

"If only I had heard him cry out—"

"He probably didn't make any crying sounds—"

"I must have been in such a deep sleep—"

"Nor any choking," the doctor continued, trying to retain his calmness and inwardly cursing for having to go through this. It was always the same. Parents staring in confusion and unable to comprehend. He sighed, wishing he could say something to comfort the grief-stricken father. Instead he cleared his throat and began again. "Mr. Roderick, there is no way anyone could have prevented his death. SIDS has no warning signs—"

"If only I had checked on him earlier—"

"We don't have a medical explanation for this," the doctor said and paused.

"I neglected him," Collin said. "I should have been in there—"

"We don't even know when it happened."

"If I hadn't neglected him—"

"We have found no evidence of neglect. We simply don't know why or how—"

"I could have done something—"

"We have nothing to indicate that you could have prevented this," the doctor said, sounding clinical and cold. This was always the hardest part, trying to steer parents away from blaming themselves. "There was nothing you could have done."

"But surely I should have—"

The doctor stood up and shook Collin's hand. "I'm sorry," he mumbled as Collin left the room.

Katherine had arrived that afternoon. He had her met at the airport where he repeated the information he had given her on the phone. He had explained what the doctor had said about SIDS.

Listening, Katherine remembered that scene as though it had happened only the day before. She had been too numbed to speak, too shocked to accept the reality of her son's death. She kept thinking that as soon as she reached the apartment, she would find the boy, lying on the floor and playing with a bright toy.

They had walked into the apartment. Katherine stood inside the door for a long moment, surveying everything. Finally she noticed the blanket across the sofa. She moved toward the bedroom and realized it had not been slept in.

"What happened here?"

"I told you—"

"You slept on the sofa?"

"Yes."

"Why?"

"I had gone out earlier. Met Loretta at the Palmer House for a drink, and after the baby-sitter left, I crashed on the sofa."

"When did you crash? Before or after Reggie—went—went to bed?"

"Afterward," he said, setting her suitcase down and locking the door behind them. "About midnight. Maybe a little later."

"How much did you drink?"

"This sounds like a police interrogation."

"How much, Collin?"

"A couple of drinks. Maybe three, I guess."

"Two or three drinks in a couple of hours?"

Then, without realizing the impact his words would make, he admitted he had probably consumed five or six.

"And you lay there, dead drunk, while my son died?"

"It's not like that, Kit—"

"No, not at all. You were so dead drunk—"

"The examining doctor said it couldn't have been prevented."

"How do you know?"

"Reggie didn't smother or have convulsions or—"

"Collin, I don't want a medical lecture."

"I'm only trying to explain that—"

"As far as I'm concerned, you are responsible for his death. If you had stayed home and not been out carousing with that blond—"

The recriminations continued. A written report from the doctor and a government pamphlet about SIDS seemed to have no effect on Katherine's perception of what had happened.

After days of recurring arguments, Collin said, "Kit, don't you think I'm suffering, too?"

She looked at him, her hazel eyes filled with anger. "Don't call me Kit again. And don't tell me about your suffering."

Katherine had placed all the blame on Collin, and he had begun to despise her.

"It took months for me to get past my grief . . . to realize that Reggie's death and my drinking had no connection. Even so," he paused and in the shadowy darkness peered into her eyes, "I've never had another drink since."

"It was such a horrible time for both of us," Katherine said.

"Yes, it was."

Katherine had refused to have a funeral, only a grave-side ceremony with a chaplain from the hospital.

That evening as they went to bed, Collin had moved close to her. He put his arm around her shoulder. Katherine had pulled away and rolled over to the other side of the bed.

"Collin, I know now you were trying to comfort me in my grief, and maybe find a little for your own—"

"But you turned away from me," he said.

"I wanted to hurt you, Collin. I blamed you for his death. I lay there thinking that if only you had stayed home. If only you had not been drinking. If only I had not listened to you and had arranged for Reggie to go to my mother's. In my grief, I wanted to punish you."

A week after Reggie's death she had lain near Collin, and when he touched her, she had pulled away. After the third time, he stopped trying.

A month later he had said to Katherine, "Haven't you punished me enough?"

"Enough? You haven't begun to feel anything yet!"

"I loved him, too."

"You loved him so much, you got drunk while he lay in there breathing his last—"

Collin turned over. He didn't want to hear it again. The next morning he asked for a divorce.

"Never. You're not going to walk out of this and just be free."

"I can get a divorce without your consent. It makes it easier if you cooperate."

"I'll never give you a divorce. I'll fight it all the way. And you'll never be free of me. I'll tell the world, if I have to, that you murdered my son!"

"Katherine, you know—"

"Murderer!" she had screamed. Over and over she shrieked it.

Without realizing what he had done, Collin had struck her across the face with his hand. She narrowed her eyes and held her hand over her stinging flesh.

"Am I your next victim?"

"You're crazy, Katherine!"

"No, I'm only trying to make you suffer for what you've done." The argument went on and on, the same words over and over.

Finally Collin said it again. "I've had enough. I'm filing for divorce tomorrow."

"Divorce? Oh, no, Collin."

"Isn't that what you want? To be free of me?"

"Ah, but I don't want you to be free of *me*," she said. "So don't try to divorce me. You won't get free of me." She walked out of the room.

Collin had never raised the question of divorce again.

"Why, Collin?" she asked him now. "Why didn't you keep demanding a divorce?"

"Would it have done any good?" he asked.

"No, I don't suppose it would have. I'd only have become more adamant. I hurt so deeply."

"So did I," he said quietly.

Katherine pulled him close to her. "I can see that now. I couldn't then. I'm sorry."

"I know you are—"

"Am I too sorry too late?" she asked, not sure she had even articulated the words.

"I don't know," he said. "I simply don't know."

Instinctively Katherine released him and moved away from him. She wanted to scream out, "Now, look who's being punished!" but she couldn't. A silence hung between them until Katherine said, "I still want a chance for us, Collin."

"I'm giving you that."

"I mean, a real chance."

"This isn't one?" he asked.

"No, I mean, forget about love and passion for a minute. Forget about the memories of closeness we once shared. If we can't remain together as lovers, can we at least pursue it on the basis of friendship? Can't we build on . . . on what we once had?"

"I don't know," he said slowly.

"Why? Why, Collin?"

"I still have too much to forget."

"I understand," she said softly, not sure she understood at all.

Katherine got out of bed, went to the bathroom, and searched through her makeup case until she found a sleeping pill. She rinsed it down with Perrier water and returned to bed. Within minutes she had fallen asleep.

Later, while it was still dark, Collin, who had not gone to sleep, heard a muffled noise at the screen. Several seconds lapsed before it registered. He raised his head slightly, cocked his ear, and concentrated on the sound. He heard it again—like the gentle tearing of cellophane paper, but with more metallic tone. In that instant, Collin realized someone was trying to break into the room from the patio.

He turned over and sat up, orienting himself in the darkness and clearing his head. He looked up just as a lithe figure pushed the window silently forward and leaped into the room. Had he not seen his outline, Collin would never have known the intruder had come inside because he never heard the sound of the man's feet hitting the floor.

Collin threw the sheet off and leaped from the bed. "Thief!" he yelled as he lunged at the intruder.

Collin grabbed an arm, and almost immediately the thief knocked him loose, and a heavy object crashed against Collin's skull. He didn't pass out, but he felt himself slipping to the floor. He made a second attempt to grab the man. This time he missed.

He felt a foot kick him in the face and realized why he had heard no footsteps—the man wore no shoes. Collin grabbed an ankle and tried to pull his assailant down to the floor with him. They scuffled.

The noise awakened Katherine, and she snapped on the bedside lamp. At that instant, the man struck Collin across the chest. He instinctively let go. The figure pulled free of Collin's grasp and darted through the window in one continuous motion.

Everything happened so quickly that Katherine saw only the dis-appearing figure. She screamed.

Then she saw Collin on the floor, his arms flailing, trying to rise and not quite able to coordinate his own body. She threw off the sheet and scrambled to the floor. "Oh, Collin, Collin—," she cried.

He dropped his arms and head and lay on the floor, dazed but awake. She scurried to the bathroom and wet a washcloth. Rushing back, she fell on her knees, lifted his head, and placed it on her lap. The blow had caused a bump on his head but had not perforated the skin. She wiped his head and had no idea of what to do next. "Please, lie still—"

His eyelids fluttered. "I think—I think a robber—"

"Please, darling, just lie quietly for a minute until—"

"You called me darling."

She leaned down and kissed him gently on the lips. "Shh. Don't say anything just now."

"Okay, Kit," he whispered.

Chapter 10

Collin opened his eyes to a sun-filled room. He glanced at his watch on the stand next to the bed. It was nearly eight o'clock. A dull headache suddenly reminded him of the robber's intrusion. He auto-matically felt for the bump.

Lying immobile in the bed, he became conscious of Katherine snuggled against him. When they had gone to bed, instead of retreat-ing to her side, she had kissed him on the cheek and lain quietly be-side him.

Now fully awake, he stroked the arm that lay across his chest. He bent forward and kissed her on the forehead. He kissed her a second time on the cheek. Her eyelids fluttered slightly.

The shrillness of the phone pierced the stillness of the room. Collin grabbed it before it had completed its ring. The noise awakened Katherine, who opened her eyes. She smiled at him and then turned slightly, burrowing her face into his chest.

"Hello," he answered. "Oh, Señor Ortega. No, uh, you didn't awaken me."

Collin continued the conversation for a full minute before hanging up. Katherine had not moved again while he talked. She lay in bed, her eyes watching him. As soon as he put the phone back on the hook, she took his free hand and squeezed it gently. "Forgive me, Collin."

"Katherine, I need to tell—"

"Just let me say this first. I was wrong—totally. I blamed you for

Reggie's death and for everything else wrong in my life. It's easier to blame than to face reality."

"I did drink too much that night—"

"I read the death report. Your drinking didn't make any difference. But even if it had," she said as she pulled herself up, close to him, "you've suffered enough."

"Don't torture yourself—"

"I need to say it. I've treated you awful—"

"We've both had a terrible time, haven't we?"

"You didn't want the baby. Remember how unhappy you were?"

"That was only at the beginning. Afterward—"

"I know, darling. But I allowed my grief to convince me you never loved Reggie—and that you were responsible for his death. It doesn't make sense. I just fell apart and had . . . had to blame someone."

"And I was the obvious target," he said.

"Yes . . . and now . . . Collin, please forgive me."

Collin rolled over and looked at his watch on the nightstand. He touched Katherine gently. "Katherine, I need to tell you—"

"Last night you called me Kit."

"I did, didn't I?"

"Will you—will you go back to calling me Kit all the time?"

"If you want."

"Oh, yes, Collin. Let's make everything the way it used to be— only better."

"I don't know if it's that simple. We both need time to change. We've drifted so far apart—"

"But I've changed, Collin. I only want a chance to prove it. Please."

"I'm willing to try."

"And, Collin," she said as she pulled slightly away from him, dropping her gaze so that their eyes didn't meet. "There's something else."

"Okay."

"Just—just don't laugh, please."

"Promise. No laughing," he said as he kissed her on the neck.

"I want to talk to the Reaves about God."

"You're sure?" he asked.

"Collin, I don't understand everything, but I know they have something special about them—something I need."

"Maybe something we both need," he answered.

The Rodericks had finished dressing when they heard a heavy rap on the door. "Anybody up in there?" a deep voice thundered.

"Tom?" Katherine said in surprise.

Collin hurriedly opened the door. "Come in! Come in!"

"Tom, how are you?" Katherine asked.

"Better."

"Honest?" Katherine asked.

"Honest," he said. "I feel fine today. As well as *fine* can cover it."

"But yesterday you were—"

"It works that way sometimes," Millie said. "He's not faking it."

The Reaves came into the room and sat on the unmade bed as Tom said, "Millie told me that she explained about my heart. We felt we owed you that much. Some days I'm worse than others. Today I feel fairly well."

"You won't overdo it, will you?" Katherine asked.

"No, but I'm not going to stay in bed either. Right now, I'm starved."

"Let's have breakfast," Collin said.

"Just one thing," Tom said. "I'm not trying to hide my problem, you understand, but—"

"But he doesn't want all our conversation to revolve around it," Millie said. "We know you care about us—"

"Oh, we do," Katherine said.

"And if you want to ask questions or talk about it, you can. Otherwise, we've faced it and have learned to live with it."

"Good. Let's go then," Collin said too quickly.

"Don't mind Collin's brusqueness," Katherine said. "When he feels deeply about anything, that's how he copes."

Millie hugged Collin, and standing on her tiptoes, kissed him on the cheek. "You don't need to explain. His eyes tell me all I need to know."

"Well, uh, let's go on, then," he said and smiled gratefully at Millie.

As they walked to the hotel restaurant, they made plans for the day. Tom would stay at the hotel, resting and reading by the pool. Collin mentioned his interview with Señor Ortega.

"That leaves you and me," Katherine said to Millie.

"I need to do one thing before we leave—buy souvenirs for the kids and a few friends back in Waukegan."

"That's what we'll do then. Collin can have his interview and add two overpriced luncheons to his expense account, and we'll shop for bargains."

"You girls can have the car," Collin said.

"We'll drop you off anywhere you want," Katherine said.

"I'll walk. Maybe grab a cab at the old market. I should be back at the hotel by early afternoon."

"We'll decide our evening plans after that," Katherine said. "Okay?"

While they sat at the table, Katherine and Collin told the Reaves about the robber and that they had reported the incident. The clerk had promised them a new screen. "He kept assuring me that they would watch everything much more closely," Collin said, laughing. "I never saw any detective or guard, but perhaps it makes them feel better."

"But . . . but there's something else we decided . . . we, uh, want to talk about," Katherine said.

"Of course," Millie said.

"I'm not sure how to start."

"Just say it straight," Collin said.

"We'd like you to tell us more about your religion."

"She means," Collin said, "that we're trying to get our lives straightened out. You two have something special—" ‚

"A quietness. An assurance," Katherine said, "An indefinable—"

Collin laughed. "My wife who writes fiction is searching for an appropriate description of what we've seen in you two."

"We want whatever it is that you've got."

"That's the nicest thing you could say," Tom answered and laid his hand on Millie's shoulder.

"You both glow with an inner faith or something," Katherine said.

"Besides all that, we need help," Collin said. "Kit and I have decided to try to make our marriage work."

"Help us. We don't want to lose each other again," Katherine said, bending forward and looking intently at the Reaves.

"If religion can help us . . . ," Collin's voice trailed off.

"Of course. We're thankful to be involved in your search," Tom said.

"How do we start?" Katherine asked.

"You already have," Millie replied.

"I mean, what do we do first?"

"You start with a need," Tom said.

"We've got that all right," Collin said.

"Then you acknowledge that you can't solve your own problems. That you need help beyond yourselves."

"We're there, too," Collin said.

"Yes, what do we *do?*" Katherine asked, realizing her voice had grown louder.

"No magic formulas," Tom answered.

"You pray," Millie said. "Just simply talk to God."

"I've done that," Katherine said and dropped her head. "I went to the cathedral in town yesterday. I prayed for help. Not very well, maybe, but—"

"Kit, honey," Millie said. "God hears what we say in our hearts. Don't ever worry about proper words."

"Seems as though you're moving in the right direction," Tom said, and he patted Katherine's hand. "Yes, in the right direction."

"But is that all? I mean—"

"God's solutions are all wrapped up in Jesus Christ. So believe in Jesus. That He's with you, that He's going to help you—"

"I—I don't know *how* to believe," Katherine said, and her hazel eyes filled with tears. "I want to. Tell me how."

"I sort of believe, I suppose," Collin said. "I mean, I don't *not believe*—"

"I'd like you to try something," Tom said. "Maybe it sounds crazy to you, but—"

"I need help," Katherine said. "I'm willing to try anything."

"I'd like you to go ahead and act as if you believed. As if you believed in Jesus Christ the way we do—"

"Sounds phony, doesn't it?" Collin said.

"Maybe, but I'd like you to try."

"Okay, tell us how," Katherine said.

"Behave as if you believed in God. We'll help you get started. Millie will give you a Bible and show you where to start. Read a little of it every day. What I'm trying to say is go through the motions of behaving like a Christian—"

"And then we'll become Christians?" Collin said. "Is that it?"

"It's not that simple," Tom said. "But that's the method I suggest."

"What he means," Millie said, "is that it gives God a chance to help you."

"Well, I'm willing, too," Collin said.

"Okay, then pray. Tell God what's troubling you. Ask for His help."

"Even when I'm not sure I believe—"

"Yes, Kit, whether you believe or not."

"Let's start by praying right now," Tom said.

Collin glanced furtively around. While only two other tables were occupied, and neither of them close by, he still felt awkward. "You mean here?"

"Sure, why not?"

"Shouldn't we go to the cathedral? I always thought you had to go to a church—"

"God's as much in this room as He is anywhere," Millie said.

"Okay, I guess . . . I guess this is just different from what I had expected," Collin said.

"Think of it this way," Tom said. "Prayer is talking to God in the same way I'm talking to you. We don't have to close our eyes or fold our hands. Just talk. Look at me or at the palm trees. It doesn't matter."

"Okay, I guess," Collin said and glanced at his wife. She nodded.

Tom tightened his arm around his wife and said, his eyes focused directly on the Rodericks, "Father, I bring Collin and Kit to You today. They want to start their lives over, with Your help. Guide them."

"Yes, Father," Millie said. "Thank You for bringing us all together. Help both of them believe and follow You."

A silence followed, and then Tom said, "Your turn, Collin."

Collin stared first at the Reaves and then at his wife. She squeezed his hand. He turned his head away from the others and looked across the bay. "Jesus Christ, I—I promise to do what I can to learn. I don't know much about praying, but I want Your help and I want what the Reaves have."

Katherine's voice trembled slightly, but she began immediately. "It's strange talking to You outloud. And especially because I can't see You. But I'm going to try. I'm going to act as if I really believe already. I guess the next move is Yours."

"Amen," Tom said, and his wife echoed his word.

"Now, throughout the day, when you think about God, just talk to Him, that's all."

"It's that simple, honest," Millie said.

As they were getting into the car, Millie said to Collin, "When was the last time you read *Forever and Ever Love?*"

"The last time?"

"Yes. When did you last read it?"

"Well, not ... not since I saw it in the galley stage. Maybe I skimmed it after it came out in print."

"Read it again. Soon."

"I know the story—"

"Do you?"

"Look, Millie, sometimes you have to clobber me to make your point."

"I'm simply suggesting that you read *Forever and Ever Love* again—especially the last four chapters."

"Millie, he doesn't need—," Katherine interrupted.

"Kit, stay out of this," she said and smiled. "And you, Collin—"

"Okay. As soon as we get back home—"

"I have a paperback copy right here." She opened her purse, took out a worn paperback, and held it out to him. "You need to read it."

"Why?"

"Just read it."

He took the book. "Okay, boss," he said with a smile. He hugged Millie. "I'll at least skim it today. Tomorrow at the latest."

Collin slipped the paperback into his hip pocket. His sport shirt covered the book so that no one would have known it was there. He immediately forgot about it.

He turned to Katherine. "I have forty minutes before my appointment, so I think I'll walk from the market."

"All right," Katherine said.

Five minutes later, Collin got out, and the two women drove off in the Fiat.

As they pulled away, Millie started humming a song. Katherine listened for a minute and then said, "I think I know that one."

"There's not a friend like the lowly Jesus—," Millie raised her voice.

"Yes, that's it," Katherine said and laughed self-consciously. "Believe it or not, I went to Sunday school as a child. Kept going until tenth grade. Then other interests—"

Millie patted her arm. "Now you're starting over again. So let's sing a bit."

"I don't know the words."

"Does it matter? Just hum." Millie, who tended to sharp her low notes, began singing "Onward Christian Soldiers." They drove down the main street of Acapulco, windows opened, lustily singing the hymns of the church. Katherine didn't care if anyone thought them peculiar. She couldn't remember when she had enjoyed singing so much.

After the fifth shop, Katherine and Millie went into the El Presidente Hotel gift shop. They walked among the counters, glancing over the displays.

"I know it's silly to come in here," Millie said, "but thanks for indulging me."

"It's fun," Katherine said, remembering when she and Collin had done the same thing years earlier. She idly fingered price tags, acutely aware of how much higher the prices were here than in the old part of the city. But, she admitted to herself, all these curios were of especially good quality. You couldn't always tell with what the street vendors sold.

After Millie had examined an endless number of place mats and stuffed iguanas, written prices on a little pad, and thanked the clerk for taking time with her, she took Katherine's arm. She leaned closer and whispered, "Can you believe the prices in here?"

Katherine smiled. "I warned you."

"You're right," she answered. "How about stopping for coffee?"

"Good idea," Katherine said. They left the gift shop and walked toward the dining area. They had just turned the corner, and Katherine glanced toward the lounge.

Katherine abruptly turned. "Not—not here," she said weakly.

Chapter 11

Katherine hurried from the El Presidente with Millie trailing behind her. She stifled the cry that demanded release as she increased her pace.

"What's wrong?" the older woman asked twice, but Katherine didn't answer.

As soon as they reached the side street where Katherine had parked the Fiat, she unlocked the door for Millie, dashed to the other side, and got in. She put the key into the ignition and stopped. With her hand she pounded the steering wheel. She swore and then laid her head against the wheel. The tears flowed.

Millie started to lay her hand on Katherine's shoulder but held back, unsure of what to do.

"He lied," she said so softly that Millie wasn't sure she had heard correctly.

"Who?"

"Collin lied. I saw him. Back there."

"In the hotel?"

"Yes." She lifted her head and pushed back her dark hair. "He was hugging Loretta Kingsley."

"Oh, Kit, are you sure? I mean—"

"I know my husband!"

"Yes, I suppose you do. But, dear, please don't jump to conclusions. I can't believe—"

"Not jump to conclusions? When a woman sees her husband nuzzling another woman in a public place—"

"It might be. . . ," and Millie stopped, realizing she didn't know at all what it might be.

"I trusted him. I trusted him, and he failed. Just like before."

Millie put her arm around Katherine's shoulder. "Oh, my dear, I'm sorry. So sorry."

"Millie, I love him."

"I know that."

"But I didn't know it. Not really. I mean, not until last night. I thought—I thought everything had been worked out. I was wrong—"

"Kit, at least give him a chance to explain."

"Give him a chance to explain? How do you explain *that?*" Katherine broke into sobbing. She turned and laid her head on Millie's shoulder. She made no effort to control herself as her body heaved with crying. For a long time the two women sat in the car. Millie said nothing, only held her friend tightly.

The heat of the day pounded on the car with its closed windows. Katherine raised her perspiring head. "Let's—let's get out of here."

She sat up and ran her fingers through her thick hair. She rolled down the window and then started the car. They drove back toward the Casa Blanca. "Oh, Millie, I can't—I can't go back there. Not yet."

"We can go anywhere you want."

She pulled over to the curb and parked. "I'd like to sit under one of the bañas for a little while," she said, nodding across the street.

"Want me to go with you?"

"It doesn't matter," she answered and pulled the keys from the ignition. She didn't lock the car or wait for any further reply. She dashed between cars to the other side of the street.

The far side of the street ran almost to the edge of the bay. From the sidewalk another fifty feet of sloping sand led to the water. It being midday, all the bañas were empty.

Katherine fell into one and leaned back. She kicked off her sandals and dug her toes into the cool sand. Millie came up behind her and sat quietly in a chair nearby. She watched in fascination as motorboats pulled gliders across the bay, making them look like giant kites. Katherine's eyes turned in the same direction, but she saw none of it.

Tears slid down her cheeks. After a lengthy silence she said, "I've made up my mind. I was a fool to think it could work—"

"You're still a fool, Kit," Millie said so softly that the impact did not hit Katherine at first.

"What?" she turned her head.

"You're a foolish, self-pitying, self-centered woman," Millie said just as softly.

"Thank you very much," Katherine answered and started to put on her sandals. "That's exactly what everyone needs to hear from her friend."

"You need to hear it. The trouble is, you haven't really heard."

"I heard all right. Foolish. Self-pitying. Self-centered. Did I forget any?"

"Maybe I ought to have added, 'and a little too judgmental.' "

"Okay, you've added that. Anything else? I'm hurting, so don't hold back. Kick me hard."

Millie took a deep breath. "Kit, you may be foolishly jeopardizing everything in your life in the next couple of hours."

"Sure. Now give me the religious lecture about forgiving and turning the other cheek and—"

"No, I'd rather give you the lecture that's called common sense."

"Thank you very much!" Katherine snapped. With both shoes now on her feet, she started striding back toward the car. "I don't know if you want to ride back to the hotel with a woman who is rude, who has no common sense and—"

"Shut up, Kit!"

"What?"

"Shut up and sit down."

"You talk to me like that?"

"It's about time someone did. Now sit down."

Katherine retreated to the baña and sat down, fuming.

"I don't know what happened at the El Presidente—"

"I'll tell you exactly what happened back there—"

"And I don't care either. Furthermore, I don't care right now about eight years ago or six years ago. I *do* know what happened two hours ago at the Casa Blanca. I also believe Collin meant it."

"So did I—at the time."

"So now you're going to throw your whole future away without even giving Collin a chance."

"I gave him a chance. He lied. He deceived me. He said he was meeting Señor Ortega."

"There you go again, Kit. Now stop it!"

"I should just smile as though nothing happened?"

"No, not at all. But you strike out at everybody. You're so afraid of getting hurt that you attack first."

"It's the golden rule of society—do unto others *before* they do it unto you."

"No, it's not that at all. It's fear. Pain. Hurt. Those are the things that make you strike out."

"Are they?"

"Aren't they?"

"I—I don't know."

"Because you're afraid of getting hurt, you hit and hit hard."

"Millie, you've got all the answers about everything."

"I didn't say that."

Ignoring her protests, Katherine asked, "Is this the way your God works? I thought He helped people."

"He does."

"This is helping?"

"He helps by giving strength in the midst of your troubles."

"Another easy answer—"

"No, Kit, no easy answers. We never tried to make it sound that way, did we?"

"No, I guess you didn't. Only—"

"Only you're confused and hurt," Millie said.

"I tried. All morning I felt so—so good. I wanted to believe and now see how it turns out."

"Nothing has turned out. Don't give up on God yet."

"Millie, don't talk to me anymore about this religion bit. It may be fine for you and Tom."

"Do you honestly mean what you're saying?"

"I took an injection. It didn't work. Now I'm immune. That's how I feel right now."

"Oh, Kit—," Millie said and then looked away, determined not to cry.

"I don't want any more sermons. Or talk about God. If you try to push me, I'll walk away. I mean that," Katherine said as her fingers dug into the chair.

"I won't say anything more . . . unless . . . unless you ask first," Millie said.

"Fine. Now, let's go back to the hotel," she said and hurried back to the car.

Katherine pulled into the hotel driveway and parked quickly. She jumped out of the car and ran back down the driveway. Millie sat silently, watching her go.

Katherine reached the road and hesitated only a second. *When Collin returns,* she thought, *he'll come up the hill.* She turned in the opposite direction. Another three minutes of half running and she reached the next road, turned sharply, and followed the street leading to the Quebrada Cliffs.

A regular performance of divers had just finished. Hawkers collected tips from tourists who wished to watch the event. They kept telling her to come back in an hour. She handed one of them five pesos and charged past. She walked down the rock-and-concrete steps. Even at the bottom it was still a hundred feet to the water and the swift currents of the Pacific Ocean.

She went to the wall and looked out to sea. She did not know how long she stood there. She had the impression of people coming and leaving again. She felt such a numbness that time meant nothing to her.

She heard someone calling her name and looked around. Dusk had come, and she could barely make out Collin's silhouette. He called her name again.

She turned away from him and faced the ocean. For the first time she became aware of a breeze blowing her hair and the sting of salt on her lips.

"I knew you'd be here," he said. He stood directly behind her and wrapped his arms around her. She stiffened, pushed him away, and then faced him. "Collin, I've been thinking—"

"I love you, Kit," he said.

"And I've decided to give you a divorce," she said.

"I don't want a divorce."

"I do," she said.

He grabbed her, his fingers digging into her shoulders. "I don't believe you."

"You've wanted it for years—"

"Kit, look me in the eyes and say that again."

She looked momentarily and then dropped her gaze. "I thought it would make you happy. You'll be free. No more sleazy affairs—"

"Kit, haven't you been listening? I love you."

"No more arguments. No silences. Both of us free."

"Kit, I don't know what's happened since this morning, but—"

"I've had a chance to think a little more," she said. "And I've decided on divorce."

He shook her and pulled her close. "Something's wrong, Kit. What is it?"

"You ask *me?*" she said. "What about Loretta?"

"Loretta who?" he said, a grin covering his face.

"The Loretta you made a spectacle of yourself with in public at the El Presidente—"

His grin disappeared. "Sorry, I tried to be funny—"

"I don't see the humor of it—"

"Kit, how did you know about Loretta and me?"

"Does it matter?"

"It matters a great deal."

"You should have thought about that sooner." A hardness crept into her voice.

He grabbed her hand. "Let's get out of here," he said. "People are filling the place up again. I want to explain."

"I don't want to hear. I've said what I—"

"Kit, you owe me that much!"

"Owe you?"

"Yes. In the past I've let you blame and accuse. You've never given me a chance to explain. This time you're going to listen— whether you want to or not!"

She shrugged and sighed. "Okay," she said. They walked up the steps together. Tourists were already jostling one another, squeezing closer to the wall. Lights went on in preparation for the first evening performance.

They found an empty spot at the edge of the parking lot and sat under a tree. The souvenir dealers and fruit vendors hawked their goods far enough away that they had a sense of privacy.

"You deserve to know about Loretta and me. Everything."

"Okay, where does Loretta fit in?"

"She doesn't fit in anywhere—"

"Oh, just a casual affair on the side—"

"Kit, how did you find out about her?"

"You think I'm stupid?"

"No, but I—well, I can't figure out how you knew ... anything," he said.

"Let's just say I knew," she answered.

"All right, Kit. But first, before I tell you about Loretta, suppose you tell me about the men in your life."

"What men?"

"Don't give me that innocent reaction. I saw too much evidence."

"Evidence?" Then she gasped. "Oh, no. The shorts and the tie!"

"How did you know? I found them by accident—one of the half-dozen cleaning women you hired accidentally put them in with my laundry."

"I—I bought those things," she said, "to get even."

"Get even?"

"Because . . . because I knew you and Loretta were. . . ."

Collin shook his head. "Do you realize what you did?"

"I . . . got . . . even."

"Kit, Kit, you almost ruined everything. Because you had a suspicious mind, you tried to make me think you were having an affair—"

"Weren't *you?*"

"Never."

"You're trying to tell me that all those meetings with Loretta were innocent little business sessions?"

"I'm telling you that nothing went on between us. Loretta threw herself at me—often. But I never accepted the offer."

"You're trying to tell me that your little rendezvous in Acapulco was accidental?"

"I'm telling you this. She knew my plans. Then she made plans later to come and meet with me. She wanted to work on my next book. At least that's what she said when I talked to her on the phone."

"Yes, I heard you call her darling."

"I knew you did—at the hotel."

"How did you know?" Kathcrine said, her total surprise obvious.

"You have a distinct clipped walk. I heard you coming behind me—"

"So you did it on purpose?"

"I decided to use Loretta's aggressiveness—just to make you even more angry—"

"But, Loretta always turns up in your life—"

"Look, Kit, I can't control Loretta. What Loretta does is Loretta's business. She's a first-class editor. I owe her a lot—"

"I'll bet!"

Collin shook his head. "Okay, I've tried." He let go of Katherine and turned.

"Wait," she said and pulled him back. "I've been so hurt. I'm afraid to trust again, Collin—"

"I'm willing to struggle with you, Kit. Just don't cut me off."

"I'll try. Honest."

"But—but what I can't understand is how you could have thought Loretta and I—I mean, even before Acapulco."

"The night . . . the night Reggie died . . . I thought you were with Loretta . . . in our apartment."

He pulled his wife closer, their faces only inches apart. Under the glow of the street light, she saw his dark eyes and the pain on his face. She wanted to say something, but words refused to come.

"I swear to you, Kit," he said, "nothing happened between Loretta and me that night. That night or any other time."

"Collin, what have we done to each other?" she said and wrapped her arms around him.

"I don't know, Kit."

"Will you—will you give me a chance, Collin?"

"Like the one you never gave me?"

"I deserved that," she said, and her voice broke.

"No, you didn't," he said, and his lips pressed against hers.

"Did you—do you love her?"

"I don't think so. I never said I did. She never asked. But she was so understanding—"

"And I wasn't," Katherine said as tears slipped down her cheeks. She took a handkerchief out of her pocket and wiped them away.

"You ignored everything except your own grief," he said. "And with what little you had left, you wrote your novels. You wouldn't even give me a chance to get close."

She closed her eyes and leaned back against the tree. "You can't accuse me of anything more harshly than what I've been saying to myself this afternoon." She bit her lip, determined not to cry again.

"I didn't mean to—"

"If you hadn't come, I think I would have jumped," she said, nodding toward the cliffs.

"Kit, please don't talk that way."

"I deserved your anger on the balcony at La Paloma Blanca. I deserve every bit of hatred you've ever felt."

"I don't hate you—"

"I ruined everything for you—for myself—," and the tears gushed out. Collin held her against his shoulder until the crying subsided.

"Oh, I'm so miserable . . . so ashamed," she whispered.

Chapter 12

"After Reggie's death, I didn't care about much of anything. I continued to write. Did more research than necessary—anything to keep myself occupied. Loretta called regularly. She also passed through Chicago at least once a month. She talked to me, encouraged my work. She listened to the problems about my writing. Finally she listened when I told her my personal problems."

"Like what?"

"Like guilt. Even though the doctor kept assuring me that I couldn't have made any difference, I kept thinking about it. If only I had checked two or three more times. If only I hadn't gone into Chicago to meet Loretta. Or had drunk less. Dozens of possibilities, but all of them trapping me."

"And my accusing you only added to your guilt?"

"If it hadn't been for Loretta, I don't know how I would have coped."

"She helped while I turned away," Katherine said, and her voice broke.

"Your grief blinded you. In a different way. Neither of us knew how to comfort each other."

"I know that now," she said, "but I didn't then. Really."

Collin kissed his wife's cheek. "That's how it went. Loretta became a friend and confidante. She didn't make any more passes, but her shoulder was available when I needed her."

"Then you found the men's shorts in your drawer and—"

"Let me tell you the rest of the story. I want you to know everything."

"And I'll listen, Collin. I promise."

"The phone call at the hotel this morning—it wasn't from Ortega—"

"I've already figured that out."

"I made it sound like him because . . . because we were finally getting our lives straight, and I didn't want to complicate things."

"You couldn't have told me the truth?"

"I didn't trust you to accept it," he said. "After all, if I told you I was going to meet her, what would you have assumed?"

"Of course, you're right," she said.

"Kit, I prayed as I walked over there. I kept asking God's help—like the Reaves told us to do. Loretta sat in the lobby, waiting for me. She hugged me, but I didn't respond. She took my hand and led me into the lounge.

"We sat down and had coffee and talked some more. That's when I told her about us."

"What did you tell her?"

"I told her that—that you and I were getting our lives straightened out. And—"

"And, what?"

"And then I told her . . . that I loved you."

"You actually told her that?"

"Yes."

"Why, Collin?"

"Because I do love you."

"You've never said it to me."

"I couldn't . . . until today. . . ."

"Why today?"

"Because I know I love you, and this time I'm going to fight for you."

"Oh, Collin—"

He interrupted her and kissed her forcefully. They held their embrace a long time. Slowly their lips parted. "I mean it. With God helping us, our love will grow . . . and be stronger than before."

"Yes, oh, yes, Collin."

"I wish you could have been there—in the lounge with us."

"I'd like to hear about it. Everything."

"Well," he said slowly, "we sat down. I hardly knew how to begin, and I told her that you and I were definitely going to get our lives in harmony again."

"Did she say anything?"

"No, she just listened," Collin answered. "Then I said, 'Loretta, I discovered two things in Acapulco.' "

"And she said—"

"Naturally she asked me what they were." Collin paused a minute recalling the details of that meeting. Then he told Katherine.

"Yes," he said to Loretta, "I love Katherine. Once I claimed to have hated her, and I think I did. But I also loved her. I don't think I ever stopped loving her. If I had, I would have gotten a divorce long ago."

Loretta smiled. "I'd already guessed that."

"You did?" Collin answered.

"I saw the way she looked at you in the restaurant. The way you responded when I came in. You didn't act like a man who despised his wife. More like an embarrassed one."

"But, I didn't know then—"

"You hadn't admitted it to yourself then."

"I suppose you're right," he answered Loretta. Then he told her the second discovery he had made. "But you won't believe this one," he said.

"Try me," she answered.

"In my desperation I prayed for God to help me. And He has. I—I feel the reality of God—or whatever you want to call it. I've never experienced such a calmness, even though I haven't worked out all my problems."

She raised her brows. "What's that supposed to mean? Have you decided to become a priest or—?"

"I said you wouldn't believe me."

"Are you afraid of dying? Guilt eating you—"

"I can only tell you that I need God's help. He's what I've been missing in my life. I've finally found peace."

"I can recommend a good shrink in lower Manhattan. Or have him refer you to one in Chicago. I went to this fellow for nearly two years after my divorce. He did wonders—"

"I've found what I need," he said.

She shrugged. "To each his own."

"Thanks for understanding."

"I don't understand so please stop patronizing me! I accept your right to foul up your life."

"Loretta, please, I—"

"Just one question. Where's the brunet iceberg in all this?"

"Struggling. Just as I am. We're both trying to give our marriage a second chance."

Loretta leaned forward and placed both her hands over his. She squeezed hard. "She doesn't deserve a second chance."

"Neither do I," he said softly.

"I've got to go now, Collin." Loretta started to get up.

"Good-bye, Loretta."

"I made reservations on the plane for this afternoon. I had hoped you'd want me to cancel."

"I'm sorry, Loretta."

"I know you are. That's why it hurts. You're the most decent man I've known or cared about in the last five years."

"Thanks for saying that."

"I mean it. And . . . and I love you, Collin. I'll get over it in time, but—," she laid her head on his shoulder and hugged him. "Just— just hold me for a minute, Collin. Only for a minute, and then I'll walk out of here, across the lobby and . . . and out of your life."

"Please—"

"Just hold me, Collin."

They both stood, and he held her tightly. He felt the moist tears on his neck, although she cried silently. She lifted her head enough to see his eyes. He started to say something, but not knowing what, he only squeezed her again. She kissed his cheek.

"So that's what happened. If you saw us, it was either when I greeted her or when she left."

"I'm ashamed," Katherine said. "So ashamed."

"I don't want you to feel ashamed. I only want you to believe me."

"That's why I'm ashamed. I believe you. I should never have doubted—"

"Kit, we've had too many rough miles between us over the years. I expect you'll still doubt me a hundred times before we're really straightened out."

"Oh, Collin, will it—will it take a long time?"

"Not if we work at it," he said and kissed her tenderly.

"I promise you something right now, Collin. If I ever doubt you again—and I hope I won't—I'll face you with it first."

"Promise?"

"With all my heart."

They stood in the darkness of the warm evening, oblivious to the world around them. Even when they could no longer see each other's faces, they stayed and held each other close.

"Kit, you know Millie asked me to reread the last four chapters of *Forever and Ever Love.*"

"I heard that. Sounded odd to me."

"But I did read those chapters. Especially the epilogue."

"She'll be pleased to know—"

"Kit, don't you remember the last page?"

"Not exactly."

"Then read it again." He pulled her hand, and they hurried down the street to a restaurant. They stood under the lighted sign and Collin opened *Forever and Ever Love* to the epilogue. He handed her the book.

Randolph stopped her when they reached the top of the cliff. They stood under the glowing street lights, oblivious to the traffic whizzing by within a few feet of them.

He stared into Hillary's eyes. "I never want to stop looking at you. I've found you . . . really found you."

"I do love you," she whispered, "I do, only. . . ."

"You still doubt me?"

"I want to believe," she said. "I want to trust you."

"Hillary, I'll never leave you again."

"What about Victoria?"

"That's over."

"What if she comes back?"

"She won't," he said.

"Are you sure?" she asked, trying not to let the anxiety show in her voice.

"She knows how I feel about you. It took me a long time to understand myself. But you're the only woman I've ever really loved."

"I want to believe you," she said.

"I love you, Hillary, with a forever and ever love."

"Oh, Randolph, I—" His lips pressed against hers, cutting off her voice. But his words kept ringing in her mind: *a forever and ever love.*

And Hillary knew he meant it.

Chapter 13

"I've been a fool," Katherine said.

"Forget it," Collin said. He took her in his arms and held her tight. He increased the pressure, and for a magical moment, both of them felt as though they were one person. Their lips found each other.

"I should have told you everything," Collin said, his face touching hers. "But I had to clear it all up first. You do understand—"

She kissed him quickly and firmly. "We've both been wrong. We've caused each other so much pain. . . ."

"But that's all behind us now," Collin said.

"All behind us . . . oh, Collin . . . ," and she kissed him deeply, while she felt her heart surging with a new warmth.

"And I understand much more now."

"Understand?"

"About us. I knew that a lot of Hillary and Randolph's story was ours. I didn't know how much."

"And how much is it?"

"It's our total story. All of it."

"I guess it is."

"You even wrote about the blond who tried to take Randolph away—"

"Yes, I did, didn't I?"

"You called her Victoria in the book—but you could as easily have named her Loretta."

"I didn't write it because I knew—"

"Nothing had happened then."

"That's right," she said.

"Anyway, do you remember how the book ended?" Collin asked.

"Of course. She was standing at the cliff, and Randolph came running to her and—"

"That's how I knew where to find you."

"Collin, it *is* our story, isn't it?"

"I love you, Kit. More than I ever thought possible."

"I love you, too, Collin, more than I ever dared admit."

Hand in hand, they walked through the darkened streets back to their hotel. They picked up the key at the desk and went toward their room. They stopped walking when they came to the spot above the fountain. The lights shone, and water poured out. "Oh, Collin, the way it was before," Katherine said.

As Collin looked toward the lobby, he saw Manuel standing by the entrance. He smiled up at them and pointed to the fountain. "Is it not beautiful?"

"More beautiful than before!" Collin said, and pulled Katherine close. They stood on the balcony a long time watching the dancing colors.

"I—I'd like to pray, Kit."

"Oh, please do."

"God," he said, "I may not do this right and if I make mistakes in how I'm supposed to say all this, I hope You'll overlook it. Mainly though, I want to say thank You. For Kit. For the Reaves. For—well, for everything."

As soon as he paused, Kit said. "God, please do something for Tom. If you still perform miracles, will You do one for him? He's such a wonderful man, and we love him."

They held each other for a long moment and then walked toward their room. As they passed the Reaves' room, they saw the door open. Millie looked up. "Oh, come in! Come in!"

"Sure," they both answered.

Tom, who had been lying on the bed, sat up slowly. He smiled.

"How are you feeling?" Collin asked.

"I'm doing all right," he answered.

"We kept the door open, hoping we'd see you tonight," Millie said.

"Oh, Millie, we have wonderful news. We're really going to get our lives straightened out."

Millie took Tom's hand, and they smiled at the younger couple.

"But you knew we would, didn't you?" Collin asked.

"I hoped you would."

"It's working out," Katherine said.

"Now, we're praying for you—," Collin said. "You need help with a problem."

"We've already begun to get the answer," Tom said. "Stanford University Medical Center called our home today, and then our daughter called us. About four-thirty this afternoon I finally got a call through to them."

"Yes? And?"

"And we're leaving tomorrow for home, and next week we're going to California."

"Does that mean—"

"No," Millie said. "That doesn't mean a transplant. It does mean he's a good candidate."

"At least they haven't turned you down," Katherine said.

"Oh, it's more positive than that," Tom said. "It means they want me there. And the chances are highly favorable."

"We're delighted." Millie said. "We believe God has answered our prayers."

Millie hugged both Collin and Katherine. "This has been one of the best weeks of my entire life."

"It's been the best for us, too." Collin said. He pulled the book out of his hip pocket. "And I want to return your copy of *Forever and Ever Love.*"

"You read it?"

"This afternoon."

"I'm glad," Millie said. "Somehow I knew you had to read it. You had to know how deeply Kit cared."

"I know now."

"I'll keep telling him in case he forgets," Kit said, reaching up to kiss her husband on the cheek.